KNOX'S IRREGULARS

J. WESLEY BUSH

ENCLAVE

PUBLISHING

Knox's Irregulars by J. Wesley Bush
Published by Enclave Publishing
5025 N. Central Ave., #635
Phoenix, AZ 85012
www.enclavepublishing.com

ISBN (paper): 978-1-62184-031-2

Published in the United States by Enclave Publishing, an imprint of Third Day
Books, LLC, Phoenix, Arizona.

This is a work of fiction. Names, characters, places, and incidents are products of
the author's imagination or are used fictitiously. Any similarity to actual people,
organizations, and/or events is purely coincidental.

Cover illustration by Graphics Manufacture (France)

Printed in the United States of America

DEDICATION

To my lovely wife, Alexandra.
After all these years, we still follow rainbows in each other's eyes.

PROLOGUE

A tyrant. . .is always stirring up some war or other,
in order that the people may require a leader.
—Plato

Lieutenant Nabil al-Hise scaled the ninety steps to the Hall of the Evolved, its turquoise-glazed dome towering overhead. When a politician came to power, it was said he had taken the ninety steps. How few of them were worthy of it.

Al-Hise chose his footing carefully – the architects had never imagined a three-meter tall armored monster would be climbing these steps and they were too narrow for his massive feet. Four meters ahead was his master, Brigadier Tsepashin. He wore no battle armor, only the black robes of the Fist of the Mogdukh, but al-Hise knew that Tsepashin was the more dangerous of the two. He had an iron belief that crushed all doubt, fear, and weakness.

They passed through towering doors and into a near-deserted vestibule. He saw only a handful of People's Deputies and clerks, most talking on coms. The rest must be in the Hall.

Surveying the area grimly, Tsepashin whispered, "Follow me, child, and do nothing until I signal."

A-Hise dipped the waist of his battle armor in a quick bow. "Tak tochno, Brigadier Tsepashin," he acknowledged, following his master into the Hall of the Evolved. Two ceremonial guardsmen parted to admit them through a mosaic-covered archway into a grand, hemispherical chamber.

Above him curved the azure dome with its shining oculus at the peak. Row upon row of People's Deputies flanked either side of the granite central aisle. The aisle led to the room's focal point, a circle of black marble centered on a representation of the sacred birch tree. Beyond the circle sat the raised dais of the parliamentary leadership.

Three hundred perfectly smooth heads turned on al-Hise and Tsepashin as they entered, three hundred searching looks following their steps. The weight of their looks was nothing to the young Lieutenant, not compared to the awe he felt for his master.

A patrician man stood in the circle, gripping a sheaf of birch branches—the Speaker's Rod. Al-Hise itched to tear him apart, especially as the Speaker jabbed the rod in their direction and called out, "You were summoned here to account for your failure to quell the disturbances. It was at your insistence that the Fist of the Mogdukh was chosen over the Scourge for this task. Many questioned the wisdom of that decision. Now you bring a weapon of war into the Hall of the Evolved? Explain yourself, Brigadier Tsepashin!"

Al-Hise halted at the edge of the circle. Tsepashin coolly crossed the line, motioning for the Rod and the right to speak. It was slapped into his hand and he turned to face the crowd. Tsepashin was silent for a long moment, his pale, almost colorless blue eyes boring into the audience. In formal robes, with his hairless scalp and chalk-white skin, he resembled the vampyri of al-Hise's childhood nightmares.

At last he spoke in a wintry voice. "Food riots. Infidel proselytizers. Civil disturbances and political dissent. The People's Deputies tasked me to combat these problems. Now I am called to account for the apparent lack of progress, and this I will do." Tsepashin beat a rhythm in his palm with the rod. "Parliament simply did not recognize the extent of the corruption—how deeply our land is riddled with foreign devils, each an enemy of the Mogdukh. Worse, many of our own citizens sympathize with these infidels.

"Now the foreigners' cleverness will be turned back against them. Despite the Hegemony's arms embargo, we have purchased a weapon from off-planet. A weapon which will bring terror to our enemies!" A hand motioned to where al-Hise stood in his battle armor.

At the recognition from Tsepashin, al-Hise felt a swell of pride. He turned to face the parliament and deployed each of the weapons from their armored recesses, smiling coldly as the politicians recoiled in their seats.

It would be hard not to be impressed when faced with tall, chitinous black armor at once simian and insect-like; hunched, its powerful arms bulging with an electric chain gun and an EMP projector; shoulders humped by twin anti-vehicular missile pods; the legs misshapen by jump-jet nacelles. A beetle-like helmet sat atop the suit, with a death's head emblazoned on the faceplate. Al-Hise grinned as he watched the decadent politicians through the visor, drinking in their nervous looks.

The silence stretched for several moments before Tsepashin continued, eyes on the floor, expression thoughtful. "The infidel is a constant threat to our way of life. However, there is something viler than an infidel: a heretic. Infidels stand outside the gates of the citadel. Heretics live within, ceaselessly undermining the foundations of the holy city. The heretic is the greatest threat to our Khlisti faith."

He began to pace slowly, fingers drumming the Speaker's Rod. "The Prophet, Master Nirsultanev, gave us a parable. All of you know it. There once was a legitimate son to a man of great wealth. Upon his father's death, the son was shocked to find his birthright stolen. Through trickery a bastard was made heir and the true son his servant. For many years the true son remained meek in his servitude. He bided his time and plotted revenge.

"Finally came the night of the long knives and his enemies lay dead at his feet. The true son reclaimed what was rightfully his."

Tsepashin's words trailed off in a fervent whisper. Then slowly, deliberately, he spoke into the silent chamber. "The night of the long knives is come."

Al-Hise's external mics caught the sound of scuffling coming from the vestibule, followed by a scream which everyone could hear. One of the ceremonial guardsmen pitched face-first into the room and lay unmoving. Something appeared in Tsepashin's hand and he turned and flung it at the Speaker. The man fell dead, the hilt of a dagger sprouting from his chest.

That was al-Hise's signal. Engaging jump-jets, he arced his way across the domed chamber, landing nimbly astride the only exit. Black uniformed troops poured in past him, each wearing a beret with death's head crest and carrying a viciously curved dagger. Al-Hise turned to face the room, prepared to cut off any escape, but he fired on no one. Tsepashin had been very clear; the cancer of these heretics must be excised by ritually-cleansed blades. But his presence wasn't necessary. The politicians sat on their granite benches, meek as doves.

As a bloc, the Purist faction rose from their position in the back corner of the Hall, pulling daggers from under their seats. Tsepashin watched, nodding his approval. His face seemed to glow with a holy light. Raising high his blade, Tsepashin's voice reverberated through the Hall once more. "Night has fallen!"

"All power to the Mogdukh!" Soldiers and armed Purists fell upon the Moderates and Rectifieds, who were easy to differentiate in their blue or green robes. In the end, the unarmed politicians fought back, al-Hise noted with grudging respect. At least they were faithful to the Khlisti way in death, if not in life. A handful sprinted for the door, and al-Hise readied himself to repel them, but two of the Purists, eyes feral and white robes soaked in gore, cut them down before they came close. The voices of the dying echoed in the perfect acoustics of the Hall. Al-Hise cut the audio in his suit, silencing the animalistic screams of both victim and killer.

This somehow made it worse – time crawled as he watched the Purists silently hack the enemy to pieces, red blades rising and falling. One young Moderate, Russian-handsome with sandy hair and a strong jaw, managed to break free of the pack and run blindly for the exit. He careened into al-Hise's powered armor and fell to the ground. The suit's tactile sensors gave al-Hise a slight reverberation in the chest to simulate the impact. A Purist dragged the Moderate to his feet and a second carved him ear to ear. Arterial blood splashed al-Hise's primary camera, plunging the world into crimson murk.

At last the deed was done. A trideo camera team hustled into the room and Tsepashin, bloody and exhausted, reentered the Speaker's Circle. "The People's Deputies are disbanded as of this moment. All constitutional authority is now held by the Guardian Council. Public gatherings and independent press organs are banned for the duration of the emergency. All foreigners and infidels will turn themselves in for deportation to the ghetto in Samarkand."

Tsepashin thrust a hand into the pocket of his robes; it emerged clutching a spherical device. The soldiers and Purists began filing out of the building. He tossed the incendiary grenade onto the Speaker's dais. In a flash, thermite set the hardwood blazing.

His features hellishly backlit by the flames, Tsepashin stared into the camera. "The ashes of the Hall of the Evolved will be the only monument to the weakness and heresy of this age. A new era begins today—an era of strength and purity.

"The disgraces of the past are cleansed in fire."

1

Diplomacy is the art of saying 'Nice doggie'
until you can find a rock.
—Will Rogers

Prime Minister Cameron Knox stood beside a hovering state car, watching an infantry colonel assemble his regiment on the landing pad of New Geneva's primary spaceport. Ferrocrete stretched for kilometers in every direction, broken only by the metal and transplas wedding cake of a passenger terminal, and a bare handful of ships still remaining landside - any merchant with sense had long since left for safer ports of call. Cold wind blew in from the north, picking up speed in the empty terrain and lashing his face with rain. He blinked it away, but kept stiffly at attention. The viewers needed to see strength and resolve.

Just behind the colonel rested a slab-sided troopship of the Terran Hegemony and two flagpoles: one bearing the tricot flag of New Geneva, the other the concentric rings of the Hegemony. Both of them whipped in the heavy wind, their halyards clanging incessantly on the steel poles.

"Open ranks... march!" the colonel shouted.

The rows of soldiers opened up for inspection.

"Dress right... dress!"

Platoon leaders sternly inspected their men. Knox imagined they would want to be sharp, especially on a day like today, with a swarm of trideodrones following their every move.

"Ready... front! Close ranks... march!" The rows reformed into their neat phalanxes.

"Present... Arms!"

That was his cue. Cementing his face with a confident smile, Knox strode out to the formation, giving the drones a wave as they shifted to cover him. The colonel faced right and offered a salute. "Sir, the men are yours."

"Thank you, Colonel. Dismissed," Knox said, taking his place at the front. He opened his mouth to speak, but was interrupted as shuttles began exiting the terminal and heading their way. The Hegemony troops were early. Apparently everyone was in a hurry to leave. Two minutes later, the shuttles were grounded and the Hegemony troops had disembarked and formed into ranks. Their commander gave an order, and they began marching in columns toward the New Genevans, punctuating each left step with a near-stomp as was their custom.

In normal times, the ceremony would call for a speech from the garrison commander, but the Hegemony was slinking away, increasingly unable to maintain order on its core worlds, let alone far-flung jerkwater planets like this one. They had no speeches for the New Genevans, but a bright-voiced tenor began singing from the rear of the Hegemony formation, with the rest answering lustily in return.

"Goodbye to New Geneva;
Off to Antares with us.
We're likely to get shot there;
but at least they'll let us cuss!

Genevans are a good lot,
to leave in such a lurch.
But not a girl will kiss us,
unless we go to church!"

The third stanza was cut short as the Hegemony troops halted and faced the Genevans. With measured step, a color guard emerged and marched to the flagpoles.

Knox kept his expression level for the sake of those watching, but felt bile rise in his throat as the color guard inexorably lowered the last Hegemony flag on the planet. Certainly he had lodged complaints against the Hegemony fleet; and granted, in election years he'd fanned discontent against the "Earthers" for votes. Every Founder's Party politician did that. But none except a handful of ultranationalists actually wanted them gone. New Geneva had flourished under the benign neglect of the Hegemony. In its sixty-year history it had grown from an impoverished colony of religious expatriates to an economic and technological marvel all out of proportion to its tiny population.

Now, that era was ending. No more would orbiting battlecruisers and the threat of bombardment protect New Geneva from its much larger and increasingly hostile neighbor to the north.

The color guard unfastened the flag from its keepers, folding and presenting it solemnly to Knox. With a final salute, they returned to their positions. At a command from the adjutant, the Hegemony unit filed aboard the troop carrier silently. Within moments, the New Genevans were left completely alone.

Facing about, Knox injected his voice with confidence, not only for the soldiers, but for the three million sets of eyes watching via live tridfeed as well. "At long last our dream of a free and independent nation is realized!" he called out, the soldiers dutifully answering with a hurrah. "We look forward to peaceful and prosperous co-existence with Abkhazia, our friends to the north, and congratulate them on their independence as well. Let today mark the beginning of a new era of mutual respect and cooperation between our two peoples."

Acknowledging the soldier's cheers, he turned and walked briskly to his state car. Not until safely hidden from sight did he slouch down in the seat, letting out a defeated sigh.

And so independence came to New Geneva.

※

"I gotta admit, Corporal, your father almost sounds like he means that rubbish. He's good."

Corporal Randal Knox laughed, glancing up from the small tridscreen his fire team was clustered around. "My old man can be persuasive when he wants to. Nearly talked me into going into politics, and that's saying something." He looked back in time to see his father disappear into a waiting car.

Randal snapped the tridscreen shut and tossed it into his pressure tent. "Show's over - best get back to work. Queue up for inspection, you lot," he said, allowing some informality since their bivouac site was well away from any higher-ups.

Grumbling, the men clambered back into their LANCER suits - Light Armored Night-optimized Combat Rig - keeping the helmets locked back. Randal looked over the team, his for eight months now, ever since Levin got promoted to sergeant. They were family – together they'd chewed dirt, marinated their livers, and even shared an explosive episode of amoebiasis after swimming in the wrong lake. First in line was Kimathi, a tall East African immigrant and the assistant team leader. Next came Rogers, the heavy weapon specialist. He was earnest, a squared-away trooper who planned to serve for life. Tavish, meanwhile, was hot-headed and quick to challenge orders, but a savant with his auto-loading mortar. Last came Sanchez, only three months out of armored infantry school and still round-cheeked with baby fat.

Stepping up to Kimathi, Randal craned his neck to inspect him. Kimathi had nearly ended up in the foot infantry - his LANCER suit was the largest the army's supplier made. Opening a panel on the armored suit's breastplate, Randal surveyed the faintly-glowing monitors concealed beneath. "That right leg still catching?"

"Fixed." Kimathi rarely used two words when one would do.

"Good." Randal moved on to Rogers, and glanced down the tube of the massive railgun affixed to the suit's left shoulder. It was locked in the "safe" position, rotated to rest diagonally across the back of the unit. Once assured it was free of obstruction, Randal knelt to check the housings on the outside of each leg. Carbon fiber spikes lodged in the housings and shot deep into the earth each time the railgun fired—the only way to keep the suit upright given the devastating recoil of the gauss effect.

Next he checked over the caseless light machine gun bulking the right forearm of Rogers' suit. Each LANCER variant had the LMG in common, though the shoulder weapon was modular and issued in one of three types: autocannon, autoloading mortar, or railgun. The cannons were vicious against light armor, the mortar good for indirect fire, and the railgunner could wreak havoc from great distances.

He heard the soft chime of his comset.

"All leaders down to fire team level are to report to the TOC for briefing," came the grating voice of the Battalion XO, Major Tarrington.

With a sigh, Randal began the long trot to the Tactical Operations Center, calling back to Kimathi, "Run 'em through battle drills until I get back. Practice reacting to artillery fire. Something tells me that'll be useful soon."

⁓⳾

Bivouacked farthest out, Randal was one of the last to arrive. The others from the armored infantry company were already unsuited, the

LANCER shells standing empty in rows outside the command tent. He shed his armor and ducked inside.

Self-inflating chairs stood in rows, turning the TOC into a makeshift briefing room. The officers and higher noncoms had taken the chairs, so Randal was left milling in the back with the rest of the low end of the military food chain.

A large someone jostled him from behind. He turned to give the guy a dirty look, but found his best friend, Jack Van Loon, grinning like a fool. Returning the smile, he punched Jack in the stomach hard enough to steal wind. "They'll let anyone in this place these days..."

Jack laughed weakly, rubbing at his belly. It had been getting softer since his wedding four years past. "Speaking of which," he said, nodding toward the front of the room where Major Tarrington had just arrived.

Randal's expression soured. Tarrington, the battalion executive officer, looked like a badger, but lacked the friendly disposition. "It's people like him that give anal retention a bad name."

Naturally, that was the moment the crowd chose to quiet down. Tarrington cleared his throat and spoke in a tone that promised many hours of extra duty for Randal. "If the junior enlisted are quite finished, I'll begin the briefing."

Sensing Jack's chuckle behind him, Randal sent an elbow back to Jack's midsection, nodding contritely to the Major. Tarrington flicked on a holoprojector and displayed a topographical map of the area. Military symbols covered it, showing what Randal recognized as friendly troops and known or suspected Abkhazi force dispositions.

The two sides faced one another across a shallow valley paralleling the Abkhazia-New Geneva border, each positioned on high points along either side. The New Genevan contingent was split in two by Crenshaw Pass, the pass being the main reason any troops were committed to the barren stretch of terrain at all. It was the smaller of the two arteries through the rocky isthmus separating New Geneva from Abkhazia. The bulk of the New Geneva Defense Force was committed to the other one, seventy kilometers to the west, astride the only major road linking the two countries.

"I've called you in because Infosec reports several attempts to hack our Nets today. Crude attempts, but I thought it best to brief you in person. Command has just raised our alert level to a four." Tarrington paused to let the muttering die down before continuing. "Keep your men in chemical gear anytime they're out of their pressure tents. Tighten up your noise and light discipline, and when your men go to the bog, make sure it's in pairs."

He called up a blinking cursor on the holo, motioning with it toward the opposite side of the valley. "Our intel assets report a heavy Abkhazi troop build-up all along the border. Our best estimate places at least two divisions facing us across the valley. That's about thirty thousand of them to the twelve hundred we've got in our reinforced battalion." Randal heard Jack mutter an oath. They were bound to be outnumbered, but it was still daunting to hear the odds.

"Events in Abkhazia are moving quickly. As you know, the Purists have been busy killing off any dissent since they took power eighteen months ago. With the Hegemony gone, Abkhazia has given us forty-eight hours to stack arms or they'll attack. Negotiation is proving difficult, as they've expelled our diplomats.

"You've probably noticed a lot of extra suborbital flights the past two days. They're deporting any foreigners and infidels they didn't already kill when they liquidated the ghetto in Samarkand. Our government has provided several of the suborbitals—the Abkhazis threatened to walk the civilians through the mountains if we didn't. The pilots are under a strict flight path that keeps them away from anything sensitive.

"I've ordered the dronekeepers to double up their surveillance schedule. In addition, Division HQ has been kind enough to attach a company from the Seventh Dragoons to us. Their armored scouts will be pulling round-the-clock recon and surveillance patrols."

The scout company commander gave an acknowledging nod. The Major continued. "This is a big job, so I'm detailing Corporal Knox's team to assist them."

He favored Randal with a small smile. That's lousy, Randal thought. Scout suits were built for extended duration patrols, but the heavy suits of his armored infantry were intended for shock assaults. Long distances were grueling.

Major Tarrington dismissed them and Randal slipped outside before the man could reprimand him. Jack caught up, still chuckling. "If he didn't have kids, I'd think Tarrington had a crush on you..."

"You only hurt the ones you love, right?"

"Just you be cautious. Your old man is Prime Minister, but Tarrington won't let something like that hold him back. I'll wager you pounds for rubles he votes Social Democrat. He just seems like one."

Randal grinned. He was a good Founder's Party man himself, but Jack was so far out on the right wing there was danger of him falling off. "I'll be careful," he promised, setting off at a dogtrot for his team.

∿∿

Reaching the bivouac area, he drew up short. Near his pressure tent stood the slender suit of an armored medic, olive drab crosses emblazoned on its shoulder plates. Its helmet was unsealed and resting on the integral backpack containing the unit's life support. The rectangular "Doc-in-a-box" issued each medic sat on the ground nearby.

His breath caught as he noticed the suit's occupant. She was lovely. Even from a distance he could make out soft brown hair and a fair complexion. The graceful lines of the medic suit were a nice complement to her features.

While she was a pleasant change from the four hairy guys with whom he spent each day, he still grumbled to himself. Whoever she was, she was the last thing he needed to deal with. "What are you doing in my area, Private?"

"I... they've placed me with you, Sergeant Knox." This was followed by a rough salute. "Private Ariane Mireault reporting as ordered."

"Corporal Knox," he amended. "And don't salute in the field. We call that a sniper check - it tells the bad guys who to shoot." He looked her over a moment. She seemed even younger than him. "Does your mum even know you're here?"

"She signed permission for me to enlist, Corporal."

That meant she'd come in at seventeen, which made her either desperate or a military enthusiast. He decided the latter option didn't seem likely. So she was desperate. Better and better.

"Haven't seen you around the battalion before. I imagine you're fresh out of Basic Indoc?"

"Yes, Corporal. They shuttled us here straight from graduation."

"Brilliant. Go re-camouflage your pressure tent – it looks like a soup sandwich. And try to stay out from underfoot." Turning, he bounded off to Kimathi and his team, the ground surveillance sensor plotting them about two hundred meters to the west.

Later, as dusk settled in, the fire team shared a meal of chicken and barley field rations. A low whine sounded behind them and moments later the sleek form of the Platoon Support Vehicle crested the ridge.

The skimmer kept to treetop-level as it flew to Randal's area, using its bottom-mounted jets to settle in between two firs.

Randal was there to greet the vehicle as the cockpit bubble slid back into its enclosure, revealing the platoon's terrible twosome— Johnny Warfield and Jeni Cho. Johnny was strapped into the pilot's chair wearing his usual jester's grin.

Jeni slipped from the dronekeeper's harness, alighting from the skimmer. "Oi, Randal!" A mischievous smile played across her lips. "I heard something interesting on the coms. The Colonel was talking to Division HQ."

Randal knew she shouldn't be anywhere near the Divisional ComNet, but pointing that out would only make her clam up. She was like some capricious goddess who wanted to be entreated for the favors she bestowed. He settled for a non-committal grunt. "Huh."

"Uh-huh," Jeni answered coyly, making a show of looking around for eavesdroppers. Just as Randal was tempted to give her a good shaking, she finally relented. "One of the other dronekeepers spotted a mobile bridge and some of the Abkhazi's new Proviso-class resupply vehicles moving into place."

After the build-up, he was a little underwhelmed by the news. "Merciful heavens, a portable bridge. We're doomed."

Jeni made a rude gesture. "You have your whole life to be a prat. Pace yourself." She took a cleansing breath. "The bridge, and those resupply vehicles, are corps-level assets. Do they seem a little more significant now?"

That changed things. "They could have five divisions en route."

She nodded, her expression sobering. "There could be as many as seventy-five thousand Abkhazis moving in across the street."

"You think they'll shuttle us in some reinforcements?"

"Doubt it. From what I gist, Division doesn't want to divide the main body. Just between you and me? As far as they're concerned, we have as much chance as Christians in the Coliseum. They won't feed more troops to the lions. If we have a war, it's important that the main army survives first contact."

Looking across the valley, the small movements he could detect took on a sinister feel. "This is going to turn into a regular Thermopylae."

"A thermo-what?"

"It was a battle. Three hundred Greeks against thousands and thousands of Persians in a mountain pass. They made us read a lot of old Greek stuff at my academy."

Jeni smirked. "Poor little rich boy," she said, rapping knuckles on his ceramic-plated chest. "How'd that one turn out?"

"Not too great if you were Greek."

She sighed, following his gaze to the Abkhazi side. "This is all gonna end badly, ducky. Try not to get dead." Stepping up on tiptoe, Jeni planted a quick kiss on his cheek and then trotted back to the hovering skimmer. She jumped up to grab a handhold and clambered inside. In a blink, she and Johnny were gone.

Randal debated telling the others as he returned to his team, but decided against it. It was better for them to spend their last night playing cards and telling lies.

As he approached, he heard Tavish telling a war story. This was despite the fact that New Geneva had fought nothing larger than border skirmishes in its entire history. The men competed to see who could tell the most outrageous ones. "There I was, knee deep in bodies, ankle deep in shell casings. The odds were a hundred to two, and they were the toughest two we'd ever faced..."

A stupid pastime, Randal supposed, but it beat brooding.

2

Let your plans be dark and impenetrable as night,
and when you move, fall like a thunderbolt.
—Sun Tzu

Two hours from first light found the team on the last leg of its recon and surveillance patrol. It had been a nerve-wracking night—six hours spent creeping through the Demilitarized Belt that extended a thousand meters to either side of the border.

Both sides had deployed a full complement of skirmishers in the Belt, both expecting trouble. More than once Randal's men received amber flashes on their Heads-Up Display warning they were 'painted' by an enemy targeting sensor. The suits' stealth technology was cutting edge; nevertheless they'd been painted often enough to make everyone short-tempered.

Randal had split the team in two: Rogers, Sanchez and himself in the first section, Kimathi and Tavish babysitting the medic in the other. The two sections were leapfrogging, one providing over-watch while the other bounded ahead.

"Corporal, movement one hundred meters ahead. Three men on foot. Our side of the border," came Kimathi's voice on the comset.

Randal was careful to emphasize every word as he answered. "Do not engage. Maintain position. We'll buttonhook around and usher them out, copy?"

"Roger that, Corporal."

He held his breath while leading his troops around Kimathi's flank, whispering a silent prayer for the men to keep cool, especially hotheaded

Tavish. Randal didn't want to be remembered as the Corporal who started a war.

Pushing aside some brambles, he caught sight of the three infiltrators. They were busily digging a spiderhole in the thick brush of a draw. Behind them sat a pile of what looked to be man-portable signal collection equipment. They obviously planned to hunker down and tap New Genevan ComNets. Randal smiled mirthlessly. Soft little Intelligence types.

Enhancing the magnification on his viewscreen, he keyed the external speaker. "You are violating the sovereign territory of New Geneva. You will leave immediately, or we will fire upon you. Do not attempt to retrieve any equipment."

The suit's night vision afforded a wonderful view of their reaction. He squelched undiplomatic laughter as the Abkhazi scuttled for the border, falling over each other like a trideo comedy. "Kimathi, police up their tech and carry it to the rear. Our spooks will want to take it apart and play with it. We'll rendezvous at the bivouac site."

An hour later, Randal rested on his stomach, looking over the hazy valley from the team's position. Down the line, Mireault, Sanchez and Rogers lay in their own hastily-scraped fighting positions. Behind them slept the rest of the team, catching an hour's shuteye before stand-to. Come first light, everyone would be awake and facing front. It was the most likely time for an enemy attack and every man was needed.

It was only in quiet times that Randal could remember life before he enlisted. For the last two years his mind had been absorbed with soldiering. Looking over the deceptively peaceful valley, his thoughts drew back to a debate from his final year at the Athanasius Academy. For his final examination in Rhetoric he'd debated his friend Pieter Haelbroeck on the making of history—Pieter arguing great men made history and Randal countering that history was created by the impact of ideas.

Both of them being good Calvinists, they had agreed at the outset that Providence guides history. The question was how Divine Sovereignty went about it.

Pieter held up Abkhazia as a clear example of great men forming history. Without the Prophet, Andrei Nirsultanev, Abkhazia wouldn't exist.

In 2028 on the world of Terra, in what was then called Uzbekistan, a new religion arose. It was one of those volatile times when economic and moral chaos reigned. The people of the region were looking for answers and the Prophet supplied them. Preaching in the name of the Mogdukh, or "Power-Spirit," he synthesized a religion from the varied strands of

Central Asia: revamped Marxism, Islam and a generous dash of pseudo-scientific mysticism.

The faith spread with frightening rapidity. In eight years Nirsultanev took control of Central Asia, Siberia, Iraq, northern Iran, the Caucuses and even portions of Russia west of the Urals. His followers came to call themselves Khlisti, or "Whips," in reference to the self-flagellation that figured prominently in their rituals.

The Prophet taught that his followers would usher in the next stage of human evolution through asceticism, collective living, and the unifying conquest of humankind in worship of the Mogdukh. Over time man would transcend the corruption of the physical and become pure spirit, as the Mogdukh was. Individual humans were nothing more than experiments created by the Mogdukh in this process of Becoming.

Through terror, the Prophet crushed dissent and seized the industrial and governmental positions previously held by corrupt oligarchs. The rigid, centralized economy he instituted failed to bring prosperity, as such economies always do, but it did elevate the poor to a common level of misery.

Even more ambitious than his economic "reforms" were the radical revisions he made upon the area's culture. He turned a demoralized region into a militaristic power bent upon converting its neighbors at the point of the sword. Over time, the Khlisti regime became a humanitarian and security crisis even the Europe Union could not ignore. This led to war with the Atlantic powers and the Khlisti Empire was broken apart.

Were it not for an "accident" of history, Nirsultanev's sect would have become a historical footnote. As his Empire was being subjugated, a joint project of Caltech and Tsinghua University made the theoretical breakthrough in physics that opened the door to faster-than-light travel. Within a quarter-century colony ships were rocketing off for distant stars and disaffected Khlisti were among the first to leave.

Abkhazia was the largest of their colonies; however, socialist economics and totalitarian control of ideas kept the planet impoverished and technologically backward. Facing hard times, Abkhazia made a fateful decision.

A group of religious settlers from Terra petitioned the Abkhazi Parliament to sell them a peninsula jutting from the southern tip of Abkhazia. It was a forbidding stretch of land—cold and windswept, seemingly stripped of anything valuable and separated from the mainland by a narrow isthmus of nearly impassable mountains.

The Moderates in power reluctantly agreed, giving the cash-strapped economy a needed infusion of capital. Once the money was spent, the economy stagnated again. Over the next sixty years, Abkhazi rhetoric toward their neighbors ratcheted inexorably toward war.

All these historical ripples were the result of one long-dead man, the Prophet.

When Randal's turn came to demonstrate the impact of ideas as the driving force of history, he chose those same religious settlers, the New Genevans, as his model.

The movement that birthed New Geneva had no central figure. Rather it began as a sentiment, a feeling by many that they were missing out on some unquantifiable thing, some vital essence of what it meant to be human.

By the twenty-third century the social forces of political unification and mass communication had created a bleakly homogenous world. A materialistic worldview was ascendant and the unvoiced assumption of society's leaders was that happiness, fulfillment and social progress could best be defined in monetary terms.

But man could not live by bread alone.

With full bellies and empty souls, humanity went looking for answers. Tribalism came briefly into vogue among young people. Luddite groups organized bombing campaigns against tech centers. Others embraced Transhumanism, seeking transcendence by fusing humanity with technology.

The most lasting impact was in a return to traditional religion. Adherence to the world's faiths had declined, and Christianity was no exception. It seemed for nearly two centuries to have lost its vigor, with the teaching of the Church devolving into a nebulous humanitarianism.

Here and there a thoughtful individual began to look to the past for answers. Some began once more to think of Christianity in terms of a relationship with a living God. Initially the number of these was so small that the early talks on the subject took place between virtual strangers in virtual rooms.

From these grassroots, a worldwide social movement sprouted. Hundreds of thousands of churches were built, but these were merely the outward manifestations. The real drama was less visible—the changed lives of hundreds of millions. Sociologists of religion christened the movement the "Second Reformation."

Reformed pilgrims went on to found numerous colonies. Coming late in the colonial period, the most desirable planets were long since claimed, so most of the Reformer's settlements were in the rim of backwater planets known as the Penumbra. Much like the first Reformation, the believers placed a marked emphasis on education, work and sober living. Work joined with frugality yielded a high savings rate; savings turned to capital and capital became the engine that prospered the colonies.

New Geneva was no exception. As their economy surged ahead, they sought to emulate their forbears, founding many universities and colleges. New technologies allowed them to access minerals in the mountains of the isthmus.

It was at this point that Abkhazia first cast a covetous eye toward the prosperous south. Economic malaise sparked a rise in Purism. These Purists soon demanded territorial concessions from New Geneva.

Thus Randal found himself looking across at tens of thousands of men planning to kill him come morning. Given the odds, they'd likely succeed. The realization made Randal's scalp tingle and a despairing sort of queasiness well up in his gut. He scowled at the moment of weakness. Man was a breath and a shadow, as Euripides had said. All that was left to him was duty. He was thankful for the classics his father had force-fed him while growing up. There was cold comfort in stoicism. Glancing up into the early morning sky, he murmured a quiet prayer asking God for courage, grace, and wisdom not to get his people killed.

In that moment there was a flash of light, followed almost instantly by several others.

A burst of static crackled in his ear, followed by Jeni Cho's voice. It sounded high-pitched and more excited than he'd ever heard it. "Third Platoon, this is Lance Corporal Cho. Satellite communication with headquarters has been knocked out. Also, a suborbital liner has strayed into restricted airspace on trajectory for our poz."

On the heels of Jeni's call came Lieutenant Kenshiro, the platoon leader. "The Old Man just put us on Alert Five status. Get everybody on the line, suits buttoned-up and looking sharp. Out."

Motioning for Sanchez to wake the others, Randal scanned the sky for the suborbital. After several moments he made it out, enhancing the image until some level of detail was visible. It was an Abkhazi model. They liked to build on a monumental scale and this craft was no exception. Oddly, there were bulky external fuel pods under the wings. All of the suborbitals he was familiar with used nuclear fuel pellets. Were times so hard for the Abkhazi that they'd resorted to internal combustion?

Then, seemingly in slow motion, the pods tumbled from the wings and fell from view. A breathless Jeni came back across the comset. "God save us! Everybody better be suited up. I think we've got gas incoming."

Randal scanned the HUD, checking his suit integrity. No problems there. Looking over his fire team, however, he noticed Mireault with the helmet of her medic suit resting back on its hinges. She was obviously still trying to wake up.

"Mireault," he growled over the speakers, "Get your flaming helmet on." She quickly locked it in place, flashing a thumbs up.

Cylindrical shapes dropped among the New Genevan positions, most of them concentrated down the mountainside where the foot infantry had entrenched. The large canisters hissed as they fell, leaving mist trailing in their wake that was vaguely yellow even in the early morning light.

The cries that soon overwhelmed the Battalion ComNet were the closest thing Randal could imagine to souls in Hell. Terrified, gurgling, howling men overlapped each other's transmissions, all of them begging for help, even for death. Adding to the terrible surreality of it all was Major Tarrington's nasally voice calling for order. As if order could be found in the face of such horror. What the devil was happening? Everyone was supposed to be airtight.

Lieutenant Kenshiro came in on the Platoon ComNet. "All teams, sitrep, over."

Giving his people a quick visual, Randal found they were mercifully all right. "Team Two, no casualties."

"Team Three, all's well."

Thank God. That was Jack.

"Team One, we're up."

"Team Four, no casualties."

It must be the foot infantry that was suffering, he thought. "Mireault, come with me, let's see what we can do," he said, surprised how level his voice held. "The rest of you maintain position."

The path down to the line infantry was nearly three hundred meters long and very steep. Randal hoped they'd given the medic at least a modicum of rough terrain drills.

Not looking back, he started his half running, half sliding descent. As always, he was amazed at the engineering that went into the LANCER suit. Sixty-five hundred microcomputers dispersed throughout the rig fed data to its artificial musculature. A virtual gyroscope in the suit's "brain" constantly updated the microcomps on exactly which direction was up. This was known as travel-by-wire.

The suit responded to the wearer's movements through a series of gel-filled sacks lining the interior of the armor. These sacks served two purposes: protecting the wearer from the impact of incoming projectiles and reading the pressure from the wearer's movements. Any body movement caused an instantaneous mimicked reaction by the suit. Some actions required finesse, and so Randal was a little worried as he hustled down the mountainside; Mireault hadn't yet had time to develop such skills.

His foot struck a rocky outcropping and he found himself unexpectedly airborne. There was a jolt as the suit's jump jets kicked in and suddenly the world was right side up again. Stumbling to a stop about forty meters from the infantry trench line, he turned to wait for Mireault.

The girl wasn't far behind. He blinked at the grace with which she moved, adroitly negotiating the broken terrain even faster than he had done. Reaching the rocky nose, she hopped from it, her jets flaring briefly as she planted a landing squarely in front of him.

"Nice descent." He couldn't keep the surprise from his voice.

"Twelve years of Cecchetti ballet," she answered simply.

"That's what I get for taking rugby. Let's go check the line-doggies."

The two approached the trenches from behind. At ten meters he halted, awaiting a challenge from the infantry. When nothing was heard after several moments, he hoarsely whispered, "Hey, straight-legs… you awake?"

There was no response.

Trying to conceal his worry, he headed for the first foxhole. Spotting no movement, he tore back the overhead cover so Mireault could work unobstructed. Two masked and chem-suited infantrymen lay inside. Their posture was all wrong. Both had limbs twisted at unnatural angles, torsos wrenched horribly, fingers clutching and frozen in place.

Mireault leaped inside and popped open her medic kit. After pulling out a rectangular device, she moved it down the length of the first man's body at a distance of about three centimeters. She repeated the process on the second, emitting a sigh. "No life-signs, Corporal."

"Nerve gas," Randal explained, remembering belatedly to call up a chem sensor readout on his HUD. There were traces of three chemicals: Martex, a blister agent; Virtus-D, a favorite nerve agent the Abkhazi stockpiled by the ton; and an unidentified solvent. He bet the solvent was what enabled the poisons to penetrate the infantry's protective gear. Each was a short-term agent; already they were dispersing to tolerable levels. "It's probably safe to breathe, but don't unmask yet."

In the next hole lay two more bodies. Surprisingly, one of the occupants still clung to life. Mireault climbed in and gently removed the soldier's mask. Perhaps he had once been handsome, but it was impossible to tell. His skin was scorched by the blister agent. It had blinded his eyes and scalded his throat so he could only emit confused wheezing sounds. His body was twisted like the others, his breathing shallow fits.

Mireault took a hyposyringe from the medical case, injecting the man with a nerve-gas counteragent and a painkiller. Settling in next to him, she pulled him gently into her arms. He croaked something, perhaps a name. Ellen... Evelyn? His arms flailed as he reached for her, his haywire nervous system refusing to obey.

Not looking at Randal, Mireault popped the seals on her helmet and pushed it back. "I'm here, honey..." she told the man softly.

A look of serenity came over the man. "Evelyn..."

Mireault looked ready to cry, taking a deep breath and stroking his hair softly. She sang to him in a whisper. The song was French and sounded like a lullaby. Her voice was frightened and a little off-key, but Randal was forced to look away, the sweetness of it penetrating his reserve. He needed to be tough to get his people through the next few hours. By the time her song was finished, the man had given up his fight. She pressed a hand to his forehead and whispered a good-bye before leaving the foxhole.

The other armored medics were checking the last of the foxholes. It was staggering—no one was left alive in the forward positions.

Someone must have given an all-clear, because the infantry pressure tents unsealed. The First Sergeant of the company closest to Randal formed up his men and started counting heads. Doing a quick count of his own, Randal was shocked to find nearly a third of the foot infantry gone. They must have been at one-third security, the remainder safely asleep in their tents. The odds in the coming battle had just gotten steeper.

Randal pitched in as the dead were policed up, tagged and bagged behind the line. As soon as the grisly task was complete he and Mireault headed back to the team's position up-mountain. The Abkhazi could have used quick-dispersing chemicals rather than persistent agents for only one reason.

They were planning on occupying that stretch of land very soon.

3

Be convinced that to be happy means to be free
and that to be free means to be brave.
Therefore do not take lightly the perils of war.
—Thucydides

First light had just kissed the western sky as movement commenced on the Abkhazi side of the Demilitarized Belt. Here and there a helmet bobbed into view or light glinted from a vehicle's viewshield. The faint sound of automatic cannon fire carried to Randal and a small orange burst exploded over the Abkhazi troops.

"I don't believe it! They got one of my drones," came Jeni's voice across the comset. "Their main body is forming up on the other side of that hill. I didn't know that many sodding people lived in Abkhazia!"

Randal smiled in spite of himself. Jeni's approach to commo etiquette was always a little left-of-center.

A *carump* sounded from behind the opposing hill. Seconds later whistling sounds presaged the explosion of an artillery shell down near the infantry trenches. A geyser of smoke and dirt plumed several meters short of them.

Weird, thought Randal. You don't see any flame like on trideo, just a big smoke puff.

A few tics and then a second round struck, this one closer. The Abkhazi walked their rounds step by step until they were falling regularly among the foxholes. The earth shook under the relentless impact of 198- and 240-millimeter shells.

Rockets streaked overhead as the New Genevans counter-fired with their own batteries. They had abandoned tubed artillery long before, favoring more effective rocket and missile systems. Additionally, scores of drones flew over the enemy positions, most with targeting lasers used to guide incoming Genevan missiles.

For several minutes a running artillery duel took place. The batteries on both sides would fire a few salvos and then frantically evacuate to another area before an answering barrage could destroy them.

The NGDF had a solid qualitative advantage over the Abkhazi, but this edge was offset by the vast numerical superiority of the Abkhazi Artillery Corps. The Khlisti saint Josef Stalin had a point when he said that quantity has a quality all its own.

Mireault joined Randal in his fighting position. She seemed restless. Medics were non-combatants and there was little to do until someone caught an unlucky round. "Are we winning?"

"For the moment, yeah. Our guys have spent a month digging in. Meanwhile, the Abbies are on the march—easy pickings for our cluster munitions."

"Here we go," called Jeni. "Main body's in motion."

Enemy forces crested the ridge. From two kilometers away, they appeared to progress almost slowly, though Randal knew they were moving full-tilt. He'd read of swarming insects that existed back on Terra before tailored viruses wiped them out. The wave of Abkhazi looked like locusts, devouring everything they came upon.

A line of tanks spearheaded the rush, both tracked and the lighter hover variants. Behind followed infantry mounted on hover-sleds and then the main body of troops in squad-wedges. Trailing the main body by a good distance was a section of black-painted vehicles. They looked to be wheeled, lightly armored and armed only with an autocannon on a swivel turret.

Those would be the Scourge of the Prophet, Randal remembered from his briefings. In peacetime they were the secret police of Abkhazia, rooting out infidels and keeping the people in check. In wartime they enforced orthodoxy among the soldiers. They were a quasi-priestly caste, rousing the troops with promises of evolution to pure consciousness should they die in battle. During combat they were there to gun down any troops who might break and run for the rear.

Johnny Warfield cut in on the Platoon ComNet. "For what we are about to receive, may the Lord make us truly thankful."

"Shut your cake-hole, Warfield. Everyone fire at will," came Lieutenant Kenshiro's order. The vanguard was still out of range for Randal's auto-cannon, but he heard the crack of Rogers' railgun from down the line.

What Rogers struck was impossible to tell. The heavy railguns of the battalion's hovertank company were working murder on the enemy by then, joined by the anti-vehicular rockets of the foot infantry. Much of the enemy's forward edge simply evaporated, the heat and force of the explosions annihilating the sled-borne soldiers. Their tanks fared little better, the hulks becoming burning obstacles to the follow-on troops.

The range-finder on his HUD placed the lead edge of the enemy at 900 meters, just within the autocannon's effective range. He and the other two cannoneers on the team opened up, spraying a hail of caseless 13.7 mm depleted uranium shells downrange.

Randal smiled coldly as his first salvo opened up a six-wheeled scout car. For the next several minutes he fell into a rhythm of target acquisition and firing. The enemy's speed ensured many shots went wide, while armor deflected others. Often it was difficult to see much of anything in the chaos. He nailed an infantry transport and it ground to a halt. Seconds later, an incoming rocket cracked it in half. He grunted in satisfaction as his cannon took apart the skirting of a hovertank - the speeding craft nosed into the dirt, main cannon bending into a useless angle.

Randal pulled back the zoom on his viewscreen, taking a moment to survey the larger battle. The surviving enemy vehicles had reached the NGDF lines and infantry transports began disgorging waves of gray-clad troops. They drastically outnumbered the New Genevans.

But conflicts were won and lost in the heart, and the enemy had already lost much of its *élan*. No one wanted to be the first to die. Caught between the guns of the NGDF to the front and the Scourge of the Prophet behind, the advance slowed to a crawl. It was truly a bizarre sight, thousands of enemy soldiers almost walking into the NGDF perimeter.

Jack apparently had the same thought. "Oh no, after you," he said over the comset with a cynical chuckle.

The foot infantry took full advantage of the situation, opening up with flechette rifles, autogrenade launchers and anti-personnel rockets at point-blank range.

Given the proximity of the enemy, Randal switched weapons and hosed the Abkhazi with the arm-mounted light machine gun. Through his sighting reticule, he could clearly see his targets dance and fall as the bullets struck, and while a detached part of his mind knew he should be disgusted, fear and adrenaline drowned out any other emotions.

The carnage was more than the demoralized enemy could bear. They killed plenty of NGDF troops just by sheer weight of numbers, but in the end they crested and broke, streaming back toward the border. The Scourge made a feeble effort to stem the retreat, but in the end decided that seeking cover might be the right idea after all.

"*C'est hyper chouette!*" Mireault called out jubilantly behind him. "We won!"

Randal felt badly for her. "That was just the first wave, Private Mireault. We haven't seen a fifth of their numbers yet. Now that they've tested us, they should hit with their full strength. They'll win by attrition if nothing else."

"*Ça craint!*"

ↀↀ

Once the enemy was back across the border, NGDF medics filtered out from the trenches. Kneeling beside Abkhazi wounded, they began treating those who moments before had tried to kill them. Brainwashed as they were, the Abkhazi struggled against their would-be healers.

Along with the danger from their patients, ammunition from the burning vehicles was cooking off in the heat, warheads firing in random directions. Randal wasn't surprised when the first explosion went off near a medic, tossing him like a child. He assumed it was a cooked-off shell.

Then rounds began falling in profusion. The defenseless medics were being slaughtered. There wasn't time for them to even consider taking cover.

"Stop them!"

Randal caught movement in his peripherals, just in time to restrain the girl before she ran off. "All you could do is die with them," he said, holding her tightly by the shoulder plates.

"But they're non-combatants," she said in a tight voice, shaking her head uncomprehendingly.

"I don't think there are any more non-combatants."

The next wave began in much the same way as the first, the surviving artillery on both sides exchanging barrages, but this time, however, the enemy committed its air power. A wing of Banshee-class attack skimmers swooped down upon the New Genevans. Though low-tech, they were respectable close air support platforms, able to deliver huge amounts of munitions with reasonable accuracy. They got their designation from the shrill keening the engines made passing overhead.

The armored infantry's position up-mountain placed them right at cockpit level as the Banshees screamed in. With the speed they were cruising, Randal would never hit them manually, so he took the risk of activating the small targeting sensor the suit supported. The active sensor could draw enemy fire, especially the anti-radiation missiles carried by the Banshees, but he felt sure the electronic clutter of the battlefield would shield the emissions.

Drawing a bead on the lead skimmer, he triggered a burst, missed.

The skimmers came in at a high angle of attack, their exposed underbellies covered with tumorous-looking clusters of munitions. Stiff ground fire and the smoky trails of surface-to-air missiles rose to meet them, swatting down several. That still left many more to release their deadly cargo.

Their first run complete, the survivors wheeled sharply to circle for another pass. According to the sensor inset on his HUD, there were at least forty of them still airborne.

"The bloody Air Marshall committed the entire NGAF to the other pass," Randal yelled to Mireault. "Even a handful of interceptors might have driven these things off. Wish he could be here now!"

He lined up his reticule on an incoming bird. The underpowered sensor refused to lock while the target was nose-on. Impatiently he waited until the Banshee presented a fat side view, grunting approval as the reticule shifted from green to yellow to red. Hearing tone-lock in his ear, he triggered the autocannon, tearing the skimmer apart.

The Banshees made three more passes before expending their payload. Less than a quarter of the Banshees survived the engagement, but the damage was done. It was difficult for Randal to make out how many troops were left below. Incendiary bombs and fuel-air explosives had set the forest alight—oily smoke billowed into the sky.

Major Tarrington came on the Battalion ComNet. "Delta Company, move forward to augment the line."

Delta was his people, the armored infantry. "It's our turn. Follow me and keep close."

The team slid down the hillside to the trench line. "Sanchez, Kimathi and Tavish take the first hole to the left. Rogers and Mireault stay with me." Up and down the line he noticed more men than he'd expected were up and at their posts.

The dense smoke made optics nearly useless. He switched the view screen to thermal, his world changing to a strange landscape of vibrant, shifting colors. The late autumn ground was still solidly frozen, spreading out monochrome blue in his viewscreen. The smoke was no longer a problem, though burning debris on the battlefield was confusing. He'd have to be sure to only shoot the bright spots that moved.

Suddenly the Abkhazi hill shifted to orange as tens of thousands of men poured over the ridgeline. At that distance it was impossible to discern individuals. Randal was given the unsettling impression of a red-orange blob oozing toward him.

His brain was too numb to muster a prayer, so he made the words of a long-memorized Psalm his own. "O Lord, my God, in you I put my trust; save me from all those who persecute me; and deliver me lest they tear me like a lion."

All his life people told him the safest place to be was the center of God's will. Watching the oncoming tide, he knew that to be the purest bunk. Sometimes God's will was martyrdom. There was no doubt in his mind that he and his men were doing the right thing, defending the defenseless. But there would be no place of safety that day. Taking a deep breath, he prepared himself to die.

For several minutes nothing had come across the comset but static. Abkhazi jamming equipment was decades behind New Geneva's, but if you built jammers big enough and made enough of them, they had an effect.

The garbled voice of Lieutenant Kenshiro came through the comset, distorted by static. "All teams move out on my mark. Work in binary teams and engage the enemy from within their formation." Randal smiled grimly. Finally he'd get to mix it up in close, no more back-benching.

This thought was cut short as a shell burst in front of his position, sending him flying. Slammed into a tree trunk, he slumped down stunned.

❧❧

By the time Randal's vision cleared, the Abkhazi were nearly upon them. The audio cutouts had dampened the blast, but there was still a persistent ringing in his ears. Kimathi's voice sounded distant and tinny as he shook Randal. "Are you alright, Corporal?"

Randal took stock. His suit was pocked with shrapnel, but nothing had penetrated. "Bruised but not broken, thanks." Scrambling to his feet, he groaned, muscles protesting.

Mireault lay sprawled out nearby. Kneeling next to her, Randal popped the panel on her breastplate. Switching to optics, he read the series of green and red bar graphs displayed beneath it. Suit integrity was nominal, respiration and pulse steady. From her lack of movement, consciousness seemed minimal.

Then came the Lieutenant's order and there was no time left to worry about her. "Armored infantry, move out!"

Randal pulled the medic down into the foxhole and then hooked up with Rogers, the other half of his binary team. The two kicked in their jets, launching into the tide of enemy troops. Along the line the rest of Delta Company was doing the same. He landed atop a hapless Abkhazi infantryman, nearly losing his footing.

He and the others began laying about with light machine guns. It was impossible to miss. Enemy troops dropped in scads.

Repeatedly he felt the impact of small-arms fire against his suit. He was thankful the Abkhazi armed their men with archaic rifles rather than flechette-firing weapons. The soft metal of their projectiles might as well have been pebbles tossed against the layered ceramic, ballistic polymer and titanium-alloy mesh of the suit's armor.

Rather than trying to hold back the enemy, the men of Delta Company waded deeper into them. Abkhazi soldiers milled around Randal and Rogers, trying to bring down the two dervishes whirling among them. He imagined it was the same all down the line; twenty eddies in the never-ending river of men and equipment flowing toward the NGDF positions.

Though Randal was careful to shoot in disciplined bursts, a flashing icon on his HUD warned of critically low ammo. Not wanting to be caught empty, he changed tactics. Extending the climbing spikes housed in both the wrists and feet of his suit, he began slashing at the surrounding troops. There was nothing subtle about killing with the spikes. It made Randal want to retch. A queasy giddiness fought against a barbarous rush inside him as he fought.

Over the heads of his enemies Randal spotted a trio of open-topped hovercraft moving quickly towards him—Razors. Though flush with adrenaline, Randal's mind was sane enough to recognize the danger the hovercraft posed.

On the back of each Razor was a twin-barreled gun on a swivel-mount. One half of the weapon was a high-powered microwave projector, the other an ultra-fast firing chaingun. To Randal it was the most fearsome thing on the battlefield. "Rogers! To your Nine—Razor!"

His warning came too late.

The gunner fired a stream of concentrated microwaves at Rogers, invisible in flight but obvious in effect. Roger's suit froze in mid-kick, internal circuitry fried by the burst.

Even above the din of battle Randal could hear the Razor's chain gun open up, demonstrating how the vehicle got its name. The heavy rounds sliced straight through his friend, blowing a huge exit hole out the rear of his suit. The knockback carried Rogers several meters.

Randal's fury didn't allow for speech, not even epithets. Instead he drained the remainder of his autocannon rounds, ripping apart two of the hovercraft. The rotary barrels were still spinning long after the last of the ammunition had cycled through.

He turned on the third Razor and leaped at the craft a bare second before the ground around him was torn apart by chain gun fire.

With a clang he landed on its open back, his momentum shifting the hovercraft enough to knock the gunner overboard. Reaching behind, he seized the pilot, hauling him out and tossing him viciously aside. He jumped from the craft, breaking his fall with a combat roll as the hovercraft collided with an armored personnel carrier.

A new voice broke through the jamming on his comset. "…is acting commander Zhao… dead. Fall back to final defensive line. This is…" The rest was lost in a burst of static.

The order could only mean the line was breaking. He called his team, but only white noise came back. He turned and muscled through the press of Abkhazi, legs churning. Engaging his boosters he jumped the final few meters to the tree line.

Everyone was dead. Already the Abkhazi foot soldiers were securing the hard-won terrain. Dashing past them, Randal searched frantically for the hole where he'd hidden Mireault.

When he found it, he saw that a team of Abkhazi had stationed a heavy machine gun inside. Several others were dragging the unconscious medic away, apparently assuming she was dead.

The machine gun opened up on him. Acting instinctively, Randal used his boosters, angling them sharply. The thrust jetted him sideways. Most of the long burst pitted the ground where he stood a blink before, but the last caught him in the arm.

The angle of deflection saved him, but not before the round scored a deep furrow in his armor. The force of the projectile spun him, flinging him to the ground. Randal rolled to the side, snapping off an LMG burst to distract them. He pushed off from the ground and rushed the nest. Once inside the hole, he made short work of the three-man gun team.

He saw Mireault lying nearby and alone. Evidently the ones dragging her had decided not to tangle with him.

After scooping the girl up in a fireman's carry, he sprinted for the final defensive line. The Abkhazi were intent on reorganizing their formation, so it wasn't difficult to outpace them, slipping out of sight amid the broken terrain of the mountainside.

After several minutes he reached the final defensive line, a saddle between two hilltops. The few remaining defenders were centered on a pair of surviving hovertanks. These were hull-down behind embankments prepared earlier by engineering vehicles. This allowed them to fire railguns over the bank without exposing their hulls.

One Platoon Support Vehicle remained. Randal was pleased to see from the skimmer's markings that it was Jeni Cho. Many of the surviving troops wore the scout armor of the Seventh Dragoons. They'd pulled strategic reserve duty and had only been used to plug holes in the line.

Passing by a tripod-mounted autocannon, he gave an acknowledging nod to the ashen-faced man behind it. The soldier's uniform was dark with blood. Given the situation, even the walking wounded were needed up front. Mireault was just starting to stir as he laid her behind a boulder. He took his place on the line.

After several minutes, Mireault walked unsteadily into view and set to treating the wounded autocanoneer. Once she'd cut the cloth away, Randal could see the angry, irregular gash where shrapnel had lodged in the man's shoulder. The medic spread a compress over the wound and pressed what Randal assumed was a stimulant patch to his neck.

A heavy hand rested on Randal's shoulder; he turned to find a friend. "It's been good to serve with you, Corporal," Kimathi said, taking a knee. "We will talk about today when I see you in Heaven tonight."

Randal followed suit, shaking his head. "I'm hoping we won't remember these things in Heaven. You and I can talk about cricket batsmen and boxing, like usual."

"*Sawa kabisa*. I will enjoy that."

Both laughed with a mirth neither felt, determined to keep up a good front until the end. Then there was nothing else to say, only to wait in silence for that end to come.

When the Abkhazi assaulted, they came as a victorious army, making no pretense of subtlety. They knew victory was theirs. But even demoralized and beaten, the NGDF troops never broke—they were simply consumed, dying in place.

Acting Commander Zhao's final order sounded over the comset. "Retreat to Rally Point Zeta. The Dragoons will rearguard the withdrawal."

Randal fired the last of his LMG ammo and began a zigzag sprint for the rear, sparing a last glance for Kimathi. An incoming rocket had taken his friend from him.

The volume of fire was intense. Everything was obscured with smoke. Entering a momentarily clear patch, Randal spotted Mireault. Several foot soldiers were trying to bear her down with sheer weight of numbers.

She dropped one with an armored knee somewhere soft, but was losing the fight to keep her balance. Vaulting a demolished hoversled, Randal plowed into the knot of troops surrounding the girl, crushing one between them and sending the others flying.

Behind them the Dragoons of the scout company made a last, gallant foray at the enemy, slowing the Abkhazi advance for a short while before being ripped to shreds.

Randal and Mireault caught up with the fleeing caravan of supply crawlers and command vehicles taking the main road southward. Here and there ran a surviving armored infantryman. Another flight of Banshees soared into view overhead. Randal braced for whatever was about to drop on him, but instead the weapon pods detached well ahead of the survivors, scattering small objects over a wide area.

It took him a second to catch on. At first he assumed they were cluster bombs ranging wide of their target. When none exploded he realized they were ADMs—Air Deployable Minefields. The vehicles were boxed in. "This way," he yelled to Mireault, pulling her from the path the others were taking. "Those were mines!"

He and Mireault clambered up the steep bank to the east of the road. Looking back, he witnessed the final moments of the battalion as hovering gunships finished what the Banshees had begun, shredding the vehicles with chain gun fire. In seconds each was a burning shell.

The two of them didn't stop running for several kilometers. Randal finally called a halt to catch their breath. Scanning behind for any sign of pursuit, he took in the skyline. It was blanketed with dark pillars of smoke.

A passage from his Greek lessons surfaced in his mind; it was the inscription over the graves at Thermopylae: "Go tell the Spartans, stranger passing by, that here obedient to their laws we lie…"

4

Gentlemen, we are being killed on the beaches.
Let's go inland and be killed.
—General Norman Cota: D-Day, 1944

No sign of movement. Randal frowned, lowering the magnification on the viewscreen. "It looks like we're the first to the rally point, Mireault," he said, motioning for her to follow. Left unspoken was, *hopefully we're not the last.*

The rally point was a hillock with a craggy north face that made it a tenable defensive position. When battalion command had chosen it, the idea was to have a place to reform for a counterattack if the NGDF should be driven back from the border. That turned out to be a sick joke, thought Randal. We'd be lucky to organize a Christmas crèche, let alone a counterattack. He assumed whoever showed up to take charge would guide them south until they found friendly troops.

At the top of the hillock was a dense stand of aspen. Their canopy would provide decent overhead concealment. It was unlikely the bloodied Abkhazi ground troops would press forward until the following day, but if he were marshaling the enemy troops he'd be sending out Banshees to harass any NGDF stragglers.

The two of them rested, both too drained to speak. He stretched out prone, turning his sensors all the way up to listen for movement.

In the quiet moment his thoughts turned inward, as always. His reaction to the whole thing surprised him; primarily that he had no strong reaction at all. The morning's nightmare was a long blur of confused images, their chronology undefined. He knew that acting natural was scarily unnatural. But thoughts came hazily, and his head and stomach had a hollow, buzzing feeling.

He heard a rustle.

It didn't come from Mireault; the girl hadn't stirred since they arrived.

Another crackle of footsteps—faint, but there. The pace increased, and it seemed to him a second or even third set could be discerned crunching through the autumn leaves.

This is not good, he thought, glancing over the lip of the hilltop. If the footsteps belonged to an Abkhazi patrol he wasn't sure what he would do. Given his total lack of ammunition, he'd have little more than caustic remarks with which to stop them.

Three figures emerged from the dry creek bed they were following for cover. Seeing LANCER suits on the trio, Randal let himself breathe again. Friendlies. Hesitant to send a comset message in case the Abkhazi were intercepting, he raised a hand, waving it until they acknowledged with one of their own.

The three troopers joined them on the hill. As they pushed back their helmets he was cheered to spot a friend. "Jack Van Loon. I knew they couldn't kill you," he said, slapping his friend's armored shoulder. Happiness flickered for a moment, but then reality snuffed it out.

"Glad to see you made it, Randal. Who's in charge?"

"You are, I suppose." Did it matter?

"Not likely, me auld. You pinned those hard stripes on first."

Randal scowled, knowing Jack was right. When two troops had the same rank the deciding factor was their date of promotion. "Just until a sergeant gets here."

Looking over the other two, he was disappointed that both belonged to other fire teams. He'd held out a slim hope that Tavish or Sanchez might have escaped. He didn't know either of the survivors well; both had transferred into the battalion recently from the Huguenot Division.

The older one, Sergei Lebedev, looked as out of place in the infantry as a socialist at a Founder's Party convention. He had a nervous, almost fawning way about him that made Randal jumpy. It was said around the barracks that he'd been a scientist back on Terra. More than his education, Lebedev's appearance made him stick out. There was a perpetual jaundiced cast to his skin and his oversized nose always seemed stuffed up. The little Belarusian might have stood 1.6 meters in his boots.

The other, David Pyatt, was an unknown to him, though he'd heard once that Pyatt had some peculiar religious views. Regardless, Randal was glad to see anyone alive.

"Where are the others?"

"It's just me and Mireault."

Jack stared at him with hollow eyes, but Randal had the feeling they were focused on events hours past and far away. "I don't know if anyone else made it out."

"You and your men get some rest, Jack. I'll keep watch."

Late in the afternoon the group was surprised by the arrival of a PSV. It settled down by the copse of aspen, the cockpit sliding open. Setting Pyatt on sentry duty, he and Jack went to greet the arrival. When the craft opened up, Jeni Cho left her harness, climbing out on the stubby wing. She plopped down and dangled her feet over the side.

"You made it," Randal said, settling for the obvious. Words were still coming slowly to him.

Jeni jerked a thumb over her shoulder. "We'd have been here two hours ago, but Johnny's been playing hide and seek with Abkhazi interceptors."

"They quit playing once I tagged a couple with brilliant missiles," Johnny chimed in. Considering the daftness of the source, Randal thought it a lucky thing that at least the missiles were brilliant.

"Jeni, we need to get word to the rear about the breakthrough. The last thing the main body needs is thirty-thousand Abkhazi popping up unexpectedly on their flank."

"Already thought of that, Randy," she said, using his least favorite of her nicknames for him. Climbing back into the cockpit, she donned a black helmet with plum blossoms airbrushed on the sides. It had an opaque silver visor Randal knew to be a viewscreen.

"With the satellites down, I'll need to use the commo drone. I can send an encrypted LR burst. It'll have the range we need, plus it's a bouncer. The bad guys will have a bugger of a time DFing us."

The canopy slid smoothly back into place and small bay doors opened on top of the skimmer. A meter-wide drone lifted out with a whir, ascending rapidly until Randal lost it for the tree canopy. It was a newer model, made in the spherical form designers were favoring in recent years. A wide assortment of communications and electronic warfare gear was stuffed inside, but the engineers had maintained a smooth, molded exterior. A drone that looked like a flying barn on a targeting screen was a dead drone.

Several minutes later the young woman guided the drone back to its berth, popped the canopy and set aside the helmet. "I let them know," she said with a shrug. "For security reasons they couldn't say much, but the gist is that the main army is on the retreat too. The good news is they're still intact, and withdrawing in an orderly manner. We're supposed to rendezvous with them north of Providence."

Randal murmured a thank you, walking back to his post, already preoccupied with planning a route southward. Providence, the only sizeable city on the isthmus, was over three hundred kilometers away. He wanted to have suggestions ready for whichever sergeant showed up to take charge. Randal didn't envy him the task—it would be a difficult passage even without the added worry of air strikes.

అఆ

By dusk, he'd lost hope of an NCO arriving to assume command. There was no sign of one, or anyone else for that matter.

His mind ran through the alternatives. There were precious few. He could simply refuse to take charge, but that wasn't really an option. A military unit couldn't function as a democracy. He could tell Jack to take command, but he knew the man wouldn't usurp even if asked. It was Randal's responsibility.

All his life he'd felt an inevitability pressing in upon him. Being the child of Cameron Knox, he was picked for leadership in everything from sports to student government. For years it was just assumed he would go into politics. Not that anyone ever asked him, it just seemed predestined. Joining the military as a grunt had looked like his only means of escape. He was beginning to scan how Jonah felt when he got tapped to go to Nineveh.

Gathering the others, he sighed resignedly. "I'm sure you've heard, we've been ordered to exfiltrate south to Providence. We'll move out at 2300 tonight. Meantime, Lance Corporal Cho will swap out your suit batteries for fresh ones and resupply you with ammo. You can pop the chests on your LANCER suits and cool down, but don't get out of them. We could still get pounced. Jeni, when you're finished with that I want you in harness, keeping an eye out for enemy aircraft."

Jeni raised a hand. "Um, Corporal Knox? I know you're doing the good soldier bit and all, but I'm military intelligence. I answer directly to the battalion commander, not corporals. It's GMLC Article Nine, paragraph two, subsection A if you need to check."

Barracks lawyer, Randal thought, resisting the urge to choke the girl. She was one of that breed of soldier who memorized chapter and verse of the General Military Legal Code expressly to find ways to circumvent it. Jeni knew every conceivable loophole in the regs.

After everything that happened that day, the pettiness of her protest exasperated him. "According to Article Twelve, in the absence of a
cohesive command structure, ranking soldier takes charge. The battalion
commander is dead, along with everyone else."

For once, Jeni didn't have an answer. Likely she never imagined he
knew the regs well enough to call her on it.

"Further, Lance Corporal, question my orders again and I'll send you
back to report to the Battalion Commander. What's left of him, anyway."
His voice came out low.

The girl wisely held her tongue.

"If there are no other questions, then rack out for now. We've got a
long walk ahead of us. Corporal Van Loon and I will stand first watch."

༒ ༒

Randal padded back to his spot after a fourth attempt to quiet
Lebedev's enthusiastic snores. "You still have those maduros in your
personal box, Jack?" he asked in a hoarse whisper, stretching out on the
ground. One kept an eye to the northeast, the other northwest.

"I was just thinking about those cigars," Jack said, reaching to pat his
suit's integral backpack. "I could really go for one after a day like this."

"I'd ask you to break them out, but they'd look like signal flares on
night vision."

"Plus that Pyatt guy would start preaching. He's a First Centy, you
know."

"A First Centy? Heaven help us." The term was a misnomer if he'd ever
heard one. In the name of the early church the First Century movement
tossed out an educated clergy, rejected any type of liturgy, subordinated
Scripture to experience and was suspicious of anyone with an advanced
degree. A lot of the Greek and Latin Randal translated at Athanasius
Academy was early church texts. In their rejection of the physical world
and their anarchic approach to church life, the First Century types much
more resembled the Gnostics of the First Century than the actual early
church. One way this manifested was in their total abstinence from wine,
fermented drink, or tobacco in any form.

Jack cleared his throat. "How you holding up, man?"

"I'm okay."

"Really?"

Randal hesitated. "No, not really. Leading a team is one thing. But this… You want the truth? I wish you'd been the one to pin on corporal first. Then you'd be in the hot seat."

"Now don't wish that. God wasn't surprised by anything that happened here today. All of this is part of the plan, even down to which lowly corporal got himself promoted first."

"It would have been nice if He'd stepped in today while His people were being slaughtered."

Jack drummed armored fingers on the hard-frozen ground. "I'm going to say something and you just be quiet and listen, okay?" He seemed to take Randal's silence for assent. "You do everything on your own. You were saved by grace, but you've never really lived by it, have you?"

"This seem like the time for a sermon?"

Jack gave him a hard look. "This seems exactly like the time. You talk a good game about faith, but you gut through everything. We can't afford for you to crack."

≈≈

At 2300 the team formed up to begin the trek to Providence.

Given the narrow trails they would be following, Randal put the team in single file. They'd be ducks in a row in the event of an ambush, but there wasn't room for a more dispersed formation such as traveling overwatch.

Both he and Jeni were concerned that the PSV might draw unwanted attention, so the skimmer would keep well ahead of them, stopping at preassigned way points to meet up. At the waypoints he could give fresh orders and the PSV would update the team on anything spotted along the way. This would allow them to maintain commo silence while on the march.

"All right. Van Loon, you take point. Pyatt, you're first on rear watch. Mireault, I want you close enough for me to hit you with a dead cat, got it?"

"Yes, Corporal." Mireault's voice was shaky and her face had a blanched quality to it.

Randal knew he should say something encouraging to her, perhaps even pull her aside a moment. But women were ciphers to him even when in an equable mental state, let alone at times like this.

Pyatt cleared his throat. "Say, Corp? My father was a wildcatter up here—I grew up in these mountains. Put me on point."

"We can do that. Van Loon will bring up the rear instead." He gave a thumbs up to Johnny and the PSV lifted off, cruising southward on vectored thrust. "Let's move out."

Pyatt set a good pace as they traveled and was careful to pass back warnings of treacherous footing with hand signals. Randal valued his experience. He'd spent a fair amount of time in the mountains himself, but his knowledge of mountaineering was the kind one picked up while thunderboarding at resorts.

Randal surveyed the terrain ahead of them. They were still in the piedmont of the range; the low ridges covered in stands of linden, hornbeam and ash. It would be another day until they reached the serious mountains.

Several hours into the march they came upon a creek. A moraine of rocky debris had partially damned the stream, forming a pool. A watering flock of partridges burst into flight at their arrival, the sudden movement causing Randal to raise his weapon. Chuckling sheepishly, he said, "Okay, we'll go down in groups of two and fill up. Everyone else stays under cover, got it?"

The team went down in pairs and refilled the internal water bladders of their suits, all of which were close to empty. The designers had needed practically every centimeter of space to jam in the assortment of microprocessors, servos, synth-musculature, electronic-countermeasures, electronic-counter-countermeasures and the other tech that modern warfare demanded. Life-support, weapons and ammunition took up much of the remaining space, leaving little room for water or waste elimination.

The team was filing back into line when Jack whispered from the rear, "Got movement."

Calling up a ground surveillance sensor window on his HUD, Randal noticed it too. It was a ghost of a contact; the target was likely stealthed. With hand signals he put the team into a 360-degree perimeter. He and Jack waited in the prone for their stalker to come into view.

A silhouette glided over the ridgeline.

"Halt. Who's there?" Randal's voice was tight in his ears.

The figure froze, keeping hands out at its side in a disarming gesture. "Private Nabil al-Hise, Seventh Dragoons Light Cavalry Troop."

Randal kept his autocannon trained on the figure. It was more than a little suspicious—the man's voice carried traces of Abkhazia and he was very late. "Tungsten."

"Albatross," the newcomer answered.

At least he knew the proper password. "Advance and be recognized."

Al-Hise approached slowly, his walk punctuated with stagger steps. Randal rose to his feet, motioning with the muzzle of the LMG. "Pop your helmet."

With a hiss of pressurized air, the helmet slipped back on its hinges. The man's wheat-toned complexion was visible even in by moonlight. His eyes were very dark and he had what looked to be a thin build. He appeared older than Randal, maybe twenty-three or so. There was not a hair on his head, not even eyebrows.

"You're Abkhazi and you took sixteen hours to get here," Randal observed flatly. He tensed, ready for the foreigner to try something rash.

Al-Hise's eyes narrowed. "I was followed. I led them away first." His knees buckled, but with visible effort he forced himself back straight.

Randal readied another question, but just then the man dropped to his knees and sprawled forward. Mireault pushed past Randal and knelt beside the fallen trooper. With a strained grunt, she flipped him onto his back.

Looking over his suit, Mireault spoke, as much to herself as to the others. "There's an entry hole, low on the torso." She opened her medic kit, taking out a slim electronic key. After feeling under al-Hise's arm, she inserted the key into a slot hidden beneath. The suit's breastplate opened with a whir, the gel packs draining into their reservoirs.

Pulling a thermal blanket from the kit, she spread it on the frozen ground. "Help me get him out," she said, waving over Lebedev. Together they slid al-Hise from the suit, laying him out on the crinkling blanket. His fatigue blouse was matted and sticky as the wound seeped from his lower abdomen. She cut away fabric to take a look.

The entry wound was small. When she turned him to the side, Randal saw no exit wound. That made him comparatively lucky. Survivable wounds for powered armor wearers were rare, since anything powerful enough to punch through layers of armor would wreak havoc on the thin-skinned human inside.

Mireault sopped the oozing blood with an antibac pad. "I need more light," she said, activating the small UV lamp on her helmet. The rays were invisible to the naked eye, but seen through low-light vision it lit the patient like mid-day.

She probed the wound gently with a fingertip. Medic suits used only a thin ballistic weave for the gauntlets, which allowed the medic most of his or her tactile sense and dexterity. "The wound is deep, well into the bowels. I think he'll get septicemia if it isn't taken care of now."

Randal frowned. Field medics didn't have anything like that sort of training.

"Oh hell," she said, a sigh coming across her suit's speakers. "It's a flechette. It needs to come out right away."

Lebedev looked between Randal and the girl. "This is possible to you?"

At this her composure slipped. Apparently she was asking herself the same thing. "I-I don't know. I just don't know. I'm going to run my suit's emergency surgical AI, but it can only give me advice. We're only supposed to stabilize the wounded for transport, the field hospital does the real medicine. This isn't supposed to happen. . ." Spreading her instruments on the blanket, she leaned over the patient. From the hitching breaths coming from her speakers, Randal thought she might actually be crying. It wasn't right; she shouldn't have to make such decisions.

Mireault's hand shook as she took up a laser scalpel. Quaveringly, she admonished Lebedev, "Do exactly what I tell you and nothing else."

Two hours later, the super-dense metal dart lay on the ground beside al-Hise. Mireault and Lebedev slid the patient back into his suit. She pressed a sequence of buttons on the electronic key and then reinserted it into the underarm slot. The breastplate closed, the gel packs refilled and the central processor shifted the suit into a supine position and immobilized it.

Mireault wiped each of the instruments clean and lined them up. She passed a handheld device over them, irradiating any bacteria. Only then did she look back to the others. "I did everything I could. The rest is between him and God." Replacing the surgical tools in the Doc-in-a-box, she added exhaustedly, "I locked his suit in place and gave him a sedative. We should be safe to move him."

The party traveled on until dawn, taking turns by twos hefting the fallen trooper. Pyatt led them to a narrow canyon where they set up camp. A rocky overhang shielded them from observation and a cold, swift-running stream ran through the canyon's center. The PSV went to ground not far upstream, in the shelter of some trees. Johnny and Jeni joined the group, reporting that the Abkhazi didn't yet seem to have moved south.

Randal asked Van Loon to stand watch, allowing the others to unsuit. He shed the armor shell he'd been trapped inside for thirty-six hours. All of his joints were chafed from constant contact with the pressure pads. Even with the suit's life support he smelled stale.

The two girls went downstream to wash away the journey's grime. Meanwhile, the men skinned down to skivvies and waded in. Being late autumn, the water was cold enough to steal breath, but no one complained. It felt good to be alive.

Afterward, the party stretched out on the sandy bank. There were only a handful of blankets in the PSV stores, so everyone huddled close against the chill. Randal's eyes closed of their own accord, mercifully ending the longest day of his life.

5

Above all, we must realize that no arsenal. . .
is so formidable as the will and
moral courage of free men and women.
—Ronald Reagan

Teamwork is essential, it gives the enemy
somebody else to shoot at.
—Murphy's 15th Law of Combat

Nightfall found the party on the move again. Progress was slowed as they left the foothills and entered the mountain range itself. The PSV was waiting for them at the first waypoint. Jeni smiled down from the cockpit, jerking a thumb skyward. "Bad news, Randy. They've got air patrols crisscrossing the isthmus at regular intervals."

That was unwelcome news, to say the least. Reluctantly, Randal ordered his people from the trail. It followed the pass and there was too much chance of being spotted while using it. He consulted with Pyatt, both reviewing topographic maps on their viewscreens. They then set out a route which added to the journey's length, but also to their chances of surviving it.

Transporting the wounded al-Hise complicated matters since there were no ropes or harnesses among the team's gear. As they followed the new path, they were often forced to backtrack when faced with excessively steep climbs.

Toward morning they scaled their sheerest cliffside yet. Randal was anxious to reach the top, because flickering light and a pall of smoke were peeking over the rim. He kicked into the rocky face, sinking a climbing spike into the brittle rock to brace himself. Van Loon stood on a narrow ledge below him, holding onto al-Hise. Above, Pyatt and Lebedev waited to haul the wounded man to safety.

Randal hung in between, a wrist and a foot spike in the cliff face, acting as the middle-man. The rock was making him nervous. It was some sort of compressed granite, and several times hand and footholds had snapped off while he climbed.

"Send him, I'm anchored." He reached down for al-Hise's suit, hooking a hand under his arm and hauling him up high enough for Pyatt and Lebedev to grab him. The two hefted al-Hise over the edge, but the shift in weight cracked the rock around Randal's wrist spike. Acting instinctively, he kicked the wall, catching himself at the last possible second. "I'm never leaving the city again," he swore as he crawled on to the plateau.

From the plateau he could see what had flickered earlier in the morning sky. Across the valley was a village lit by flaming buildings. It rested atop a rounded spur which jutted from the opposing mountainside. With all the smoke he could make out few details, just the boxy forms of prefab buildings, a few of them burning brightly. On full magnification he could see tiny figures battling the fires.

Calling up the map on his viewscreen, Randal identified the village as Burnley Gap. That put them a full klick from where they should be. When Abkhazi sat-killers knocked down all of New Geneva's satellites they did more than just disrupt communications, they also rendered useless the global positioning system. Every soldier was trained in land navigation using only digital map and compass, but in practice everyone just relied on their GPS. Randal was getting a remedial lesson from hard experience.

The mountains were full of settlements like Burnley Gap, each sustaining itself through either independent mining operations or "wilderness encounter" tourism. The party had passed two other settlements already, but this was the first they'd found unevacuated. "Looks like something pasted them pretty good," Jack said, walking to Randal's side.

"It's too far south for ground troops, I'd wager strike craft got to them."

"Banshees." Jack made the word sound like a curse. "We should see if our medic can help."

Not thrilled with the delay, but knowing it was the right thing to do, Randal assented. Equally reluctantly, he broke commo silence. "Cho, this is Knox."

The answering voice sounded surprised. "You rang, Randy?"

"Way point four changed. Rendezvous at grid coordinate 2107-5496 at 0630. How copy?"

She repeated the order back to him. "See you then. Cho out."

The group descended the plateau, on a shallower grade than the opposite face. Gravel piles made footing slippery, but aside from a few slides the group made it down without incident. At that altitude the undergrowth was scrubby—mostly hardy grasses and gnarled trees. From what Randal understood, the terraformers who made the planet habitable had selected foliage from nearly every highland region of old Terra.

The terrain was open most of the way to Burnley Gap. If there were any Abkhazi hiding out there, the team would be badly exposed to incoming fire. Randal split them in two, one group keeping to the long, early-morning shadows and prepared to provide covering fire, the other bounding to the first available cover.

Leapfrogging, the team crossed the danger area until they were all lying prone in an erosion-created ditch near the village. The ditch ran perpendicular to a well-worn dirt road which traveled from the center of town, down the hill and southward into the mountains.

Randal was leery about just walking into town for two reasons. First, the village had just been bombed. He wasn't keen on death at the hand of a trigger-happy militiaman. Second, no one was yet sure the New Genevans were still in control of the town.

"Corporal Knox, to your three," Pyatt said, pointing.

Shifting his attention, Randal spotted what had interested Pyatt—a man walking the perimeter in a cumbersome-looking suit of powered armor. It was easy to spot, as its entire surface area was gleaming white. Randal supposed it had last been painted in a winter month, which left its owner looking like the polar bear holo Randal had seen at the Terrarium in Shiloh. "Oi—that's a first-generation suit. I thought they'd retired all of those."

Jack high-crawled over and joined the conversation. "Most of 'em. Some they gave to militia commanders. My neighbor got one."

"Well, that solves one worry. At least they're on our side. We shouldn't all go up though. They're liable to think it's safer to ask forgiveness than ask questions."

"I'll go." Jack rose to his feet.

"Careful, Jack."

"I've got a wife and kid. I'm always careful."

"And that's why you joined the infantry."

Jack didn't answer, intent upon entering the open as slowly and unthreateningly as possible. Keeping his hands well in the air, he began climbing the spur to the hamlet. Any vegetation on the spur had long ago been stripped away by the village, leaving a barren kill zone for Jack to cross. The villagers spotted him almost immediately, excited shouts carrying to Randal and the others. Armed men ran to the perimeter.

Randal wished he could just raise them on the comset, but it was useless trying. The armored infantry used high-level encryption for all their communications. The coms issued to the militia were also encrypted, though on a simpler level. All either of them would receive from the other was squawks and gibberish.

At about 200 meters from the perimeter, Jack halted and called out, "I'm a good guy. Please nobody put any holes in me." Two militiamen in hunting clothes walked out to Jack and escorted him inside the village. He reemerged several minutes later, gave a thumbs-up and motioned for the team to join him.

As Randal approached the perimeter, he saw the hard eyes of the village defenders peering from their fighting positions. Mountain people were a tough lot, in his experience. Mounds of fresh dirt sat beside each hole. The militia needed to smooth them out; the piles were signposts for where the fighting positions lay.

The team filed into town. Jack met them in the square, standing between an enormous, balding fellow in the obsolete powered armor, and a whip-thin man in a clerical collar. Flipping back his helmet, Randal led his people up to the trio.

"Corporal Randal Knox," Jack said formally, motioning to the large man on his left. "This is Mayor Jowett. He heads the militia here. And this is the Reverend Hauptmann."

Randal nodded respectfully. "Pleasure to meet you, goodmen."

The two gave him odd looks, not returning the greeting.

It took Randal a couple of seconds to realize what was going on. "Yes, Cameron Knox's boy," he said, forcing a smile to set them at ease.

The two glanced at each other. "This is a surprise," said the mayor. "We're all great admirers of your father."

"I am too," he said, anxious to change the subject. "Did you get caught by air strikes?"

"We did." Reverend Hauptmann motioned to the gutted buildings Randal saw burning earlier. "Some families lost everything, but thanks be to Christ, no one was killed."

The mayor rumbled in a deep basso, "There was only a pair of aircraft. We drove them off after the second pass. They didn't expect so much ground fire, I imagine."

"It looks like you have the fires in hand, but can we provide any other help? We have a medic," interjected Jack.

"No, we were fortunate. The woman and children were in the mineshaft you see beyond the church there, and the men were in their holes. However, I see that you've a wounded man of your own," the reverend said, looking to al-Hise.

"We got hammered pretty hard at the border," Jack answered quietly.

"Well, you can rest in the church and we'll put on coffee. We're hungry for news. The town is in a trideo dead zone with these mountains and our satellite comsystem hasn't been able to get anything for two days."

That explains why they haven't evacuated, Randal thought, not relishing the bad tidings he was about to deliver.

The reverend and his wife, a plump, cheerful woman in insulated nightclothes, set them up in the church sanctuary. Like all buildings in the town it had been prefabricated and delivered by cargo dirigibles. These were slow, but cheap to produce and maintain, and capable of efficiently moving tons of cargo over otherwise impassable terrain.

Since a limited number of firms built prefab structures, one little mountain town looked much like another. This church had the same stained glass windows and synth-wood pews he remembered from the chapel at the winter resort he frequented in childhood.

Seated on sleeping mats, their armor arranged along the wall, the group sipped coffee and updated the mayor and reverend on recent events. An hour later they heard the whoosh of the PSV landing outside. Randal grimaced. He'd forgotten to warn the militia about Jeni's arrival.

"Nice, Randal." Jeni strolled into the sanctuary with Johnny at her heels. "Those hicks almost shot us." Abruptly she noticed the two villagers. "Greetings and salutations. What a charming outpost you have! I love the . . . trees."

"Mayor, Reverend, this is our dronekeeper, Lance Corporal Cho, and our support vehicle pilot, Private Warfield."

Johnny shuffled his feet a bit, spiking up his blond bangs in a habitual gesture. He returned their greetings with a grin. Randal suspected his mental capacity was overtasked with suppressing snickers at Jeni's gaffe.

Jeni plopped down next to Mireault, nudging her out of the way. "Bad news, Randy. The Abbies finally got resupplied, or whatever was holding them up. They're on the move now in a big way."

Frowning, Mayor Jowett cut in. "Are they likely to come here?"

Biting the inside of his cheek thoughtfully, Randal considered the question. "The road they'd follow is several klicks to the east. But they won't leave an unpacified village along their supply route. We're going to need to evacuate you." He sighed inwardly. Taking charge of the NGDF survivors had been an unwelcome enough surprise. Nursemaiding a hundred-odd civilians through occupied territory was definitely not covered in Basic Indoc.

To his credit, the mayor didn't protest, instead merely slapping his thighs and standing. "I'll inform the village elders. It'll take a few hours to get things together."

❧

Randal awoke mid-morning. He stretched and wandered over to Mireault. The girl was kneeling next to al-Hise, changing his dressing. She didn't look up as he approached. "I'm worried about him."

"What's wrong?" He took a seat on the nearest pew.

"I can't get his fever down. He must have a secondary infection or something. It was dark, and there was dirt everywhere..." She trailed off, fingers clearing strands of chetnut hair from her eyes. "I'm doing the best I can."

Randal wished Jack were awake. He was so much better at talking to women. Safely married, he had nothing to fear from them. "You're doing a great job. We're all thankful to have you here, Mireault, really." Not sure what gesture would be appropriate, he settled for giving her shoulder a companionable squeeze.

The girl started at the contact. "Thank you, Corporal Knox," she said, setting aside the soiled dressing and returning to al-Hise.

"Hang in there." With a parting smile he left her, pushing out the double doors of the church. On the stoop he found Jack meditatively rolling two dark, fat cigars between his palms.

"Be your best friend if I get one of those," Randal said, taking a seat and resting back against the railing.

"Who do you think I was waiting for?"

He took the cigar and cutter from Jack and sliced a wedge-shaped section from the endcap.

"Here's a light."

"Thanks." Sparking up with the electric lighter, Randal took a soulful drag and evaluated the end of the cigar critically to ensure he had an even burn.

The two smoked in silence. Around them the villagers bustled, loading cargo crawlers with supplies and packing away valuables. For the two men it was a tranquil moment, time slowing into the lazy curl of cigar smoke. Randal savored each mouthful, taking it in slowly, appreciating the faint cedar undertones.

Down the center of town a line of crawlers was forming. These rugged, tracked vehicles were the primary means of transport in the highlands. Though slow, their low center of gravity and powerful engines were ideal for the rough terrain. The crawlers were piled high with crates, canisters and miscellanea. Bewildered children squalled as parents strapped them onto the removable benches lining the cargo beds.

Jeni's voice sounded over the PSV's external speakers. She and Johnny had spent the morning sleeping in harness. After the Banshee strike of the previous night, Randal wanted early warning of any follow-up attack. "Randy, we've got company. I count six flyers inbound."

Stubbing out his cigar, Randal hustled back into the church, manually activating his suit's comset. "Fast movers?" That would be nice—interceptors wouldn't pose much of a threat to the village.

"Wait one, battlecomp is still IDing them." A whispered curse. "Tentative identification—it looks like troop carriers."

Crunching the numbers, Randal calculated the odds they faced. A forty-man platoon per transport meant a full company would be arriving soon. Worse, if they were air mobile they weren't grunt infantry, but the Theocratic Guard.

Randal ran to the door. Outside, the mayor was directing the loading of one of the cargo crawlers. "Mayor Jowett, we need to get these people moving! The Abbies have Theocratic Guardsmen inbound!"

He ducked back inside the church. The others were looking to him for orders, and he stalled for time while suiting up. What in the world did he have to tell them? Whatever orders he gave, people were going to die.

At least he could ensure that no women would die by his order. "Listen. . . Mireault, you'll travel with the convoy and provide medical support. The rest of us will stay behind to buy time for them to escape."

"Corporal, are you sure?"

"I am. You're too valuable to risk in a skirmish like this. The civilians will need you along the way."

As they left the church, the mayor was already sending off the convoy. Whatever wasn't loaded would have to be abandoned. He apparently had the same idea as Randal; the majority of the men were remaining behind while a small detachment of militia was detailed to guard the women and children.

Mireault knelt down, hefted al-Hise, and carried him to the nearest crawler. She fastened him in and gave the group a wave as the vehicles rumbled into motion. A gaggle of rangy-looking mountain dogs trailed in the dust of the crawlers, their howls echoing from the mountainside. Soon the convoy rounded the mountain, following a road that looked like a glorified game trail.

The rest took their places on the line.

That morning the militia had improved the defensive positions, deepening their holes in the frozen ground and piling scrap metal to frustrate enemy fire. There were sixteen militiamen holding the line in groups of four, one group on either flank, the remaining two in the center. Randal dispatched Jack to the right flank, himself to the left. He wanted the added firepower of Lebedev's railgun and Pyatt's autoloading mortar to shore up the vital center.

The Platoon Support Vehicle was kept well to the rear. While it mounted defensive armament, he wasn't willing to risk it for a temporary tactical advantage. There was always the danger of interceptors skulking behind the shuttles, hidden from sensors in the acoustic clutter of the mountains. Each LANCER suit was dependent upon a recharged power pack from the PSV every seventy-two hours. There were adapters so the suits could recharge from ordinary power sources, but there were few of those in the wilderness. Losing the PSV would mean abandoning their armor.

"Three klicks out," Jeni updated them. "Should be in visual any second."

Six black, snub-nosed shuttles appeared on Randal's viewscreen. Their noses pitched upward as orange thrusters fired from beneath, the pilots pulling a quick deceleration. Mentally extrapolating their course, Randal realized they intended to land right in the middle of the village. Expecting only lightly armed militia, they apparently thought themselves invulnerable.

Their mistake.

Lebedev's railgun boomed across the valley, the magnetically-propelled projectile slicing through the air toward the lead transport. The craft was in a landing posture, its wide underbelly fully exposed. The projectile's force of impact split the thing nearly in two, igniting its propellant in a bright orange ball of flame. Burning wreckage rained down on the town, the fuselage leaving a black smudge against the mountainside.

Randal and Jack opened up with their autocannons, each targeting the same transport. Fire danced along its hull, a snub wing shearing free as the shuttle curved into a steep dive. Trailing smoke, it plowed into the ground, digging a long furrow. The loading door had just opened when the craft exploded.

With more alacrity than Randal expected, the four remaining shuttles broke off their landing, winging away like vultures driven from carrion. For several minutes they disappeared into the mountains, apparently reevaluating the situation.

"Look lively, guys, they're back!" Jeni called over the comset.

The shuttles flew around the plateau Randal and the others had scaled the previous night. Keeping as close to nap-of-the-earth as they could, they landed at the base of Burnley Gap's spur. Immediately the shuttles disgorged a wave of troops in silt-gray uniforms.

Theocratic Guard units were considered elite forces by the Abkhazi military. While discipline was brutal in these units, pay and prestige came with membership. They were much better trained and equipped than the grunt soldiers of the Abkhazi line infantry. This was evident as they swarmed up the hillside, keeping up a good volume of fire even on the move.

Randal resisted the inviting targets the grounded shuttles presented, instead setting up grazing fire with his LMG. Squeezing off controlled bursts, he kept the rounds about a meter off the ground, ensuring a hit even on the ones keeping low.

Over the crackle of small arms fire he could hear the mortar and rail-gun joining the fight. The small mortar shells took out clusters of troops with shrapnel, while the railgun made craters where soldiers once stood.

Nearby, the reverend squeezed off shots from one of the militia's flechette rifles. At the same time he shouted Psalms to bolster the men around him. "Praise be to the Lord my Rock, who trains my hands for war! And my fingers for battle!" A pause for breath, followed by a dead-accurate shot. "He is my loving God, and my fortress!" Another Abkhazi brought down. "My stronghold and deliverer..." Drop clip and reload.

The mountaineers were all excellent shots, but their success was hampered by the body armor of the Theocratic Guards. Again and again Abkhazi went down, only to rise to their feet and return fire. The enemy troops exacted their own pound of flesh. An old timer next to Randal pitched backward, killed instantly.

There was a flash down the line from Randal, followed by a thunderclap and an expanding gray cloud. When the smoke cleared, only Lebedev still held the position. Randal spotted the rocketeer down the hillside, the missile tube smoking on his shoulder. He blasted the Abkhazi and hailed Lebedev on the comset. "Sergei, still with us?"

"*Shto sluchilos, Kapral*?" The Belarusian answered, sounding dazed. "I think am okay."

Things were not okay. In fact, they were quickly becoming ugly. The Abkhazi were dividing into three detachments. The largest of these was in the prone, putting enough pressure on the New Genevans to keep their heads down. Meanwhile, Randal could see the other two detachments scuttling to the flanks, intent on catching the defenders in crossfire.

The convoy had enough of a lead. It was time to run. Randal called Pyatt, frustrated at the communication security measures preventing him from talking to the militia directly. "Pyatt, tell the mayor to start pulling back. We'll run interference for them."

"Lucky us. I'll let him know."

The armored infantry blew off their precious ammo freely, holding the enemy at bay long enough for the surviving militiamen to lose themselves in the mountain trails. Then it was only for Randal and his men to outpace their pursuers.

&

"I still don't understand. They had us beaten – why didn't they follow us?"

Randal didn't have a good answer for the mayor. He took a bite from his dry ration bar and considered the question.

Jeni leaned in past him, resting an elbow on his knee. "Cause a bunch of raggedy civilian types don't worry them. They just needed to eliminate a potential strongpoint on their supply line. Once you lot became refugees there wasn't any sense losing more people coming after you."

A memorial service for the dead had finished earlier and now sleeping families were spread out around the camp, bundled up against the frigid night air. The convoy was encamped in a depression surrounded by several good high points. The rest of the team was helping the militia set up a perimeter.

Cupping hands over his mouth, Randal breathed out to warm his numb fingers, steam leaking between them. "Even so, the Abbies know you're out here somewhere. They might not commit ground troops to following you, but it would be a cinch to call in an air strike. One fuel-air bomb in exchange for a lot of dead infidels would seem like a good trade."

The mayor looked between them, clearly out of his depth. That look made Randal nervous. He didn't want the fate of ninety civilians on his hands.

"What do you suggest then?" the mayor asked, as Randal knew he would.

Rubbing at the tension lines developing on his forehead, Randal shrugged. "I'm suggesting that it's too risky trying to make it to Providence. Even without air strikes there's the possibility of an early snow. I don't want you ending up another Donner Party."

"Another what?" Jeni and the mayor asked simultaneously.

"It would just be bad. Do you have a place in the mountains where you can hole up?"

The mayor scratched at his bald head, lifting the padded hunting cap he wore even inside his armor. "There's a fairly large cavern system not far off. We could head there. But this won't be popular." The mayor rose, clapping Randal on the shoulder with a huge hand. "But popularity isn't what being a leader is about, is it?"

That thought kept Randal awake for the next two hours.

6

Avenge, O Lord, Thy slaughtered saints, whose bones
lie scattered on the Alpine mountains cold.
—John Milton

A few minutes in the cavern were enough to remind Randal how much he disliked enclosed spaces. The stretch he and his militia guide were inspecting was crammed with stalagmites and stalactites, hemming him in. The ceiling was low, seeming poised to press down on them with its stony teeth. He would have given half a month's pay to see open sky. Worse was the strange, blue-glowing fungus coating the walls. "What is this stuff, Goodman Fisher? It's creepy."

His guide laughed, scraping a sample free from an upthrust piece of rock and then laying it out on his palm for inspection. "Phosphorescent lichen. Ghost moss they call it. It's one of the few native plants to survive the terraformers, sir."

"Just call me Corporal. I tried out for officer once, but got rejected when they found out I had a work ethic." Randal plucked the fungus from the goodman's hand. "This stuff is disconcerting."

"You get used to it, s—Corporal."

"I hope not to be down here long enough for that to happen. Let's finish this section." They split up, picking their way through the large chamber.

"There's a sizable crevice over here," his guide called. "We'll need to mark this one."

"Got it."

The system permeated much of the mountain, but the segment where the villagers would be resettling seemed secure. Teams of two had been organized to identify any physical hazards, as well as to remove any animals they found. This was necessary, as the terraformers had released higher-order predators into the mountains such as bears, wolves, and a feisty hybrid of the lynx and puma.

"Let's head topside and give the all-clear for this section."

Once the system was secure, the villagers were led inside. The mouth of the cavern extended tunnel-like for some distance before opening into a wide chamber. This chamber sloped downward at a slight grade to the bank of an underground stream. There were a couple of good fords to the stream. Beyond it the room rose once more, branching into a divergent series of tunnels.

To the left of the main room was the side chamber Randal and his guide had inspected. The opening to it was narrow and entry easily controlled. Mayor Jowett stood nearby with the village elders. Inside the cavern he looked even more ursine in his hunched white armor. "This will be the village storehouse," he told them. "Get a group of men to stash the stores right away. We just received our wintering supplies, but rationing should still be strict. Set guards on this entry—best to keep temptation to a minimum."

Dull yellow beams of light pushed back the darkness as the crawlers entered the cavern, gathering in the center of the main chamber. As the families disembarked the mayor did his best to keep order. "Goodman La Grange, your people will be in that far corner. Your children make up about half the school-age population, so take all the space you need. Ah, Goodwife Patel. How about here by the storehouse?"

The families set about marking off and organizing their living spaces. Rolls of the polymer used to insulate the village orchard during cold months were passed around and used to line the floors of the family quarters.

Pyatt and Jack joined Randal, lugging a chemlamp, a couple of mattresses and some other equipment. "Private Mireault wants us to set up an aid station over by that cave blister in the corner," Pyatt told him, passing off some of the load.

"The what?"

"The big white thing," Pyatt said over his shoulder as he headed in that direction. "It's made of egg-shell calcite. Anyway, it looks like a good, dry spot for our medic." Randal joined the work on the improvised aid station. Afterward, they carried over a semi-lucid al-Hise and laid him beside the mattress.

Pyatt gave the room a gimlet eye, nodding approval. "It's an active cave, so they've got running water for drinking and sanitation. Between the geothermal air flows and the insulating rock, they won't freeze this winter. Food won't be a problem. They weren't planning on new shipments 'til spring anyway, not until the passes are unstuck. All in all, they're going to be more comfortable than we're likely to be."

"What's that little medic talking with the mayor about?" Jack asked, gesturing across the stream.

"Dunno, give me a sec." Randal donned his helmet, keying up the external pickups. Even with sonic filtration, the sound was still fuzzy. The acoustics were terrible inside the cave.

"…alcove would be good. The last thing you want is a cholera or dysentery outbreak." Mireault brushed back her bangs in what Randal was coming to recognize as a nervous habit. "What do you have in mind for a latrine, Mayor? I can't see digging one in this rock…"

"We can consolidate some of the plastic drums they use to ship our oils and grains to us. Cutting a few of those in half will do nicely for outhouses, and we can string up sheets for privacy. Thank you, Miss Mireault." The clap he gave her on the back rocked her a bit, in spite of her armor.

Mireault smiled as she approached the aid station. It was a nice smile, Randal thought, but it only increased his impression that there was something melancholy just behind it. "The clinic looks great. I appreciate your help with this."

It didn't look bad, considering what they had to work with. They'd elevated the mattresses on storage crates. The Doc-in-a-Box sat on a pressurized juice keg next to the bed, alongside a chemlamp and a large plastic stand.

"Let's see how our patient is doing." She inserted the electronic key into al-Hise's suit once more and the breastplate opened. The men laid al-Hise on the mattress and Mireault gave him a mild stimulant.

After a few moments she knelt by the bed, touching al-Hise's arm lightly. Since their time in the village his periods of consciousness were longer, but still confused. "Hey there. How are you feeling?"

Al-Hise's eyes opened slowly, his pupils taking time to focus. A hint of recognition showed as he looked up at her, until the strange surroundings registered. "Where have you taken me?"

"It's a cavern—you're quite safe."

His thin face darkened. "The last time, you said I was wounded. How badly?" Al-Hise was one of the most intense people Randal had ever seen, his frame instantly taut, nearly vibrating with energy.

"A flechette was lodged in your intestine. I took it out. But there's still a fever. I'm trying to keep it under control." Her words came off apologetic. Randal couldn't blame her. Al-Hise seemed to have the same effect that peace officers did, making you feel defensive whether you'd done anything wrong or not.

"Unimportant. How soon until I can fight again?"

Mireault stared a moment, nibbling at the skin of an index finger. Randal could see the nail was already chewed down to the quick. "*Euh...* Two weeks?"

"*Poshyol ti!*" Al-Hise tried sitting up. Randal knew the pain of the wound would lay him flat almost immediately. Somehow it didn't. Face contorted by the pain in his abdomen, Al-Hise sat on the edge of the bed.

"Please, you'll tear the sutures. Lie back down."

Reluctantly, al-Hise reclined, letting out the breath he'd been holding. "Perhaps a couple of days' rest. But no more."

Mireault asked lightly, "Do you have an engagement to rush off to?"

"I need to kill those—" he said something in his mother-tongue that Randal was grateful not to understand. "First though, I will show them pain." The grim upturn of his lips was chilling.

"You hate them?"

Al-Hise spat on the ground beside the bed. "Hate is too weak for what is in me. I would rip the hearts from them if I could. All of them—from baby to babushka."

Mireault looked back at Randal and the others. He thought she might ask for help, but instead she turned back to her patient. "Please try to stay calm, Private al-Hise. Getting worked up is the last thing you need right now." She took a deep breath, and then said quietly, "I've heard it said that hate is like taking slow poison, and then waiting for the other person to die."

His glare set her back a step. "Stupid girl. You know nothing of what's been done to me, or to my people. *Za kneiss, glupaya devka.*" Randal moved closer, half expecting al-Hise to make a grab for the medic.

"Forgive me, Private al-Hise..." Mireault said, turning and pushing through Randal and the others in her haste to leave.

Randal could feel Jack's eyes on him. He made a sour face. "I know... I know. I'll go talk to her." Trotting after the girl, he caught her up near the far wall. She looked ready to crack. There was more bothering her than just al-Hise, but he wasn't about to delve into whatever it was. "Alright, Ariane?"

Her arms were folded around herself. "Yes, Corporal. But that was clumsy back there, the way I handled things."

Randal scowled, glancing over at the aid station. "That guy's a psychopath. You didn't do anything wrong."

"No, I did. I jumped in with advice before even listening to him. I'm always trying to fix people. No matter how right my thoughts might be, they're just going to sound like platitudes to him, you know?"

Platitudes were something he understood. Right then, they were all that came to mind. "He'll be in your aid station for the next two weeks. That's plenty of time to listen."

∾ ∾

In order to keep everyone's circadian rhythms in order, the village elders established lights out at 2200. For an eight-hour period each night they hooded the chemlamps and kept noise to a minimum. Reverend Hauptmann organized a prayer vigil for the hour before lights out. Randal was pleased to see nearly all of his team represented, with the exceptions of al-Hise, who was sleeping fitfully at the aid station, and Pyatt, who had made it clear he thought the rest of the team were heathens. First Century types often shunned anyone who wasn't baptized in their church.

The murmuring of the crowd died as the reverend took his place. "I have no sermon for you tonight. No words of wisdom or easy answers. All I have to offer you is my faith, my assurance that our God is not afar off. He will hear the prayers of his people."

He paused, looking over his little flock, obviously feeling more than he had words to say. "We'll begin with a responsive reading, and then anyone who feels burdened can pray. I'll close with a passage from our Book of Common Prayer. Come, let us seek our God together."

From memory he recited:

"We sinners do beseech Thee to hear us, O Lord God."

"We beseech Thee to hear us, Good Lord."

"That it may please Thee so to rule in the heart of your servant, the Prime Minister, that he may above all seek thy honor and glory."

"We beseech thee to hear us."

"That it may please thee to defend the fatherless children and all who are defenseless and oppressed."

"We beseech thee to hear us."

"That it may please thee to forgive our enemies, and to turn their hearts."

"Have mercy upon them, O God."

"Amen."

For the next hour everyone took turns praying, some for the war effort, some for national forgiveness, and others for more practical worries. Many of them cried, kneeling in the muddy wetness of the cavern floor, paying it no mind.

Randal wished he could be like them. All his life he'd watched people give themselves over to God completely. But his heart could never make the leap. There was a reserve inside of him. It was something he learned growing up under his father's watchful eye. From Randal's earliest days his father molded him to be a future Prime Minister. Randal had no doubt the man loved him, but he was ruthless in perfecting his son. As a defense against the constant barrage of trials and criticism, Randal had evolved a deep stoic streak. He just refused to let it touch him.

The sound of muffled laughter brought him from his thoughts. Jeni's hand was cupped to Johnny's ear, and both of them were making commentary from the back of the gathering. It took only a moment to find the source of their amusement. Mireault wore a look of serenity, obviously given over wholly to the prayer. Hands at her side, she swayed slightly, lips moving silently. She reminded Randal of a holo he'd seen of Thayer's Angel.

In time the volume of prayers slowed, and the reverend raised hands in supplication over his people. "O Lord, God of Hosts, stretch forth thine almighty arm to strengthen and protect the soldiers of our country. Support them in the day of battle. Endue them with courage and loyalty; and grant that in all things they may serve without reproach; through Jesus Christ our Lord, Amen."

❧❧

Through the clinging fog of sleep Randal heard voices speaking Russian. Abkhazi soldiers? Still half asleep, he rummaged through the bedroll for his sidearm. After a moment, his mind cleared enough to remember that his 10mm Kinyo was packed away and the voices were familiar ones.

Cracking his lids, he saw the rest of the cave was already up and about. He must have crashed hard. Scowling at the sour taste in his mouth, he tugged on fatigue pants before leaving the sleep sack.

He wandered over to the grounded PSV. Lebedev and Jeni sat atop it, staring into an open access panel and jabbering in Russian. Jeni's intel training emphasized the dialect spoken by most Abkhazi. While pockets of them clung to Tajik, Kazakh or Farsi, they unified around Russian as the language of commerce.

Randal's Russian was worse than his French—he caught perhaps every third word as he approached. "Something wrong, Jeni?"

The slender Korean woman looked up with an exasperated huff, shaking a spanner at him. "We can't send or receive LR messages. We took the drone outside and I tried all morning to raise HQ Providence. Nothing."

Lebedev wiped at his nose with the back of a hand and gave Randal a wave. He was really suffering in the caves. It was bad enough out in the field—he was the first infantryman Randal had ever met who was allergic to dirt itself—but the spores from the ghost moss were torturing him. "I've looked over the drone, Kapral Knox. Is working fine. But ship's receiver is bad. Without a new one, we're *kak po-angliskiy*? Out of luck."

"Have you checked for spares?"

Jeni cut the Belarusian off before he could answer. "Yeah. We don't have any."

"You're quite sure? Let me check. Second set of eyes and all that." Randal popped the hatch to the main storage compartment.

"That's not necessary. Really."

Something was wrong. There were a few containers presumably filled with electronics, but in the center of the space was a translucent plastic container with a liquid of some sort. He pulled it out, setting it on the floor. Oddly, behind the jug was a bag of charcoal, two copper kettles connected by metal tubing, and a bag of potatoes.

"Oh, aces," came Jeni's voice from above.

"Bathtub vodka?" Randal was incredulous. "You left equipment behind to make vodka?"

Jeni clambered down the handholds to hover protectively by her cache of liquor. "Johnny and I get thirsty. Like we were supposed to know the stupid part would burn out."

Randal's hand twitched with the urge to smack the side of her head. Eventually, the absurdity of it all overcame his anger. Jeni Cho wasn't so much a person as a force. And like tornadoes or floods, the object wasn't so much to control as to survive her.

"You're in real trouble…" He pointed a finger, the tip almost pressing her nose.

She took a step back.

"…unless I have a cup of that in about two seconds."

Jeni grinned, turning to rummage in the compartment for a cup. "Belly up to the bar, Randy." Wiping out a cup with her dusty fatigue blouse, she poured him a drink, then one for herself. He took a swig. The stuff was foul, but he thought it might mix tolerably with the punch powder that came in their rations.

He motioned with the cup. "I've got a question for you. Do you really buy into that Abkhazi being a cavalry scout? It still seems dodgy to me."

Her face took on a hooded expression, the kind that told him he was straying into Classified territory. "Al-Hise's all right, Randy. A bit of a nutter, but he's on the level. You don't have to worry about him."

"How do you know?"

Jeni didn't answer, instead changing the subject with a casual, "So. You fancy the little medic?"

Randal coughed, both from the awfulness of the vodka and the question. "What?"

"C'mon, Randy, I've seen how you look at Miss Prim. Think she's ever been kissed?"

He felt like he should defend Mireault somehow, but that would only encourage Jeni's prodding. "I don't look at her any way. She's just a friend. Honestly, she's not even a friend."

"Uh-huh."

"She's not hard to look at. Can we drop it?"

"As long as I get to be a bridesmaid." Jeni sipped her vodka, smirking at him over the cup.

He stalked off, mind turning to other things. With their long-range commo deadlined, they'd be walking into Providence nearly blind. The rest of the day would be spent planning the safest approach. He expected the Abbies would have the north end of town staked out by the time they arrived. It would be tricky to filter through enemy lines and make it to friendly forces.

❧

Unable to sleep, Randal read a copy of Augustine's Confessions from his datapad. Hearing someone approach, he glanced back. The footsteps belonged to Mireault, returning from checking on al-Hise.

The girl sat down cross-legged on the edge of his bedding. "Having trouble sleeping, Corporal?"

"You can call me Randal when it's just us, Ariane. And yeah, a bit tense. Jeni Cho—"

Ariane smiled, seeming as amused by Jeni as the other woman was by her. "What did she do now?"

Randal told her about the spare parts, omitting the talk about brides-maids. "She really has no concept of social niceties, have you picked up on that yet? She's une belle dame sans merci." He grimaced at his own pronunciation.

Ariane's eyes lit up. "You know Keats? I love the Romantics."

"Really? I know hardly anyone who's read them." His eyes glanced upward as he grasped for a long-ago memorized passage. "I saw pale kings and princes too, pale warriors, death-pale were they all; they cried—'La Belle Dame sans Merci hath thee in thrall. . .'" For once he didn't feel at a loss for words with her.

"Ah, bien sur. Whenever I'm down I read them—Byron, Gautier, even evil old Baudelaire." She admitted with a grin, "Especially evil old Baudelaire."

He watched her as she spoke, though he was careful not to look at her in that way, whatever it was. "I usually turn to Augustine or one of the Stoics." He tapped the datapad. "What made you join the Defense Force, anyway? Don't take it wrong, but you don't seem all that militant."

Her smile faded. For a moment she sat quietly, fingers twisting the fabric of his sleep sack. "Jean-Marie."

"Was he a boyfriend of yours?"

A melancholy laugh. "Non, he's my little boy."

Randal blinked, words tumbling out before he could weigh them. "But you aren't married."

The smile she gave was a tired one. He was sure this wasn't the first time the fact had been pointed out to her. "You don't have to be married to conceive a child."

"I know that," he answered a little too quickly. "I just haven't known many people personally who did. Listen, I spoke without thinking…I'm sorry."

"It's okay – I get it a lot. I was stupid. This boy, he said he was going to take care of me, that we were going to get married and I could get out of my father's house." Her voice was distant. "He said a lot of things."

"Until you got pregnant."

She nodded. "He was in the Diplomatic Service Academy. There were only a few months until graduation and acknowledging me would have gotten hurt his career. So I kept quiet. When he was posted to the embassy on Tanganyika Mpya he promised to send for me. *Hélas*, he never wrote."

"But your parents, they wouldn't help you?"

Another pause. "My father is a senior director for the Haelbroeck Corporation in Providence. I humiliated him. He would barely even talk to me after Jean-Marie was born."

The Haelbroeck Corp was owned by his friend Pieter's father, along with half of the rest of Providence. They had a mammoth set of complexes. To reach a director slot was impressive.

"Have you talked to your family pastor? Your father needs to forgive you."

"My father is an atheist and I'm still new to faith. When I got pregnant he rubbed my nose in it. He's a very hard man. It wasn't the morality of things – it was just that I'd spoiled all his plans for me, and embarrassed him with his friends." Pressing palms to her forehead, she pushed back her bangs and twisted them.

"Who has Jean-Marie while you're here?"

She winced, and he could see the worry in her eyes. "My mother is watching him for me. You don't think the Abkhazi would hurt civilians, do you?"

Randal smiled, lying for her sake. "Of course not. They're only worried about the Army." Impulsively he reached out and gave her hand a squeeze. "You'll have to introduce me to Jean-Marie when we get to Providence."

Ariane brightened a little. "I'd like that."

7

Once we have a war there is only one thing to do.
It must be won. For defeat brings worse things
than any that can ever happen in war.
—Ernest Hemingway

The next two weeks seemed endless as they waited for al-Hise to recover enough to travel. Nerves frayed in the dim, blue-green world of the caverns. Pyatt needed to be pulled off of Johnny and once even Ariane snapped at Jeni when the passive-aggressive needling got to be too much. Worse for Randal was his claustrophobic streak. Long walks above ground helped a bit, but inevitably he had to return to the close confines of the caves. It felt hard to breathe down there.

Finally, though, all was ready for them to leave.

The reverend organized a prayer service and everyone raised entreaties for their protection. Once suited up, they filed out, Johnny deftly threading the PSV through the entry tunnel.

Outside, Mayor Jowett shook each one's hand. When he came to Randal, he paused. "Good luck, son. Thanks for your help back at the village. You're a good lad." Randal was surprised to see the big man was a bit misty.

"Once we link up with the Army, I'll pass word to the right people about your situation," Randal promised, though he wasn't sure what anyone could do about it.

The mayor smiled knowingly. "I appreciate it, but I doubt we'll rate high on the priority list. We're mountain people. We can do for our own."

The wind was bitterly cold. After another quick round of good-byes, the mayor hurried back into the cavern. Once more the team was on its own. Soon the entrance was out of sight, its safety and warmth a memory.

Randal pushed the team hard on the march, anxious to reach Providence. He didn't relish a return to combat, but if they missed a decisive battle he knew it would always haunt him. Their progress was slowed by the necessity of following back trails to avoid detection. Despite this obstacle the team performed well, covering nearly forty kilometers a night. Randal was relieved to see that discipline hadn't suffered too badly during the slack time with the villagers. Given the motley composition of his squad, he'd been concerned.

The forward edge of the battle area was well to the south, and they didn't run into any Abkhazi ground forces. Three times during the march to Providence flights of enemy air units tickled the PSV's sensors, but none strayed too close. One thing that still troubled Randal, however, was how exactly to get his team through enemy lines and into friendly territory.

A steady stream of suborbitals traced overhead, small silver pinpoints against the night sky. Their arrival in New Geneva demonstrated more engineering prowess on the part of the Abkhazi than Randal would expect of them. Each suborbital was longer than a football pitch. Hewing a landing strip for the craft in mountainous terrain during combat conditions was a marvel.

The end of the fourth night found the team about fifteen klicks out from Providence. They encamped in a deep draw, while Jack guided down the PSV with flashes from his UV headlamp. As soon as the skimmer touched ground, they began covering it with vegetation pre-cut for the task. That they weren't already caught by an Abkhazi patrol indicated that God was looking out for them, but Randal didn't want to be presumptuous.

"Jeni, this is for covering of doors," Lebedev said, the last of his words lost to a sneeze. "Please take quickly, they are allergic to me."

The dronekeeper took the branches, camouflaging the doors. "It looks good from up here, Randal. Ready for me to pop a commo drone and see who answers?"

"Please do. But keep the transmissions short and be careful."

"You're going to make someone a wonderful mother someday." She climbed into the harness and launched the drone. Six sets of eyes followed it anxiously. Randal paced the campsite, nervously flexing armored hands.

"Randal, c'mere," Jeni said a few minutes later, waving him over to the open cockpit of the PSV.

"What did they say?"

Jeni set the dronekeeper's helmet aside, sighing. "I couldn't raise them."

"Grand. You mean the short-range commo is fritzing now, too?"

A slow shake of her head. "No. Like there was no one there to answer me." His face must have reflected his stunned incomprehension, because she spelled it out slowly: "There. . .is. . .no. . .one. . .out there. The Army isn't here."

"Oh. Well." That explained the suborbitals. The Abkhazi hadn't built a landing strip—they were using the spaceport at Providence itself. It took a moment to absorb. There were nearly a quarter million civilians in the city, what was their fate? "Try picking up civilian radio or trideo transmissions. Maybe we can get an idea how far south the Army was pushed."

"I thought of that too. Either the military censors have a media blackout going, or the transmissions are being jammed."

Feeling like his wind was knocked out, he leaned back against the PSV and smoothed a palm over the rounded dome of his helmet. "The militia. Can you try hailing one of the militia cells? Maybe they know something."

"That won't be easy. Each cell is autonomous, with its own frequency and encryption. And their freqs hop on a pre-set pattern. On top of that, they're gonna be paranoid and our story is a little thin."

"Any better ideas?"

She shrugged. Donning the opaquely-visored helmet, she switched on a panel Randal remembered was devoted to decryption. "The coms they issue the militia only operate on a narrow freq range. I'll have to narrow the search pattern." Jeni didn't bother to explain anything further and Randal didn't ask questions. She was being cooperative, no sense in tempting fate.

The girl set the receiver scanning in the target band. It didn't take long to find a transmission with the characteristics they were looking for. "I think I've got one. Turn around while I hack it. This part's classified."

"Huh? Don't be silly."

Her small chin elevated slightly. "Am I going to have to get cross with you, Randy?"

With a sigh, Randal averted his eyes. Jeni was fertilizer for the spiritual fruit of longsuffering.

After a bit, Jeni reached out of the cockpit to smack his helmet. "Bow before your queen. I am good." She switched the audio feed from headset to speakers. Terse messages were being transmitted back and forth, most of it difficult to understand without context.

Jeni broke in. "This is Lance Corporal Cho, NGDF. How copy?"

The next voice to speak was panic-filled. "It's a trick, Marcus. Don't answer! Turn off your com!"

Silence.

Twice more she contacted militia cells, only to be rewarded with dead air. "This is making me mad. Climb in Johnny's spot, Randy. You can talk to the next bunch."

After shedding his armor, Randal slid into the pilot's seat and donned the headset hanging on the stick. Static filled his ears, followed by a confused jumble of digitized sounds. After a while these coalesced into clear speech.

"Providence militia, this is Corporal Randal Knox, NGDF. We are behind enemy lines and in need of assistance."

The line was immediately taken up with answering transmissions. In their haste to silence each other, the members of the commo net stepped on one other. Only fragments of speech came through, much of it profane. These tapered off into silence.

Randal couldn't blame them. In the event of occupation, the militia was intended to go guerrilla. Self-containment was their only defense against the enemy using the capture of one cell to hunt down the others. "Try one more, Jeni. If this doesn't work, we'll go catch some rack time. I'm exhausted."

"Roger that."

It took her some time to slice an active channel. "Go."

"This is Corporal Randal Knox, NGDF. Please listen."

"Even if you are, you're violating protocol. I'm signing off."

Another voice came across the com. Something about it struck Randal as familiar. "Did you say Randal Knox?"

"That's a rog."

"Then tell me how you broke your leg six years or so ago?"

Randal grinned. "This nutter I knew amped the juice on my board without warning me." He wasn't surprised to find his friend Pieter hooked up with a guerrilla cell. The boy joined any club that would have him.

"I don't believe it - Randal Knox! Haven't seen you for yonks, Kipper!"

Randal shot a warning look as Jeni erupted in snorting giggles at his prep academy nickname.

She spoke up on the channel. "Keep it short. Even dumb Abkhazi can plot you if you chatter long enough."

"Pieter, we've been incommunicado for days. I'd like to meet with you. Can you get out of town? Remember the hunting stand on Capshaw Mountain where I took that buck?"

"Yes and yes. And I shot the big buck there."

"You always had a vivid imagination. Anyway, meet you there. I'll be in place by 2100 tonight."

"See you then, Kipper. Stay sharp."

Randal set the headset aside, rubbing tiredly at his eyes.

"Kipper? You must have been quite the lady-killer," Jeni said, laughing so hard her eyes closed.

"It was prep school. Everyone had a nickname."

"Undoubtedly, Kipper." She struggled to catch her breath. "We should get some sleep."

"Keep calling me that and it might not be safe for you to sleep," he grumbled, climbing from the cockpit. "Thanks for the help with the commo."

"No worries, ducky. Sleep tight."

≈∽

The rustle of feet on dry underbrush carried to where Randal and Jack lay hidden beneath a leafless elm. A snapping twig spooked an owl into flight. Pieter and his friend weren't woodsmen. Randal clucked his tongue to get their attention.

The two were edgy, freezing as soon as they heard the noise. "Knox?" Pieter asked softly, training his autorifle on the shadows around him.

"Yeah, over here."

Randal and Pieter talked while Jack and Pieter's comrade kept watch. "It's good to see you, man," Randal said, shaking his hand warmly. "Where's your group holed up?"

"You know P-city used to be an Abkhazi mining center, right? The land underneath the city is just riddled with shafts for kilometers down. We call them the Catacombs. Our militia cell is in the tunnels, and we've seen signs that other groups are operating from there as well."

Along with much of the rest of New Geneva's legal system, the militia statutes were based on the old U.S. Code from Terra. The militia consisted of "every able-bodied male ages sixteen to fifty not convicted of a felony." However, New Geneva took the law seriously, issuing each militia member a weapon. In a city like Providence, that meant thousands of armed men. Randal had wondered where they were hiding.

"Is there much of a Resistance in place?"

"Not really. When the Abkhazi first came there was a lot of street fighting. Heavy casualties for us and them. But once it was clear the army was abandoning the city most of us went underground."

"Abandoning?" Randal was surprised at the bitterness in his friend's voice.

Pieter made a disgusted sound. "They fled south when the Abkhazi came. Word is they decided their position was 'untenable', and chose to trade land for time." His eyes focused in the direction of Providence. "People for time you might say."

Randal could understand why NGDF command had made the choice it did. No one had expected the savagery with which the enemy attacked, or how swiftly they advanced. Likely the NGDF wasn't able to reinforce sufficiently before the enemy fell upon them. Faced with the option of losing the army or evacuating, they made the only decision they could. The destruction of the main NGDF force would have meant defeat and ultimately the end of their way of life. He imagined it was the kind of decision armchair generals would debate forever, provided any of them survived to do so.

It wasn't the time to point any of that out. "I'm sorry, Pieter. Was there time for many civilians to escape?"

"No. Once the Abkhazi saw the army was bugging out, they flew in those gray-suited troops in the shuttles and blocked off all the southern routes."

"We're all that's left from the battalion they posted at Crenshaw Pass. They've ordered us to link up with the main body. Do you have any idea how far to the south they ended up?"

Pieter shook his head, putting up a hand to forestall him. "Don't. Most of my cellmates have families. We sent three runners south to find a path to evacuate the women and children. They watched the front lines for a week trying to find a weakness. Only one of them made it back. The NGDF is dug in down at the Firth of Farel. The isthmus is so constricted there the Abbies are practically standing shoulder-to-shoulder. My men got hit before they were even four kilometers from the line. You'll be signing your people's death certificates."

As usual, Jack saw and heard more than he seemed to. Over a shoulder he interjected quietly, "He has a point, Randal."

It was true. Slipping past enemy defenses around Providence was one thing, but Farel would be a nightmare. The NGDF had been wise to pick it—the natural bottleneck there made it easy to defend.

"Come wait this out with us." Pieter flashed his most agreeable smile.

Randal returned the smile, but behind his eyes he thought, I'm not waiting anything out. And neither are you if I can help it. "That sounds like the best plan, but I'll have to talk to my people."

"Give me a jingle when you know the answer."

"Oh, Pieter, I meant to ask—how are your parents weathering things? I hope they weren't caught in the chateau?" Randal loved the Haelbroecks like they were his own parents.

"Thankfully, no. They were vacationing down at the Cape when the balloon went up. What in the world does that mean anyway? Balloons don't seem terribly militant to me."

"Back on Terra, balloons were used for observation and signaling in warfare. Listen, glad to hear your folks are safe. I'm sure my father has put yours to work with the war effort."

Pieter laughed. "No doubt some juicy sinecure—Undersecretary for Mobilization of Cocktail Parties or something. The beasts have taken over the chateau, though. Staff cars are constantly flying in and out. I pity them if they break any of mother's china. She's vengeful."

≈∽

"I know this isn't exactly SOP," Randal told his people after explaining their predicament. "But I think we should vote on staying in Providence or continuing south."

"I'm staying," Ariane said abruptly, drawing surprised looks. "I want to stay."

"Staying here is the wisest option. We won't do our country any good getting butchered crossing the front lines," Jack weighed in.

"You don't get to make that call, Van Loon. None of you do." Pyatt stood from his crouch, looking ready for trouble. "Our orders say to link up with the main body. All of you should stow your cowardice and get moving."

That brought Jack to his feet. "Try using some sodding common sense once in a while - you might just live longer. It isn't cowardice to avoid walking into a meat mincer." He spat on the ground between them. "And come over here and call me a coward where I can reach you."

"Easy, Jack. Easy. Pyatt gets a vote too."

"I'm for staying. So is Johnny," Jeni said, looping an arm around the pilot's shoulders.

"Well, I'm not so sure . . . Hey that hurts! Yeah, let's stay here."

"Lebedev?"

"Nothing waits for me in south. I am content to remain."

Everyone looked to al-Hise for his answer. "I will not hide like a rabbit, Corporal. Either here or in the south, I will have my revenge."

"You'll have your revenge. That I can promise you. I'll feed you vengeance until you choke on it." Randal tossed aside the stick he was stripping of bark and walked away from the group. His answer drew a few questioning glances, but he ignored them. A plan was forming in his mind and he wanted time to think it through.

The team separated to bunk out for a few hours. Ariane flashed him a smile in passing. He believed she might have deserted if the vote had gone differently, but he couldn't blame her. Her little boy was trapped somewhere in the city. Ever since they'd learned of Providence's fall there had been a haunted look to her.

Jeni commed their answer to Pieter, along with a request for tools and a cutting torch. He seemed surprised by the request, but promised to do what he could.

Several hours later, three militiamen arrived at the draw toting the needed equipment. Randal's hope was to salvage what he could from the PSV. It wasn't feasible to try sneaking the thing into the city, let alone transporting it through tunnels.

Aside from the ammunition and supplies, the easiest thing to secure was the recharger for the LANCER suits. The PSV was designed to be the forward support center for an armored infantry platoon. In theory, a full maintenance bay could be hundreds of kilometers away, so repair work needed to be as simple as possible. Consequently, most of the major components on the PSV were modular and quickly replaceable. The recharger was no exception. It was completely self-contained and compactly constructed. The removal of eight bolts and three cables freed it from the ship.

Jeni and Lebedev set to cutting other needed parts from the PSV. A sullen Johnny watched from nearby, wincing each time something was cut away from his ship. In the end they managed to salvage the recharger and good portions of Jeni's dronekeeper gear.

The militiamen led them through the forest, shadowing a paved road that led to town. Al-Hise trotted up next to Randal. "Corporal, I've got movement on the hardball. Get everyone down."

Randal didn't hesitate a second. "Everybody down, now! Hit the dirt." The NGDF people complied without a moment's pause. A heavyset militiaman, Drummond if Randal remembered correctly, simply pressed himself up against a tree, peeking around the edge. Snarling, Randal high-crawled to the man. He reached up, grabbed hold of his workmen's coveralls and pulled him to the ground.

The man let loose a string of unmentionables. Randal pinned him, pressing his visored face close to the man's. He had the rheumiest eyes Randal had ever seen, and the florid face of a hard drinker. "They might have infra-red detectors. Keeping down behind this bank can help conceal us a bit. When I tell you to do something, just DO IT."

The lesson had to be cut short as the rumbling of armor on the road intensified. Once they were well past, Randal risked a look. As expected, he saw a trio of the six-wheeled light tanks the Scourge of the Prophet favored. They were ideal for hunting down partisans and deserters. It was a rare stroke of luck, or the grace of God, that they hadn't spotted his people. Giving Drummond's chest a sharp poke with a fingertip, Randal climbed off.

Other than a sulky look, Drummond let the matter drop. He led the group to a culvert, where filthy water ran into a drainage canal. Beyond the banks of the canal rose the massive storage tanks and buildings of a factory—the Haelbroeck Petrol Refinery. It was the largest of the plants owned by Pieter's family. Pieter had spent a summer there as an intern, during one of his father's sporadic attempts to teach him responsibility. Around the factory were the silhouettes of modest-sized houses, the beginning of Providence's sprawling suburbs. Sprawling by New Genevan standards anyway, thought Randal. A megalopolis on the planet Terra often teemed with over forty million people.

The team waited while the militiamen conferred with the sentries at the tunnel's entrance. "I remember that spot," Ariane said, resting next to Randal. "We lived there back when it was just a grassy field. My family had moved here from the Swiss Province on Terra during the boomtime. That area was covered with pressure tents because there was a huge housing shortage. We stayed in one for months."

Randal smiled at that. "Really? That was like nine years ago, right? I was in P-city then too. I spent the summer with Pieter up at the Haelbroeck house." He felt slightly relieved; it was the most Ariane had spoken in two days.

The sentries signaled for them with a birdcall. Randal grinned, motioning for his people to follow. He wasn't sure how furtive a quail call actually was, considering the birds never strayed that far north.

The culvert led into a maze of sewage tunnels, some barely passable in powered armor. Randal activated his onboard comp's mapping program. This used the ground surveillance sensor to develop a 3-D view of the surrounding terrain. Here in the tunnels that included both the main route they followed, as well as side tunnels for as far as readings could be received.

"Turn left here," their guide said, gesturing with his chem-lantern. Off to the side of the walkway was the dark mouth of a tunnel. Randal could see where the steel bars sealing it were cut away. It looked like an abandoned mineshaft. Rather than the smooth walls of the sewage system, these were rough-hewn.

After many turns, and one needed backtrack, their guide brought them to a chamber. Whichever ore men had sought, there was obviously once a rich vein at that spot—the chamber extended easily 200 meters ahead of them. Pillars of rock were left in place to act as supports, dividing the chamber into sections. Chemlamps rested on improvised sconces along the walls. The militia had expanded to fill much of the space; bedrolls and personal gear were spread haphazardly everywhere.

Randal and the others pushed back their helmets, pausing at the entrance. About thirty men were in the chamber, killing time. A group of four sat near the entrance playing euchre. Pyatt muttered darkly about the "devil's picture books" as he spotted the card players.

With a wry look, Randal led his team into the room.

Pieter glanced up from where he spoke with two older men and stepped over to greet them. His eyes slid right past Randal, affixing on Ariane. "Hello there, I'm Pieter Haelbroeck," he said, flashing the same smile he gave every girl he ever found standing next to Randal.

Ariane seemed unimpressed, which was atypical in Randal's experience with Pieter and women. "Ariane Mireault," she answered coolly.

"Ah! Enchanté," he said, air kissing her cheeks. Pieter's accent was much better than his own, Randal noted glumly. Pieter turned, clapping loudly to gain the militiamen's attention. "Everyone, these are our new arrivals."

The men wandered over unhurriedly. Randal thought they looked beaten. Their clothes were unkempt, their expressions flat as they approached the NGDF troopers. "This is Corporal Randal Knox; I'm sure all of you know him. I'll let him introduce his people."

A low murmur passed through the crowd. His father had been Prime Minister for the last twelve years. There had been puff pieces about Randal on the trideo since he was a child. Then two years ago he'd graduated from Saint Athanasius. It was common knowledge the Founder's Party was holding a safe provincial legislature seat for him, intended to groom him for higher office.

To the shock of the pundits, as well as his father, he'd declined to announce his candidacy. Instead he enlisted as a private in the infantry. It was national news, of course.

When interviewed he'd said only that he didn't feel ready for public office. The truth was, the prospect of making life-changing decisions for other people terrified him—the awful responsibility of it. Worse was the sense that his life was planned out for him while he was still in grade school.

He was learning that you couldn't run from destiny. As the Khlisti saint Trotsky had once said: if you wanted a quiet life, you picked the wrong century to be born in.

The militia stared openly as he introduced his team. Their faces reflected a mixture of resentment at what he represented, and curiosity at being in the presence of a celebrity.

"Thank you for giving us shelter," Randal said, choosing his words carefully. "I regret what's happened to your city. I'm so sorry we weren't able to protect you better." Perhaps a few hard looks softened at the apology. "But it's important for me to be honest with you. Our war is not over by a long shot. If you allow us to stay with you, we may very well bring the war to you. I intend to keep hitting the Abkhazi until my team is dead or Providence is free."

"Whoa, Randal," Pieter muttered out the side of his mouth. "Throttle back a bit."

Randal ignored him, pressing on. "I invite each of you to fight with us. God has given us an opportunity. To the south our countrymen fight for the survival of New Geneva." He paused, feeling his pulse pounding. No turning back now. "Here we have been placed by the hand of God, deep in the soft heart of the enemy. We can strike where he is vulnerable, hurt him in places the regular army cannot. Together we can bleed him to death with a thousand tiny cuts! I'm asking you to join with me. Please, help me to liberate Providence."

Swallowing, he quieted, watching them expectantly. After an initial silence they murmured in small clumps, heads shaking, hands gesturing rapidly.

"So let me get this straight," said a stout man with the pale complexion of a miner. "You army types want to just stroll in and take over. And we're supposed to listen just 'cause you're real army? You jokers had your chance."

Randal shook his head, catching the man's eyes and locking onto them. "No. There will be no regular army, no militia. Only patriots of New Geneva."

Others asked questions, more respectfully than the first. He answered them patiently, amazed at how right the situation felt. It was the same sensation that came over him in a rugby match—his conscious mind was utterly not in control, yet everything was working out.

Pieter cleared his throat. As Randal spoke, he had sidled away to join the assembly. "There are only forty of us, Kipper. Aren't you being a little grandiose?" Then came the ironic look that Randal always hated.

But this time it didn't put him in his place. Randal turned on his friend. "No, I'm not. I'm going to unite the militia cells and build an army."

Pieter retreated a step, an eyebrow cocked. "You're living in a dream world, chum."

"*You* are living in a dream, Pieter Haelbroeck. You and any of the rest who think to hide down here while the war goes on without you. Do you think the Abkhazi will overlook you forever? Or your neighbors and families up above? The only reason everyone above isn't dead already is because they're more valuable as laborers than corpses.

"These fanatics aren't fighting for our land, but for our destruction. Their religion promised them supremacy, that they would rule over all others. The fact that our civilization thrives while theirs declines makes us a living contradiction of all their beliefs. They must destroy us. Such men can't be reasoned with, only resisted.

"Join with me. Better to die now as men than to spend the remainder of your days cowering like rats in this sewer." He turned, motioning for his people to exit the chamber. "We'll return for your decision in fifteen minutes."

8

The guerilla must move amongst the
people as a fish swims in the sea.
—Mao Tse-Tung

Pieter was nothing if not clubby, and his air of collegiality returned as soon as the militia cell signed on to Randal's plan. If anything, he sought to co-opt the vision, eagerly throwing himself into things. He christened the composite group "Knox's Irregulars" and insisted everyone use it.

Randal ordered his people out of their powered armor and requested civilian clothes for them. He wanted to blend the two forces immediately and common dress was an important first step. A pair of university-aged militiamen brought over armloads of trousers, jackets and shirts. "We don't have any women's clothing, I'm afraid," one of them said apologetically.

Randal started to answer, but was cut off as Ariane spoke up from behind him. "I'll get some. I'm going home."

It wasn't a surprise. "Just give me a moment. I'll go with you." Randal took up an outfit that looked like it should fit and ducked behind a stone pillar. After donning the civvies, he tucked his sidearm into the waistband of the rough workmen's trousers and stepped out. "Mind guiding us topside?" he asked one of the collegians. Ariane gave him the street address.

"That's an upscale area. Abkhazi officers live in most of those houses now. It's thickly patrolled."

"Still, I have to go there," Ariane said, a little more urgently for the new information.

"I can get you close."

The young man led them through the tunnels, holding a chem-lantern before them. Randal felt odd out of his armor; he missed the enhanced senses it gave him. Along the way the trio passed food wrappers, ash piles from small fires, and other signs they weren't alone in the Catacombs. The surrounding walls smoothed as they breached the sewer system once more. He was relieved to see that walkways lined both sides of the sludge.

"Hold on," the guide said, pulling himself up to peek out a drain. "We're off-course. Wait here while I figure out where we are exactly." He disappeared into the darkness. That close to the surface they'd been forced to hood the lantern.

"Randal?" Ariane asked, scooting a little closer in the gloom. "Can I ask you a question?"

"Of course."

"Don't you ever have problems with being both a Christian and a soldier? I mean, all the parts about blessed are the meek and turn the other cheek and all?"

He blinked. "That was random."

"I've been thinking about something. Well, don't you?"

"Van Loon and I have talked about that quite a lot, actually. We always end up back at Romans 13, where it talks about the powers of the magistrate. 'For he does not bear the sword for nothing. He is God's servant, an agent of wrath to bring punishment on the wrongdoer...'" He shrugged. "I'm the sharp edge of the state's sword."

Ariane listened and then pulled her knees up to her chest, hugging them. "I want a gun."

"We'll get you one from Pieter."

The scuffing of boots on gravel announced their guide's return. "This way. I found where we took a wrong turn."

He led them through the city's underbelly for another twenty minutes, halting them by a group of handholds set into the wall. He climbed up and pushed aside the cover with a grunt. After popping his head out briefly, he hopped back down. "This is it. I'll wait here one hour."

Randal and Ariane scurried across the suburban street, stopping behind a row of hedges. Alternately crawling and walking, the two made their way in the direction of her house. "There it is," she said, taking a step toward her home, seeming oblivious to everything else.

"Wait," Randal hissed, yanking her back out of an orange pool of streetlight. He covered her mouth to stifle protest and pulled her to the ground behind a privacy fence. The hum of a patrol drone carried on the night breeze as it made slow progress down the street. Randal prayed he'd spotted it in time.

The drone didn't slow as it passed, nor did it give any audible alarms. That didn't necessarily mean all was well, but it definitely beat klaxons and flashing red lights.

Once things seemed clear, the two dashed across the street and down the alleyway that ran between the backyards of the rows of houses. The two hit the ground behind her father's house, frost-covered grass crackling beneath them. "You guys don't have a huge French dog named Hugo or anything, do you?" Randal asked, raising his head to scout for one.

"My father hates animals. He'd never allow one."

"Hates animals? I'll bet he's smashing at parties. He just sounds fun and frolicsome."

She ignored him, eyes fixed on the rear door.

The two crept across the backyard, and Randal got a better view of the house. It was done in the Glasgow-School Revival style that was all the rage a few years back. From the rough siltstone walls to the 'romantic' asymmetry of the architecture, down to the sapling ornamental trees, it all spoke of newfound wealth. "Nice house," he observed politely.

Ariane rapped knuckles on the back door. "He worships money."

Randal kept a hand on the flechette pistol in his waistband. If an enemy officer was living there now, the Abkhazi chain of command was about to have a hole in its roster. The curtain pushed aside after a moment, and a rounded face appeared. The magnetic lock disengaged as the man cracked the door fractionally. "Daughter, why are you here? And in that uniform. You'll get me shot! Come inside!"

Opening the door, he ushered her in. He paused, seeming unsure what to do with Randal. Apparently deciding that keeping him outside was more of a risk than in, he opened the door wider. "Keep your gun in its holster."

Taking them into the parlor, he covered the divan with a cloth and then allowed them to sit. Ariane started to speak, but he shushed her. "Un moment, s'il te plait." Opening a cabinet he took out a bottle of Scotch, pouring himself a generous amount. Downing it, he repeated the process. "Very well, daughter, I am prepared to listen now."

Fidgeting impatiently, Ariane blurted, "Mother and Jean-Marie. Where are they, father?"

After filling a second glass, the stout man took a seat in the armchair and handed the drink to Randal.

"Father, tell me where they are."

Monsieur Mireault cupped his drink, watching the swirling amber liquid thoughtfully. "Your mother is dead, Ariane. I'm very sorry. She was shot in retaliation for the attacks of la Résistance."

The girl's lips moved silently, her eyes growing shiny. Working hands together in her lap, she asked in a broken voice, "And Jean-Marie?"

"Jean-Marie is safe. The Abkhazi have placed him in a special school where he is being cared for."

"*Es-tu ivre ou fou?*" Ariane's voice rose sharply in pitch. She stood and paced the carpet. "What kind of school? How could you let them take my little boy?"

The remainder was incomprehensible to Randal as they began shouting in rapid-fire French. The two exchanged harsh words for several moments before she switched back to English. "So you will prostitute yourself to these men… to these, to these butchers who killed my mother, just so you can be comfortable?"

Her father came out of the chair. "Will getting myself killed bring back your mother? Would I have been able to stop them from taking that little bâtard of yours? Non! I am doing what I must to survive."

Ariane raised herself up, seeming poised to strike him. Slowly she lowered, stepping back. Through clenched teeth she said softly, "You're a coward. And you are not my father."

She turned and swept from the room. To her back the man called out, "You are my daughter. But you are a disappointment! You have made nothing of the life I gave you!" Retaking his seat, he seemed to remember Randal was there. "The Scotch, is it to your liking?"

Randal blinked at the sudden shift. "Oh? Ah yes, an Islay, isn't it?" He preferred the drier bite of highland malts, but it didn't seem like a good time to mention it.

"Indeed." The man's eyes narrowed a bit. "Your face is familiar to me. We have met?"

"Just one of those faces, I guess."

"You have the bearing of a soldier, despite your clothes. You are one of the religious jingoists who've brought this war down upon us, I think." He seemed to be looking for an outlet to take out his annoyance with his daughter.

"This is a war of self-defense—and you know it, Monsieur Mireault. Don't try to excuse your collaboration with sophistry."

"The larger picture, young man, the larger picture. Religion causes war. It is the religious who kill one another. Both New Geneva and the Abkhazi are quite religious, *non?*"

Randal steepled his fingers, pressing them to his lips a moment. He felt as if he was sitting next to the hearth at Saint Athanasius all over again, sparring with Professor Lambrix. The old prof had loved playing devil's advocate. "Always the religious? Which century would you like me to pick to refute that? The Eighteenth, with the enlightened French revolutionaries and their Terror? Or the Twentieth, when Communism killed over a hundred million people? Perhaps the Twenty-Third, when Eco-Liberationists spread hantavirus on Leewynn to cleanse the planet of its 'human infestation?'"

Monsieur Mireault waved it off angrily. "What kind of God would allow all of this? Would allow men such suffering? Read Hume someday, boy. Or Sartre. If God is even out there, He's evil."

"God uses the evil choices of men to work out His righteous purpose - Judas's betrayal is a perfect example. And I have read Hume's *Inquiry*. What he fails to factor in is the afterlife, Monsieur Mireault. God will make things right once this world passes away." He watched the collaborator for a moment and felt sudden pity for him. "There will be justice for your wife's murder."

"*Bah*!" The man took a long drink of the liquor, turning red eyes on Randal. "I have no need of such comforting myths."

Too weary to argue, Randal simply shrugged. "Let's just enjoy our drinks."

Monsieur Mireault smirked, but raised his glass in agreement. "*À votre santé.*"

"To absent friends."

Ariane reappeared in the open double-doorway. Randal thought she looked pure revolutionary chic in the clothes she'd picked out. A ribbed charcoal sweater and black pea coat were worn over black synthleather slacks. She had a civilian-style beret pulled down over her chestnut locks. It took Randal several moments to remember to breathe.

"We should be going." He drained the last of his whiskey, the heavy peat tasting like liquid smoke. "Thank you for your hospitality, Monsieur Mireault."

The stout man shook his head as they walked to the back door. "This one has a brain at least, Ariane. That's better than the other one." She didn't answer, merely giving her father a world-weary look before stepping outside.

"Take care of my little girl."

"I will, sir."

Neither of them spoke on the way back to the base.

❧❧

"That's the way. Good. First man kneels and pulls near-side security. Meanwhile, the second man crosses the danger area, does a quick box patrol to check for bad guys and then watches over the far side. After that, everyone else crosses singly and as quickly as possible. You're second man, Drummond. You got all that?" Jack got a curt nod from Drummond in response.

Watching from the sidelines, Randal was impressed with how well Jack had brought the hard-headed miner around during the previous three weeks. How well he'd brought all their people around.

The NGDF regulars had divvied up the militia among them, forming them into fire teams and acting as cadre. They taught them the rudiments of urban warfare: how to cross danger areas; how to avoid detection from windows and basements; the least dangerous ways to clear a building; and other tricks of the trade. Randal drove them relentlessly. There was so much they needed to know and so little time to learn it.

During the training certain men came to the fore as natural leaders. Randal brevetted them to sergeant, instituting a chain of command among the previously anarchic militia soldiers. In turn they'd started calling him Captain. It was all they called him, at least to his face.

In addition to infantry tactics, the men were training in communications, first aid, explosives, and other needed skills. Across the chamber a group clustered around Ariane, half of them wrapping makeshift bandages around the upper arms of the other half, elevating and putting pressure on the simulated wounds. One man had been pulled from each squad to train as a combat medic.

Scuffling sounds pulled Randal's attention back to Jack's group. Drummond and one of the younger men were locked up on the floor. The miner had the boy's jacket up over his head and was working his ribs and kidneys with short, vicious hook punches.

Jack grabbed him by the collar, dragging him back several meters on the rock floor. "Now stay there. I'll be right back." Drummond seethed, but he stayed put. In Randal's experience, Jack rarely used his size to bring people around to his way of thinking. That just made it much more imposing when he did. He walked over to Randal, pulling him in close and whispering, "These are civilian volunteers, not regulars. You're pushing them too hard."

"There's too much to cover, Jack. They need to suck it up."

"Don't be your father. You're pushing them too hard and yourself as well."

"I'll be as hard as I have to, Jack, and so will they. I need to go check in on Jeni, just do what I ask of you." He could feel Jack's stare as he walked away.

He found Jeni in the small grotto she shared with Ariane. She was hunched over one of the drones, an electronic warfare model, arguing with Lebedev. Clearing his throat, Randal gave Jeni a skeptical look. "You uh, someone did something to your hair." It looked like she'd attempted to dye the tips blonde, but instead they had come out an orange hue not native to any human-inhabited world. It was pulled into bunches and tied off with red twine.

"You like?"

"It's not exactly stealthy. . ."

She beamed a Cheshire smile. "We're irregulars now, Randy. And I'm more irregular than most."

He was speechless in the face of such reasoning.

"The communications training I'm giving the militia is going well, by the way. I've got my little soldiers doing print message dead-drops, one-time pads, ciphers, the whole gamut. I'm also working on standardizing their commo procedures. To listen to them, you'd think they were nine-year-old girls chatting on vidphones, but they're making progress. It really is amazing what you can train them to do these days." She smacked Lebedev's hand as he adjusted a valve. "Not so much."

"But...But is not yet enough."

"You're not too old for me to turn you over my knee, Sergei. Behave." She glanced back up at Randal. "Once this is back online I can pull electronic warfare duty."

"Brilliant." Randal wrinkled his nose. "What's that smell, anyway? Is the drone leaking something?"

"I am sometimes working on explosives." Lebedev brushed at his hooded black pullover. "Is benzene and propylene fluid, for the making of jellied fire. That other idea I had, with the cleaning supplies and permafoam was a little, how to say? Wolatile."

"We remember," Randal said, covering a grin. "That incident was why you and your assistants were moved a hundred meters from everyone else, remember?"

"That and the smell," Jeni added helpfully.

"You are right, of course. Well, things are much improved. Soon they will know making of detonators and caps for blasting. Soon we can blow big things into many small things."

"Good man. You two meet me in the TOC in an hour. I've been thinking."

≈ ⋙

The senior staff filed into the chamber set aside as the Tactical Ops Center. Three collapsible tables set end-to-end and surrounded by chairs and crates served in lieu of a conference table.

Once everyone was seated, Randal took his spot at the head of the gathering. "I've been thinking. We're going to reach a point where inaction dulls the effect of any further training we give these guys. Van Loon seems to think we've reached and breached that point already. I think it's time to launch our guerrilla war." Randal looked instinctively to Jack for his opinion.

His friend considered it. "I agree. But it won't do any good to just send men out and hope they find targets. We need information. Wandering around will just jack up our own body count."

"Van Loon's right, Randal; we can't send them out blind. I've been giving some thought to that," Jeni said, absently twisting one of her black-orange tufts. "Guys can't move freely 'cause the Abbie's consider all of them militia and arrest and execute them. But women are safe as long as they keep covered up like a ghost. How about we use the men's wives as our eyes and ears? We could teach them what to look for and how to do message drops. I've shown the goodmen that much already."

Randal nodded. "Good thinking, Jeni. And thanks for volunteering; you're a natural to head up our new intelligence network."

"Hey! Wait just a—"

"I'm glad that's settled." He thought a moment. "Pieter, some of the men have scoped hunting rifles. I want you and Pyatt to pair each of them with a spotter. Until we get more experience, most of our ops should be two-man sniper teams doing hit-and-run attacks. We'll keep things simple for now."

"What in the world do I know about snipers, Kipper?"

"Pyatt can help with that. My advice would be to fake it 'til you make it. It's gotten me this far." He grinned as his friend gave an exaggerated huff. Pieter would do fine, he just needed the right push.

Over the next week Jeni put together her "Kitchen Klatch," as she insisted on calling them. The women proved to be excellent scouts with a good eye for detail. Each evening before curfew they dropped note-filled bottles into specified sewage drains for retrieval.

With these reports, the Irregulars put together a composite picture of Abkhazi force dispositions. Every night thereafter, three or four sniper teams would go topside. They would shoot from long distance, at their target and only their target, and then flee back to the safety of the Catacombs. Over the course of a few nights they turned what the Abkhazi must have considered a pacified city into a free-fire zone.

❧

The enemy response came several days later. The Irregulars kept two men near the surface twenty-eight hours a day to monitor the dry, propagandistic radio and trideo broadcasts in hopes that something of intelligence value might slip out. It had paid off a few times already. One of the monitors ran into the main chamber, looking around wildly until he spotted Randal. "Captain! Captain, you need to see this. I recorded it off the trid." A group gathered around curiously. Randal took the datapad, tapping the play icon on the recorder. He held it up so everyone could see.

The pallid visage of an Abkhazi officer came into view, his gelid blue eyes frightening even on the small screen. The camera panned back and they could see he stood outdoors, wearing a black uniform with death's head insignia on either collar. Randal's gut twisted. Having that man in town was nothing short of discovering that Death was your new next-door neighbor.

"I am Brigadier Gregor Tsepashin. Remember my name and learn to honor it. Due to the cowardly and warmongering actions of terrorist groups in this city, I have been appointed as garrison commander. Mogdukh be praised. The craven attacks of these infidels cannot be ignored. Many of the Pure have died at the hands of the Unevolved and justice must be exacted," he said in uninflected English, his voice full of the calm reasonableness of the madman. "If you wish to prevent further reprisals against the civilian population, please report any knowledge of terrorist acts to your nearest security sub-station."

The jittery image from a hand-held trideo camera panned over to a line of fifty-odd civilian women. They stood holding hands, weeping and praying.

"*Raz... dva... strelyai!*"

Autofire sounded from off-screen and the women collapsed like marionettes. Tsepashin came back into the picture, speaking smoothly once more. No one listened.

A heavy silence hung over the group, the tension a palpable thing. The crash of a bottle shattering against rock made everyone jump. "Sod it, I didn't sign up for this."

"Too right!"

Randal knew he was in danger of losing them. "Listen," he said, keeping his voice low so everyone would have quiet down if they wanted to hear. "What just happened was sickening. I'm sure some of you are thinking about quitting right now. It's only natural. But quitting will only ensure those women died for nothing. If we let the Abkhazi win then every civilian in Providence will eventually share their fate."

He tapped the datapad screen with a finger, making hard eye contact with the bottle-thrower. "Do you want payback for this? Well, do you?"

A slow, grudging nod.

"You'll get your payback. Tomorrow we take the war up a notch. Sergeants, please join me in the TOC. We've got an ambush to plan."

As the leadership team headed to the meeting, Randal caught sight of al-Hise. He looked pale and wobbly, like he'd been sucker-punched. It was understandable; every non-Purist in Abkhazia lived in fear of the midnight knock that might be Tsepashin and his Fist of the Mogdukh.

9

Every normal man must be tempted at times to spit upon his hands,
hoist the black flag, and begin slitting throats.
—Henry Louis Mencken

The 'eathen in 'is blindness must end where 'e began.
But the backbone of the Army is the non-commissioned man!
—Rudyard Kipling

It was that loneliest time of night, the brief period before dawn when
everything was still and frozen. The morning fog glowed in the mer-
ciless lights of Security Sub-station Number Eleven. Formerly Trinity
Classical, a secondary school, it had been impressed into military service. The school office now functioned as a headquarters, the classrooms
drafted into barracks duty, housing a full company of Scourge secret
police. The Abkhazi had divided the city into precincts and locked it down
tight with dozens of similar headquarters.

Randal's scouts reported that the Scourge had converted the football
pitch to a buzkashi field. He noted the twin poles placed at opposite sides
of a circle drawn in lime. Buzkashi, the Abkhazi national sport, literally
meant "goat-grabbing" and was known for its brutality. Normally played
on horseback with lead-tipped whips, the object was simply to move a
headless, sand-filled goat carcass from one pole to the other. Central
Asian tribes had played it for centuries. In Providence they had adapted
to the lack of horses, playing on foot but keeping the whips.

Every morning the Scourge company assembled on the buzkashi field
for physical training. Randal intended that morning to be a memorable

one for them. He and his team squatted in the alleyway across the street from the school. Over the headset he'd appropriated from a militiaman he said, "Pyatt, this is Knox. Are your people in place?"

"Gimme two mikes."

"Roger, out."

Outstanding—the sniper teams were nearly ready. He'd kept the plan simple for the benefit of the recently civilian. There would be time for more complex missions later, but for their first platoon-level operation he wanted as few potential foul-ups as possible.

The Irregulars were set up for an L-shaped ambush—two lines of troops meeting at a right angle, anchored at the joint by the unit's light machine gun. Snipers formed the base of the L, hidden in an abandoned cannery across from the football pitch. Pyatt and Pieter were in charge of that section.

Autoriflemen hiding with Randal in the alley formed the back of the L. None of Randal's people were in powered armor. He wanted to save that surprise for a special occasion. The only available cover was a line of vehicles along the street. These had been impounded with the onset of martial law, the groundcars chock-blocked, the nozzles of the skimmers booted or simply cemented shut.

With a painful opening screech, speakers blared the Abkhazi national anthem. It was a militarized adaptation of the Russian-Kazakh composer Lilya Katseppova's piece, Moyo Otetchestvo. Randal doubted Katseppova would appreciate the revisions, or the people using her work.

Men poured from the barracks and dashed madly to formation. In spite of the frigid air they went bare-chested, wearing only workout shorts. They stacked their rifles to the rear of the formation and scurried into their assigned places.

The last man to find his spot was brought to the front. A senior sergeant beat the man with a baton until he crumpled at his feet. Dragging the fallen soldier to the side to regain his senses, the senior sergeant led the men in callisthenic drills. As the men exercised, he circled like a predator through the ranks, striking anyone who seemed lax in his performance.

You get it first, Randal thought. He'd established code words with the machine gunner, the man who would initiate the attack—Mayhem if it was a go, Declension in the event of an abort. Before giving the go-code, he glanced at Ariane, who crouched nearby. She was along as medic for the op. The trim submachine gun slung over one shoulder still seemed awkward in her grip. He gave her a nudge. "Just stay close to me."

With a quick smile he looked back to the pitch, motioning for the autoriflemen to take position. As one, they slunk into place behind the impounded cars, keeping out of sight. Just then the senior sergeant paused in mid-swagger. Randal would never know whether it was a glint from a riflescope or a flicker of movement, but suddenly the enemy noncom started barking out orders.

The Abkhazi, conditioned to instant obedience, rose to their feet. Seeing his advantage about to disappear, Randal called "Mayhem, mayhem!" over the com.

The loud retort of the machine gun broke the pre-dawn silence, followed by the snipers firing in quick succession from the old cannery. Autoriflemen popped up from behind groundcars and skimmers, spraying the massed troops with 5 mm rounds.

First to fall was the senior sergeant—Pieter's snipers had remembered to target the chain of command.

Chaos erupted as the enemy soldiers scrambled over each other to seize a weapon from the stacks. Many gave up and dashed toward the school building, but there was no safety to be found.

Strangely, one soldier sprinted not toward the school, but in the direction of Randal's riflemen. His hands were in the air and he was shouting frantically. Whatever his words, they were lost in the tumult. "Nobody shoot the runner – he's surrendering!" Randal called over the headset.

Then he forgot the man as a handful of Abkhazi returned fire, using a pile of their dead compatriots for cover.

He killed one with a carefully aimed shot, but took no pleasure in it. There was nothing honorable or glorious in guerrilla warfare, no matter how effective it might be. He felt pity for the young Abkhazi dying helplessly in their gym shorts.

Beside him Ariane fired burst after burst at the enemy. The one glance he'd caught of her made him worried; she looked sick with guilt. He wished he could tell her a comforting lie, maybe that her weapon was useless at such a range, but there was no time.

The volume of fire slackened and then died as all movement on the football pitch ceased. Now they needed to evac the area before enemy reinforcements arrived. "Everyone start pulling back. I want you off-site in three minutes."

"Randal, this is Pieter. We've got a man down—head wound."

"I'll send the medic." He turned to Ariane. "I need you to move with a purpose over to the cannery. One of the snipers took a head shot."

The girl winced. Randal didn't envy her having to work under such conditions. "Tell Pieter I'll be right there." He watched her run off, a slim girl with an oversized medical kit and a gun. It was a beautiful sight.

Belatedly he remembered the surrendering Abkhazi. Had he survived? "Anyone on this ComNet—any word on that Abbie who ran toward us?"

An anxious voice came back to him. "Captain Knox, we're to the north of you. Sergeant al-Hise, he... I think he's going to kill the prisoner."

Randal cursed. Al-Hise didn't have a militia com and there was no way to call him off.

He sprinted northward and found the Abkhazi soldier kneeling with hands behind his head. The ternate stars printed on his gym shorts marked him as a light colonel, the cat-of-nine-tails below it placed him with the Scourge of the Prophet.

Looming over him was Nabil al-Hise, the muzzle of his rifle propping up the man's chin. Off to the side stood a skinny militiaman Randal remembered the others calling Rickets. "What's going on here? We're expecting enemy counterforce troops in two minutes. Why are you two lollygagging?" Randal's blood was still up from the fight.

"Captain Knox, he's going to kill him!"

"Sergeant al-Hise, stand down. Lower the weapon now."

Al-Hise didn't look up. "He's a swine and he deserves to die like one." The weapon shook in his hands, the muzzle tracking wildly around the prisoner's face.

There was no time for negotiations. Randal pointed his flechette rifle at al-Hise. "One more chance."

The enemy officer began speaking in slow, measured tones. His English was flawless. "I'm with the New Genevan Intelligence Service. I'm deep cover, please believe me. I wanted to make contact with you."

This startled al-Hise enough to lower his weapon. "He's lying. But if you would kill me rather than this swine, then very well. I will remember!" With a contemptuous look he trotted off to join the escaping Irregulars.

Keeping a safe distance from the Abkhazi, Randal knelt down to eye-level with him. "You're probably lying. Either way, I don't shoot prisoners so this is your lucky day." He paused, debating internally before adding, "If you're on the level, then be at the hovertram stop at Cedar and Leominster at 1700 this evening. If you double-cross us, believe me that my snipers are very, very good. You'll never leave that spot alive." He stood, freeing his sidearm from its shoulder rig. "Now close your eyes, I have to give you an alibi."

With a resigned sigh, the Abkhazi officer leaned forward, covering his eyes. "Just make it quick."

Flipping his pistol to hold it by the barrel, Randal struck him as carefully as possible on the back of the head.

"Oi! That really hurts."

"Sorry! Never really done this before." The second hit sprawled the man out. To the enemy troops who found him it would appear he was captured and left for dead.

After checking the Abkhazi's pulse, Randal sprinted to join his team. The rumble of oncoming armored vehicles grew loud as he dropped into the welcoming safety of the Catacombs.

❧ ❧

At 1700 a Korean woman enshrouded in the shapeless burqa distributed by the Khlisti authorities sat by the hovertram stop at Cedar and Leominster. Behind her rose the pink stone buildings of Abraham Kuyper University, the pre-war research hub of New Geneva. She pretended to read a copy of Istina, or "Heavenly Truth" from a datapad. Her eyes flitted over the top of the screen, scanning the thin crowd surreptitiously.

An almost deserted hovertram pulled into the kiosk, expelling a rush of air as it settled down on its rubber skirting. The door accordioned open, a lone passenger in Abkhazi fatigues descending the steps. Ternate stars were sewn onto the collar of the blouse. An oversized flechette pistol rode low on his hip.

Jeni set aside the datapad, favoring him with a wave that would be a tip-off if he was the man she was to meet, and merely interpreted as flirtatious if not. He was a handsome one, if not tall enough for her usual tastes.

He took a seat beside her. Pulling up his sleeve, he eyed a small electronic device strapped to his forearm. "Other than the microtransmitter on your person, there seem to be no other listening devices in the area. We can speak with relative freedom," he told her softly, slipping an arm around her shoulders. Officers were allowed liberties with the civilian population and she knew the physical closeness would keep any other Abkhazi from disturbing them.

Jeni made no apologies for the transmitter. It was the only way to alert the security team hiding in the sewer below if trouble arose. "I'm with military intel, so don't assume I'm a bit of fluff. How do we know you are who you say you are?"

The man shrugged. "Any details I give you to authenticate myself would also be known to a false flag agent. You'll know I'm real when the things I tell you come true."

Jeni nodded, not entirely satisfied. "All right. But my transmitter has a live trideo feed. My people know what you look like. You double-cross us and every sniper on the payroll will be looking for you." She flashed the oversize button of her purse at him, ostensibly the micro-cam. It was a total bluff—the transmitter was actually a mic taped to her throat, but he seemed to buy it.

"Very well. What information would you like first?"

That stymied her momentarily. It was only supposed to be an introductory meeting and the team hadn't expected him to be so forthcoming. Moved by a generous impulse, she asked on Ariane's behalf, "The Abbies are stealing children. Where are they taking them?"

"There's a boarding school, near the university. They've turned it into an academy for Janissaries." His eyes never left hers as he answered. He was either telling the truth or a masterful liar.

She had no idea what a Janissary was, but trusted that Randal would. "Alright. We'll communicate through dead drops, of course. Here's a set of locations and times."

He nodded assent, pocketing the list. "You will call me Onegin in our correspondence, and I shall refer to you as Tatyana. If by chance our messages are intercepted, I can easily explain you away as one of my moles in the Resistance."

Deftly lifting her veil, he stole a quick kiss from her lips. "Just for appearances," he said with a twisted smile. After a quick bow he was off, rounding a corner and out of sight.

⋖⋗

Ariane sat wrapped in a coarse synthwool blanket in the Irregulars' makeshift infirmary. This consisted of three folding cots, a poorly stocked medical cabinet, a pile of linens, the Doc-in-a-Box, and a chiropractic-turned-operating table Pieter had scrounged up.

Her patient slept on the cot to her right, wrapped in the warm embrace of a sedative. The only casualty of the morning's ambush, he'd caught an improvident ricochet - the round had grazed his skull, and then buried itself in the meat of his left shoulder. He would live, but the joint would never be the same. Ariane simply had neither the equipment, nor the skills she needed, and that fact plagued her constantly.

With a soft wrap of knuckles against the stone of the infirmary entrance, Nabil walked in. "Good evening, Private Mireault," he said politely, taking a seat on the empty cot.

"Nabil," she answered, feeling wary.

"I heard of the death of your mother and came to express my sympathies. I lost my parents to those butchers as well." His voice held no trace of emotion, his eyes seeming to search her face for something.

"*Merci*. I'm sorry about your parents."

His shoulders elevated millimetrically. "They are being avenged. Perhaps now you see that forgiveness isn't the panacea you thought it was, no?"

Ariane smiled a glum little smile. She knew she should be mad at his cynical little thrust, but instead felt a sort of pity for him. "I'm angry at what they've done, Nabil. But hating them won't bring her back. Hating them only hardens me – it won't hurt them at all."

"Perhaps you didn't feel as strongly for your mother as I did for mine," he said, pursing his lips. "If you did it wouldn't be so easy for you to sympathize with her killers."

That got her attention. "Easy? They have my little boy. The easiest thing in the world would be to give in like you have." She came halfway out of her seat. "There's something dark in you Nabil. And it won't be happy until I'm just as hateful as you. Misery really does love company, I guess."

She paused for breath, standing and starting to pace the floor. Nabil watched in silence, dark eyes narrowed to slits. Turning back to him, she stooped to meet his eyes. "There's another reason you keep coming to me like this—some small part of you knows I'm telling the truth. The part that knows the Abkhazi are no bigger sinners than you once were in the eyes of God."

Quicker than she could imagine possible, his hand was pressed flat to her chest and shoving her backward. "Don't bring our God into this, stupid girl!" he said, springing to his feet and pushing past her.

Ariane trudged back to her cot and slumped into bed. Nabil's games were the finishing touch on a wretched day. She sobbed away the day's misery into a thin pillow, grateful it was finally over.

❧

Now that Pieter's crew was functioning well as a team, Randal decided it was time to press on with his plan to unite the militia cells into an organized resistance.

He knew it wouldn't be easy. STA—Safety Through Autonomy—was one of the key tenets driven home to the militiamen during their monthly training days. It was a great theory, but the reality on the ground was something else. The Army's retreat from Providence had left the cells so demoralized that few were still in the fight. Other than occasional reports of distant autofire from his snipers, and spoor and trash in the Catacombs, the Irregulars found little evidence of their fellow cells.

Randal believed that someone with vision could bring them back. With the right instruction the cells would be much deadlier united than separated. At times he worried it was hubris driving him on, but his vision for a partisan army wouldn't let him alone.

Even if he could find them, he had other another worry: constant hiding bred paranoia, and approaching the cells without getting shot might be problematic. Even once contact was made, Randal doubted that most cell leaders would cede command as readily as Pieter.

Taking his concerns to Jeni had proven to be a good idea. For the previous two days she and Lebedev had sequestered themselves in the Belarusian's workshop. Fishing for hints about her plans only rewarded him with maddeningly enigmatic smiles. Jeni had scared poor Lebedev into silence as well—leaning on him for information had only made him more squirrelly than usual. Thus it was with great relief that he heard Jeni say, "Randy, check it out," as she and Lebedev joined him in the TOC. The Belarusian carried an improvised electronic device.

"You're finished?" he asked, careful to keep his voice level. Sounding excited would only make her coy.

"Uh-huh. Sergei and I cannibalized the DF gear from one of my drones. Then we tore the guts from one of the deadlined coms and used its housing. Next, Sergei hooked up this little monitor we found with some cable lines. He's so clever." She goosed Lebedev, nearly causing him to drop the device.

"Dee-Eff. So I can direction-find the militia coms with this?"

Jeni nodded. "Uh-huh. But only when you know what frequency to scan for. That's where I come in. I'll use a drone to find signals, decrypt 'em to make sure they're friendly, and then tell the team with the hand-held set what freq to look for."

Parts of it began to make sense to Randal. "Like triangulation."

"Exactly like triangulation. My comp will tell me the direction the signal is coming from. Then the hand-held set will give its people a back-azimuth for the signal. We plot lines on the map from our locations in the direction of the source. Wherever my line meets theirs, we've got our target to within about ten meters. I'll call ahead to warn them you're coming, and then your ground team moves to contact." She elbowed Lebedev lightly. "'Simpler than a steamed turnip' as you Slavs are always saying, right Sergei?"

The man only managed a nervous smile.

Randal took the device from Lebedev, turning it over to examine it. "This little box might be worth a regiment to me. Thanks."

"Anything for my loyal subjects," Jeni said regally, leaving him with a wink.

The next day Randal assembled a contact team. He planned to lead it himself, hoping his notoriety would give the team's proposition some much-needed credibility.

He brought Pieter with him, since he was also a well-known personality around Providence. Rounding out the team was the rail-thin secondary school student the men called Rickets. He'd earned a good reputation bird-dogging for the snipers. Also, Rickets looked about as intimidating as a Pomeranian. There wasn't much chance of a militia sentry mistaking him for an Abkhazi warrior and getting trigger-happy.

At nightfall they crept from underground, activating the direction-finder. About a kilometer away another team was placing Jeni's drone atop an abandoned building to give it needed elevation. They'd been unable to salvage the flight controls.

Randal's team hid in an alley while they waited, keeping low behind a pile of uncollected garbage. After nearly an hour Jeni's voice came across the headset. "Hardly anyone's talking tonight. I finally have an active channel. Go to three-eleven point eight-seven."

Pieter punched in the freq. The small monitor cast a greenish glow on his features as he studied it. "It's processing..." he whispered.

They all ducked as a pair of gunships soared overhead, vectored thrust kicking up debris in the alley, pelting them with garbage. Fortunately they were in a visual dead zone and the gunships' searchlights never brushed them. Randal badly missed his LANCER suit–the flechette rifle he carried would do little to stop the gunships–but he was still keeping the armor in reserve.

"Okay, it's showing numbers. Um...Two-seventy-one point four."

Randal relayed them to Jeni.

"Okay, Randy. Your prize awaits you at grid coordinate eight-seven-one-four, nine-nine-five-two—give or take."

"Roger, out."

Pieter pulled a datapad from his waist pack, calling up a topographic map of Providence. As a cell leader, he'd received up-to-date military maps. He entered the grid code, then glanced up, frowning incredulously. "They're in my church, Randal. That coordinate is spot in the middle of Kirk of the Hills."

The trio dropped back into the sewers and started working their way downtown. Randal knew before long the Abkhazi would grow wise and start monitoring the main arteries, but until then it was safer traveling underground than above. The closest sewer access to the church was in the middle of a major thoroughfare, so the contact team backtracked to a side street. After slipping out, they kept to the shadows, creeping to within sight of the old church.

Pieter cursed under his breath, echoing Randal's thoughts. They'd seen evidence the Abkhazi were torching all reminders of Providence's religious roots, but neither had wanted to believe that Kirk of the Hills had shared that fate. Massive walls remained like a brick ribcage, piles of rubble spilling out like intestines. The wood beams and antique shingles of the roof were a memory.

What saddened him most was the loss of the gorgeous rose mosaic glass window that once sat over the main doors. It was a relic of Terra, depicting the resurrection of Christ in thousands of microscopically thin glass wafers layered in painstaking detail. He'd spent an entire afternoon one winter just watching the light of the revolving sun shift and nuance the colors of the glass.

Another thing the Abkhazi would be called to account for.

"They must be in the basement level of the church. You really have to admire their cheek, setting up residence in the middle of downtown," Pieter said over Randal's shoulder.

Rickets nodded. "Bet it's the last place the Abbies would think to look."

Randal hailed Jeni, giving her the go-ahead to contact the cell in the church.

After a few minutes, she came back with, "No luck, Randy. Had 'em five-by-five, but they went cold as soon as I made contact."

"Do they know we're coming?"

"Doubtful. I messaged that you were approaching, but they likely flipped off their coms."

Randal scanned the street for enemy patrols and then dashed across to the first available cover, Pieter and Rickets on his heels. They threaded their way to the church steps. "NGDF. We're friendlies," Randal whispered urgently. The shadowed mounds of rubble made no reply.

"We can't stay out in the open for long," Pieter said. "I can still hear those gunships circling."

"You two keep put."

Letting the flechette rifle hang across his back by the sling, Randal started the climb, arms out and palms empty. The broad, stone steps led into the remains of the church narthex. He squinted into the gloom, but could make nothing out. Meanwhile, he was a sitting duck, silhouetted in the entryway by the ambient city light. "NGDF. I'm here to make contact."

"Hands behind your head." The gruff voice came from nowhere. Randal fought the impulse to skin his sidearm and then carefully laced fingers behind his skull.

Shadows began to move and form into men. A face emerged, blackened with soot, from not three meters to his right. These chappies were good. The militiaman gestured for silence and then smashed the butt of his rifle into the side of Randal's head. He hit the ground in a lump, choking on ash. Through the haze of pain, Randal saw other men run past, drawing down on Pieter and Rickets.

Then people seized him under the arms and frogmarched him down into the basement. They passed through a candlelit corridor and reached a set of double doors. A peephole was carved into the left one. After a callsign and password, the doors opened and the captors dragged Randal and the others inside a long meeting hall. None too carefully, they planted the Irregulars face down on the tile floor. "Stay put."

Quiet voices murmured in the corridor and then Randal felt a boot nudge him. "Turn over."

Randal rolled to find a solidly-built older man in hunting clothes. Looking closer he realized they weren't hunting cammies at all, but rather old-style fatigues the NGDF hadn't issued in at least a decade. He flipped a skinning knife and caught it by the antler grip. "NGDF, you say? You fellows all bugged out for the south. I guess that'd make you a deserter."

"We're not—" Rickets started to say, earning a short kick to the ribs.

"I was talking to this one."

"We're not deserters." Randal spat blood on the dusty floor. "Our unit got wiped out in Crenshaw Pass. We hooked up with the Providence militia."

"I'll admit you don't sound like Abbies. So what authorized you to violate STA?"

"Autonomy was intended to protect cells during guerrilla ops. How many are still in the fight?"

The man motioned with the knife. "You three can get up. Just keep your hands clear."

Randal stood and took stock of the room. It was probably once the social hall, but now it served as barracks, dining facility, and aid station. Chem lamps hung on the wall, bathing the room in an unnatural yellow glow. Out of an original strength of forty men, he could see less than twenty remaining, including three wounded on cots. "The war's been hard on you."

"We're still in the fight. Just reduced our operational tempo once it got hopeless." He jammed the knife away and stuck out a hand. "Sergeant-Major Wheeler, NGDF retired."

"Corporal Randal Knox."

"Of the Irregulars," Pieter broke in. "He's a captain now."

"The Irregulars. And why are you violating STA?" He definitely *seemed* like a sergeant-major, with a bullet-shaped head and the menacing attitude the military issued a man upon achieving the rank.

Knowing hesitation meant disaster, Randal answered as coolly as he was able. "We're putting together an army. You're just the sort of leader I've been looking for, Sergeant-Major."

The old soldier chuckled. "Come again, son?" If he was impressed with Randal's parentage, he hid it well.

Randal stood his ground. "It's time to get the cells back into the war. The main body of the enemy is far to the south, and we're sitting smack in the middle of their supply lines. A partisan army in Providence would be—"

"—completely unthinkable!" Wheeler scratched the bristles of his hair. "Imagine the logistics of it. Feeding them, arming them, training them. . ."

"I have thought about it, Sergeant-Major." Randal pulled the datapad from his rucksack, called up a file, and tossed it to him. "I've laid out organizational charts for the force, worked up a roster of needed positions, and outlined everything else I could think of. You're right, it'd be near-impossible to pull off. That's why I need you."

Wheeler scanned the document and for awhile it was as if the rest of them weren't even there. Then he let out a short bark of a laugh and pulled Randal over to him. Tapping the screen with a thick, stubby finger, he nodded. "You might be on to something, boy. There are a few things I would change."

For the next three hours Randal and the Sergeant-Major huddled in a corner, and argued, debated and discussed. By the end, the old man seemed rather taken with the idea. "Now for the real test," Wheeler said, walking away to join his men. "Theory is one thing. Let's see if anyone will actually sign on to this crusade of yours. You can bunk down in the corridor while we discuss it."

Militiamen set them up with blankets, and Pieter and Rickets were racked out in minutes. It wasn't so easy for Randal. He stewed, straining to hear anything through the thick wooden doors. Only the occasional angry voice squeezed through them. After an hour or so, four men left the hall and went topside, relieving the watch.

Just as Randal was ready to smother Ricket's snores with a flak vest, the double doors opened.

"Here's a com, son," Wheeler said, tossing a battered set to Randal. "If we're teaming up, we'll need to be able to get in touch with each other. But don't tie it up with chatter. If you lot can find us, I've no doubt the sodding Abbies can too."

"We'll get a medic up here for your wounded post-haste, Sergeant-Major, along with some rations."

"Much appreciated. As discussed, we'll sit tight for now. Don't keep me waiting long – I'm ready to get these men back in the fight."

Randal was jubilant as the trio sneaked back to the Irregulars' base. Noncommissioned officers were the backbone of an army, and Sergeant-Major Wheeler had devoted his career to making them.

⋰⋱

Over the next three weeks Randal repeated the process nearly every night, bringing Pieter and Rickets with him. Many nights Jeni was unable to raise a channel that was active for more than a handful of transmissions—too short a time for their improvised DF system to zero in on a location. Other times the cell would refuse to come out of hiding. But perhaps a third of the time they were able to meet with a cell leader. All but two of these were convinced to join the Irregulars.

The nightly harassment by Irregular sniper teams had stirred up the Abkhazi. During the weeks of the outreach to the cells, Randal saw an ever-increasing number of patrols—mechanized, foot and air. He knew they were pushing it to keep going topside every night, but success spurred him forward.

On what he had decided would be the final night of their initial push, Jeni picked up a good, solid signal. It was tantalizingly close. Despite an uneasy feeling up the back of his neck, Randal led the contact team in the signal's direction. They moved swiftly through a dormant business district, keeping to the streets. More than once they'd missed contacts by taking the slower underground route.

"My map plots them in an office complex," Pieter said, stowing the datapad. "It's probably empty at this point."

The whole district is abandoned, thought Randal. With martial law in place, commerce was dead. Looted and abandoned business towers loomed over them, the wind howling through vacant streets like the ghosts of vanished capitalists.

Sound carried in the near-silent city. Even far off troop carriers and gunships sounded nearby, giving Randal the uncomfortable feeling of being surrounded. Making matters worse, his snipers reported motion sensors and cameras in places the Abkhazi thought guerrilla activity likely. The alley they were traversing was just such a spot, Randal noticed.

He called softly up to Rickets. "Keep a sharp eye out for cameras."

The boy looked back, giving a thumbs-up.

Just then his shin broke a micro-thin tripwire. Randal noticed it gleam as it snapped. The tripwire looked as if it followed a crevice between the bricks, traveling around the corner. That thought raced through his mind the instant before a light like a small sun blinded them. The keening wail of an alarm came with it. Randal's heart stopped and he felt his gorge rise in his throat. It took a second to realize it wasn't an explosion, but a warning device.

Randal seized Rickets by his collar, yanking him back roughly. Turning, he stiff-armed Pieter's chest. The man was frozen in place, stunned by the unexpected light.

"Ground flare! Move!"

Every Abkhazi for a kilometer would be on them in a blink. Randal got the other two moving, sprinting away from the damning flare. They hopped the fence into the parking lot of a three-story office building and dashed across the open space.

A wheeled, low-slung scout car barreled around the corner. It braked for only a second before accelerating and crashing through the gate. A casemate turret swiveled atop the car, its medium machine gun belting loose a stream of bullets and pocking the wall. The trio ducked behind the building for cover.

Coughing on concrete dust, Randal yelled, "Run for the back fence!" Only his flechette rifle had any chance against the vehicle. He rolled to fire from the prone around the side of the building, targeting the tires. The left side wheels popped loudly enough to be heard over the machine gun. The vehicle lurched to the side.

But it didn't stop.

Randal ground his teeth in frustration. It had run-flats. Seeing the turret sighting on him, he winced, anticipating the machine gun slugs about to fly in his direction.

Instead they struck about ten centimeters overhead. Sharp pieces of concrete and plaster bit into his neck and scalp. The turret couldn't depress far enough to hit him at such close range. He took advantage of that, spider-webbing the driver's window with flechettes.

The driver was quick-witted, shifting fire to the two runners. Clearing the side of the building, he had a clean shot. Pieter and Rickets were just scaling the fence when the rounds struck. Most went wide, one tearing the top bar of the fence in half, dumping Pieter into the ditch on the opposite side.

Rickets wasn't as fortunate. Two bullets found him, his thin frame barely slowing them down. The boy hung bonelessly, his ragged jacket caught on a fence post.

Randal scrambled to his feet, rushing the car and firing on the move. He filled the driver's window with holes, still shooting even after he was sure nothing survived inside. Then he rushed to his fallen man and eased him to the ground, kneeling to examine the damage. Ripping open the boy's shirt, Randal fought down the urge to be sick—the exit wounds looked like angry red mouths erupting from his chest. Air bubbled and hissed from one of the holes, the collapsed lung struggling to function.

Randal pressed his hands over the wound, beginning emergency aid. He soon saw it was futile. Already the rise and fall of his chest was slowing, the eyes losing their light. "Stay with me Rickets, look at me. . ." Taking the boy's hand, he squeezed it tightly and prayed quietly over him. Rickets was gone before the amen.

He took a grenade from the boy's webbing, disengaged the secondary safety and pulled the pin. Rolling Rickets over, he wedged the grenade under him. When the Abbies collected his body, Rickets would have the last word.

Slinging the boy's autorifle, Randal stepped over the broken fence to join Pieter. He hated leaving Ricket's behind, hated the awful pragmatism with which he had to act, but he forced aside the feeling. He needed to be hard to see his people through.

"I hear gunships," Pieter said, setting off at a run. The two of them followed the ditch to where it flowed into a culvert. Wading into it, they entered the embracing darkness of the Catacombs.

❧❧

The following days seemed to blur, one into another. With the challenges of integrating new cells into the Irregulars, Randal's life narrowed down to a never-ending series of meetings and planning sessions. From having forty-six souls in one spot to care for, he now had nearly three hundred in seven locations. One cell had no central location at all. Instead, the troops lived dispersed in the attics of militia sympathizers around the city. It would have been a logistical headache even without the constant threat of Abkhazi patrols. During those brief times he was permitted to sleep, Rickets' final moments played a repeating loop in his head.

Their latest crisis was a supply shortage. An army runs on its stomach, and a few crates of pilfered rations and some preserved fruits wouldn't keep it going for long. Of the senior staff, only Jack and Jeni were in the Catacombs, so Randal sent runners to bring them to the storage chamber. Jack came immediately, a flechette rifle slung across his back. Jeni ambled in at her own pace.

Catching Randal's worried expression, Jack eyed their dwindling stock of provisions. "My wife's been telling me to diet."

"You're in luck then. I thought recruiting the cells would be the hard part, but that's easy compared to equipping and feeding them."

"Devil's in the details, Randy," Jeni chimed in brightly. "We're overextended. We don't have anything like the support network we need to keep this army in the field. We need supplies, safe houses, intelligence…"

He knew she was right. It was the part of the job he hated most. Big ideas came easily to him; niggling details were another matter. "Believe me, I know. You have some ideas?"

The girl splayed out her fingers, examining the nails critically. "We have a sympathetic population just waiting to be asked. They're in this as much as we are, after all. I could start by getting the addresses of likely candidates from the militia guys. I do have a certain knack for these things."

"And you're welcome to it. Keep me posted." Randall turned to Jack. "Van Loon, I need you to spend a few days with the Brighton District cell. They're shot up so badly it'll take a miracle just to reestablish unit cohesion. I'm hoping you can work one. Take along one of the new noncoms; he can learn by watching you." He sat down on an ammo box. "In addition to the Brighton cell, pick a second one. You, al-Hise and Pyatt are each going to take a newbie sergeant. We'll divvy up the cells, two for each of you. You'll be responsible for getting them organized. Agreed?"

Jack nodded. "I was thinking along those lines. But that's only the first step. We can drill them on combat basics, but they'll still need someone to train them further. We need to bring Sergeant-Major Wheeler into this."

"Definitely. When you and the others are working with the new cells, keep an eye on who naturally stands out. We'll attach them temporarily to the Sergeant-Major. He's going to be our one-man NCO academy."

"Sounds good," Jack said. "Now what should we do about the cell over in the abandoned metro station? They're split right down the middle between those two yobs who both want to be the boss."

"Kick one of them upstairs."

"How's that, Jeni?"

"Promote one of them to some meaningless HQ position where he can't do any damage. Assistant Deputy Lieutenant Signals Officer or something. That'll take him out of the equation."

"It just might work." Randal was always amazed how Jeni could go from vapid to brilliant in the blink of an eye. "Oh, and I want you to liaise for me with the Korean cell, Lieutenant Shin's people."

"I like that guy—he's crazy," Jack said, chuckling. "Though I wouldn't let him give me a shave. He seems a little too infatuated with that knife of his."

"They're calling themselves the Headhunters. Sometimes I worry they might be taking the name literally."

"I'll make contact with Shin tomorrow." Jeni stood, kissing the top of Randal's head. "I'm for bed. G'night, boys."

After she was gone, Jack scooted his ration crate a little closer. "I hear Rickets died last night."

"It was a mess."

"How you feeling?"

Randal shrugged, not sure he wanted to get into it. "It was one thing losing Kimathi and the others, but this kid was a fourth form student. I should've been walking point. I keep thinking over and over what I could have done differently. But what really bothers me is that I should feel all broke up about it, but can't seem to. Like if I let it touch me I won't be able to keep things together." The words came easily as he spoke to Jack, as they always did. He couldn't imagine what he would do without his friend.

"I've told you from the beginning, mate, you're trying to gut through this. God makes a better God than you do."

Randal chased a pebble absently with the toe of his boot. "I worry sometimes that even if I survive this war, I won't be the kind of person I'd want to be around."

"Don't worry. I'll still hang out with you."

10

The battlefield is a scene of constant chaos.
The winner will be the one who controls the chaos,
both his own and the enemy's.
—Napoleon Bonaparte

We're surrounded. That simplifies the problem.
—Chesty Puller, USMC

The next month was a mad one for Randal, a constant sense of trying to keep too many balls in the air at once. At least his people were making progress. They'd organized the new cells into squads and positioned them around the city, placing freshly-minted noncoms from the Sergeant-Major's basement academy in charge.

Jeni had assembled an exceptional grassroots network from among the goodwives of Providence, and her intelligence-gathering resources were formidable now. She'd even managed to enlist New Genevan women forced into clerical or labor roles by the occupiers, giving her glimpses inside the Abkhazi war machine. No one ever paid attention to secretaries or cleaning ladies.

For the time being the supply problem had abated. The Irregulars had knocked off one of the enemy storage depots, netting not only food, but also hand-held rocket launchers, small arms, and munitions.

While the professional side of life was making gains, on the personal side he could feel Ariane slipping away. It was funny, but not until she was absent did he realize how much he liked having her around. Ariane was the first girl that didn't leave him searching for words. Other than

Jeni of course, but she was just like one of the guys. Saint Athanasius Academy had been a boy's school. The infantry was basically just a school for overgrown boys with machine guns. Out of sight, out of mind; he'd never really had to deal with females. But now Ariane was often in his thoughts.

He knew why she was pulling away. They'd known for some time where her son was, yet hadn't rescued him. Randal had explained his reasons for waiting: the complicated nature of hostage rescues, the inexperience of the new cells, and the difficulty of relocating over a hundred children. Rational arguments held little weight. He knew she wasn't angry, but Randal was still the man keeping her child in Abkhazi hands.

So he was glad to finally bring her some good news. Standing in the infirmary entrance, he cleared his throat softly.

Ariane set aside the copy of Blake she read by chemlight, a genuine printed book she'd gotten from Pieter. From the darkness under her eyes it was clear she wasn't sleeping much. "Come in."

He shook his head, giving her a gentle smile. "I've got planning to do. Just talked to Van Loon and the Sergeant-Major. We've decided it's time to rescue the Janissary children. I thought you'd want to know."

Her nose pinked and she pressed fingers over her lips. "Thank you, Randal. Thank you."

They held one another's eyes, neither speaking.

Randal knew anything he said would spoil the moment, and took leave with an inclination of his head.

Reaching the ops center, he sent runners to gather Jeni, al-Hise, Lebedev and Pieter for a briefing. Once they were assembled around the table, he distributed hardcopies of the plan he and the Sergeant-Major had put together.

"Pieter, I need a cast-iron watch on the Janissary school for the next few days. That means a warm body with electronic binos scoping it every second of the day, got it?" Pieter was now heading up the Irregulars' scouting, with al-Hise's oversight. "I need to know everything—guard shift changes, static defenses and especially any holes in the patrol routes. Can you handle it?"

His friend huffed, seeming offended by the question. "We're talking about me, Kipper. Of course I can."

"Jeni? Oh, Jeni..." The girl was smoking one of her bidis again. She was lost, watching the strawberry-scented smoke drift away. The stink from the rolled-leaf cigarettes was cloying in the small room.

"Wha—huh?"

"I need your Kitchen Klatch to start putting out feelers. We'll need safe places to relocate these kids once we spring them."

"No worries, ducky. I've got a few contacts out in the country that might be ideal. I'll keep you apprised."

A sneeze reminded him of Lebedev's presence in the corner. The gray little man was easy to overlook. "Sergei, first of all, congrats on the coating for the powered armor."

Lebedev waved it off. "No mentioning it, it vas easy." Easy or not, it was a huge help. The rubberized coating he'd developed for the feet of the LANCER suits muffled the noise they made on city streets. Better, it stopped them from skidding wildly on concrete. The NGDF had overboots for the suits, but they were never issued on the border. No one had planned to end up in Providence.

"Sergei, I need you and your people to cook up a couple of anti-vehicular mines for me. Make them look like debris. And try not to bring the cave down on us when you're doing it."

The Belarusian laughed wheezily at that. "*Nu ladno*, I am always careful. You will have your mines soon. I have just the thing."

"Okay, everyone look over the plan, and we'll reconvene in two hours to get feedback. When you're done reviewing it, make sure your copy ends up in a burn bin. Are there any questions?"

Jeni waved a hand. "Yeah. What's a Janissary, anyway?"

Randal sat forward, folding his hands on the table. "Back during the Crusades, on Terra, the Muslim Turks used to capture Christian children. The most gifted of these were put into Janissary schools where they were brainwashed and taught a fanatical hatred for anything Christian. It's said that when the Turks finally sacked Constantinople, the Janissaries led the way, slaughtering their own people." He let that sink in a moment. "This is the fate from which we're rescuing these children. This is the nature of the enemy. Let's get this op rolling."

эс

Randal trailed behind al-Hise and Pieter as evening fell. They were moving through a neighborhood of row houses and condominiums just north of the Janissary academy. The Abkhazi was giving Pieter an impromptu lesson in scouting. "Just remember the acronym NATE and you'll be fine. . ." he was telling him. "Number of troops, their Activity, the Time you spotted them, and what Equipment they've got. It's easy to get excited and start rambling when calling in a spot report. Keep to these basics unless it's something vital."

For two hours they had reconnoitered the area around the Janissary school. Randal had faith in his scouts, but nothing compared with putting your own eyeball on a piece of terrain. Plus it got him out of the Catacombs, which was always a relief.

A woman popped her head out of a doorway down the street and the three Irregulars hunkered down behind a low boundary wall. It was the first sign of life they'd seen on the street. While it wasn't likely she would turn them in, the collaboration of Ariane's father made Randal chary about trusting strangers.

Al-Hise motioned over his shoulder with a thumb and spoke quietly. "This is a good spot for the northern Security Team during the raid. The stoops of these buildings would give good cover for our shooters, and there are plenty of ground-level windows to snipe from."

"I was just going to say that," Pieter said amiably. "Plus these buildings have sandstone walls. Bulletproof, I should think. That'll keep down the number of civilian casualties." His voice lost some of its enthusiasm as he caught a dark look from al-Hise. Apparently, civilian casualties were not a legitimate factor in the equation.

Risking a peek over the top of the wall, Randal could see the woman anxiously scanning the street as if looking for something. Then, he detected the faint rumble of vehicles. "Shh. . .Hear that?"

Al-Hise cocked his head and nodded. "Several large ones. They're getting closer."

The trio high-crawled to a nearby alley. It opened to a tree-filled park and a maze of back streets where they could lose themselves if needed. A convoy of troop carriers and some livestock crawlers rolled into view down the street, a lone figure in black leading them. Randal noticed it wore powered armor of a type he'd only seen in holos, armor which dwarfed the LANCER suits of the New Genevan military.

"I didn't think the Abbies used powered armor," Pieter whispered. "That thing is enormous!"

"They only issue it to their special forces, the Fist of the Mogdukh." Randal frowned as things clicked together in his head. "And since we haven't seen any sign they're stationed in Providence . . . Oh, Lord. That must be—"

"Brigadier Tsepashin!" Al-Hise's hiss cut him off. The young Abkhazi was fingering the trigger of his autorifle, face frozen in an expression that looked equal parts rage and terror. His eyes could have been targeting lasers, never straying from the black armored figure. Randal placed a restraining hand on al-Hise's shoulder, afraid he might open fire.

The convoy halted in front of the row houses, and soldiers swarmed from the rear doors of the troop carriers. Rather than running in terror, the woman stepped down to meet Tsepashin and began pointing to the buildings around her. Tsepashin gave directions to some waiting non-coms. Soldiers began ransacking the neighborhood, kicking in doors and dragging the screaming residents from their houses. It seemed to Randal they were being queued by building. Soon hundreds of women and children huddled under gunpoint, shivering in the cold evening air.

Disgust welled up inside him as he watched the collaborator follow Tsepashin down the line, apparently helping to verify that everyone was rounded up. Randal's own helplessness was the worst. Even if he somehow took down the infantry company, Tsepashin would still be waiting in his near-impregnable armor. Armed only with flechette rifles, it would be little more than suicide.

"We can't just sit here. . ." Pieter whispered in a disbelieving voice. But there was nothing to be done. Eventually the civilians were all herded into the livestock pens on the back of the crawlers. With dark satisfaction Randal watched Tsepashin snatch the collaborator up by the collar and toss her in with the rest of the prisoners. He could imagine the reception she'd receive.

It wasn't until the convoy started moving that he really believed it was happening. Until then his mind had held on to the irrational hope that something would intervene. Fighting back angry tears, he motioned for the others to follow and slipped into the shadows.

を❦❧

Preparation for the assault on the Janissary school took more than a week. Scouting evacuation routes, finding homes for the children, estimating enemy response times, prepositioning equipment—the list of pre-op requirements seemed to grow without ceasing. Even once the prep was done, Randal was left with an anxious sense that something was being overlooked. Nothing in his training had prepared him for such a mission.

As soon as it was dark, sappers began clearing the locations where the security and assault teams would set up. They disabled trip-flares, swept the areas for booby-traps, and estimated the observation span of cameras so they could be avoided.

Randal and Jack monitored their progress from the Irregular safe house that served as a staging area for the mission. A call came in on the coms. "Oh man. Base, this is Javitz. Murph just stepped on one of those toe-popper mines. God help me. His foot's all chopped up!"

"Calm down, Javitz," the Commo Officer said soothingly, looking to Randal for guidance.

"Tell him to find a place to hole up and then call us with a location. I'll get them a medic." With a flash of guilt, Randal realized he was hoping they wouldn't be taken alive if found. Alive they would be interrogated, dead the Abkhazi had no reason to link them to a larger operation. His soul was progressively being replaced with a calculator.

At thirty minutes to H-Hour, the Irregulars filtered into position. Circumstances had necessitated dividing the troops into seven teams, an utter command-and-control nightmare.

Four were Security Teams. One would emplace in each cardinal direction to deter the expected Abkhazi reinforcements. The largest of these would be to the north, since the nearest security sub-station was there, barracking two full companies of mechanized infantry. Randal was heading this northern team himself, with militia NCOs directing the others.

The Assault Team had the actual task of freeing the children. Al-Hise would lead the assault, with Ariane providing medical help if needed.

Overwatching the Assault Team was the Support Team. This primarily consisted of Lebedev's railgun, along with one of the few medium machine guns in the Irregulars' arsenal. One of the diciest steps of the raid would be getting the children from the school to the Catacombs. Randal hoped the Support Team would buy them time.

The last group was a mix of Irregulars and goodwives. These waited underground to receive the children should the raid succeed.

At twenty minutes, Randal gave the go-code to Johnny. "Taxi Driver, get us some wheels. Call me when you're up."

Three minutes later Johnny's voice came back across the comset. "This is Taxi Driver. I stole us a fast crawler. It's got this huge bloody trailer on the back."

"Copy that, Taxi Driver. I'm leaving this ComNet. Just standby for your cue from Pied Piper." He switched over to the northern Security Team's net, grinning at al-Hise's call sign. He doubted the surly Abkhazi appreciated a moniker like Pied Piper.

❧ ❧

Randal watched as one of his snipers pushed open a basement window, clearing his line of fire. The northern Security Team was setting up in the same area the Abkhazi had depopulated a few days earlier. What was once a working-class immigrant neighborhood was now a ghost town. The houses were darkened, many of the doors still open from when the Abkhazi tore the inhabitants from their homes. From what Jeni's Kitchen Klatch could piece together, they were rounding up the city's population a section at a time. Randal believed they were only proceeding slowly because military transport priorities outweighed ethnic cleansing. Each day, however, suborbitals were taking people away, likely to labor camps in Abkhazia.

Ironically, the enemy had hurt themselves by clearing the area. The Irregulars had the run of the place now, with no worries about collateral casualties. Tsepashin had eliminated the very collaborator who might have given warning of the ambush.

Movement atop a row house caught his eye. That would be one of the anti-armor teams. He'd learned his lesson with the scout car. All of the rocketeers were placed to fire either from rooftops or basement windows. Hopefully they would be either too high or too low for the heavy Abkhazi weaponry to sight on them.

An Irregular set a spherical object on the flat roof of a condominium, one of Jeni's drones. The girl was back at the staging area, nearly a klick away. She was a non-combatant's non-combatant and war for her was a trideo game. Tonight she'd be working electronic warfare, mostly signals jamming and meaconing—the sending of false data or messages to an enemy unit.

Down the street, Lebedev's people were prying open the hatches to a pair of groundcars. Then they hauled containers out from hiding places, stacking them inside the vehicles. One of the acolytes slipped on compacted snow, nearly dropping his load. Randal's audio pickups caught the soldier's near-perfect Lebedev impression. "Must be careful—is wolatile!"

Randal allowed himself a breath. Everything seemed in place: the snipers, the anti-armor teams, the flanking teams on both side streets, and the spotter by the sub-station. He and Pyatt, finally back in their LANCER suits, would be the shock troops of the ambush.

Then there was only to wait and to pray.

৵৽

Watching Nabil glide in his armor was humbling for Ariane. Granted, the scout suit was optimized for stealth and agility, but there was also a predator's stalk in his movements that she could never match.

Signaling for a halt, Nabil crouched against the hedge encircling the perimeter of the school. Ariane and the ten Irregulars took up position behind him. Each carried a snub-nosed submachine gun liberated from the Abkhazi and equipped with zip silencers. Lebedev's people had concocted them from empty grenade canisters, pipe fittings and cotton batting. There had been no time to test the silencers and everyone was just hoping for the best.

In his other hand Nabil gripped his cruelly curved guldor pichok dagger. The ivory hilt was inlaid with gold, the blade etched with whorls. It didn't seem to Ariane to be from any recent century.

Ahead was the front entrance to the school. Wooden sentry stations bracketed either side of the lane. "Wait here," Nabil said coolly to the Irregulars. He and Ariane walked in a crouch to the entrance. From that close, she could see the thermal signatures of the sentries through the hedges. There were four of them, all out of their booths and smoking, the cherries of the cigarettes glowing brightly as they puffed. The acrid smell of Abkhazi tobacco was strong on the wind.

Nabil didn't bother to give her warning, springing around the hedge and charging the sentries. Ariane caught up in time to watch them die, Nabil's movements a flowing blur.

The first collapsed before anyone even realized Nabil was there. The scout spun, pulling the guldor pichok free and slashing a second man. The guard dropped his weapon with a clatter, clutching at his throat. Thrusting his foot backward, Nabil kicked his third victim with a bone-crunching thud. By then the last man had managed to unsling his assault rifle, drawing a bead on the dervish who had dropped among them.

Ariane cut off a warning shout, not wanting to give the team away. Watching Nabil in action, she'd forgotten the subgun hanging at her side. She triggered a silenced burst from the still-unfamiliar weapon. The rounds crackled through the hedge behind the Abkhazi, distracting him and winning time for Nabil to take him out.

Ariane froze, blanking on what should happen next. "Hide the bodies, girl," Nabil growled, dragging two off into the guard shack.

Berating herself silently, Ariane tugged her two into the other stand. Nabil motioned around the corner for the rest of the troops, who quickly joined them.

The clock on her HUD said it was nearly time for the next phase of the plan, a mad sprint across open lawn broken only by the occasional shade tree. The academy was built atop a small hill. It was fortress-like, constructed in an imposing Tudor style.

Peeking beyond the guard shack, Ariane watched a roving patrol head toward the rear of the academy. Between the two guards stalked an ovcharka, the enormous breed of dog the Abkhazi military favored. Soon they were out of sight. "Pied Piper, it's clear."

The group dashed across the snow-covered lawn, zigzagging in case someone opened fire. Reaching the wall of the school, they pressed against it.

"You know what to do. Do it."

Ariane had thought Randal's leadership style was minimalist, but he was chatty next to Nabil.

One of the men slipped a coil of thin, knotted rope from his shoulder. Taking hold of its improvised grappling hook, he tossed it at a second-floor balcony railing. The hook's claws were muffled with the same rubberized formula Lebedev used on the suits. It fell back to ground with a thump, earning him a barely audible curse from Nabil. The second try was successful.

A pair of Irregulars ascended the rope. Four others peeled off to breach the food service entrance, while the remaining two teams moved to the large bay windows on either wing of the building. They would wait until the shooting started and burst in.

Nabil and Ariane would go through the front door. None of Jeni's Klatch had ever been inside the school, so the Irregulars had zero idea what to expect. They'd elected to disperse as widely as possible, hoping to take down the guards before they could harm the children.

The children. Jean-Marie. He was so close she could almost feel him.

They high-crawled through the landscaping toward the front entrance. Heavy oaken doors were set deep in the stone archway. As Ariane crawled, a second Abkhazi patrol came into view, walking the perimeter. She was amazed the dog couldn't hear them burrowing through the fresh snow. The wind must be for them.

Before they could move to the doors, a low whine sounded from the dog. Ariane glanced back down at the patrol. They were nearly to the sentry shacks and one of the patrolmen called to his friends. After no one answered, he peered inside. Immediately he shouted at the top of his lungs, looking around wildly. It seemed to Ariane that he spotted something. Then he and his partner started shooting at the academy building.

An anguished sound came from the balcony. Ariane heard a clatter as one of the Irregulars fell to the ground.

A second later the two Abkhazi and their hound were gone. A small crater and a large mess had taken their place. The guard shacks were blown over by the blast, and a shock wave rattled the school windows.

"Idiot! That railgun was heard for kilometers!" Nabil snarled at Lebedev over the com, following it with a string of invective.

"I thought they needed to be stopped," Lebedev said, sounding flustered.

"Nabil out." He ripped open the front door, the deadbolt snapping easily with his suit's augmented strength. The sentry on the other side was alert from all the noise. He stitched autorifle slugs across Nabil's chest, staggering him but failing to pierce his armor. Close on Nabil, Ariane ended the soldier with a burst.

The next instant seemed to slow endlessly. She nearly dropped the weapon, disgust welling up inside for the thing. The guard fell slowly, lifelessly to the ground, his face frozen in surprise. Her knees buckled as she was hit by the knowledge she'd just taken a life. The room was fuzzy and a light, tickly feeling crept over her brain like fingertips. She stumbled back against a marble bust, toppling it from the plinth.

Her helmet rocked as Nabil's armored hand gave her a smack. "Girl, let's go. Your son is waiting."

That got her attention. She stood, nodding drunkenly. "Okay."

They left the foyer, confronted by long halls on both sides and a central staircase winding before them.

"Which way?"

Shouts and autofire echoed from upstairs before Nabil could answer. "Follow me," he said, hustling for the stairs.

⤳⤲

The faint sound of gunfire reached Randal from the south, sounding almost like firecrackers. Moments later the hollow boom of a railgun rolled through. Randal winced. He'd hoped things would stay quiet longer than they had.

For several minutes all was peaceful in his AO. Distantly he could make out one of the other three Security Teams engaged, though it died off quickly. Hopefully it was just a patrol vehicle responding to the clamor at the academy. The Security Team would have made short work of it.

"Captain, they're moving. Good Lord, they've got a lot of stuff." That was Devin, his forward observer watching the sub-station.

"Thanks for the head's up, Dev. Knox Out."

Now that Lebedev and Jeni had succeeded in breaking the encryptions, the commo systems were finally compatible, and regular army could talk to militia. When speaking, Randal kept his voice cool and even, allowing a slight drawl to creep in. They needed him to be omni-competent and in control, no matter how badly the thousands of kilos of approaching steel terrified him. "Look lively, Irregulars—the enemy is on his way. We have to hold."

When the Abkhazi arrived, it was fast and with no regard for defense. Their only concern seemed to be reaching the academy.

An explosion flared from the roof of one of the row houses, a sizzling orange streak colliding with the lead vehicle, one of the infantry fighting vehicles the Abkhazi nicknamed korobachka—"box." The armor-piercing rocket struck the thin top armor of the vehicle. Its warhead burst, injecting white-hot phosphorous into the armor, boring through to spray the inside compartment. A nanosecond later it ignited the cannon shells in the ammunition stores. The metal coffin ripped in half, its fate obscured by the thick black smoke engulfing it.

The first rocket was joined by others, flashing from basement windows and rooftops. A stricken korobachka ground to a halt as a track blew off. One rocket misfired, fizzling off randomly and another deflected from the oblique-angled side of an IFV.

The second volley was more successful, three of the korobachkas exploding in a brilliant pyrotechnic display.

The thirty or so surviving IFVs pulled up sharply. Back doors fell open, expelling a dozen troops per vehicle. Unable to spot any of the hidden Irregulars, they fired at the buildings around them, milling behind the scant protection of the troop carriers.

Abkhazi vehicles poured rounds into the row houses. The korobachkas mounted an autoloading 78mm cannon while the anti-aircraft crawlers had vicious quad-27mm chain guns. A few of the IFVs looked optimized for urban warfare, with high-power plasma projectors.

From the windows, Irregular snipers dropped the Abkhazi infantry in droves. So far, so good, thought Randal. He watched the three men he'd placed behind a boundary wall not far from the enemy. They were supposed to toss grenades and then move out.

The grenades were devastating, bursting squarely in the middle of a massed section of Abkhazi. But before they could escape, other enemy troops cleared the wall, enfilading them. Randal rushed forward to give cover fire, but it was too late. He cursed himself for his poor judgment.

As if there wasn't chaos enough, Lebedev's people chose that moment to detonate the two car bombs. Shrapnel and liquid fire flew everywhere, homemade napalm coating everything around it, burning without respite. To Randal, the street looked straight from the mind of Bosch – a hellish inferno engulfing buildings, vehicles and men.

"Randal, this is Pyatt! Where do you want me?" He hazily recognized the voice, noticing Pyatt's LANCER suit nearby.

Peeking over the low wall, he got his bearings. The Abkhazi infantry was spreading out, and before long they'd start digging his people out of hiding. Worse, the plasma cannons were setting buildings on fire, torching his people where they hid. The Abkhazi chain of command might be overly rigid, but it was holding them together.

"We've got to disrupt them. Into the fray, Pyatt."

"After you."

The two ran full-tilt, diving into the dismounted infantry, their machine guns firing steadily. There wasn't a shortage of targets—in fact, they were surrounded by them.

A threat whistle sounded in his ears—someone had targeting lock on him. Legs pounding, Randal scooted behind a korobachka. The whistle stopped, thank God. There was no time to hit back. The fight moved on relentlessly.

Running alongside the IFV that sheltered him, he tore it open with autocannon fire. Clearing it, he felt the thud of what must be rifle slugs against his back. He ignored them.

The commo net was jumping with messages. They kept distracting him from the business of staying alive. Men nagged at him for orders. He mumbled answers reflexively, hoping in the back of his mind they were good ones.

All the while, like a mantra, the thought kept playing in his mind— we have to hold. We just have to hold.

∾ᖶ

Nabil halted at the top of the staircase, dropping flat to peer either way down the hall. The shots they'd heard earlier had crescendoed into a full-scale firefight.

Ariane heard him laugh, the sound like dry leaves. "They've got our man pinned out on the balcony. Pity none of them thought to watch their rear." He rose and practically sauntered into the hall. Ariane followed, keeping her submachine gun ready.

Casually he killed the Abkhazi with blade and bullet. Ariane doubted they even guessed the source of their deaths. Nabil had the clinical air she'd expect of an executioner. He wiped his guldor pichok clean on a dead man's jacket.

"All clear," Nabil called to the Irregular on the balcony. Nudging one of the corpses with a toe, he added reflectively, "I missed center mass on this one by four centimeters. Getting sloppy."

Ariane wasn't interested in his self-critique; she wanted her child. Opening the door to her right, she glanced in cautiously. Inside were rows of bunks. Children sat on and beside them, most hiding their faces, all screaming.

The doorjamb exploded into splinters. Ariane backpedaled, stepping into Nabil. "They... Someone's in there!"

Nabil kicked the door wide open, diving into a combat roll to clear the entrance. Coming up, his LMG tracked for targets. Ariane followed, crouching low as she rushed in.

Along the back wall stood an Abkhazi officer. One massive, almost furry arm encircled the waist of a young boy. His other hand pressed a machine pistol to the child's head. With queasy relief she saw it wasn't Jean-Marie.

"*Ukhodi...Ukhodi!* I will kill!" He was plainly unnerved, bald dome pouring with sweat, the hand clutching the pistol shaking violently.

Nabil preempted anything Ariane might have said. "Put your weapon down, Ariane, he means it." He knelt slowly, turning the weapon flat to place it on the floor.

The SMG kicked once in his hand, and he was standing again. A long red smear pointed the way to where the Abkhazi officer's corpse slumped against the wall. There was a hole in his forehead that hadn't been there a moment before.

Pandemonium erupted as soon as the firing stopped, the older children bolting for the exit. Ariane stood dumbfounded as the surviving Irregular from the balcony stormed into the room. "Block the door!" Nabil yelled to him. None got past.

Ariane unsealed her helmet and threw it back. "Children, children, please! It's all right; we're here to help you." She spoke soothingly, promising them their parents and safety. Her demeanor was as important as her words. There were at least fifty children in the room and she searched their faces desperately for Jean-Marie. He wasn't among them. What she did see were hollow eyes and gaunt cheeks.

Eventually they were able to line the children up holding hands. They were mostly older, a few into their early teens. The older led or carried the younger.

Swallowing her acid disappointment, Ariane said with forced cheerfulness, "Now then, children. We're going to walk outside now. We get to ride in a big crawler. Everyone stay together, please." Passing Nabil, she was tempted to ask how he knew he'd hit the Abkhazi rather than the young hostage, but she knew the answer—he hadn't cared.

Shortly after, a call came in from one of the other teams. "Pied Piper, this is Leavitt. We got about fifty of the little buggers in here. We're down to just me and two others, but all the hostiles are dead."

"Excellent, we're the same. Meet us out front," Nabil said, pausing a moment and then calling Johnny. "Taxi Driver, we're ready for you."

He turned to Ariane. "Get these outside. I'll see if there's anyone left to mop up."

Ariane led the children down the stairs and out the front. Outside, the sounds of a small war to the north were very loud. The children began wailing again. "Let's sing 'Jesus Loves the Little Children,' okay?" A few of the older ones joined in raggedly.

Down the lane Johnny careened past the guard shacks, sideswiping one with the cargo crawler.

"Here's our ride. Everyone queue up now. Our friend Johnny is going to take us home."

"Wait for us," a voice said behind her. An Irregular walked out, leading a second string of children. These were much younger, the militiamen having a hard time herding them all. It took her a moment to recognize the sobbing toddler he cradled.

"Jean-Marie!" she cried, sweeping the child from the astonished soldier's arms. Then she wasn't aware of what she said at all, murmuring nonsense in French while covering the boy's face with kisses. She barely noticed Johnny screeching to a stop behind them. Squeezing Jean-Marie tightly, she pressed her face to the top of his head, inhaling the familiar scent deeply.

A hand clapped her curtly on the back. "Didn't you hear? Jeni just called. Gunships are coming."

～｡▱ ｡～

Randal was pinned down behind a burning korobachka, trading fire with one of the nasty anti-aircraft crawlers. It didn't seem deterred at all by the fact he wasn't flying, the quad-mounted chain guns tracking him relentlessly. Its sensors were powerful enough to target far-off and stealthy aircraft—his LANCER suit must look like a blimp on the gunner's screen. He couldn't expose himself long enough to get a clear shot.

"Oh, Randy?"

"What?" he answered testily.

"Just thought you'd wanna know, I've plotted a gunship inbound for you, and another one for Nabil's team."

"Fan-bleeding-tastic."

"Well said. I'll see what I can do, Cho out."

Randal cringed as another blast from the anti-aircraft crawler rocked the vehicle he was using for cover. "Pyatt, can you drop something on this AA track for me? I'm pinned!"

The only response was a distracted grunt, but an instant later Pyatt's autoloading mortar shells struck the open-top vehicle, disabling it.

Something ripped through the air over the battlefield, slamming into the row houses nearest Randal. The second floor exploded outward, glass and rubble flying everywhere. On its heels came several more rockets, leaving smoky trails as they struck the buildings. Several row houses collapsed, spewing clouds of dust and smoke into the street. Randal was temporarily blind, but he was sure at least three of his rocket teams were gone.

The gunship floated into view over a rooftop. Its vectored thrust was vented so as to make it near-silent. Watching it glide overhead, Randal was reminded of the sharks of Terra he'd seen on trideo.

He froze, not wanting to draw its attention. A soft giggle sounded in his ear. "I pulled a voice intrusion on him, Randy." Jeni sounded pretty self-impressed.

"Huh?"

"You know, I faked out the gunship pilot. I hacked his commo and digitized the voice of the guy giving him orders. Then I sent him a command saying the rebels had taken over the armored vehicles and to blast away at them. And then I jammed the ComNet so their boss couldn't amend me."

Randal spotted an Abkhazi raising a shoulder-fired rocket, muzzle in his direction. He took him out with an LMG burst, ending the threat. A glance confirmed the hovering gunship had taken no notice. Hopefully the pilot was confused enough to hold his fire.

When Randal didn't answer, Jeni asked curiously, "So is it doing it?"

"Doing what?"

"Blowing up the korobachkas."

"No, it's just hovering. Waiting."

She seemed put-out by that. "But my forgery was perfect. You're sure?"

Randal made an exasperated sound. She really had no clue it wasn't all an elaborate trideo game. "Um, yeah."

"How disappointing. Though I suppose it is preferable to them shooting at you."

"Indeed. Knox out."

Randal keyed up Pyatt. "Hey, you got any illumination flares left in your mortar munitions?"

"One or two, why?"

"You heard Jeni has the gunship confused. Get me a distraction while I angle for a shot."

"Rog. Give me a minute."

Pyatt fought his way from a side street, downing an Abkhazi fire team along the way. "Get ready, Knox." Smoke belched from his shoulder-mounted mortar and an instant later a bright-white flash burst in front of the gunship. The pilot must have jerked the stick in surprise, because suddenly the attitude of the craft went sharply nose-up.

Randal wheeled around the side of the demolished korobachka and sighted on the gunship. The reticule on his HUD settled over the craft, the onboard taking a second to achieve lock. His suit shuddered as the autocannon let loose with a stream of rounds.

The gunship listed, its pilot seeming to fight for control. This was complicated by the loss of several nacelles on the right side which Randal had blasted free. Trailing smoke, it veered away, shearing off a dormant electronic billboard from a roof.

Randal whispered a thankful prayer, turning his attention back to the ground battle. He had no idea how many of his men were left. The battle had degenerated into individual firefights with little organization on either side. Soon sheer weight of numbers would overwhelm his people. "Pied Piper, what's your status?" he called over the comset.

"Loading the children. Give us two mikes and then disappear."

When no end was in sight, the fight had passed in a blur. Knowing that he could soon escape made the next hundred and twenty seconds seem endless.

At least the enemy vehicles weren't advancing, thanks be to God. They had pulled back about a hundred and fifty meters to regroup. Someone had taken out their command vehicle, a large IFV bristling with dishes and antennae. Its remains smoldered about fifty meters to Randal's front. With such a rigid chain of command, knocking out a link condemned lower echelons to paralysis.

Though they weren't advancing, the vehicles were keeping up a heavy volume of fire into the buildings. Also, the Abkhazi infantry was still working its way house to house. They would be oblivious to the death of the higher ups—grunts only worried about what their team sergeant was saying.

Randal drew down on one of the plasma projector IFVs, scoring a hit on a storage tank and bathing the vehicle in its own superheated energy. He glanced at his HUD. The two minutes were finally up. "Devin, Dev... You still awake?" Or alive?

His forward observer answered after a moment. "Pop the flare?"

"Pop it and get clear of the area."

A green star cluster burst over the battlefield, the parachute-mounted flare descending leisurely out of sight. For anyone who was still alive and listening to their headsets, Randal yelled out, "That's the signal! Disengage and evade. Reform at rally point Lambda."

He and Pyatt stayed behind, keeping the Abkhazi occupied to buy time for the retreat. Eventually he commed Pyatt, "I don't think the Abbie's have anything left to shoot at except us. Let's go."

"Follow me. I found a good route earlier." Pyatt boosted over an apartment building to a side street. Randal followed, nearly draining his jets. They slipped away, leaving the decimated mechanized companies licking their wounds.

11

War is the unfolding of miscalculations.
—Barbara Tuchman

The Irregulars slammed shut the rear doors of the crawler, leaving Ariane alone in the dark with a hundred caterwauling children. She didn't mind, her attention only for Jean-Marie. A dull pounding reverberated in the metal box. Something heavy was scaling the cargo compartment. "Is that you, Sergei?" she asked tentatively over the comset.

"Da. Getting ready for incoming gunship."

With a screech of metal on metal, objects punched through the roof. She flipped on her helmet and activated the UV-headlamp. Above she could see four metallic spears driven through the ceiling—twin climbing spikes and the long braces tucked away inside the legs of all railgun-equipped suits.

Lebedev came on the comset again. "How far out is gunship, Jeni?"

"You should see it any second."

"Very well." He sounded resigned to his fate.

The little Belarusian never ceased to amaze Ariane. He always smelled a bit musty and there was a terminally bewildered look to him, but he saw things in ways no one else did. This explained why he was now a human anti-aircraft turret atop a cargo crawler full of ex-hostage children.

Johnny gunned the engine, the cargo vehicle accelerating with a jerk that set the children to shrieking. Ariane braced as best she could, afraid she might hurt one of them with her heavy suit.

Centrifugal force pulled everyone to the side as Johnny thudded around the circular drive. She felt a thump as they left the drive and hit open road. It was surprising how much speed Johnny could coax from the large vehicle.

"Gunship is behind us! Is shooting!"

Five holes appeared high on the wall of the cargo compartment, matched by five ragged exit holes on the facing side. For those in the compartment, it was like sitting in a cathedral bell while a madman hammered it.

The impact of heavy-caliber rounds rocked the vehicle, its metal body shuddering. The response from Johnny was immediate. Far more rapidly than she would have believed possible, the world shifted about 90-degrees, the crawler tilting at the sudden turn. Ariane huddled over Jean-Marie, praying quietly.

Lebedev's running monologue played in her ears. Did he know he was still transmitting? "Davai, you foolish thing! Lock! *Nyet, nyet, nyet… Idi syuda…* Come around… *Blin!* Ah… little more…"

A deafening BOOM! filled the compartment. Ariane cried out, sure they were all dead. Opening her eyes, she checked Jean-Marie with frantic urgency. He was unharmed.

Above, she saw night sky. Fresh snow flurries swirled into the long furrow torn in the roof where Lebedev once rode. The ceiling was peeled back like a can.

She set Jean-Marie carefully aside. Giving a hop, she caught the lip of the roof and hauled herself up for a look. The remains of the gunship were spread over a snow-covered playground, the largest section burning cheerily in the canopy of an old cedar.

A dark lump lay on the sidewalk, unmoving. Lebedev.

"Johnny, stop! We lost Sergei."

The crawler rumbled to a halt. Pulling herself out through the roof, Ariane leapt from the back of the vehicle, hurrying to her fallen friend. He was just starting to stir when she reached him. "*Bozhe moi…*" he moaned, reaching a hand up to her, pawing the air as he missed.

"You did it, Sergei! You saved us." She helped him to his feet and opened the cargo doors. He climbed gingerly inside, groaning. When he saw the roof he laughed, a high-pitched, wheezy sort of laugh. "I think I might have misunderestimated the recoil."

"Perhaps a bit?" Ariane said politely, pulling Jean-Marie back into her lap.

Johnny drove to a prearranged rendezvous point. The children were ushered underground, past the watchful eyes of a full Irregular platoon and into a broad mineshaft. Pallets had been set up in anticipation of incoming wounded.

Keeping to themselves was a group of goodwives. They looked ill at ease in the unfamiliar Catacombs. Having been told to wear dark clothing for the mission, many were dressed in odd combinations selected for color rather than style. One stepped from the group, smiling kindly at Ariane. Even in the shabby surroundings she maintained a dignified air, her gray hair neatly coiffed. "I'm Goodwife Alston. May I help you with the children?"

Ariane nodded, brushing ballistic-weave armored fingers through Jean-Marie's hair, wishing she could unsuit. "Oh, please. We need to learn if there are any siblings among them."

Goodwives shepherded the children into the center of the chamber. Irregular medics treated the few who had received light wounds during ride. All seemed traumatized, though they showed it in different ways: some stared sullenly at the ground, others cried, and still others yelled and jabbered excitedly.

Ariane watched in admiration as Goodwife Alston gained their attention. It was obvious she was a mother, gently but firmly quieting them. Ariane felt a pang. Her own mother would never be able to pass along mother-wisdom in that quiet way she had had.

After several minutes of reassuring the children that they were in safe hands once more, the goodwife asked, "Does anyone have a brother with them here today?"

Several raised their hands, including one towheaded set of four brothers.

The goodwife took charge, pairing two children to each of the women who'd volunteered to shelter them. Siblings were kept together. At the end she stood by the four brothers, smiling. "My husband and I have a sugar beet farm well outside the city. No one has seen fit to bother us. The work is hard, but I also have six children of my own for you to play with."

A guide led each woman back to the surface with her new charges. Whenever possible, their parents would be informed that they were alive, but not where they were being kept. The chance that the Abkhazi would come looking for the Janissary children was simply too great.

Ariane kissed Goodwife Alston on either cheek. "Thank you for your help. I couldn't have—"

"Yes, you could have. But it was my pleasure. Take care of that baby," the older woman said, stroking a thumb down Jean-Marie's cheek. "You all should be proud of what you did tonight. I think it's just marvelous." Turning, she motioned to her new boys. "Come along, young goodmen. We have quite a hike ahead of us."

Watching them leave, Ariane caught herself smiling. It was a marvelous thing they had done.

Too soon, cries of "Medic! Medic!" echoed down the shaft. A flashlight beam ricocheted its way toward Ariane and two Irregulars shuffled into the area, carrying the broken body of their comrade between them. Her elation withering, Ariane let a sentry guide her to the aid station.

A never-ending flow of dead and wounded streamed into the primitive hospital throughout the night. She and a handful of assistants were quickly swamped. Out of necessity they established a harsh triage, with many of the gravely wounded placed in a nearby chamber, comforted by friends. There were no painkillers to spare. The lightly wounded were also separated, though volunteers worked to keep them from falling into shock, giving them warm drinks and elevating their legs.

Those with moderate wounds received first priority. Ariane struggled to save those she could, working as fast as she was able with the help of the suit's medical AI. Nevertheless, many from that group died of injuries before she reached them.

By the end, patients no longer had faces, only wounds. The post-adrenaline crash had left her queasy and weak. The universe had fallen away, and her world was the operating table—blood, confusion and the appalling variety of suffering that man could inflict on man. But outsiders kept intruding. The mindless howls of the dying filled the corridors; her assistants kept pressing her for advice—as if she knew what to do.

Many, many hours later all that could be done was done. Finding an unoccupied pallet she collapsed upon it, heedless of the gore-soaked sheets.

∾∾

Randal paused quietly outside the chamber Ariane shared with Jeni, listening as she spoke to Jean-Marie in the nonsensical patter that is the common language of infants and adults. It was jarringly normal after the previous night's madness.

He spoke through the sheet the girls hung for privacy. "It's Randal. Mind if I join you?"

"Come in. . ." Ariane sat on her pallet, playing with the boy's toes and making him giggle. The twenty-month-old seemed to be weathering events surprisingly well.

"Just wanted to check on you," Randal said, taking a seat on a folding chair and feeling like he was intruding. "How are you faring?"

The girl smiled at him. He was amazed how much she could say with a simple expression, the smile at once tender and world-weary. "Better," she said, elevating a shoulder incrementally. "I'm so thankful to have Jean-Marie home. But..." She paused, waving it off. "You have enough to worry about, and it's selfish of me to complain."

He shook his head, reaching out for her hand. "I care about you—I want to hear." Hesitating, he added, "You're one of my troops. It's my job to listen."

The look she gave made him feel as opaque as transplastic. "Your job," she said, giving his hand a squeeze.

"And we're friends. Naturally. Now tell me what's wrong."

"It's just. . . We lost almost a quarter of the Irregulars last night. Any idea how many people died in surgery last night because of me? People keep looking to me for help, and I'm a mess." She chewed her lip thoughtfully. "Do you know what that feels like?"

As he always did at such times, Randal wished Jack were in his place. He was better at this sort of thing. "Ariane, you're doing a fine job. We're all impressed with how you're handling yourself in a tough spot."

She let go of his hand and stared at the wall. "I don't need a pep talk, Randal. I need someone to listen to me."

He shifted uncomfortably on the metal chair. It was tempting to hide behind a leader's need for detachment and drop the conversation. He might even be justified in doing it. But he knew it was a decision he would regret later. "I do know how it feels. Are you kidding? I've elevated self-loathing to an art."

"You? You always seem so sure of yourself."

He laughed cynically. "It says in the manual that I'm supposed to. But plenty of those Irregulars are dead because I don't know what I'm doing. They're my mistakes, but other people get to do the dying. So yeah, I know a little of what you're feeling."

"Between the two of us, it's a wonder anyone survives this place at all."

Randal smirked, unlimbering from the chair to sit facing her on the pallet. She set Jean-Marie off to the side, giving him a mess tin to play with.

"You're doing an amazing job, Ariane. All stirring speeches aside, you really are. You have from the beginning," he said, breath tight in his chest. He reached forward, brushing a strand of hair from her eyes.

"Vraiment? I thought you hated me when we first met."

"No, I never hated you. You just put me off-balance. One look and it was clear you were going to mix up my well-ordered life." He shrugged. "I knew I could fall for you if I wasn't careful."

There. It was out in the open.

She regarded him mutely, dark eyes searching his face.

Dreading silence, Randal pressed on. Her level look only pushed him that much closer to babbling, so he closed his eyes. "But it happened, you know? I think about you constantly. I'm sorry, I'm really bad at this sort of..."

His flow of words was stemmed by the soft pressure of her lips.

Eyes popping open as if spring-loaded, Randal broke off the kiss in surprise. That close, her breath was sweet and warm on his face. He could make out the natural scent of her hair and the clean, soapy smell of her skin. His body felt charged the same way it did during combat.

Pressing a hand softly to her cheek, he kissed the corners of her mouth, then tilted his head to kiss her fully. Menelaus had always seemed impetuous to him, but while kissing Ariane, Randal could understand launching an armada for the sake of a woman.

For a long while he held her tightly, thrilling at the closeness of her. He didn't speak, not wanting to complicate the perfect simplicity of the moment. Even Jean-Marie seemed to sense it, playing quietly with the mess tin and exploring the chamber.

"I win the bet, Johnny. I knew they were a couple."

Ariane and Randal both froze, eyes darting to the door. Jeni and her sidekick stood in the entry wearing identical grins.

Flushing six shades of red, Randal tried to keep his voice light. "She had something in her eye."

"Totally plausible, Randy. I give my blessing to this, but remember what I said before—I get to be a bridesmaid."

Ever Jeni's mascot, Johnny chimed in with, "Right. And Ariane has to name her firstborn after me."

An awkward silence ensued.

Jeni jabbed him viciously with an elbow. "Nice one, plonker." Turning back to Randal, she favored him with a wink. "Leave six inches for the Holy Spirit."

Once they were gone, Ariane and Randal shared a nervous laugh. "Well."

"Well indeed. I'd best go check in on Pieter. He's had scouts near the spaceport and was supposed to brief me."

"I understand."

He kissed her on the cheek and tickled Jean-Marie's round belly. "Talk to you soon." Ariane nodded, not seeming to know what to say either.

As he walked the corridor to Pieter's chamber he could still feel the delightful pressure of her lips. His handful of summertime flirtations gave no perspective on the happy commotion he felt inside. Nearing Pieter's quarters, he did his best to wipe the silly look from his face.

Not bothering to knock, he wandered into Pieter's room, taking a seat on the pallet.

Pieter was dressed in dark fatigue pants and a black sweater bearing the Saint Athanasius Academy crest. He looked up from the piles of hastily-scrawled NATE reports surrounding him. Swirling a tulip-bulbed glass at Randal, he asked cheerily, "Care for a cordial?"

Randal craned his neck to read a note about MagLev supply trains. "Huh? No, thanks."

"A martini then? It'll have to be a Monty, as vermouth supplies have fallen to emergency levels."

"No luck in scrounging vermouth?" He was continually amazed at Pieter's knack for expanding his liquor cabinet. The week before, he'd traded an extra pair of boots for a bottle of Armagnac—a major coup.

"Not as of yet. I've been reduced to making them dry as the bloody Samarkand Desert. But we all must make sacrifices for the war effort."

"It's a noble cross you bear, my friend."

"Sure I can't tempt you? I've some Drambuie and a spot of applejack left."

"Thanks, but I have to talk with Pyatt after this. One whiff of demon liquor and he'll get irate."

Pieter shuddered. "He's disagreeable, though that al-Hise character is the true piece of work."

"Nabil has his ways," Randal said with a shrug. "How's your scout training with him going?"

"Quite well, actually. He's an excellent teacher, apart from looking fit to eat my liver every time I make a mistake. My scouts have learned a great deal."

"Brilliant. Speaking of your scouts, what did the Recon and Surveillance team come back with from the spaceport?"

Pieter brushed aside the bangs of his meticulously sloppy hair and rifled through the scattered reports. "Let's see... Security is tight on the north side out to three kilometers. Static defenses, dogs, patrols, you name it. But Alvarez, our retired pilot? He says given the trajectory of those birds, we can be ten kilometers out and still swat a suborbital."

"That leaves plenty of room for mischief. I'll send Van Loon up with a team tonight."

It was stellar news. The primary means of resupply and reinforcement for the Abkhazi military was the spaceport. Even this was limited to suborbital flights; the big spacefaring cargo ships were interdicted by an unusual source—the sea.

By the middle of the twenty-first century, offensive technology had relegated surface fleets to the pages of history, but subsurface ships still played an essential role in modern warfare. The New Genevans deployed scores, and the Abkhazi hundreds, of unmanned submarines. Each was small, fast-moving, and equipped with every stealth technology in its nation's arsenal. Efficient fusion engines allowed them to stay at sea for years at a time, with automated repair systems keeping the ships on-line.

These weapons platforms served two chief functions, both of which paradoxically saved lives. The first was the prevention of total war. Both sides knew that unseen ships lurked off their coasts, each carrying an array of strategic weapons they had no hope of stopping. Neither side would ever use them, knowing there would be no winner in such a war, only survivors.

The other benefit was that the submersibles kept conflicts localized. Combatant nations couldn't draw neighboring planets into the dispute for the mere fact that no one could hope to land on the planet. Any spacecraft bold enough to enter the atmosphere would have little chance against the hypersonic missiles of the subs. The seaborne killers also reduced suborbitals to low-level travel as their only hope of survival, since the subs were primarily equipped to engage high-altitude targets.

This put the precious, thin-skinned airframes of the suborbitals within striking distance of the Irregulars.

"We've only got a few surface-to-air missiles," Pieter said, quaffing his brandy.

"I know. But after we knock down a suborbital or two, they'll switch to ground transport. We'll be able to start hitting fat supply convoys come spring."

Pieter nodded, staring off into the gloom. The corners of his lips played up, though he was visibly trying to restrain them. "Jeni was in here before you arrived."

Randal did his best to keep his expression level. "Really."

"Oh yes. I must say though, Kipper, you never seemed the sort for romancing the kitchen help."

"It's nothing like that. Besides, you're one to talk."

"I larked around with the trollops—I didn't pledge my troth to them. Besides, you've seven more years 'til the 'Good and Orderly' statute kicks in. There really are less painful ways of dodging it."

Twenty-eight, in the lives of young people in New Geneva, was second in importance only to sixteen, when they attained their majority. The law specified that: "Whereas marriage is that founding pillar of good and orderly society, and seeing that young adults unconstrained by family or matrimony are a source of much mischief and public disorder, all citizens of New Geneva shall be married by the day of the twenty-eighth year of their birth, or present just cause to their local magistrate why it be not so. A levee of five pounds will be exacted for each day in violation of this statute."

"I'm not dodging anything. I care about her. Besides, it's not as if our banns are being proclaimed tomorrow. We just kissed."

"You care about her," Pieter said flatly. "Isn't that just a bit infra dignitatem? She's damaged goods. Come now, the tramp's already whelped a sprog. What will your Old Man say about this tart?"

Clicking his teeth together loudly, Randal did a slow five-count. "If you use one more word starting with T to describe her, I'm going to put you in the infirmary. Look in my eyes and tell me if I'm joking."

Pieter met his eyes, neither of them blinking. Randal could see the gears turning in his head. He was either struggling to find another slur beginning with T, or weighing the odds of taking Randal. Not that it was a real likelihood—Randal had played scrum half on the Saint Athanasius rugby team and the military hadn't exactly dulled his muscle tone.

Finally Pieter dropped his eyes, smiling sheepishly. "Hey, it's your life. And you'd never take me in a fair fight—it wouldn't be fair chasing me down and beating me senseless while I screamed like a girl."

Grinning, Randal leaned forward, slugging him hard in the shoulder. "I gotta run, it was good talking with you."

As he left he heard Pieter mumble, "If you date the help, do you still have to pay them Christmas bonuses?"

∽⧟⧟∽

Jack clenched his jaw to keep teeth from chattering, lamenting for the hundredth time that his LANCER suit had recently been deadlined. Its layer of gel-pad insulation would be a godsend in the bitter cold.

Winter was upon the isthmus in earnest now, and the glare from unbroken drifts of snow was almost blinding in the daylight. An incessant, cutting wind carried the powdery stuff, reducing visibility to virtually nil. In any other year, independent prospectors would be flooding into Providence to await the spring thaw.

With numb fingers, Jack pulled the face mask up just far enough to press a canteen to his lips. He choked down a few sips. They had added foul-tasting minerals to the water to keep it from becoming a solid block of ice. Quickly he yanked the mask back down, his lips already blistering from the chill.

After tucking away the canteen, he inspected the slender, tubed weapon he held across his lap. The trigger mechanism looked clear of ice. Peering down the tube, he ensured no ice was forming inside, either. After two days of battling frostbite, he didn't want to blow himself up with a barrel obstruction when he finally got a chance to shoot something.

Only twenty minutes more and Aldrich would be on duty. The snow cave they had hollowed at the base of an ash tree seemed as luxurious as a suite at the Hotel Placide just then.

Taking up the thermal binoculars, he did another sweep of the northern horizon. They couldn't use the targeting sensor on the launcher to track for suborbitals—any active sensors would alert the Abkhazi and bring down a world of hurt in minutes. At the same time, migrating snow drifts made the naked eye useless. Instead they were relying on frequent sweeps with the binos to pick up heat signatures. Once they spotted a suborbital, there was a narrow window when they could activate the launcher and fire a shot before the craft was out of range.

A lot was riding on the operation. Eliminating the suborbital flights could temporarily hamstring the Abkhazi war machine. With blizzards clogging the mountain passes with unstable mounds of snow, these flights were the enemy's only reliable source of supply.

Boosting the magnification, he did another hopeful sweep. Still nothing.

In spite of the cold, he was thankful for the solitude the mission provided. Since coming to the Catacombs there'd been no time to be alone, to collect his thoughts. He realized that it was at least a day since he had thought of his wife or his boy. Soon Tobias would be turning four. Would he recognize this strange, battle-weary man when he came home?

It was late afternoon, dinnertime. He pictured Hannah teaching Tobias his catechism after the meal. He wished to God the Abkhazi would go home so he could too. Being apart from Hannah gave him a constant, low-grade sense of loss. They had met for the first time the night his parents arranged an "introduction." Only six years had passed, but already the time before Hannah was blurring around the edges. He had made her promise to remarry if God called him Home during the war, but he knew she never would.

Something tickled at the back of his mind, and he pressed the binos to his goggles again.

There. A small orange spot rapidly grew larger. Dropping the binos to hang by their strap around his neck, he scrambled to his feet. Though he'd mentally rehearsed the launch prep for two days, his icy fingers felt clumsy as he went through the process of disarming safeties and activating the weapon.

Hefting the tube to his shoulder, Jack pointed the muzzle northward. He pressed the targeting scope to his eye and growled in frustration. Ice covered the tiny screen. He had forgotten to check it.

The huge airframe of the suborbital passed overhead, trailing a maelstrom of snow and debris in its wake. That close to touchdown it was practically hugging the earth. Struggling to keep upright, Jack turned and triggered a launch. He hoped the missile's guidance was smart enough to catch the suborbital even without a lock.

He need not have worried. Much like the first interstellar ships sent out by Terra, the suborbitals utilized a nuclear pellet fuel system. The heat generated by the propulsion drive was astronomical, a broad and easy path for the heat-seeking warhead to follow.

In the event of an impending crash, safety cut-outs would engage, killing the engines and preventing a nuclear disaster. A lull in the wind allowed Jack to see the final seconds of the doomed craft. Forward thrusters were firing, the control surfaces shifting for a landing, the wheels only meters from the ground as the warhead impacted the tail section.

A light brighter than a hundred suns flashed, consuming his world and frying his retinas. Searing pain shot through his eyes to his brain. He screamed, clawing vainly at his eyes. An instant later the shock wave struck, tossing him like detritus into a snow bank. He fell into the mercy of unconsciousness.

❧❧

The next thing Jack was aware of was a jerky, rocking motion and the disconcerting sensation of moving without touching the ground. His head felt ponderous, like it was full of sand. He tried opening his eyes to see what was happening, but they felt glued shut.

"He moved a little," said a voice he knew he should recognize.

"It's about time. We've had to carry him for ten klicks already. Hey, wanna see something amazing? Check out that sunrise."

"Would you look at that? It's all the dust in the sky from what our Van Loon blew up. Really catches the light."

"I know. Just wish it would stop falling on us. It smells awful."

Somewhere in the deep well of his disorientation, Jack made a connection. He remembered the suborbital. He'd blown it up. The cut-outs must not have worked. He opened his mouth to warn his teammates about the fallout, to tell them to leave him and find shelter. Only a creaky sound came out.

The grip around his ankles shifted painfully as his bearers almost dropped him and then he lost his tentative hold on consciousness.

❧❧

Randal and al-Hise crawled the last few meters to the crest of the ridge, careful not to skyline themselves. Peering down the slope, Randal was bewildered to find the trees scythed for nearly a kilometer around the spaceport.

The spaceport itself seemed fuzzy, indistinct. He'd expected to make out buildings at that range. Adjusting the focus, he saw why. There was no more spaceport. A vast, glassy crater sat in place of the runway, the earth fused by unimaginable heat.

Between the sketchy information Jack's teammates were able to deliver and the reports of a bright flash to the east of town, the Irregulars had surmised that the suborbital's dying explosion was of a higher magnitude than expected. But this was… insane.

"What the deuce? There's nothing left, Nabil. What's your monitor reading?" Standard infantry suits didn't mount Geiger counters; it was one of several advantages to having a scout suit around.

"The area is hot, hotter than anything we've seen so far. Ariane was right about the radiation sickness."

Randal winced, feeling as if judgment had just been passed on him. It had been a nuclear accident. Even with terrorism as widespread as it was among the colonies, there were only a handful of accidents on record. Were the Abkhazi callous enough to skimp on safety equipment? The command team had assumed the safety cut-outs would keep the suborbital from this.

Nevertheless, it was his order that sent his best friend to fire on it.

Already three days had passed and Jack was still comatose. Twice Ariane had restarted his heart with her medkit's defibrillator. The other two men were wasting away—hair shedding, vomiting uncontrollably.

"That's a lot of cremated Khlisti down there," al-Hise observed with abiding satisfaction in his voice.

"Yeah." Randal felt too miserable to remind al-Hise the Khlisti were also God's creations. "I should have known there was a risk factor. This was wrong."

"Spare me the sentiment, Knox. The spaceport is going to be unusable for months. They can't land suborbitals without a tower. Don't pretend there's anyone you wouldn't trade to cut their supply lines like this."

Randal itched to blast al-Hise, wanting to mute the insinuating voice that sounded so much like his own conscience. There was a part of him that rejoiced at the scene below. Who knew how many lives at the front would be saved by stemming the flow of enemy men and matériel? He hated himself for being so calculating.

But who was it that accused him?

"You know," Randal said quietly, swiveling his helmet to look over the scout. "You hate the Khlisti so much, but I don't see much difference between you."

"That sounds like something your girlfriend would say. I expect better from you, Corporal."

"You know, you're right. Actually, I have more respect for the Khlisti. At least their religion encourages them to hurt their enemies. But you're vicious even to your fellow Christians. Whatever the Abkhazi did to you, you'd do back tenfold just to see the expression on their faces. So tell me what moral high ground you stand on when you look down on the rest of us."

He tensed, not at all sure how the hot-tempered scout would react. A windswept peak overlooking an irradiated disaster area seemed like a lousy place to die.

Instead the man muttered something profane in his mother tongue, stalking back the way they had come.

The next week was a busy one, something Randal was grateful for as it kept him from brooding. Even under martial law information gets around a city and word of the Irregulars' successes at the Janissary school and the spaceport was too big to be quelled. The goodwives of Jeni's Kitchen Klatch helped spread the news as they warned their neighbors to stay indoors during the worst of the fallout. Randal was no longer canvassing for new cells to recruit. Instead, the once reclusive Indies were coming to him. Fortunately there was an established NCO cadre to deal with the influx.

He'd avoided Ariane since their kiss. With the imminence of Jack's death hanging over him he couldn't imagine romancing her, but she was never far from his thoughts. Nor was Jack. He'd come out of the coma, but that was the limit of the good news.

His hair was gone, his skin parchment-thin. The radiation had damaged portions of his brain, making his speech slow and confused. The worst was his eyes—they were scabbed and sealed as if he'd been on the Damascus Road. But Randal was no Ananais, and Jack Van Loon would never see again.

He paused outside the infirmary, catching Ariane's attention and motioning her out. "How is he?"

Ariane looked sadly back to the room, pitching her voice low. "It's bad, Randal. His abdomen is hard, like it's filling with fluid. His skin has all kinds of splotches. I'm sure he's hemorrhaging and there's nothing I can do but watch while he unravels..." She held her hands up helplessly, words dying off.

Randal swallowed, nearly choking on the gob in his throat. "The other two?"

The girl made an exasperated sound. "They seem to be getting better. But without a dosimeter there's no way to know how much exposure they had." She crouched, cradling her head. "I've got the Irregulars using only ceramic filters for their water. I at least know those will strain fallout. But I had only a twenty-minute lecture on nuclear stuff during medic school. This wasn't ever supposed to happen..."

Randal knelt by her side, slipping an arm around her shoulders. Neither spoke for a long while. He kissed her temple softly and stood, smiling down at her. Just like with Jack, here was a person who didn't need him to fill the air with words to understand him. She smiled back, brushing lips to her fingertips and extending them toward him.

"Hey Jack," he said with unfelt cheeriness as he entered the sick chamber. "You're looking better. Want me to keep reading from Ecclesiastes?"

A barely perceptible nod came from his friend. Much of what Jack said these days was garbled, but on that he'd been adamant. Randal could recognize why. The message that everything in this life is ultimately dust must be a comfort to the dying man. Despite all the white lies people were telling him, he knew his own condition.

Randal read the short book beginning to end for his friend, pausing a few times when he seemed to drift.

"Ran—Randal," Jack rasped, the first time he'd spoken all day. "I don't want you blaming yourself anymore." He took a breath, his head shifting side to side as he searched for words. "I don't regret."

It was the most lucid Randal had seen him. He thought of dementia patients sometimes recovering their wits just before they died, their soul collecting itself a final time. It frightened him.

"I messed up bad, Jack. Please forgive me." He leaned in close to his friend.

A hand rose, searching the air blindly before settling shakily on Randal's head. "I forgive you," he said, intoning absolution. "It's not bad, you'll see. We're just pilgrims."

Randal wept unashamedly. "Jack, please don't. You're the only real friend I've got. I can't do all this without you."

He could hear a little of the old Jack in his voice as his friend chided him gently, "I'm not your strength. God is. Tell my boy . . . you tell him what I did on that hill, hear me?" The hand lifted from Randal's head, trembling. "Letter, to Hannah. In my box."

"You can tell Tobias yourself when you see him."

The blistered lips twitched in a ghastly smile. "Not gonna happen. Now go on, I'm feeling tired again."

Randal embraced him as tightly as he dared. "I'll see you again, Jack. This world or the next."

❧

Randal fixed his eyes on the candle he held. It kept him from seeing the shroud-covered bodies moldering around him in the chamber. Bodies his orders had put there. He dimly heard the young seminarian they had called as their Chaplain as he spoke the liturgy of burial.

Instead he remembered Jack back in Basic Indoc. Though only a few years older than the rest of them, he'd had a wife and a child and seemed ages more mature. He was the one who usually kept them out of trouble when they left the base on pass and the one to talk them out of trouble the rest of the time. He had a quiet dignity that even military police respected.

As the Chaplain came to the end of the liturgy, Randal and Lebedev placed the body on a rocky shelf.

"Unto God Almighty we commend the soul of our brother departed, and we commit his body to these depths of the earth; in sure and certain hope of the resurrection unto eternal life through Jesus Christ our Lord."

"Amen."

The Chaplain extinguished his candle. The mourners did the same, plunging the room into utter darkness. For a time all was still and black.

Then a candle was relit, and in turn lighted another and another until the room was illuminated again. "Let these candles serve to remind us of the hope we have of the life to come and the covenantal unity which binds us together in this life."

"Amen."

As he filed out with the others, Randal felt a small hand take his own, squeezing it. "You'll see him again."

"I know, Ariane. I know."

12

We all agree that your theory is crazy,
but is it crazy enough?
—Niels Bohr

When asked what forces drove an economy, a venerable Terran thinker once replied: "Animal spirits."

That phrase played in Randal's mind often in the weeks following Jack's death. The resistance movement took on a life of its own, growing from a handful of cells to dozens. The early days of harrying Abkhazi sentries with snipers seemed a lifetime ago. With each operation the Irregulars grew bolder and more proficient. Men who were accountants and mining engineers just months before now commanded platoons.

The focus of the missions was also changing. Rather than merely trying to wear down the enemy by plucking a soldier here or there, strategic points were targeted for destruction: communications centers, modes of transport, unit commanders and so on.

It was heady to see his vision taking shape, but at the same time the pace of events always looked just this side of disastrous. Jack would tell him to trust God and trust his people. That was easier said than done.

Case in point, he thought bemusedly, spotting Lebedev and a sinewy Asian man crossing the floor of the main chamber. "So Sergei," he called, setting aside the propaganda leaflet he was reviewing. "How did it go at the MagLev control station?"

The Belarusian blew loudly into a handkerchief, tucking it inside his cowl-hooded pullover. "*Builo prekrasno*, Captain Knox, you should have seen explosion! Everywhere train cars and people flying. Was it not, Lieutenant Shin?"

Shin grinned a wide, feral sort of smile, nodding. As always, Randal found the expression disconcerting. The man had filed his teeth down to points.

In the autumn, Shin had been a prosperous and unassuming actuary with a wife and children, from what Randal heard from Jeni. Now, at mid-winter, he was the leader of the Headhunters. They were all-Korean and prided themselves on assassination. Extremely insular, they set themselves apart with the facial and body tattoos used to initiate recruits. A unit takes on much of its commander's attributes and that was obvious with Shin. He was aggressive and proud; even in conversation he was imperialistic, constantly inching closer into the space of whomever he was talking to. Randal half expected Shin to promote himself from lieutenant to warlord.

When Lebedev requested Shin for the attack on the MagLev lines, Randal had been skeptical. Lebedev was an odd bird in his own right; the idea of setting him loose with a madman like Shin was alarming. "Nothing went wrong?"

A laugh from Shin.

"Well…" Lebedev said, motioning vaguely. "One of the trucks of explosive blew up on way to site. Otherwise… no."

"Anybody hurt?"

"*Nyet*, our man got out. And important thing is mission vas successful. Even if they replace tracks, station is gone. *Sovsem unichtozhena.*" He brushed his hands together as if washing them.

"Excellent, Sergei. I'm continually amazed what one can do with fertilizer, cleaning supplies and petrochems. Who knew they were so versatile?" He gave Lebedev's hand a shake, settling for a bow with Shin. Last time the man had tried to lay a bonecrusher on him.

Watching them leave, he marveled at what war brought out of a person. Some of the loudest braggarts in the militia were the first to freeze when the lead started flying. At the same time, the war revealed strength in Ariane no one had ever noticed before. And then there were men like Shin or Nabil—ordinary men twisted by extraordinary circumstances into something unnatural, something that wouldn't know how to live when peace came and there was no more killing to be done.

Sometimes he worried he might be one of them. Over and over he thought of what Nabil had said on the mountain. Was there anyone he wouldn't sacrifice to hurt the Abkhazi? Was there anything he wouldn't do?

Everything in him was invested in liberating New Geneva, in breaking the Abkhazi. He thought of Jack, killing himself in the very act of destroying his target. Randal wondered if he was doing the same thing, just much more slowly, and on a level where the wounds weren't physical.

The beefy quartermaster tugged on his pointed van dyke beard for what seemed like the hundredth time. The man was nervous, though Randal thought it was understandable with people like Shin and the Sergeant-Major in the audience asking direct questions. It was no easy task keeping the Irregulars in beans, bullets and bandages.

The command group had taken to calling itself the "Little Council"—a tongue-in-cheek reference to Calvin's government in Geneva during the First Reformation. In addition to the Sergeant-Major and each of the former NGDF regulars, it was composed of the leaders of the Irregulars' reconnaissance, special ops, supply, and internal security sections, as well as the company commanders. The militia cells were now organized in fours as companies.

"We can't just let the civilians starve," said one of the company commanders angrily, as if the Quartermaster were somehow advocating it.

The Quartermaster mopped sweat from his forehead, looking overwhelmed. "I didn't say they were starving. Yet. But with the suborbitals stopped, the little food the Abkhazi were giving our civilians has stopped too. I've barely enough in store to keep our own troops going, let alone a whole city."

The Abkhazi were getting desperate as their problems mounted. The countryside was providing few supplies; the MagLev train connecting them with their armies in the south was destroyed; and no help would come from Abkhazia until spring. They had taken to going house-to-house, confiscating anything edible for use by the army. The people of Providence might not be starving yet, but the writing was visible on the wall.

All eyes looked to Randal. "From now on, no destroying supply crawlers or storage facilities. We'll prioritize seizing them intact and securing provisions." He paused for thought, hoping it wasn't too obvious he was coming up with it on the fly. "We'll train Jeni's Kitchen Klatch in rationing, and use them to teach others and distribute the food we score."

"Speak of the devil and she appears," Jeni said, bustling into the room. "Sorry I'm late, Randy. Onegin, our man on the inside, sent word that we needed to meet." She walked to the head of the group, giving the Quartermaster a long look until he relinquished the floor. She paused before speaking, raising up on the balls of her feet and lowering slowly, building the suspense. "The honchos from the NGDF sent a message to us."

A low murmur filled the room. It was big news. For so long the Irregulars had been totally isolated, feeling no part of the "real" war to the south. Now the regular army was contacting them.

The Sergeant-Major thumped the table. "Out with it. What'd they say?"

"Well, first of all, the Prime Minister expresses his gratitude on behalf of the country. Which is nice. Oh, and your mum says hello, Randy."

Jeni leaned back against the damp rock wall, folding her arms. "The rest of the message is a bit dicier. They want us to kidnap the science faculty at Abraham Kuyper University. That and blow up Pieter's biggest factory. And they want it all done within seventy-two hours."

"What?" Pieter nearly came out of his seat.

"It's not like it's doing you any good these days, Pieter. I'm talking about the benzkamen facility. Very strategic."

It was strategic. Randal was surprised he hadn't thought of hitting it himself. Benzkamen was a shale-like rock that yielded respectable amounts of oil when refined. While most vehicles in New Geneva ran on electric, the great majority of Abkhazi still used petroleum-based systems. Before the war, nearly all the petrol produced in New Geneva was shipped north.

Now, with their supply lines broken, the benzkamen plant must be vital to the Abkhazi army.

"She's right, Pieter. I'm sure your father has it insured anyway." Randal winked at Jeni.

The woman's smile faded and she pushed off from the wall. "There's something else Onegin wanted to tell me. The Fist of the Mogdukh are here now. They've come for us."

The former civilians shook their heads uncomprehendingly, but the soldiers all took on the same worried expression. "The Fist of the Mogdukh," Pyatt explained glumly. "Abkhazi special forces. They make regular troops look like a children's choir."

"Worse," added Jeni, "They've got powered armor. Bought off-planet. Not as technical as ours, but wicked tough."

An anxious quiet descended on the group.

"It's quite flattering, really." Pieter said thoughtfully, pausing to take a pull from his hip flask. "Much better than being killed by some second-string bad guy, don't you think?"

"I move to adjourn," Randal slugged Pieter hard in the shoulder.

"Seconded," everyone answered in unison.

❧❧

Randal found Pieter in the large, round chamber that served as the Irregulars' rec hall. Clumps of men sat on the improvised furniture talking, smoking or dicing. Shouts echoed from a group of Koreans playing five-field kono in the back of the room, pebbles and shell casings filling in for markers.

Pieter lay in a hammock slung between pitons driven into the opposite ends of an alcove. He didn't look up as Randal approached, busily laying out cards on the blanket resting across his legs.

"Better not let Pyatt see you, Pieter. He'll keep you up half the night explaining the evils of card playing."

"Highly unlikely, Kipper. Take a look over there."

Randal scanned the line of crates serving as the Irregulars' pub and recognized a slumped form with thinning red hair passed out at the bar.

"I watched him. Four drinks and he went to sleep like a kitten."

"If a First Centy is strung-out enough to drink, it's not a good sign. I'll talk to him tomorrow after his headache wears off."

"Your girlfriend was in here looking for you earlier. She had good news. That al-Hise fellow's last Geiger reading came back almost clean. She's OKed the drinking water, though milk is still on the No list."

"Well, given our lack of subterranean cows, that isn't a real concern. I came by to talk to you about the benzkamen factory. Have a few?"

Pieter gathered up his cards. "That was the plant where my father made me intern. Remember his crusade to teach me responsibility?"

"Of course. A rousing success."

"Shut it. Anyway, I've been thinking. Half of our job is done already. That factory is a gigantic bomb just waiting to go off."

"Really? Show me." Randal untucked the datapad from under his arm.

After clearing the screen, Pieter began scrawling lines, squares, and circles. "See this box? The feed prep area. Crawlers dump the raw benzkamen in here. Conveyors then pull it up to this big square. They call this square the MTP – don't ask me what it stands for, I just know what it does. It heats the rock to six hundred centigrade, liquefying it."

"So then it's petrol?"

"Not yet, it's kerogen," Pieter said, drawing lines to another box. "Pipes bring it to this place—the Kerogen Processor. At this point it's still lacking a hydrogen atom. Over here…" He added a circle. "This is a liquid hydrogen tank."

"Beauty. That'd be rather flammable."

Pieter grinned cheekily. "Too bad for them, eh? And the kerogen is vaporized to add the hydrogen, which only increases the explosivity. Explosiveness. Explosivefulness. Whatever, we can have fun with it."

He scribbled a bit more. "This is the petrol reclamation point, where it's separated into various grades. Then it goes to these day-tanks and then ultimately to these holding tanks. They're much, much bigger."

"All of which adds up to the mother of all explosions," Randal said brightly, taking the stylus. "So planting charges on these holding tanks and the hydrogen tank should disable the plant, right?"

"Only temporarily. If you really want to set off wailing and gnashing of teeth, you'll need inside here." Pieter added a small square well away from the complex. "The control center. I imagine that damage to the rest of the plant could eventually be repaired by cannibalizing factories in Abkhazia. But they'll have a real job trying to replicate our controls."

"Security is pretty tight there?"

"That's a dead cert. We were always paranoid about terrorists, what with the plant surrounded by suburbs these days. The place has chem sniffers, magnetic anomaly detectors, and a pass card system. And that was *before* the Abbies took it."

"We can get the senior director to slip us in. He'll have a master passkey."

"Use your head, Kipper. Even if he's still alive, they'd certainly have changed the codes by now."

"Uh-uh. Laurent Mireault is a sodding collaborator. All that's changed for him is the name of his boss."

"You're serious?" Pieter huffed. "The man was nothing when he came to us, just Earther trash. Good help really is hard to find these days." He tilted his head, giving Randal a curious look. "How do you know, anyway? And if he's sold out, why would he help us?"

"Because he's Ariane's father."

"You certainly can pick them. An illegitimate child and a collaborating father." Pieter's shoulders shook in silent mirth. "Oh well, you can't choose your in-laws, right?"

"I'm going to hurt you now. This'll just take a minute."

Pieter shielded his face, still laughing.

Randal stood, tumbling Pieter from the hammock. "I'll go talk to Lebedev about charges for the storage tanks. You'll be on the team hitting the university, so get started on your pre-ops."

∼∽

Randal descended the thick, knotted rope to the lower level. After one of his accidents nearly brought down the headquarters, Lebedev and his acolytes were exiled a couple hundred meters down and away, placing any innocents out of likely blast radii.

He dropped to the floor and started down the corridor toward the mad Belarusian's den. Along either side were small chambers, most of which contained either sacks and jugs of raw materials or twisted constructs of beakers and tubing.

Ahead of him sounded a shoom, followed by a gush of smoke from a side room. One of Lebedev's followers tumbled from the chamber, a young, red-haired woman wearing the hooded pullovers they all seemed to favor. A cloth was pressed over her mouth and nose. "Don't breath the fumes, don't breath the fumes!" she yelled, rushing past him without slowing.

Tucking his face into the thick field jacket he wore, Randal sprinted through the haze, eyes stinging powerfully. He didn't stop until he reached Lebedev's main shop. Once inside, he let himself breath again, gratefully sucking in lungfuls of air. Lebedev emerged from behind a monstrosity of glass and hoses, watching Randal with his sad eyes.

"Sergei," Randal said once his breath was caught. "I've got a job for you." He swept aside the clutter of small electronic pieces on the table and set down his datapad. Calling up the crude map Pieter had drawn, he explained the basics of the op to Lebedev.

"And so basically, I need this hydrogen tank and these big holding tanks here to explode," he summarized, tapping the screen with a finger. "Oh, and the bombs need to be small enough to get manpacked in."

He expected protest from Lebedev on that last part. It seemed like a tall order, making bombs small but powerful enough to do the job.

When Lebedev didn't answer, Randal glanced up, anticipating a skeptical look. Instead, the man looked near tears. "Thank you, Randal. I am so happy. Is so boring always making the mines and booby traps."

Randal patted his shoulder, forestalling what he sensed was an impending hug. "No worries. So you think it's possible then?"

The man waved dismissively. "Will be like shooting the puppies in a barrel. On hydrogen tanks a scabbling foam will be used. I have just the thing."

"Scabbling? Do you mean spackling?"

"Eh? *Nyet*... scabbling. Instead of putting bomb in one spot, person sprays explosive foam over big area. Stick on a detonator and cap, and boom! Whole section blows up. Ve can remove big piece of tank all at once, making explosion bigger."

Randal whistled softly. "You're a scary guy, Sergei. Will the scabbling work on the holding tanks?"

A shake of his head. Lebedev pointed to the holding tanks on the datapad. "*Smotri*. Probably very thick walls on these. To us will be necessary shaped charges with molded explosives." He shifted, no longer speaking to Randal but himself. "*Ili polusharia, ili truba... mozhet buit veyer...*"

He drew a semi-circle on the datascreen. "I'm thinking a, how to say? A hemisphere." Adding radiating lines to the curve he said, "Or maybe fan pattern. Either one should open up side of tank."

Randal looked at him in wonderment. "Sergei, what were you doing in the infantry with us dumb grunts?"

Lebedev laughed, the high-pitched sound of it walking up Randal's spine. "Is funny-sad story. I come here from Minsk, in Belarus Province of Terra. Very bad there. Whole city owned almost by one company, NovTechProm. I work first as chemical researcher, then in electronics. Ven I apply to leave, they try stop me, but government says okay. So they pull dirty trick on Sergei. I come to New Geneva, but encoded in documents it says I am big-boy felon."

He hocked and spat on the floor. "So Immigration Ministry decide to deport me. I find lawyer who tells me if I join Defense Force I can get exemption. Now Sergei is a soldier. Crazy, nyet?"

"No crazier than anything else around here."

❧❧

Randal stooped by Ariane's pallet, watching her sleep. Chestnut bangs lay across her eyes; he brushed them away with a fingertip. She was curled around Jean-Marie, one arm encircling him protectively. Randal placed a hand on her shoulder, acutely aware of Jeni's bemused presence a meter away on her own bed. Jeni's watchful eye, and his cumbersome cold-weather gear only increased his awkwardness. "Ariane, wake up. It's Randal."

She sat bolt upright, careful even in sleep not to disturb Jean-Marie. "What is it? One of the patients?"

"Oh, no. I was hoping you'd go topside with me for a bit. To talk… It's okay if you'd rather not."

"No, that sounds nice," she said, her voice thick with sleep. "What about Jean-Marie?"

"Aunt Jeni will watch him, if that's okay," Jeni piped up.

A ready nod. "Wait outside while I get dressed."

From the hall he could hear whispers, nervous giggles, and more than one "Hush, he'll hear you." Finally, she appeared. It was worth the wait. She was bundled in a midnight blue, fur-trimmed parka. With a nubby gray scarf around her neck all he could see were two amazing dark eyes, but they were enough. "Where are we going?"

"It's a surprise."

Shouldering his satchel and flechette rifle, he set off. Together they walked the tunnels for a solid hour before he led her out a well-camouflaged exit into open country. From the fence they encountered it was likely once a sheep pasture. Only a thin sliver of a moon was visible, the night sky clear and black, the stars shining as brightly as he had ever seen them.

Coming to a road, he listened for several ticks before sending her across, covering her with his rifle. Down the way were the charred remains of two infantry fighting vehicles. He followed her across and they came to a steep incline made treacherous with ice. Though he knew it wasn't necessary, he made it a point to offer a hand whenever he could. Near the top was a wide outcropping of rock which gave a clear view of Providence. Finding a spot in the lee of a boulder, he spread out the thermal blanket from his satchel. "Have a seat?"

Then came the dilemma of where to sit: behind her, right next to her, or should he leave some distance? Any of them could be misread. In the end he plopped down next to her, placing a palm behind, but not technically around her.

"Look at that view. *C'est merveilleux!*" Both were keeping their voices low. The spot was remote, but one never knew. "You can see the whole city. From up here you'd never know there was a war on."

"I know. We found this spot during an anti-vehicular ambush the other night and I thought of you."

Ariane smiled. "That would have sounded strange not long ago. Now it's strangely... romantic." Her smile faded as they looked out over the city lights. "I loved this city. Before they made it an abattoir."

"The war can't last forever. Providence will be restored. We're Calvinists after all—too bloody stubborn to ever give up."

"People should hire you to write mottos."

"Oh, I almost forgot." Slipping a hand into the battered satchel, he fished out nonushka flat bread and some pickled cheese, both liberated from an Abkhazi ration pack.

"You brought provisions! Now if we only had some wine."

"O ye of little faith," he said, pulling out a half bottle of Malbec and two plastic tumblers. "Chaplain let me borrow this from the communion stores. RHIP and all that."

"RHIP?"

"Rank hath its privileges. Though this is the first one I've discovered." He eased out the cork while she worked on the cheese and bread. Then they sat quietly, drinking the dry red. Early morning fog was settling over the city, giving it a dreamy quality.

"What are you thinking?"

He laughed. "Wishing I had some light artillery. This spot would be perfect."

"Really?"

"No, not really. Just thinking about us. It would be a lot simpler in peacetime, wouldn't it? You'd have like ten chatty girlfriends along so I could be quiet instead of rambling like this."

She nudged him lightly. "I think this was a sweet idea. Besides, in peacetime my father would be around. He can be a little intimidating."

"So I noticed." Nibbling at the flatbread, he grimaced. "Not hard to tell their army bought these from the lowest bidder."

"They're not so bad," she allowed generously, though her nose wrinkled at the taste.

Fast-moving, fingerlike clouds were moving in, obscuring Alshabel, the only of the twin moons visible that early in the morning. Hopefully the clouds presaged warmer weather.

"You know," Ariane said quietly, "when I was little, clear skies used to depress me. I hated them."

"That's odd."

"From the time I was little my father told me that we were alone in the universe. The cosmos isn't watching and it certainly isn't going to help me. He would always say a person has to carve their own niche in the world, and that's the only immortality a person can hope for. I'm sure he thought he was preparing me for life."

She kept her eyes on the moon. "I can remember being eight or so and staring up into the night sky. It went on forever. The idea that I was all alone in that vastness terrified me. After that, I loved cloudy days."

Randal poured them each a refill and corked the bottle. "How did you come to believe, anyway?"

Ariane took a handful of snow, molding it absently as she spoke. "I made a lot of Christian friends when we emigrated here. Providence is worldlier than the rest of New Geneva, but still very religious. My friends weren't afraid of open sky, *tu comprends*?

"In time I came to understand that there was an amazingly benevolent Person out there. I wasn't a Christian yet. My father controlled everything I did and at thirteen that didn't leave a lot of room for trouble. So I didn't feel the need for a Savior that others do."

She paused, sipping the wine and collecting her thoughts. "Over time I came to see that I did the same sins as everyone else. Mine were only pettier. Next to the perfection of God, my goodness meant nothing." She laughed, running a glove over her face. "You talk. How did you become a Christian?"

Releasing a long breath, he watched the steam billow away in the icy air. "Me? I can't really remember a time I wasn't. They baptized me at a week old and from then on it was just part of my world. I grew up in the Covenant. There isn't a time I can point to when God wasn't there.

"About three years ago, after vespers, I rededicated myself. Before then my beliefs were largely based on what I was told, but they were more mine afterward. Does that make sense?"

"Sure. I think you have to do that with everything when you grow up."

Randal reached down, taking her hand. It seemed terribly small through the thick gloves. He felt her give a squeeze. Dreading it, he finally screwed up the courage to broach the reason he'd brought her to the mountainside. "I kissed you."

"I was there." Was there a smile in her voice?

Good, she was keeping it light. Light was good. "Since then I've kind of been avoiding you, 'til I could figure out where things should go between us."

A soft laugh came from beneath her scarf. "I was avoiding you for the same reason. Have you figured it out yet?"

He hesitated before answering. "Not yet. Things are so crazy now. But I've never felt like this for anyone before. I care about you a lot."

"I care about you as well." She wasn't doing anything to make it easier for him, he thought.

He sipped the Malbec. By now it was cold enough to make his teeth ache. He wanted very much to say he loved her, that he was ready for a commitment. Self-doubt gnawed at him: doubts about his motives, was it really love or just needing warmth in the midst of war; doubts about becoming an instant father; but most of all, doubts about creating a war widow. He didn't expect to outlive the war. Was it loving or fair to ask her to don widows' black just so he could be happy for a little while?

She misread his silence, he realized, as she spoke. "Listen, Randal. Please. I mean it when I say care for you. I've only loved two other men— my father, and Jean-Marie's. Both of them broke my heart. Don't act like one of those spoiled Academy brats who treat us like toys. I'm a real person. And I don't think I can go through that again." Her back was to him now, knees hugged up protectively to her chest.

Randal sighed, rubbing a frost-encrusted glove at his forehead. "It's not like that, Ariane. I just have some things to sort out."

Some of the stiffness seemed to leave her spine. "I'll be waiting when you do."

Silently, he gave thanks. For a moment he'd feared losing her. He would have made any pledge, no matter how ill-advised, to stop that. "You know," he said, still a bit unsteady. "It's always coldest just before first light. Would you like to sit closer?"

Feeling her nestle in close to him, his hand running absently down her side and along the contour of her hip, the drumbeat of doubts receded to a faint tempo in the back of his mind.

13

You get more with a kind word and a gun
than you can with a kind word alone.
—Al Capone

Nabil looked himself over, checking his reflection in one of the few intact
window panes of the Miner's Trust, the largest bank in Providence. He
pulled the Abkhazi-issue field jacket a little tighter, covering the twin
bullet holes through the front of the fatigue blouse. It was still stained
black with the blood of the previous occupant. Lastly he cocked his
helmet at the proper angle, using two fingers to set the distance from
the brim to the bridge of his nose. The helmet seemed ridiculous to him,
designed with a wide brim that left the ears exposed to shrapnel and
concussion.

Quit stalling, he chided himself. He knew the others believed nothing touched him, but that was far from the truth. Long experience only
taught him to keep his worries quiet. Walking into an Abkhazi camp
with only his guldor pichok, a standard-issue sidearm, and his wits for
protection worried him plenty.

Taking a deep breath, he rounded the corner and crossed the street
to the checkpoint. Beyond it lay a wide, snow-covered yard bisected by a
wending avenue. From his vantage, Nabil could see the first of Abraham
Kuyper University's imposing gray edifices.

As he neared the trio of guards at the gate, he was careful not to make
eye contact. Instead he worked at the settings on his timepiece, seeming
only to notice the lowly guards when he needed to, as any officer would
do.

"*Dobriy dyen*," he said in answer to their greetings, snapping a crisp salute back to them. Given his age, he was forced to imitate a very junior officer, and they were always thrilled to receive a salute.

That was the easy part, he thought, taking the sidewalk. Many of the dorms were being used as barracks now, which meant a good deal of coming and going through the gate. The real security would be at sensitive points like arms rooms, commo centers, and of course, the scientists the Irregulars intended to rescue.

Abkhazi vehicles plied the lane as he walked: rail-gun tanks, korobach-kas, and multi-barreled anti-aircraft crawlers. Being surrounded by his ex-countrymen brought back a life he had buried with his murdered parents. He had left all of this, and it made his skin writhe being around it again.

Knox's words came back to him, however, like a canker sore he couldn't help worrying at. What did make him better than the Abkhazi? Yes, the Khlisti killed his parents for their faith. But what if his hatred was betraying the very thing for which they died?

Worse were the comments that little chit Knox was dating had made about forgiveness. She had lost her mother also, yet while she mourned, he had seen no evidence of hate within her. He watched for it avidly, encouraged it to bloom, but no black flower appeared.

If Knox's words galled him, the thought that the girl might be his superior in some small way shamed him to the core. He held Scripture in reserve against the day they confronted him again. Long nights he'd searched the Book. Eye for an eye, tooth for a tooth, repay tenfold and the like. In his heart, though, he feared it was smoke.

Shunting away depressing thoughts, he snapped a salute to the leader of the patrol he passed. They were heavily armed, looking for trouble. He hoped fervently that the Irregulars would give them plenty.

Passing in the shadow of the first university building, he could see it was dormant. No attempt had been made to cover shattered windows with transplastic. The front doors were sealed with chain and a large magnetic lock.

The next several buildings were the same. The cafeteria was operating, as was the university recreation center. Inside, several Abkhazi watched the stale, censor-approved trideo programs he remembered from his life in Abkhazia. Back when his parent's friends taught him English, he remembered how difficult it was for them to communicate the concept of "fun" to him. The Abkhazi dialect had no such word. Enjoyment, sure, recreation, yes, but no understanding of purposeless pleasure.

Making a note that the recreation center would be a first-rate bombing target, he pressed on. To either side of him rose two sets of dorms, each at least eight stories high and full of Abkhazi regulars. His hand strayed to the sidearm riding his hip. It held only sixteen rounds.

Though it was mid-afternoon, the near-constant overcast and the deep southern latitude meant darkening skies. A streetlamp blinked on above him. The Irregulars had decided against destroying the city's main fusion plant: it was virtually impregnable, for starters, and if they succeeded the civilians would have to survive winter without heat. Many would not.

Leaving the dorms, he faced down the slope. All the remaining buildings were dark except one. The scientists were imprisoned there, he hoped.

He became aware of other people nearby.

"Do junior lieutenants no longer show obeisance?"

Resisting the urge to bolt, he whipped out a sharp salute, turning to take in the Colonel he'd just inadvertently ignored. "Forgive me, Colonel!" He didn't need to fake the panic on his face.

"What company are you assigned to, you illegitimate goat?"

He knew he could drop the fat officer and his twitchy-looking aide before they could blink, but he had a mission. The Colonel wanted to know what unit he was with. Jeni had briefed him on his shoulder insignia, which one was it?

"Third Battalion, Astrakhan Regiment, my Colonel."

"Go immediately to your captain and request punishment. Can your unevolved mind comprehend this simple order?"

Inclining his head, Nabil murmured a "Yes, Colonel" as subserviently as possible. He backed away, carefully not to dishonor the officer by turning his back on him. That would likely get him shot.

As soon as he was out of sight, Nabil sprinted to put distance between them, laughing under his breath. For once the Abkhazi's brutal discipline worked in his favor. The Colonel would never verify if Nabil reported to his commander for punishment. Terror would ensure any real Abkhazi soldier's compliance.

Circling around slowly, he approached the building he suspected housed his quarry. Guards stood to either side of the entrance, each shouldering heavy flechette rifles and full combat webbing. Several lights were on inside and steam rose from vents atop the building. More significantly, he could see light emanating from the frosted windows of the building's basement. He'd bet his guldor pichok the scientists were down there.

Returning the guards' salutes, he walked casually around the corner of the building, melding into the shadows. After dropping his helmet to the ground, he freed the balaclava and gloves from his cargo pockets, donning them

Hugging close to the chimney, he started his ascent. The wall was constructed of rough, irregularly-hewn rocks; the mortar set deeply enough to allow his fingertips purchase. It wasn't his easiest climb, but certainly not the hardest. Not with the training he'd undergone. Nabil pulled himself up the last meter to the roof.

Holding fast with toes and one hand, he pulled off a glove with his teeth. Slowly, slowly, he moved it over the rim of the roof and then pulled it back down, narrowly keeping his hold on the wall.

He flapped it lightly. It seemed intact. That was good—no midge wire waiting to slice him apart before he even knew it was there. After stuffing away the glove, he took out a small, black box from his cargo pocket. He flicked it on and held it between his teeth.

His feet were starting to cramp from keeping him in place. If he didn't move soon the enemy would find him broken at the base of the chimney. Grasping the edge of the roof, he pulled himself up far enough to scout.

No one was there. He'd hoped for live guards. No guards meant technological defenses and he hated that. Hauling himself up, he lay on the meter-tall border and then dropped flat to the roof itself.

After strapping the faintly-vibrating black box to his wrist, he took out the two remaining items from his pocket: a monocle and a small aerosol.

Thus equipped, he headed for the maintenance hatch. Lebedev swore the box would defeat any motion sensor he encountered, provided he moved slowly. The man had mumbled through a detailed explanation of ultrasonics, but that it came from Lebedev was enough; Nabil held his technical skills in almost shamanic respect.

Every couple of meters he sprayed the aerosol, pressing the monocle to his eye. It looked scavenged from a civilian night-vision device. Together, the two allowed him to spot the skein of laser sensors crisscrossing the area. Evading them required all of his gymnastic ability, but somehow he reached the door, thankfully without triggering any of the pressure pads likely distributed around the roof.

The maintenance hatch was a flimsy one, meant to keep mischievous students inside, not bloody-minded guerrillas out. Finessing the primitive mechanical lock was quick work for his well-worn set of picks. It and the guldor pichok were his only remembrances of Abkhazia, souvenirs of a time when he'd held common scouts and infantrymen in contempt. No other warrior stood above a Fist of the Mogdukh.

Nabil descended the short flight of stairs. When he had approached the building earlier the top floor had been dark, but there was always the danger of roving sentries. Pulling up his jacket, he slid free his dagger with a well-oiled snick from the scabbard concealed in the small of his back.

He peeked his head into the hall, glanced lightning fast left then right and then pulled it back before anyone could shoot it off. Closing his eyes, he made himself recall what he had seen without a second look. There wasn't always time for a second glance, and relying on one made you sloppy. Sloppy made you dead.

The wing he was in extended a good thirty meters in either direction. The hall was deserted. A stairwell stood at both ends and the silver double doors of a lift were in the middle. Classroom doors lined the hall, broken only by the lift and a small alcove with couches and potted plants.

He pulled off the balaclava and stowed it away. Swiveling the hilt of his guldor pichok, he pressed the curving blade along the inside of his forearm. If his luck ran out and someone challenged him, he planned to bluff first. If that failed, the blade would go to work.

He stepped to the stairs and descended them gingerly. It was an open stairwell, with no doors at the landings—any noise he made would easily reach the wrong ears. At the third floor he paused, glancing down the length of the hall. All clear. His goal was floor two; he'd seen a lone classroom or office with lights burning when he reconnoitered.

A light bobbed on the walls below and trudging boot steps echoed up to him.

He went into the darkened hall, trying the first door. It was locked. So were the second and the third. The footsteps were nearly to his floor. He could hear the low murmur of chatter. At the alcove he flattened out, slipping under one of the couches. Painstakingly slowly he eased out his pistol. If the guards took him, it wouldn't be alive. He knew too much.

The footsteps stopped at each classroom; he assumed the guards were shining the light through the small window inset in the classroom doors. When they reached the alcove he closed his eyes. They might reflect light and he needed every edge he could get. "Blind their eyes that they may not see," he prayed, moving his lips without sound. They paused nearby. He cracked his eyelids, ready to come out shooting.

They didn't seem to have spotted him. The click of an electric lighter sounded, and soon the stench of stale tobacco filled the air.

He grinned with relief. They were sneaking cigarettes. Smoking was a grave indulgence in the Khlisti faith, though one routinely broken by enlisted troops. They'd find the soles of their feet beaten with rods if they were caught. Finally they moved on.

Nabil padded down to level two. The second floor rooms were walled with reactive glass which could be adjusted for privacy. It only took a moment to find the occupied classroom.

A small "window" was programmed into the opaque glass door of the room. Allowing himself a single peek, Nabil saw a tweedy fellow diagramming something on a large trideo screen mounted on the wall. The New Genevan professor looked hard-used and in need of a square meal. Probably half a dozen Abkhazi civilians watched from their desks, flanked by an equal number of guards.

His scan didn't allow him any idea of what the old man was charting, but it didn't matter. Nabil's scientific curiosity extended little beyond combat applications. Springing the lock on a nearby room, he waited for the lesson to end.

Several hours later, it did. Catfooted, he shadowed the group, giving them plenty of lead time. At the bottom of the stairs he went to his belly and peered around the corner. People often missed movement when it was low enough.

In the center of the hall, where the main entrance should be, a trio of guards sat around a desk. Uniforms of silt-gray serge and the dark-brown berets folded and tucked into their epaulettes marked them as Theocratic Guardsmen—tough, battle-hardened troopers.

Beyond, he saw the professor and two guards split off and file through a doorway. It shut with a solid thud. He assumed the professor was being taken to the basement; it seemed likely the other academics were being held there as well. He wanted very much to get a look past that door.

Common sense held him back. If the Abkhazi discovered that the Irregulars were sniffing around the scientists, it wouldn't be a trio guarding the front door but a platoon. Reluctantly, Nabil went back up the stairs. Once more he crossed the trap-laden rooftop and climbed down the wall. Down was always worse than up, but he managed.

Getting to the perimeter was no problem for the scout. Security wasn't directed at keeping people in and the enlisted troops he passed weren't likely to challenge an officer.

He had chosen his exit before going in, a row of shrubs along a side street. Across the street lay demolished apartments, their residents long since deported or killed. Past the rubble was an entrance to the Catacombs. An hour prior to the infiltration he'd removed the cover and swept the area thoroughly for traps.

A reedy, tremulous whistle came to his ear, the melody an Abkhazi folk tune he remembered from childhood. Soon a gangly private strolled into view. He looked barely old enough to shave and carried his assault rifle like it was a fowling piece.

Nabil's smile was a cruel twist of the lips as he slid free the guldor pichok. He concealed himself behind a bush, biding his time.

As the young soldier passed, Nabil struck, adder-fast. A hand went to the throat, to quell the boy's frightened scream; a foot to the back of the knee took him down; and a short, upward thrust of the blade ended his life.

In a blink, the deed was done, the corpse stretched out behind the hedge. Nabil took time to clean his blade on the boy's shirt before sprinting across the street.

Picking his way through the rubble, Nabil felt his insides churn. Where was the exultant rush that always came, the flash of vindication? He could see the boy's face—the sightless eyes, the stilled lips that seemed to mutely accuse.

Twice he stopped to empty his guts before reaching headquarters.

Melted snow had long before soaked through the knees of Randal's black coveralls. He only hoped his joints would obey when the time came to move; they felt frozen in place. He could see no static defenses from his position behind the Mireault house, but security had been beefed up since his last visit. Two different guards had walked the perimeter so far. He assumed there were only two and they were alternating rounds. If a familiar face made the next pass he'd know.

The foot patrols told him something encouraging: no sound or motion sensors, or else the guards would trip them themselves. There was a motion-sensitive light on the back porch that stayed on about thirty seconds after someone passed. He'd need to wait until the next round set it off before he could make his move.

Despite his whinging knees, he felt good. In a little under sixty-eight hours his people had formulated workable battle plans for two very complicated ops and performed the necessary reconnaissance and technical prep. Even with the factory surveillance showing a thornier situation than they'd hoped, the plan was still green-lighted.

Unfortunately, it all depended on the cantankerous man in the house before him.

Randal patted the folded hardcopies in his breast pocket, smiling mirthlessly. These were fake messages cooked up by Jeni, and ostensibly transmitted from Laurent Mireault to the Irregulars. The information was all gleaned from other sources, some of it based on sketchy inference at best, but it would be damning for the man if found.

If Mireault proved intractable, Randal would let him know that the next Irregular corpse the Abbies searched would be holding the messages. Ariane had no idea of the plan.

The back light flashed on. A guard wandered into view, the same one he'd seen earlier. He had a limp and his web gear rattled with each step. The man didn't know how to secure it properly at all. Once the guard rounded the corner Randal moved, sprinting across the yard. At the back door he sighed in relief; the locking mechanism hadn't been changed.

He reached into his waist pouch, taking out the crude lock slicer contained inside—a standard pass card connected by optic line to a sequencer. It was simple to operate. A single button both activated the slicer and set it to work.

Slotting the pass card into the electronic lock, he pressed the button twice. Numbers flashed on the display much faster than they could be read. Fleetingly he wondered why Lebedev bothered with a display at all, though it did reassure the user that the machine was doing something. He chewed the inside of his cheek, hoping the slicer would work as advertised. An alarm in that part of town was a death sentence.

The lock popped and Randal was inside, closing the door softly behind him.

He tucked away the slicer and then freed the flechette pistol dangling from his shoulder rig. There could be more guards inside. He passed through the kitchen to the atrium, keeping low as he moved—all his stealth getting into the house meant nothing if someone spotted him through a window.

Static hissed from the parlor. Taking a look inside, Randal found the man sunken into a plush reclining chair. Mireault's eyes rested vaguely on the trideo, which was tuned to nothing at all.

He looked terrible. His suit was slept in, his cheeks hollowed and sprouting several days' stubble. Head turning in Randal's direction, his expression didn't change as he took in the ugly black gun pointed at him. "I hope you're here to kill me," he said tiredly, draining the last of the amber liquor from his glass.

"Actually, I've come to ask for your help, Monsieur Mireault." Randal edged into the room.

"C'est dommage. Come have a drink." He refilled his highball, motioning with the bottle to Randal.

"I thought you would want to know—Jean-Marie is safe. We rescued him. Ariane is also doing well. I can't tell you how many lives she's saved." He squatted not far from Mireault, keeping his attention on the room's entrance.

The man smiled faintly at that, mumbling to himself in French.

In a flash, his expression shifted. He sat forward with a slosh of ice cubes, fixing his gaze on Randal. Where before he was hazily pleasant, he was now all angry intensity. Randal feared the man might be crazy. That would be disastrous: he needed Mireault sane for their plan to work.

"Why are you here, boy? Are you trying to get me killed? Is it not enough for you to take my daughter, will you take my own life as well?"

Randal lifted his pistol in line with the man's forehead, letting the 10 millimeter muzzle work its soothing effect. "If you don't be quiet, you'll rouse the guards and get us both killed. Can't let you do that."

The man's mouth snapped shut. Apparently he wasn't as ready to die as he'd imagined.

"You're the most foolish man I know, Monsieur Mireault," Randal said coolly, flicking a glance at the door. No guards so far. "The Khlisti religion has been around for over three hundred years. Do you think this is the first planet where this has happened? They even have a term for people like you. It translates roughly as 'useful fools'."

Mireault started to interject. A motion with the pistol silenced him.

"How long do you think they let these useful fools live once they've consolidated power? Answer: not very sodding long. First of all, you're an infidel. And second, if you'd betray your own people, how could they ever trust you? You'll only live as long as you're needed." Randal smiled easily, giving a beneficent wave of the gun. "Your turn."

"This is idiocy. . . Madness! Why should I go live in holes just so I can be shot down like a dog? New Geneva is doomed, and so is this ridicule rebellion!" Mireault's fire flared a moment and then dimmed to resignation. "At least here I am comfortable until my time comes."

Randal sighed, shaking his head. "In the south, the Abkhazi have only managed to advance eight hundred meters in the past month—less than a kilometer. The Irregulars have cut their resupply and reinforcement to a trickle. They're being squeezed from front and back, and spring is a long time coming."

They had gleaned the information about the bogged-down advance from Station Liberty just that morning. The Abkhazi maintained constant broad-band jamming, but occasionally a broadcast slipped through.

Mireault ran the flat of a hand across his bald pate and down his face. "Why is this happening, my friend? I want only to live in peace in my own home. I don't understand why…" His mouth continued to work soundlessly, eyes settled on the bottom of his highball as if to find an answer there.

Seeing him like that, Randal felt compassion for the man. But he couldn't let him go to pieces. He needed him intact.

"You're an atheist, Monsieur Mireault. You don't get to look for ultimate meanings." Remembering Ariane, he softened his tone. "But your daughter told me what you used to say to her. How making your mark in this go-round is the only immortality you have? I'm offering you a chance, the only one you're likely to get. Let your life mean something."

The front door opened unexpectedly.

Randal scuttled behind Mireault's chair, hunkering down. He pressed the muzzle of the pistol into the back of the recliner, certain the man could feel it through the padding.

Booted feet thumped on the wooden floors. There was a sliding sound to the walk, probably his friend with the limp. "You are here, that is good," he heard the guard say. "I will log in report. My relief will check to your safety in the morning."

Waiting until the guard was out of earshot, Mireault muttered, "Good for you," followed by fragments in French that Randal couldn't translate and was certain he would not want to. Emerging from behind the chair, he gave Mireault an expectant look.

The man's eyes were clear as they settled on him. "What is it you want from me?"

14

Against the rigidity of classical methods of fighting,
the guerrilla fighter invents his own tactics at every minute
of the fight and constantly surprises the enemy.
—Che Guevara

Randal peered over a windowsill of the fire-gutted cafe the infiltration team was using as a staging point. Behind him he heard the snap of black tape being ripped in lengths. Pyatt was helping Johnny and Ariane with some last-minute soundproofing on their gear.

Pieter crouched to his right, both watching the university through heavy snowfall.

"One set of eyes in the wrong place, Kipper."

"And we're spotted, I know. But attacking in force would be suicidal. We'd lose all the Irregulars, not just the five of us."

It was something they'd debated during the planning stage. Pieter wanted to hit them hard, with a full-on assault. Randal was adamant—guerrillas survived through stealth and ambuscade. Pitched battles with regular armies allowed the other side to find, fix, and destroy the guerrillas with superior firepower. No guerrilla army in any history he'd read ever won a war without the aid of a regular army. And when the guerrillas confused their role with that of the regulars, disaster inevitably followed.

"I just have a bad feeling about this. If NG Intel wants these boys so badly, why don't they come get them?"

Randal didn't answer. He was hungry, exhausted, and was afraid he might bite off Peter's head. Besides, Pieter was just working through his pre-op jitters. He knew why the mission was so vital—his father's company had certainly benefited from the astounding technological developments coming from the Abraham Kuyper science faculty.

The military had benefited as well. From the layered ceramic armor of the LANCER suits to the propulsion systems of the latest generation of unmanned submersibles, few weapons in the NGDF arsenal lacked a contribution from AKU.

For centuries, the Terran Hegemony's policy was to keep Penumbra colonies as technologically primitive as possible. Such colonies were kept permanently undercapitalized and restricted from importing advanced tech. There would be no wars for independence so long as colonial governments had only twenty-first century tech with which to challenge the orbiting battlecruisers of the Hegemony.

While coming nowhere close to the level of the Core Planets, New Geneva had developed far beyond the typical Penumbra colony. Ideas had consequences. Contrary to the "don't polish brass on a sinking ship" mentality of many Christian theologies, the Reformed worldview found value in this life, not only in the life to come. The universe was the "theatre of God's glory" and education and free inquiry were cherished. AKU was the pinnacle of an educational system researched and applauded by experts from as far away as Centari and Terra.

Now the cream of the university was in Abkhazi hands. The long-term implications for the war effort were dire—their technological advantage was the only edge the New Genevans held.

Randal had kept the plan to rescue the scientists as straightforward as possible, but there were still more variables than he liked. In a few moments, mad Lieutenant Shin and his Headhunters would begin a diversion on the far side of the campus. Big variable number one was whether Shin could pull enough attention from the infiltration team's section of the perimeter to get them inside.

Next to him, he sensed Pieter flinch as the sharp crack of a rifle rent the night air. Several more followed close upon it. Each of the Headhunters carried either a military-grade sniper weapon or a high-powered hunting rifle.

"That's our cue," Randal said over the headset, pulling down his primitive Abkhazi night vision goggles.

They high-crawled across the street in file. Randal gave thanks for the snow banks packed to either side of the roadway. Once over the snow banks, he led them along the hedges in a crouch. Their goal was a break in the hedge up ahead. Jeni's spies had spotted a trail of footprints in the snow there during daylight. This was essential—there was too much likelihood of mines and midge wire if they blazed their own path.

Approaching the spot, he leaned forward to peer through the break.

Two Abkhazi troopers walked through the bushes, nearly into him. Backpedaling, Randal's feet slipped out from under him on the ice, pitching him back on the concrete. Overhead he heard the throaty whisper of Pyatt's silenced SMG as he dropped the two.

"Thanks," Randal said as they pulled the bodies under a hedge and shrouded them with armloads of snow.

"No worries."

Tentatively, Randal took another peek. It looked clear to the next available cover. "Let's move." Keeping carefully to the trail, they low-crawled to a tiny, demolished prayer chapel. A half-meter of snow lay on the ground, their white wraps blending with it seamlessly.

From the chapel it was slow progress through the jumble of abandoned buildings and offices leading to the science center. Avoiding contact often meant waiting long minutes for the opportunity to dash a few critical meters.

The Headhunter's attack had long since tapered off, though occasional rifle cracks could be heard, answered by autofire. The plan was for the Headhunters to break contact and circle to a rendezvous point to support the evacuation of the scientists. Either Shin was improvising, or the Abkhazi were pursuing more tenaciously than they'd hoped. It was just another variable to worry over.

Eventually they made their destination, taking cover behind a snow-covered mound. "Burned books," he heard Ariane whisper disgustedly.

Brushing aside a bit of snow, he made a sour face. She was right; the mound was actually a huge pile of scorched books. To their right was the brick-and-stone facade of the university library. It amazed Randal. Even in the midst of war the Abkhazi censors never rested. Across the narrow walk was the science building, two hulking Theocratic Guard soldiers standing watch on the stoop. If Nabil's intel was current, another trio awaited them on the other side of the doors.

"I'm going car shopping," Johnny whispered.

"Roger. Let me know when you get lucky."

Johnny's job was to steal a transport while the rest of them sprang the prisoners. The pilot crept out of sight, black plastic tool case in hand. Randal wondered how many times he had boosted vehicles before joining the military. He certainly had a knack for larceny.

"Pyatt, these Theocratic Guard types wear ballistic armor. Make sure you go for a headshot."

The response came back wryly. "Mummy, can you come show me how to take my gun off safety, too?"

Randal grinned, lining up sights on his guard. Pyatt had really loosened up. It was important to get a headshot though. The subsonic rounds the SMGs fired were much easier to sound suppress than other ammunition, but they were useless against a decent ballistic vest. "Okay, on three. One, two..."

Both gently squeezed a three-round burst. Randal's guard pitched backward, while Pyatt's just sort of crumpled where he stood.

"Go!" Randal grabbed Ariane's waist belt, encouraging her along. The team sprinted to the door. Each pushed back their night binos. Inside, the light would overwhelm the systems, reducing their vision to a green blur.

Pieter threw open the door. Randal entered low, Pyatt high.

As he crossed the threshold, Randal hoped fervently that Nabil's intel was right.

❧ ❧

Lebedev was miserable. Not only did each corner of the freshly harvested benzkamen seem intent on poking him somewhere sensitive, but he'd found in the shale-like substance an entirely new allergy to add to his list. The dust cloud filling the enclosed bed of the crawler made his eyes sting and choked him with sneezes despite the filter he wore. Worse were the hives he felt forming from hairline to ankles.

In the dim light he could just make out the beaming face of Miriam. His young apprentice seemed to find the experience exhilarating. For his own part, he would never have come at all, except the mission was too important to entrust to children. His apprentices amused him: they'd drawn straws to see who would get to accompany him on the reckless errand.

Through the back opening he could see neat rows of suburban houses, each nearly identical to the last. They looked new—likely the area was wilderness when Haelbroeck first built the factory.

He felt the crawler decelerate. "Nu, Miriam. Time is for burrowing." The two pushed aside narrow trenches in the rock and then wriggled into them, covering themselves as best they could. With their dark clothing they should pass any but the most thorough inspection.

Someone clambered up the back of the crawler, shining a high-powered hand torch. Burrowed near the front of the bed, the light barely reached them. "Clear! Proceed!" the guard barked in Russian. He hopped back down, slapping the gate. With a jolt, the crawler moved out.

Lebedev watched the twin guard towers recede. Next, the large retaining pool holding waste water from the factory's MTP section went past. Soon would come the factory's Feed Processing Point.

The crawler swung in a wide loop and then began backing slowly. Lifting his head, Lebedev saw the dark mass of the feed pile. "We must move, now. *Buistro, devochka!*"

He and the girl scrambled back over the rubble. The timing was tricky—jump too soon and get spotted; jump too late and be crushed beneath tons of rock. The bed started tilting. Miriam leaped out, lost to sight in the dust cloud.

Stepping up on the bed gate, Lebedev flexed to jump. And overcompensated. And dove headfirst out the back.

Landing with an oof! he heard the releases on the gate give way. He sighed fatalistically and prepared to be flattened.

Strong hands grabbed him by the collar, hauling him back as an avalanche of rock poured from the bed. He was dragged through the rubble, his hands firmly pressed over his face. "Doctor Lebedev, you're alright." Tentatively, he pulled the palms from his eyes. The voice seemed to be telling the truth, he noted, patting his legs and torso.

Miriam smiled down at him, offering a hand. The willowy tech was certainly stronger than she looked.

"Euh, *spasibo*," he said, accepting the help up.

He readjusted his headset as the two skirted the mound of raw benzkamen. Miriam was an inky contour ahead of him, he noted with satisfaction. He'd insisted they both dress in dark blue. Military types always favored black out of a totemic belief that it was somehow tougher, but scientifically Lebedev was convinced that blue camouflaged better at night.

Lights stabbed through the darkness. A rumbling vehicle was headed their way. They dove behind a benzkamen pile, ready for trouble. The vehicle shifted rightward and its hulking silhouette came into view, one of the tracked industrial 'bots used to feed the conveyor belt between the feed point and the MTP. In his shock from almost being crushed, Lebedev had forgotten their existence.

Keeping in the shadow of the conveyor, the two crept toward the MTP. The structure towered over the landscape, at least six stories in height. Inside he could see the glow of flame as the benzkamen melted into a petrol-like fluid called kerogen. Steam poured out funnels atop the structure and a sluice kept a steady flow of waste water pumping down the channel to the holding pond.

On several of the catwalks circling the MTP he saw guards pulling watch. Hopefully none had night vision gear or they were likely to be spotted. Luckily, night binos were in short supply in Providence .

They sheltered under the conveyor. "Now detka," he said softly, though the grinding of the belt overhead would drown him out past a few meters. "You know how to correctly set charge, da?" In a fatherly impulse he brushed black powder from the girl's nose.

"I do, Doctor Lebedev. I won't let you down—I promise."

"Clever girl! Call me after charge is set. And good luck to you."

The girl grinned impishly, flashing the strange, four-fingered hand sign he'd noticed his apprentices using with each other. Awkwardly, he repeated it back. In a moment she was gone, off to demolish the petrol holding tank on the far side of the plant.

He shifted attention to his own task. The liquid hydrogen tank sat on a tall, concrete pedestal. Reaching it meant climbing to the second floor catwalk and then crossing the gantry from the MTP to the tank. Unfortunately, a guard paced squarely in the middle of the gantry.

Dodging from one support beam to another, he made his way to the external staircase. Just before starting up he heard footsteps ring on the catwalk overhead. A tan-coveralled workman descended the stairs right above him. As soon as he was gone, Lebedev climbed the stairs, crouching at the top. A pair of guards disappeared around the corner, chatting in Russian. Roving patrols injected a troubling element of randomness into the equation; he must be swift.

He charged the silenced pistol, feeding a round into the chamber as he stepped out onto the gantry. He took a deep breath and leveled the weapon at the guard. The Abkhazi dropped his rifle in shock as Lebedev squeezed the trigger.

Click sounded the pistol.

"Nyet! Not again!" He had charged the weapon with the safety on. It wouldn't work that way. He was always doing that.

With a frustrated growl, he tossed the weapon at the soldier's head and charged across the gantry. The man's hands were high to protect his face as Lebedev collided with his middle. With all the force his spindly legs could muster, the pint-sized Belarusian drove the larger man backward, spilling him over the low railing. The guard struck the concrete below with a hollow crunch.

Lebedev barely stopped himself from following the guard in his fall. He pushed off the railing and turned to the liquid hydrogen tank. Out came the canister of pressurized explosive. With broad arcs of his hand he coated the side of the tank with explosive foam.

"I've always wanted to try this. . ." he said to himself conversationally, finishing the coating with a flourish. The pyromaniac in him cartwheeled in anticipation of the upcoming detonation.

Suddenly, a deep voice barked from below. "You there! Stop! Do not move!"

ڡ ڡ

Nabil followed behind Ariane's father, running a finger under the tight collar of the formal Abkhazi tunic. Even as a civilian he'd hated wearing business attire. It felt constricting.

Laurent Mireault stunk of fear and alcohol. In spite of the frigid air the man's bald head ran with sweat. Nabil worried he might be weighing betrayal. He hated collaborators with all his guts—the Abkhazi used them back home in their purges. If Mireault gave them up, Nabil's last act would be to kill the traitor with his hands.

He cast a sidelong look at Mafouz, one of several ethnic Abkhazi in the Irregulars. Mafouz was a descendant of one of the many families that chose to stay on the peninsula when the land was sold to New Geneva, rather than return to the Khlisti-run "paradise" to the north. He had volunteered for the mission. The two of them were posing as new arrivals from Abkhazia needing training from Mireault, the plant director.

Mafouz did not seem any more comfortable in his business tunic than Nabil, giving him a shaky smile. He carried a briefcase identical to Nabil's, though the handle looked absurdly small clutched in his hammy fist. The man stood well over two meters, with the build of a champion buzkashi player.

The architects had built the factory control center with anything but aesthetics in mind – three stories of ferrocrete surrounded by hard-frozen ornamental plants. Its windows were narrow slits covered with bars, the main entrance a sliding blast door flanked by soldiers.

Mireault held his badge aloft as he approached them. "These two are with me," he said in answer to their questioning looks.

Only one seemed to understand English. "Where are their badges?"

"They are fresh arrived from Abkhazia and I was told to begin training them immediately. The security office won't open until morning. I'll have badges made for them at that time."

Nabil was relieved. Mireault looked to be playing straight, so far.

The guards deliberated, chattering rapidly in gutter-level Russian. Finally the English-speaker punched a code on the door panel and it slid open with a hiss.

Inside, guards patted them down and searched their briefcases as well. Nabil noticed the sensors of a magnetic anomaly detector surrounding the doorframe as he entered, as well as the intakes for a chem-sniffer. Anyone bringing in a bomb or gun would be nabbed immediately.

Good thing none of them were packing.

"Go in," the guard said flatly, opening a much lighter transplastic door for them to enter the main level of the center.

Once past security, Mafouz pantomimed using the urinal. "Which way is bathroom?" he asked, deliberately mangling his English.

"Down the hall and to the left," Mireault answered. He looked between them, likely searching for a cue on what to do next. Nabil had kept him in the dark on the remainder of the plan, not trusting him a millimeter.

Mafouz went to the lavatory while Nabil kept an eye on Mireault. He returned a few minutes later, and Nabil headed for the bathroom. Inside, he popped open his briefcase, ripping out a long piece of its interior. What before looked like molding was revealed to be an improvised blade, whittled to razor-sharpness from a piece of extremely dense polymer. Magnetic Anomaly Detectors were practically infallible with guns, but useless against plastics. He wrapped the base of the knife in coarse tape to make a grip and tucked it up his sleeve.

Now armed, they had Mireault lead them up to the control room, an open chamber with a raised area in the rear. Workstations covered in digital gauges filled the floor, though few were manned so late at night. A gray-suited Theocratic Guardsman kept watch in each corner of the room, unmoving as a statue.

An Abkhazi with the red security badge Nabil was beginning to associate with management walked over to them. Mireault explained the situation to him, mopping at his forehead with a palm. The management type seemed satisfied with the answers.

Now all that was left to do was go through the motions of training and wait for things to start blowing up out on the factory grounds. Nabil hoped the weird little Belarusian came through, or things were going to end ugly.

"Well then," Mireault said, clapping his hands together and smiling a sickly smile. "Let's begin with an overview of reporting procedures, shall we?"

❧ ❧

Entering low, Randal fired from the hip, tagging one of the seated guards. Over him, Pieter squeezed off a burst, stitching rounds across the other guard's chest before he could even reach for the autorifle propped against the table. The force of the rounds rocked the guard off his seat, though they didn't penetrate his armor. A follow-on burst ended him.

It looked like Randal's man might still be moving, so he double tapped him. Totally against the Hegemony laws of war, but those were not worth the parchment they were printed on any longer.

They paused in the foyer, the stench of expended rounds thick around them. "Where's the third one?" he heard Ariane ask in a small voice.

The answer came bouncing around the corner.

Seemingly in slow motion, the group watched as an ugly, oblong-shaped Abkhazi grenade rebounded off the wall and clattered across the floor toward them.

Randal was shoved from behind, hitting the tile floor hard enough to loosen teeth. Pieter vaulted over him, reaching for the grenade. Randal's peripherals caught sight of him scooping up the deadly object, tumbling forward in a roll and tossing it back around the corner.

A half-second later an explosion shattered the air.

Awareness returned slowly to Randal. His eardrums throbbed and spasmed and his brain felt like a poached egg. Plaster dust and smoke clouded the air. He thought he must have checked out for a few seconds. Around him the others were starting to stir.

He crawled to Pieter and rolled him over. His friend was alive, but white-faced and stunned. Blood trickled from his left ear.

"We've got to move," Randal croaked back to the other two. "Ariane, see if you can help him. Pyatt and I will head down." His vision still swam, but by moving slowly it might be possible to walk without falling down or vomiting.

Passing the desk, he took up one of the autorifles. Stealth wasn't a big concern any more.

The basement door flew open and an Abkhazi soldier ran out. He skidded to a halt, eyes wide at the demolished hallway. Pyatt killed him before he could recover his wits.

Randal edged open the door with the autorifle muzzle and peeked down the stairs. It looked clear. The two made their way carefully into the basement.

"What a shop of horrors," Pyatt said, disgust filling his voice.

It was indeed.

A large mahogany desk had been called into service: restraints for wrists and ankles were crudely attached to the top and a metallic box with electrical leads running from it sat on one end. Beside it sat a wheeled tray covered by a towel. Surgical tools lay across the towel, gleaming coldly in the fluorescent lighting.

Near the windows hung various contraptions made of welded metal poles—some inverted triangles, others twisted into even more sinister-looking shapes. Brown patches that had to be dried blood pooled under several of them. "Where are the professors?" Pyatt sounded antsy, with good reason. Enemy reinforcements should be there any time.

Randal scanned the room, spotting what looked to be a janitorial closet at the far end. "Over there, I think."

Just then they heard a scuffling from behind the furnace. The furnace sat to their rear atop a concrete platform, shadowing everything in that corner of the room. Randal and Pyatt broke right and left, both training their weapons on the furnace and taking cover. "Move where we can see you!" Randal called out in Russian. At least that's what he hoped he had said.

Out stepped a grandfatherly-looking gentleman in a lab coat. The man watched them impassively, holding a scalpel loosely at his side. He gave a small bow and asked in a caring voice, "May I help release you from the prison of this life?"

Randal knew him instantly for what he was, an interrogator for the Scourge. Expression never shifting, the man unexpectedly charged, stabbing with the scalpel. Stomach twisting, Randal shot him down. Red wounds blossomed across the spotless white of the man's coat. Not a man—a monster.

Fists beat against the closet door and they could hear voices calling from inside. The two of them sprinted to the door. Randal broke the lock with the rifle butt. Opening the door they met twelve faces, all blinking at the sudden intrusion of light into the pitch-black of the closet. Every face showed marks of abuse and the tell-tale signs of exhaustion and starvation.

"Please, everyone remain calm, we're going to get you out of here," Randal said, trying to sound encouraging. "Is everyone able to follow me upstairs?"

"M-most of us…" said a gaunt-faced older man. There were patches missing from the hair on his head, as if they'd been ripped out. "Those who can will help the others." A few heads nodded in agreement.

"Randal!" came Ariane's voice across the headset. "Pieter's awake, but very groggy. Some soldiers just came in to investigate. I shot at them and they ran back out. I'm sure they're coming back!"

Almost on top of her came Johnny's transmission. "Sod it, Knox! So much for being sneaky. I heard you all the way 'cross campus."

"We got pounced. Talk to me, Johnny. Are we happy?"

"Yeah, yeah. I got us transport, are you ready for me?"

"Ariane, we're on our way up." He paused a tic. "Johnny, come to the back of the building now. You'll be coming in hot, so be ready."

It was all a matter of timing. He hoped they could evacuate the scientists before the Abkhazi tried their luck against the lone girl holding the front entrance.

So many variables.

15

If you gaze long into an abyss,
the abyss will gaze back into you.
—Friedrich Nietzsche

Lebedev froze as the guard yelled from below. "I am cleaning!" he called back, setting down the empty canister of explosive foam.

Apparently, the guard was unconvinced. Likely the dead body on the ground had made him suspicious. Bullets spanged off the tank near Lebedev. He drew in a deep breath. In theory only an electric charge would detonate the scabbling foam, but it was still a little frightening to watch bullets strike next to it.

"I say do not move!"

"*Nu ladno*, I am staying," Lebedev said, easing a hand into his fanny pack. Activating the detonator, he slipped it out and slapped it onto the foam. He turned and dashed across the gantry, stooping to take up his pistol in passing. Autorifle slugs sparked on the metal grill beneath his feet.

Ahead lay the narrow entryway to the MTP. The open door was solid metal; it looked like a bulkhead hatch on a no-frills spacecraft. Waves of heat and a hellish orange glow emanated from the building.

He heard boots pounding on the staircase. His acquaintance, the guard, would be there shortly. A glance to the right revealed yet another trooper running the catwalk in his direction.

Diving into the MTP, he was assaulted by the oppressive heat. Abkhazi techs stared as he ran through the level, though none moved to stop him. He paused behind an open vat of molten benzkamen, holding back sneezes as the vapors filled his nose.

Dropping the magazine into his palm, he worked the action of the pistol, ejecting the misfed round. Just as he was reloading the piece he heard a brusque voice questioning the workers.

Lebedev popped from behind the vat, firing wildly at the two guards. They scattered, taking cover as their prey unexpectedly turned on them. Not squandering the opportunity, he ran out the opposite side of the MTP, squeezing off a couple more shots to keep them at bay.

Exiting the room, he turned to dash down the catwalk, nearly running into a roving sentry. Apparently the noise of the factory had dampened the weapon retorts coming from the other side—the guard looked as shocked as he did.

Both sprang back, raising their weapons quickdraw-style. Lebedev's light pistol trumped the guard's rifle and he fired first. Despite his best efforts his eyes closed, as they always did when he shot at people.

He heard a scream, followed by a thump. Cracking his eyes he saw the guard laid out with a painful but nonfatal wound in the shoulder. Lebedev stepped over him and hopped the railing. He hugged the support beam and slid to the ground.

"Doctor Lebedev, the charges are set," Miriam said over the headset.

There was no sign of fresh pursuit as he ducked into the shadows. The guards were likely still looking for him several floors up. "Excellent, detka. Blow charge when ready and meet me at water tester."

"Yessir!"

If his young apprentice set the trumpet charge correctly, the area where he stood would soon be filled with flaming petrol. Taking a last look for guards, he made a break for the water tester. This was an automated contraption at the midpoint of the sluiceway running from the MTP to the wastewater pond.

The flash of Miriam's charge caught his eye, and a second later the sound reaching him. A plume of flaming gas climbed forty meters into the sky. Lebedev ran faster, an absurd part of his mind self-conscious about how he ran even while trying to escape immolation. If only his knees wouldn't bang together the way they did.

Small geysers of dirt kicked up nearby. It took him a second to realize people were shooting at him from the factory.

With a trembling hand he took out the remote detonator, flicking up the safety cover with a thumb. Wincing, he pressed the red button at the center of the remote. From behind him the liquid hydrogen tank tore itself apart in a spectacular explosion. There was a moment to reflect that he wasn't nearly far enough away before the shock wave hit him.

As if a giant child were having a tantrum, he was tossed like a plaything. He somersaulted in the air and came down hard on a shoulder, feeling something give. Lying on his back, wheezing for breath through the pain of cracked ribs, he watched his handiwork unfold.

The liquid hydrogen burned hot enough to ignite the materials used in the factory's construction—pipes, catwalks and the rest caught fire. The burst apparently ruptured the vats inside, as lava-like liquid started oozing out of the building. Countless liters of refined petrol poured down the slope from the burst holding tank, feeding the conflagration.

Lebedev wept, the quiet pride in his heart growing as the flames climbed into the night, thick clouds of oily smoke roiling.

It was... beautiful.

He realized he needed to join Miriam. Regretfully he picked himself up, turning from the scene and limping toward the water tester. He mentally added a broken collarbone to his list of injuries. Nearing the water tester, he spotted Miriam. She was waving excitedly. With his good arm he waved back. She did it again, yelling something. He frowned. It would be necessary to reprimand her—yelling wasn't very tactical.

Then she raised a pistol in his direction. "*Nyet*, is me!"

She fired several shots.

A yelp sounded from behind him. Looking back he saw several guards running across the field toward them, their silhouettes flickering in the light of the inferno.

At a shuffling run he reached the girl. "Into the channel, hurry!" he called, giving her a tug with his good arm. The two leaped feet-first into the sluiceway. It was shallow and the grade to the pond was steep.

With the destruction of the factory, the flow of wastewater was a residual trickle. The sluiceway was coated with centimeters of slick scum. They flew like luge riders, eventually splashing into the viscous water of the holding pond.

Crawling from the pond, he spat out a mouthful of its contents, wondering vaguely how many different carcinogens he had just ingested. Miriam's watch cap was gone, her red curls matted to her head. "We should go. They'll be waiting for us."

"After you, my dear," he said through gritted teeth. The slide had played murder on his injuries. "But walk slowly."

৵৽

Everyone ran to the main window as the factory blew itself apart. Although he'd been anticipating it, Nabil still flinched at the scope and suddenness of it all. The four Theocratic Guard troopers shouldered everyone aside, gaping at the disaster. The one with sergeant stripes shouted into his headset. Nabil sidled behind the sergeant, giving a go-ahead nod to Mafouz.

Letting the blade slip from inside his sleeve, Nabil twisted it into a firm grip. With a bound he was on the trooper, one hand grabbing the collar, the other thrusting the blade. Made to stop fast-moving slugs, the trooper's ballistic weave did little to slow the blade as it slid between his ribs.

The guard shuddered, death spasms ripping him from Nabil's grip.

The guard nearest him reacted immediately, despite the confusion. Nabil's vision went white as the man's rifle butt glanced off his forehead, knocking him to the ground. A shot went off somewhere, but there was no time to think about it.

He kicked blindly. His foot connected with the guard's rifle as it lowered for a killshot. Instinctively, Nabil flexed his knees, tightened his abdomen and kipped up to his feet. His vision still foggy, he thrust the shiv where he sensed the guard to be.

The guard was quick; his torso twisted as the strike landed. The blade skittered along his armor uselessly. Reversing the twist, he came back with another buttstroke with the rifle. This one caught Nabil's jaw. Hard.

He fell poleaxed to the ground. Knowing what was coming, he curled up in a defensive ball. A string of rifle shots rang through the room. Nabil shouted in anticipated pain.

Strangely, he didn't seem to be hit. Rubbing his jaw, he blinked to bring the world back into focus.

The guards lay dead nearby. Mafouz's enormous head loomed into view, staring down at him. "One got me too," he said in Russian, grimacing. A dark stain was spreading from down low on his left side. He was gutshot. Painful, but likely survivable for hours, an aloof part of Nabil's brain recollected.

As he stood, trying to ignore the throbbing in his jaw, Nabil saw Mireault emerging from behind a workstation. "I-I'll disengage the emergency overrides," the man said, giving the dead guards a dazed look.

The civilians were wisely keeping to the floor as Mireault stepped over the shift manager, appropriating his workstation. Entering a handful of codes in sequence was all it took to lockdown the control room, sealing the heavy blast doors. It was a delicious irony, Nabil thought. The building was a veritable fortress. With the barbarians inside the gates, the defenses worked equally well against the owners.

"I won't need to override the safety protocols," Mireault called to them, reviewing the monitors on the station. "The devastation is total." Next he pointed out critical systems to Nabil and Mafouz, who obligingly shot them to pieces. Nabil menaced the Abkhazi civilian workers while he sabotaged the place, but he didn't harm them. His strange reaction to killing the young guard at the university was still fresh in his mind.

"That should be it," Mireault said, sounding a little out of breath.

"If any of you follows us," Nabil roared at the civilians, "we will do to you as we have done to the guards!" Nabil pushed out through the fire door, followed by Mafouz and Mireault into the cramped stairwell. This too had conspired to help them, for there were latches only on the interior sides of the doors.

Reaching the ground floor, Nabil waited for a huffing Mireault and a wounded Mafouz to catch up. Easing the door open, he sneaked a single look and then shut it. In his mind's eye he reviewed what he'd seen.

The building was surrounded. Worse, one of the gigantic anti-aircraft crawlers was flashing around a floodlight. They wouldn't make it five meters before they were cut down.

"Leave the rifles."

"Huh?" Mafouz sounded skeptical.

"We're surrounded; we can't fight through that many."

"But we're as good as dead if we surrender," the big Abkhazi protested.

"Not so hasty, they might just imprison us," Mireault said softly.

"Just trust me," Nabil told Mafouz, ignoring the collaborator. "Drop the gun and conceal your blade."

Holding his breath and gritting teeth, Nabil drew the tip of his blade across his own forehead. Warm blood poured down his face. Scalp wounds bled like mad, but they didn't hurt much. And they always looked worse than they were. "Follow my lead."

Pushing out the fire door, he held his hands high, yelling in Russian, "Oh my brothers, it is terrible! They are killing everyone!" He heard the other two add their laments to his own.

Mafouz dropped to one knee, pressing a hand over his stomach. If he was exaggerating his injuries Nabil doubted it was by much. He looped an arm around Mafouz's shoulders. "My friend, he has been shot! Please, please... is there a doctor?"

Soldiers bustled them away from the building, leading them to a man wearing the crossed dagger insignia of a Captain. He seemed much more concerned with crisis management than with wounded civilians, angrily directing that they be taken to the infirmary. They were herded into a light, wheeled transport. Behind followed a second vehicle carrying a quartet of guards.

Midway through the drive across the compound, Mafouz casually bashed the driver and tossed him from the vehicle, while Nabil grabbed the controls to keep the thing on the road. Shots punctured the rear gate of the vehicle as their escorts caught on. Nabil slid into the driver's seat, weaving to throw off their aim.

No one fired from the guard towers as he speeded out of the compound. Likely they were off vainly fighting the fire. The driver's rifle rested by his leg, butt on the floorboard. He handed it back to Mafouz, who started plinking away at their pursuers.

The two trucks raced through the abandoned suburbs, exchanging poorly aimed shots. He couldn't blame Mafouz; firing from a moving vehicle was difficult.

Suddenly, the rear end of the truck slid sideways, the whole thing bucking as a rear tire shredded itself, cored by an unlucky shot. By some miracle, Nabil kept it from rolling, bringing the vehicle to a sliding stop in the middle of the street.

The other vehicle skidded to a halt about thirty meters behind, troops diving out and taking cover behind it.

No plan survives first contact with the enemy, thought Nabil. But this one was turning into a real dog's breakfast.

∾≪ ≫∾

While Ariane and a shell-shocked Pieter ushered the scientists out the back, Randal and Pyatt held off the Abkhazi probing the front. So far their response time was slower than he'd dared hope—the majority must be out playing hide-and-seek with the Headhunters.

"We're loaded, Randal," came Ariane's voice across the headset.

"Roger, we're moving." Firing a last burst from the autorifle he'd taken from a downed guard, Randal led Pyatt out the rear exit.

Johnny and his stolen transport were waiting. The primitive internal combustion engine rumbled inside the thing, belching fumes which hung heavy in the freezing air. It was one of the three-axled, wheeled variety the Abkhazi favored. The squinting, bewildered faces of the scientists peered out the back.

He climbed up into the cloth-covered bed, finding a spot near Ariane. Pyatt teetered on the lift gate and then fell inside as Johnny took off without warning. The pilot charted his own course, tossing everyone around as he narrowly averted disaster several times, slaloming madly between buildings and obstacles.

Randal found Ariane's hand. She squeezed back tightly as Johnny sideswiped a building, the screech of it horrible inside the space.

Round holes appeared in the cloth of the cover, spears of light shining in from the streetlamps. It took Randal a second to realize they were taking fire. "Everyone down!" He impelled Ariane to the floor, covering her body with his own. They clung to one another in the darkness.

Someone grunted nearby. Randal heard the meaty thud as a round struck whomever it was. Sticky warmth made the floor slick, soaking through his fatigues. Selfishly, he hoped it wasn't one of his people.

He lifted his head for a look and saw they were nearly clear of the campus. From there it was only a short trip to their destination, a skimmer Johnny had prepped several hours before the operation. Their pursuers were receding from view, the speeding truck leaving them far behind. It all looked to be working out nicely.

When the mine first exploded, Randal wasn't sure what had happened. One moment the truck was bouncing across open field, the next it was hurtling uncontrolled through hedges, across the street and through a storefront. The journey bled off much of the truck's momentum, but everyone still ended up in a tangle of limbs at the front of the transport bed.

No one moved for a time, molded together by the crash into a dazed, unthinking lump. Positioned near the back, Randal and Ariane were among the first to recover and tumble out of the truck. "I'll see to the injured," Ariane said, holding onto the bumper to steady herself. Randal felt a flash of admiration at her presence of mind.

"I'll check on Johnny."

Afraid of what he might find, he tore open the crumpled driver's door. The pilot lay slumped over the instrument panel. His forehead was one big bruise from the looks of it. Randal had to give him credit though; the controls were still gripped in his fists. After laying Johnny out next to the truck, Randal belatedly remembered to check on their pursuers.

Looted pharmacy shelves lay helter-skelter in the truck's wake. He clambered over them on his way to the store entrance, scanning the street for enemy soldiers. Dozens of Abkhazi were crossing the field in columns, taking the safe passages through the minefield.

Unslinging his rifle, Randal downed one. The others dove for what cover they could find. He shouted over the headset, "Pyatt—Johnny is down. Can you handle a skimmer? We've got to get the brain trust out of here!"

The reply sounded reluctant. "Yeah, yeah I can. Somewhat."

"That's more than I can do. I'll hold these off. You go grab it riki tik, okay?"

"I'm on it."

Randal ducked below the sill as a welter of incoming rounds struck near the window. He keyed a different freq on the headset. "Lieutenant Shin, what's your sitch?"

"We've finally broken contact. En route to rendezvous point."

"Negative, negative. We're pinned down in a pharmacy on Leominster Street, just south of the campus. How soon can you be here?"

"Perhaps ten minutes. The Headhunters will come for you. Shin out."

Randal rose up, sighted quickly, fired and dropped back down. He thought he winged one, but didn't want to be exposed long enough to see. He would have to shoot sparingly—there was only a single clip for the autorifle, and the SMG was nearly spent as well. Keeping low, he crawled to a new firing point. They had him clocked at the first one.

Plaster chips stung his cheeks as more near-misses impacted around him. Ten minutes might as well be ten years. He couldn't hold that long.

A dark thought began to form in his mind.

The brain trust was too important to be allowed to fall back into enemy hands. The knowledge they held would allow the Abkhazi to field a nightmare array of new weapons. He couldn't let them be recaptured.

What were twelve souls when weighed against the lives of an entire nation?

Popping up to take another shot, he shoved the temptation angrily aside. Such moral calculus repulsed him. Still, the thought returned unbidden as he reflexively fired, shifted position and fired again. When the time came, he wasn't sure what he would do.

❧

The three crouched behind the broken-down transport, Mafouz clutching their sole weapon.

Nabil risked a look around the nose of the truck. The Abkhazi weren't advancing yet, but it was just a matter of time. "We'll have to make a run for it."

"Please don't leave me behind," Mireault said, a pleading note entering his voice.

"No one is getting left." He answered him scornfully, but the collaborator wasn't far off the mark. If he wasn't Ariane's father, Nabil would cheerfully have cut him and chummed him to the sharks pursuing them.

"No, I'm staying."

They both looked at Mafouz in surprise. "What are you talking about? Prepare to move out."

"I cannot run like this. And without covering fire they will cut you down before you even make the sidewalk."

Nabil swallowed hard, nodding. The logic was unassailable; Mafouz would stay.

Clasping the man's hand in his own, he said softly in Russian, "Greater love has no man than he lay down his life for a friend. Your sacrifice will be remembered, brother." The two embraced, kissing each other's cheeks.

Mafouz fired over the nose of the vehicle while Mireault and Nabil ran for the nearest cover.

As they disappeared into the safety of snow-covered suburban lawns, Nabil spared a last glance backward at his friend. Mafouz stood recklessly, trading shots as bullets rocked and cratered the transport.

Nabil and Mireault eventually reached the rally point. Inside the garage of the appropriated house waited two fast groundcars, blankets, and the stewed birch bark that substituted for tea those days. A relief team was stationed inside the house. Nabil gave them Mafouz's location, but knew sadly what they would find.

One of the apprentice medics was bandaging his scalp wound when a battered-looking Lebedev stumbled in. Both shared a tired smile. The redhead with Lebedev flashed him a victory sign.

It was then Nabil realized they had actually done it. Losing Mafouz had loomed so large he'd lost sight of that fact. His friend died accomplishing something glorious—Nabil refused to mourn that.

And with dawning recognition, Nabil realized the fires of his vengeance were gone. Mafouz had shown him another way. While he didn't fully understand it yet, he knew he could move on at last and let the dead bury their dead.

❧

The rifle kicked against Randal's shoulder, but stopped abruptly. A short burst.

In denial, he flipped the rifle to its side, howling in frustration. The readout blinked EMPTY. He tossed the useless weapon aside.

The Abkhazi were almost upon him and it was at least five minutes until the Headhunters would arrive. By then he'd be a corpse and the brain trust captive again. The only alternative was to kill the scientists before they could be captured. It was murder, plain and simple, but he saw no other way. People said that sin was a choice, that God always left a way of escape. Those people had never fought the Abkhazi. With a queasy feeling, he unslung the submachine gun.

He crawled back the few meters to where the unsuspecting scientists waited, unaware their defender was soon to turn on them. He couldn't let the Abkhazi have them. They were huddled together, sheltering beside the truck. They looked like sheep. No, he thought, like lambs. A shudder twisted up his insides.

"I'm so sorry," he said, standing over them. "The Abkhazi are going to take us, and I can't allow you to fall into their hands again." His tone sounded so reasonable in his ears. Madman reasonable. Why tell them at all? What was he looking for... absolution?

They turned their faces away, a low wail rising collectively from the group.

Randal was only hazily aware of Ariane tugging at his arm as he raised the SMG.

"Are you insane, Randal? What are you playing at?"

"Leave off, Ariane. This has to happen."

"You aren't God! These people are innocent—you can't do this!"

"God's had enough chances." Randal tore his arm from her grasp and tracked the SMG over the scientists before settling on the first victim. His finger tightened on the trigger.

From outside the store came a flash of light, followed by the shock wave of an explosion.

The blast pulled Randal back from the abyss and knocked him to his knees. The strange, red miasma slowly cleared from his mind. He turned and ran back to the storefront, taking cover behind rubble. It was hard to see what was happening for all the debris in the air.

Another explosion sent dirt fountaining up across the street. Then the throaty growl of a chain gun erupted; screams of the wounded filled the night.

The Abkhazi turned from the pharmacy, settling into a firefight with Randal's unseen rescuers. Small arms crackled on both sides, drowned out repeatedly by the booming of the cannon. In the face of the withering cannon and chain gun fire the Abkhazi broke, retreating in disorder back to the campus.

A tank clanked into view, one of the giant Behemot-class models. A dozen Headhunter guerrillas rode on the back. Lieutenant Shin stood peacock-proud in the officer's cupola, his shark-tooth smile visible even from a distance. "Sorry we are early! After we killed the tank's owners, they no longer needed it!"

Randal was too numb to do anything but raise a few fingers in greeting.

"Knox," came Pyatt over the headset. "I'm inbound, ETA two mikes. What's the sitch there—is the LZ hot?"

"Negative. Just put her down. I'll ready the passengers."

He trudged back to the others. The look of horror he saw on each face mirrored his own feelings perfectly.

16

Never despair, but if you do, work in despair.
-Edmund Burke

Euphoria was the only word to describe the mood. Rather than just nipping at the enemy's heel, the Irregulars had taken a chunk of his throat and it felt good. A victory party was in full swing with anyone not on duty crowded into the common room. The quartermaster had even broken open the stores for snacks. It didn't seem to matter that this was little more than stale cookies and vitamin powder punch.

The unit's portable sound system was pulsing so loudly it threatened to bring the rocky ceiling down on the partiers. Everyone had come in their brightest civilian clothes. Dancing was a group affair in New Geneva and the dance area was a whirl of colorful lines and circles.

In a dark corner of the chamber, Randal rested back against the wall, his feet slowly drumming the omnifuel generator he sat upon. Faces of the nearly-murdered scientists kept rising in his mind like Banquo's ghost, reminding him of how very far gone he was. How could he ever trust his own judgment again; how could anyone?

"Why the long face, Kipper? I'm the one that feels like I've got a knitting needle poked in my ear."

Randal managed a smile. He owed Pieter that and a lot more. "What's the prognosis?"

"Your girlfriend is a good little medic. I like her." Pieter took a swig of homebrew from his mug. "Unfortunately, that grenade took out the hearing on this side. After Everything I'll need a new eardrum. It'll only take a week for a clinic to vat-grow me another one."

"After Everything" was the reigning euphemism those days for "If we survive."

"Thanks for saving our tails back there, Pieter. Tossing away that grenade was quick thinking."

Pieter shrugged modestly. "All in a day's work for us true-blue hero types, you know. Just be sure to tell my father when you see him. He'd never believe it from me."

"Still like that, is he?"

"Are you kidding? The man thinks you hung the moon. It'll be good for him to hear I'm not completely witless."

"The least I can do."

Pieter squinted, tut-tutting under his breath. "Will you look at that carousing swine? Who knew Lebedev was such a ladies' man?"

Randal glanced in the direction of Lebedev's party. His acolytes were clustered around, all garbed in the same dark hooded pullovers, all watching him raptly. The man himself looked battered, with taped ribs and an arm sling. Apparently he was relating a story, his excited state making the gestures of his good arm almost paroxysmal. Two women orbited him—one a tall redhead, the other a pinched-looking brunette wearing spectacles of all things.

Randal chuckled in spite of himself. "His people have their own hand sign now. If they start minting membership rings or collecting the Sacred Sayings of Sergei I'll have to step in."

"When the mass suicide comes they'll probably do it with a bomb."

A commotion drew their attention to the far corner. Jeni was keeping Johnny and a much smaller Asian man from each other. Randal could see other Headhunters rising to their feet.

It wasn't hard to guess what had happened. The Headhunters liked their privacy; the whole celebration they'd stayed off by themselves. Jeni, being Korean, was able to mingle freely with them. Very freely. For ages Randal had suspected that Johnny was inarticulately in love with the girl. Likely, he'd had enough of watching Jeni flirt.

"Pieter, would you please go rescue Johnny? This isn't the kind of thing a commander should get in the middle of." His friend rolled his eyes, strolling off unhurriedly.

For the next hour or so, Randal just let the noise and music of the party wash over him. He had no energy to deal with people just then, but he dreaded solitude. The clamor precluded thought; alone he would brood.

Ariane was still nowhere to be seen. Since the mission she had avoided him. He couldn't blame her. Crises revealed what was inside a person, and now she knew what he had hoped to hide for so long—exactly how far he had fallen. It was not just fear or awkwardness holding him back from committing to her; it was the cold lump at his core. He had always had a stoic streak that held his heart back from God and everyone else, but now it was aggravated by war. It was what let him look in the shaving mirror each morning after sending other men to die. Each day his heart became more scarred—twisted, hardened and unfeeling.

The Sergeant-Major's gray, crew-cut dome moved through the crowd in his direction. He walked with his head and chest jutted forward, striding unswervingly toward Randal, knowing that everyone would step aside for him. Randal frowned, well aware that his miserable mood wouldn't deter the Sergeant-Major if there was something on his mind.

He tossed a half-salute to Randal as he neared, stopping a couple paces back. "Good afternoon, Captain Knox." The man always managed to sound like he was standing on a parade ground.

Randal sat up a bit straighter to show respect. "Sergeant-Major."

"Is young Pyatt back from delivering the brain trust to Burnley Gap?"

"Not yet. The villagers are friendly, they have plenty of food in their cavern, and their male-to-female ratio is a lot more favorable than ours. He won't hurry back."

The Sergeant-Major chuckled, though his expression turned pained. "What is that noise those lads are blasting, anyway?"

Although the sound system's memory held a reservoir of forty thousand songs, Randal had noticed nearly everything played came from either the Dream Reality or Psi-Beat music trends beloved by his generation. None of the boys commandeering the system looked old enough to legally vote. Suddenly, Randal felt old. "You're the top enlisted man, Sergeant-Major. Go tell them to program some Malloy Trio or something."

"Ha! Not worth the effort. I actually just came to deliver some news. Sorry to talk shop at the party, Captain." He drew a mem chit from his pocket, tossing it to Randal. "I drew up rosters for our contact teams. Thought you'd want to review them and sign off before I inform the lucky frostbite candidates."

"I'll slot it after the party. How many teams?"

"Two score, four men to a team. There's at least one real woodsman with each."

"That sounds solid. This plan could really pay off come the thaw."

The Sergeant-Major merely nodded, his eyes narrowing. "Not to speak out of turn, but you look like death sucking on a stim-tab, sir. How are you holding up?"

"Me? I'm right as rain."

He didn't seem impressed with the answer. "Uh-huh. Just ensure the Captain doesn't fall into the delusion that he's responsible for everything around here. That's why God created NCOs."

Though it was said jokingly, Randal knew to take it seriously. "Message received, Sergeant-Major. Thanks."

"Don't thank me, son. Thank your recruiter!" Tossing another near-salute, the older man wheeled and made a beeline for the exit, pausing only to bark at a hapless scout to get his hands out of his pockets and stand up straight.

Randal tucked away the memory chit, laying odds on whom the Sergeant-Major might have selected. Though Randal didn't envy the men who were about to be sent into the wilderness, he had seen the wisdom of the plan as soon as the Sergeant-Major had presented it. The Irregulars would soon begin expanding beyond Providence, establishing guerilla units in the surrounding mountains.

It was a good decision on a number of levels.

For one, things were getting cramped in Providence as the movement grew. Even with the cells dispersed throughout town, both above and belowground, too many men were being lost to Abkhazi hunt-and-kill teams. Over time the enemy was honing his skills at ferreting out the Irregulars. Lowering the guerrilla population density could only help. Plus, there was ample forage and game in the mountains. Food was getting scarce and the quartermasters would not mind a few less mouths to feed.

The primary motivation was strategic. Come spring, convoy after convoy would descend from the north on New Geneva, bringing supplies and reinforcements to the beleaguered Abkhazi army. When that time came, Randal was intent upon owning the countryside. Hundreds of small hamlets dotted the isthmus. Undoubtedly most were pacified by the invaders, but it was hoped that many were holed up in the mountains to wait out the war. The plan he and the Sergeant-Major had put together entailed making contact with the villages, enlisting their militias and then welding them into a rural partisan force. From what he knew of history, rural guerrillas were often even deadlier than their city-based cousins.

It was a tall order, but they'd agreed to send some of the better lieutenants and noncoms to oversee things. Their absence would be felt, but if the plan worked it would pay big dividends.

He faked a smile as two young troops congratulated him on the evening's successes. If he had to give that plastic smile one more time he was afraid his face would crack. Hopping from the crate, he went to find Ariane.

The curtain to her chamber was open and he ducked his head inside. Monsieur Mireault sat on a pallet, holding Jean-Marie overhead, tickling his belly with moustache and goatee. The child squirmed in the man's grasp, kicking his chubby legs and calling *"Non, non, non!"* through his giggles. Ariane watched with a bright smile, though she hovered protectively.

"Oh, I... excuse me."

Mireault set the toddler aside, glancing between Randal and his daughter. He seemed to sense something in the air. "Please stay. I was about to take my grandson for a walk. Just let me bundle him up." He wrapped the boy in a jacket and scarf and carried him out, giving Randal a nod in passing.

He seemed a very different man than the one Randal had spoken with not many hours before. Whether it was the reunion with his family or the shock of the previous night's operation, something had shaken Mireault out of his angry despair.

Once they were alone, Randal cleared his throat softly, suddenly unsure why he was there. "I'm sorry to interrupt."

Ariane didn't meet his eyes. "It's good to see you."

"Is it?"

Her chin rose a little at that. "What do you want from me, Randal? You didn't see your face last night. It was terrifying. I don't even know how to act around you right now."

Randal leaned back against the wall, folding his arms. "Please don't pull away from me, Ariane. I need you. You and my faith are the only things holding me together right now."

Ariane gave no answer, sitting down cross-legged on the pallet. Her eyes were shiny when she looked up. Randal felt like a verdict was about to be read. She pointed a finger at him, her hand nearly swallowed by the sleeve of the oversized turtleneck. "Everything you just said is a total lie, Randal."

Recoiling, he didn't even trying to hide his shock. "What?"

"Maybe you've convinced yourself it's true. But I'm not holding you together. Honestly, Randal, you won't let me hold you at all. I'm always at arm's length with you. As soon as I get a glimpse of what's behind your eyes, you slam shut on me again."

His eyes dropped to the floor. There was nothing for him to say.

"As for your faith, were you relying on God when you were about to murder those scientists? It looked more like you were playing God."

Her words tumbled out, as if she were afraid of losing nerve if she paused. "And you're not holding it together. I think you're about one crisis from cracking up."

Eyes closed, Randal ground his teeth. She sounded like Jack. But contrary to what she thought, he'd let her in more than he had anyone else. She stung him in a way Jack never could.

Her voice softened. "I'm not going anywhere. When you get your head on straight, I'll be here waiting for you."

For a long moment they looked at one another. There was so much he felt, so much he wanted to tell her, but there was a block, a disconnect between heart and mind. Everything that came to him sounded either trite or as if he were just trying to mollify her.

In frustration he slammed the meat of his fist against the wall and stalked out of the room.

≈≈

The three-kilometer trek to the surface was interminable. Interminable was a word that played often in Randal's mind those days, almost always in relation to the winter. There seemed to be no end to it—the slate gray skies, the bitter cold which reached even into the belly of the world where they hid.

The exhilaration following their twin victories at the factory and university had long since worn off. In its place had descended a bleakness. The movement had lost its innocence. There was no glory to be won any more, only bare survival to cling to. It was hard to get excited about the wounds they inflicted on the Abkhazi when they only rebounded on defenseless civilians in grisly transference. Pieter's scouts reported mass graves outside the city. Each looked large enough for hundreds upon hundreds of victims.

Trudging toward the surface, Randal did his best to ignore the rumbling in his stomach. Hunger was now a constant companion for all of them. The ancient Greeks had believed hunger taught many lessons, but he wasn't sure what he'd learned so far, other than that he hated it. It was even worse for the civilians—out of necessity the Irregulars kept more of the scarce food they captured than they passed on to others. Some of the elderly and weak were already succumbing to malnutrition.

Always the handmaiden of famine, disease was everywhere. Immune systems weakened by starvation fell prey to illnesses long thought to be eradicated in New Geneva. Ariane's people were surreptitiously making the rounds, but if the situation didn't improve soon the outbreaks would become pandemic. Ethnic cleansing would be unnecessary for the Abkhazi—the Horsemen of pestilence and famine would do the work for them.

The military situation looked just as dark. In the aftermath of the factory raid the enemy had doubled the number of troops stationed in Providence. Granted, they were pulled from the front lines which helped the war effort, but Randal found that was minimal comfort when they were shooting at him.

Worse, as Onegin had warned, the Fist of the Mogdukh had arrived. The Abkhazi special forces were everything rumor and trideo made them out to be.

For the first time in the war the enemy was using Randal's own tactics against him. Each night he still sent teams topside to hunt and demoralize the enemy. Each night, the Fist hunted them in turn. Their commander, Brigadier Tsepashin, seemed to have an intuitive knack for locating his teams. The bodies were always left to be found, every one bearing the Fist's calling card—a black flyer emblazoned with a grinning silver death's head. Not content to play cat and mouse, Tsepashin was also hunting down the guerrillas in their dens. An entire cell of Irregulars had been wiped out on the east side of Providence. With no new recruits available in the city, each death brought the Irregular's a step closer to extinction.

Losses to the Fist's depredations were high, but they weren't worst of it. What was truly harmful was the toll it took on morale. The Irregulars no longer owned the night. Every raid was a run through a gauntlet that might have near-invulnerable armored monsters waiting at the end.

Twice Randal set ambushes for them, dangling his men like live bait. Both times Tsepashin sniffed out the trap, pulling his men before it could be sprung, once even managing to snatch the bait while doing it. Three more deaths for Randal's conscience.

The only bright spot was the sporadic news which filtered in from the south. It was said that Abkhazi morale was awful and desertions were a growing problem. Word had it that the battle lines were stalemated, the crawling advance finally ground to a halt.

He wanted to believe it. It might all be true. Or it might be a way for New Genevan Psy Ops to buck up partisan morale. Who could tell?

Either way, events in the south wouldn't bring him one more bullet for the guns or one more mouthful of food for his hungry troops. Duty kept his field of vision shrunken to the here and now. The war down south might as well have been on one of the moons.

Complicating things, the Abkhazi had partially reopened their supply lines. Despite constant harassment by the Irregulars, they'd succeeded in hacking out an airfield outside Providence and cobbling together the needed ground controls. Fortunately, the low-altitude transports they used were obsolete and there weren't many in their arsenal. Things could be worse.

However, now they seemed poised to turn worse. The wife of one of Randal's men worked in a processing center for the occupation forces. Early that morning the woman had smuggled word to the Irregulars— one of the recent flights from Abkhazia had brought tower components for a suborbital pad.

If true, it had the potential to break the stalemate at the Front. With ready supplies the Abkhazi could launch an early offensive. In spite of heavy losses, their numerical advantage was still crushing.

The suborbitals would be harder to destroy this time. If they were bringing them in, the problem of the reactor cut-outs was obviously solved. Also, new defensive counter-measures were appearing on even the low-altitude transports: multi-directional pulsing lasers to blind incoming missiles; shrapnel packs to destroy them in-close; and canisters which sprayed a cloud of dense chemical mist to block laser-guidance systems. Randal expected to see all of these on the suborbitals.

Their spy knew only that the tower components were stored in a warehouse on the outskirts of the Abbey District, the cultural center of Providence. Luckily there was little commercial zoning in that area and Pieter believed his scouts had the structure pinpointed.

The group reached the main sewer lines about a half kilometer from their target. As they passed through the Abbey District, Randal caught occasional glimpses through the sewer drains—here the Handel Conservatory, there the Terrarium. Abruptly, the man in front of him halted and Randal pulled up short. He had to be careful. Two-point-three meters of armored suit could crush a man's foot without trying.

They were going in heavy for the raid, with Pyatt, Ariane, Nabil and himself all in their LANCER armor. In addition, a squad of Irregulars was included in the op. One of these had enough technical knowledge to differentiate suborbital controls from an automated salad maker, which was more than Randal could do. There wouldn't be any second chances; they needed to destroy the components on the first pass. Once installed, they'd be shielded in a ferrocrete bunker and then even Lebedev's railgun would not be able to touch them.

Nabil was point man for the op. He climbed the metal rungs to the surface, disappearing for several minutes and then sending an all-clear. "Come up. Something around here is interfering with my sensor suite, but that happens a lot in the city. Visual checks clear."

The team formed up in sight of the warehouse, skulking in an alleyway. The building itself was settled on a wide concrete pad cluttered with crates and palletizing equipment which would shield their advance. In front of the building sat two dormant loader 'bots and a group of wheeled delivery transports.

"Two guards out front, two at the back door," Nabil whispered as they circled around to listen. "Low security. They must be relying on secrecy."

"Or else it's a trap," Pyatt said.

Randal scowled. "That's a chance we have to take. There's no option – we have to proceed as if the threat is real. We can't let them reopen their supply lines."

"Maybe we should take a moment to pray for guidance?"

Randal turned his back on the suggestion. "You can pray if you want, Ariane. The rest of you get moving before we're spotted."

Randal and the other armored troopers provided overwatch as the straight-leg Irregulars moved noiselessly toward the warehouse. Each carried a silenced autopistol.

Ten pistols coughed bullets and the guards dropped to the ground.

The armored troops moved in. Without the need for further orders everyone went to their pre-assigned places. Pyatt and a quartet of Irregulars shifted to cover the back, while Ariane and Nabil anchored the defense at the front.

Randal and his technical adviser, Zimmerman, went to the large sliding doors. When planning for the raid they had enhanced the visuals from Pieter's scouts, so they knew what to expect. Holding the door in place was a biometric lock with a retinal scanner. Those stymied even Lebedev, so the plan called for non-technical means. Seizing the lock in an armored fist, Randal then wrenched it right and left, twisting it to scrap. No bells erupted, but undoubtedly silent alarms were being received somewhere. Speed was essential now.

Randal pushed the doors apart and stepped inside, his LMG tracking for enemy troops. No one took a shot at him. Everywhere sat pallet after pallet of ration boxes. His heart sank a moment. Was the intel bad?

"Over there. Those crates by themselves."

He looked to where Zimmerman pointed. "Good eyes. Let's check them."

Extending a climbing spike, he pried the lid from the first crate. Some larger ones say nearby. "I.D. this stuff quick so I can blast it. We have to move." Both peered into the crate as he pulled away the lid.

At the bottom rested a single leaf of paper. It was utterly black. In its center, a silver death's head caught the light.

"It's a trap!" Randal screamed into the comset, making for the exit. "Split to binary teams—Go E and E!"

Escape and Evasion was their only hope. Whatever the ambush entailed, staying and fighting was suicidal.

He half-turned. Zimmerman was still staring into the empty crate, stunned. Beyond him, Randal watched as three of the larger crates smoothly fell open. There was only a second to register the hunched forms that emerged, their matte-black carapaces giving them the look of predatory insects. He was temporarily frozen by the gray death's head emblazoned on each helmet.

A rain of autocannon shells tore into Zimmerman. Engaging jets, Randal leaped behind a tall stack of rations, buying time.

Pyatt's voice rang loud in his ears. "My God! The Fist! We're taking..." The message was lost to static. Jamming, Randal realized bleakly, searching about frantically for a way out.

He switched to his active sensor suite, no longer worried about being detected. The motion sensor showed three wispy readings, all advancing cautiously. Randal gave thanks. Though only marginally, his sensors could overcome the electronic counter-measures of the Fist suits.

Sidestepping, he hunched as incoming fire ripped open the rations above him. He had to act fast, divide and conquer. Soon they would be on him and together they would pull him down like wolves.

17

All combat takes place. . .in a kind of twilight,
which like a fog or moonlight, often tends to make things
seem grotesque and larger than they really are.
—Carl von Clausewitz

Don't let it end like this. Tell them I said something.
—last words of Pancho Villa

Ariane watched Randal and Zimmerman disappear into the warehouse. She and the other half of her binary team moved over to a stationary loader 'bot. Her teammate was a man with the improbable name of Hiranyagarbha Calvin. Since coming to New Geneva, she had met many who had taken on the surname of one of the great churchmen. His was certainly one of the more curious combinations she had encountered.

Stretching out prone behind the 'bot's thick metal loading mandibles, she propped her flechette rifle in place. Nearby, Hiranyagarbha took cover behind one of its manipulator arms.

Across the front lot sat three delivery vehicles. The other Irregulars squatted down behind them. As long as everything went smoothly, Randal should have the components destroyed in no time and they could slip safely away.

A solitary pigeon landed on the loading 'bot and bobbed its way toward Ariane. She eyed it ravenously.

"It's a trap! Go to binary teams, go E and E!" yelled a voice over her comset.

Randal's words froze her heart. Worse was his tone. He sounded frantic. She'd never heard him like that before and whatever could panic him would certainly terrify her. Ariane looked to Hiranyagarbha. He looked at her. It dawned on her that neither of them knew what to do.

That was when the shooting started.

Cannon fire reverberated through the plastic walls of the warehouse. She had the impulse to run inside to Randal, but too much was happening at once. Firing erupted from Pyatt's side of the building. "My God, the Fist! We're taking..." The transmission cut off. Was Pyatt dead?

Wait. The Fist.

Ahead of her, shadows began to move, take shape, and solidify themselves into nightmares. As they crept from the dark places where they hid, Ariane could see them clearly with low-light enhancement. They looked like every fairy-tale monster she had ever been afraid of amalgamated together and put on two legs. They were hulking monsters with chitinous black bodies, oversized arms tipped with claws and an eerie, scuttling walk.

With a whoosh, Hiranyagarbha's anti-armor launcher fired, the laser-guided missilette blasting one of the Fists. The remaining ones opened fire. Ariane yelped, stretching flat behind the loader 'bot. The multi-ton machine shook violently as depleted-uranium rounds riddled it.

Pyatt and two Irregulars hustled around the corner, exchanging fire with pursuers out of her line of sight. Nabil was moving in her direction, zigzagging nimbly and firing on the advancing Fists.

Fighting off the terror threatening to paralyze her, Ariane raised up and shot the flechette rifle almost blindly. It didn't seem likely she had hit anything. She dropped back down.

The sound of tortured metal drew her attention to the rear—just in time to watch the lift gates of the three delivery vehicles being ripped open from within. The two nearby Irregulars barely registered the emerging Fists before they were cut down.

Pyatt turned, letting off an extended burst from his shoulder-mounted autocannon. Two of the Fists dropped.

Her brain freezing in denial, Ariane watched as Pyatt took a stutter-step, his fast-moving gait turning awkward. The armored suit rocked as a second shell punctured it and then a third.

And then the suit froze, still resolutely upright.

"No!" Ariane screamed, raising her rifle. She knew Pyatt was dead already, that the virtual gyroscope of the suit's travel-by-wire system was keeping it upright in spite of its lifeless occupant. The Abkhazi blasted Pyatt's suit once more, knocking it to the ground.

Ariane fired on full-auto. Sparks flashed from the Fist suit as the flechettes deflected uselessly from its tough hide. She nearly shot Nabil in surprise as he dashed into her field of vision.

"Girl, let's go. I'll cover for you." True to his word, he took a knee, driving back Pyatt's murderer with well-placed bursts.

The net was closing in on them. Ariane, Hiranyagarbha and Nabil sprinted toward the Abbey District. The others tried to evade to the south.

As they tore down a narrow alleyway, Ariane was tormented with images of the black-suited demons pursuing them. The tall buildings looming to either side only reinforced the feeling of entrapment. She knew that Hiranyagarbha was slowing them down, unsuited as he was and lugging the rocket launcher. But she couldn't leave him to those things.

"Keep running, don't look back," she heard Nabil say as he dropped behind. His tone brooked no protest. She half-obeyed, watching over a shoulder while continuing to run.

Five or six Fists entered the far side of the alleyway. She watched in awe as Nabil charged them.

&⁓&

The three blips on Randal's motion sensor split up, looking to box him in.

Body checking the tall stack of rations in front of him, Randal sent the mass tumbling on a luckless Fist. Wasting no time in celebration, he dashed to meet the trooper flanking him on the left.

Though imperfectly, his sensors were able to get a lock despite the ground clutter and electronic countermeasures. He fired the autocannon without a visual, trusting his equipment.

It didn't let him down. Dehydrated rations were little impediment to his cannon shells as they flew true, punching into the Abkhazi. An anguished scream came over the Fist's speakers and he went down.

Facing about, Randal watched in surprise as bullet impacts traveled the wall of boxes behind him—seemingly in slow motion, they walked a line in his direction.

The inertia of the chain gun round spun him as it struck the brassard of his arm. Ceramic armor crumbled, blood, flesh and fragments flying.

Acting on instinct he ran, scrambling away from his attacker, hoping to lose him in the labyrinth of crates.

As he ran, his external mics caught a strange whine. An instant later his leg servos pulled a punch-drunk stagger and started moving sluggishly. He ducked into cover, heart racing.

The pain in his arm was intense. The armor was slick with blood. His lower tricep area was mangled, jagged pieces of armor protruding from the wound. Although the round could have taken his entire arm, that was small consolation just then.

He felt the surviving pressure pads around the wound tighten, the life support in his suit working to stem the flow of blood. A sharp stab smarted his hip. A moment later the pain in his arm dulled to manageable levels and a feeling of crisp alertness came over him. The condition monitor had just contributed an analgesic and a stimulant to his bloodstream.

Able to think clearly again, Randal made the connection between the odd noise and his suit's unresponsiveness. The rumors of a man-portable EMP unit must be true. A near-miss of electro-magnetic pulse had scrambled the microprocessors in his suit's legs.

Staying and fighting was lunacy, but the Fists stood between him and the door.

Then he noticed the thin shafts of light entering through the bullet holes in the wall. Of course! The warehouse was essentially a thin plastic shell. After firing off a couple bursts to keep them dancing, he ducked his head and charged the wall, ramming it hard with a shoulder. The brittle plastic shattered, pieces bursting outward.

Coming out on the street, Randal glanced at the sensor projection on his HUD, expecting multiple blips. Nothing showed.

Somehow that bothered him more than if they were waiting for him. They must be stalking his people out there. Stalking Ariane. He looked over the maze of possible routes she might have taken, trying vainly to discern which way she had gone.

A wave of dizziness struck him, and he pushed his worries aside. He needed to reach a safe house before blood loss put him down. The bum leg loosened up as the travel-by-wire system rerouted to bypass the damaged processors. Making for the nearest safe house, he gave thanks to God that he saw no medic suits lying among the dead.

For the first time in weeks he really prayed. "Merciful God, please watch over her."

৶৽

Just as the other scout troopers had done in the mountain pass, Nabil charged impossible odds to save his compatriots. Ariane saw one of the Fists fall to his assault. Another seemed to stagger. Strangely, though their arms were extended toward him, the others didn't seem to be firing at Nabil.

He was almost on them. She saw his jets engage and the scout suit arc through the air. He was jumping into the middle of them.

The graceful parabola was cut short as he plummeted to the ground, falling like a stricken raptor.

There was no time to mourn. Running past an abandoned bistro and a looted digital art gallery, she and Hiranyagarbha came to the Terrarium. "This way," she called to him, nearly losing her footing on ice as she changed direction. "We can lose them in here!"

Shooting out the glass plating on an exit of the Terrarium, she led him inside. The room was wide and high-ceilinged. A few overhead lights were left burning. Holographic projections of famous Terran historical figures stood on stone pedestals around the room. Nothing looked damaged or missing from the place. Apparently, relics of earth didn't offend the Khlisti censors.

Whenever the Hegemony had colonized a planet, they inevitably built Terrariums. Holding together an empire spanning hundreds of star systems required more than just battlecruisers; cultural memory was needed, a vestigial sense of loyalty to mother Terra. Terrariums were a core part of that endeavor—half museum, half temple to the glory of distant Earth.

Before they'd gotten far she heard shouts outside in guttural Russian. "We can't outrun them…" Hiranyagarbha sounded winded.

You can't outrun them, Ariane thought, but repressed the selfish impulse. Nodding, she took up a position behind one of the stone pedestals. Her partner did the same, sheltering under the hologram of a man in flowing blue caftan. Looking up, Ariane saw an Asian figure in black lacquered armor holding a curving sword. His nameplate was printed in both Latin letters and what looked like kanji script. Tokugawa Ieyasu, it read. She looked away quickly; it reminded her too much of the things outside.

A ratcheting sound came from Hiranyagarbha's direction as he chambered another missilette from the boxy, top-mounted clip on the launcher. "I will take the first one," he said, "You target the second."

"All right."

"We will hit them and then run."

The first Fist through the door took the missilette squarely in the breastplate. Between the warhead and the ammo explosions it set off, the suit burst open like an overcooked sausage. Smoke from the launcher's backblast filled the room.

Not even breaking stride, the second armored trooper stepped over his fallen comrade. Ariane fired on him. She was still a terrible shot, but she saw flechettes strike home, mostly in the arm. Then the rifle cycled empty, dying in her hands.

Extending an arm in her direction, the Fist took aim with its cannon. Before closing her eyes in dread, Ariane noticed the weird angle of its barrel.

There was an explosion. Ariane opened her eyes to see the Fist running crazily in a wide loop, one arm dangling limply to the side. Then it fell, face-first.

"You bent the gun barrel—he blew himself up!" she heard Hiranyagarbha yell. "We had better get moving."

Suddenly, a gray death's head emerged from the smoke cloud obscuring the exit. The bulky suit moved with deceptive swiftness, leaping on her instantly. It plucked the useless rifle from her grip and snapped the stock as if it were a twig.

Hiranyagarbha pointed his launcher at the Fist, yelling in what Ariane thought must be Hindi. He had no time to fire as the thing pounced. Its free hand grasped him in curving talons, raising him to eye-level.

Ariane skittered backward, using the distraction to escape.

Glancing over a shoulder, she saw poor Hiranyagarbha struggling to free himself until the thing tossed him dismissively against the wall. A low laugh rumbled behind her. "Where are you going, child? The fun is only beginning."

≈≈≈

Nabil woke up dead.

The world around him was one of impenetrable darkness. It was soundless. And worse, it was not void—it hemmed him in, immobilizing him.

He thrashed against the metaphysical prison. It couldn't be! Where was the heavenly light? The White Throne of Judgment? Perhaps it was Hell. Maybe his hard heart had kept him from Paradise.

He struggled once more to move. It was futile. Howling impotent rage, his words came back to him after traveling no distance at all.

Sweat stung his eyes. The air around him was stale. He breathed shallowly. None of it made any sense. It wasn't until he felt himself being moved that the truth came to him. Only then did he recognize the feel of the pressure pads against his skin and the familiar smell of the suit's plastics.

He was a prisoner inside his own armor. It had lost power. He was blind with no viewscreen; deaf without external mics; mute without speakers. And he had an awful suspicion who was toting his armored coffin.

The sensation of movement stopped after a time. A vibration coursed through the suit, making his teeth chatter. They were cutting him out with a vibratool. He lay still as the dissected sections of armor were pulled free. Whoever his captors were, they'd be on guard just then. Better to wait for an opening than be gunned down in an empty gesture.

He raised an arm to shield his eyes—it felt like they were shining a searchlight at him. Someone pressed a weapon to his temple. "A familiar face," he heard a voice say in Russian. "The Brigadier will be pleased. Very pleased, indeed."

The weapon was pulled away from his head. Its owner pistol-whipped him and then he felt nothing.

꒰꒱

As Ariane ran, the chilling laughter followed her. The Fist didn't gun her down, as he easily could. In fact, he did not even seem in a hurry.

The next section of the museum was a retrospective on flight, with digital projections and physical models of man's progression to space travel. She took no notice of these, mindful only of what lay behind her. Coming to an intersecting hallway, she turned to the left. If only she could find an exit!

Feet pounded on the synthetic marble floors. The echoes grew quickly louder.

She darted into one of the darkened side rooms. Filling the room was a large, white, model of a ziggurat. It was multi-tiered, with statues on the corners of each level. It would be perfect cover until her pursuer ran past. Then she could slip away.

"This impressive building is called the Congressional Palace. It is the meeting place of the Hegemony Senate," a pleasant female voice said, the holographic projection of a young woman appearing beside the model.

Too late, Ariane noticed the motion detector on the display. She searched frantically for a way to turn it off. Inexorably, the virtual guide continued. "The actual Congressional building is located in the European Provinces of Terra, in the city of Brussels."

The light coming from the doorway dimmed.

A black mass blocked the entrance. Now Ariane could see the crescents emblazoned on the thing's shoulders. Crescents for brigadier, she remembered with horror. She was face-to-face with Brigadier Tsepashin himself.

Tsepashin gave a playful sort of hop toward Ariane and then froze. He was toying with her. She ran to the other side of the model, knowing how futile it was. He could take her any moment he chose.

He advanced deliberatively, extending and retracting his claws. "I think I'll make you hurt first. Medic, heal thyself..."

Oblivious, the virtual guide motioned to the various tiers. "The statues on each level represent a different stage in man's development. Here we have hunter-gatherers, a primitive time when mankind survived by preying on animals, and each other."

The Brigadier's jets flared briefly and then he was beside her. It never occurred to her to run or fight. Inside was only a feeling of resignation, of surrender to an inevitability. He seized her by the shoulders, sweeping her to the ground and pinning her. The locks on his helmet popped and it lifted back with a puff of pressurized air. "You rob the game of interest when you let me win."

The face that admonished her would have been frightening even were it not for the eyes, but they were by far the worst – the limpid blue of a frigid winter sky.

Huge hands grasped her helmet, wrenching it open and nearly taking her head with it. He reared back, surprise registering on the impassive face. "What is this? This changes the game." A razor-sharp talon stroked down her cheek. "Your captured friend is a dead man. But you, oh you my dear will be my war prize."

Ariane trembled. Her arms felt powerless, terror enervating her.

And relentlessly the guide kept talking. "Each tier grows progressively more civilized until one reaches the pinnacle of the Congressional Palace. There stands the crest of the Hegemony, the five concentric interlocking rings symbolizing unity. It was sculpted by famed artist Qi Jinghan. The

Hegemony stands at the highest peak of man's development, a glorious era marked by peace, enlightenment, and mutual respect of all persons."

Brigadier Tsepashin's lips curved in a bloodless smile. "I have worked so hard for the Mogdukh. So very hard. Now he has rewarded me." He pressed a massive, armored hand to her forehead, pulling her hair taut and covering it up. She realized what he was doing—imagining her without hair, which all Khlisti found repulsive. He tilted his head, examining her critically. "You will bear many strong children for the Mogdukh, once your genes are cleansed."

That galvanized her. Dying was better than being made a monster's spoil of war.

Gingerly, she eased a hand beneath her back. Tsepashin took no notice. To him she wasn't even there, not really. She was chattel.

She shuddered as his bulk lowered. He sniffed at her, his nose settling in the hollow of her neck, snuffling like an animal.

Fear-numbed fingers skimmed along the contours of the suit's integral medical pack. Hitting a release, she felt a small hatch pop open. A cylindrical object fell into her hand. Biting down on her lip, she swung the tube up swiftly, pressing it to the man's neck. He shouted in pain and surprise, lurching back and pressing a hand to where the hyposyringe had injected him. "Chyort vozmi!" There was barely time to cover her face before the armored palm rocked her. Reality went blurry for a time.

When the cobwebs cleared, she saw that he had fallen to the side. With his central nervous system going haywire, Tsepashin's body started flopping around uncontrollably.

Ariane scooted back out of reach. Tsepashin gave anguished, animalistic yells, firing wildly, junking the model. She ran from the room, sobbing. Behind her the man was leveling the place, shouting twisted fragments of sentences as his tongue refused to obey.

Though she despised him, the effects of the chemical were terrible. When administered to a nerve gas victim it was lifesaving. Given to someone healthy it was almost as bad as the thing it was meant to cure. Ariane ran blindly, wanting only to escape the screams before they drove her mad.

༺༒༻

Pain shot the length of his wounded arm as Randal shifted on the lumpy mattress. If there was a comfortable spot on the thing, he'd yet to find it. It took up nearly the entirety of the tiny room in which he lay.

The candle resting on the nightstand flickered on slanted roof beams only a meter above him. Claustrophobic by nature, he fought the urge to escape.

Nevertheless, he was thankful. Given the pinch he was in, the safe house of Goodwife Onodugo was a godsend. The old woman was not a medic, but she had a cool head and a steady hand with needle and thread. His arm might throb like the devil, but the bleeding was staunched.

The Irregulars had put in a lot of time on the bolt-hole. To make the room they had built false walls on both sides of the attic to keep it symmetrical. After creating the door, they had camouflaged it almost perfectly. And best of all, they had scrounged a load of insulation not long before. If the Abkhazi came through with thermal sensors, as they often did, it would take a ton of what the heathen called luck to spot heat signs through the thick insulation.

With immediate concern for survival gone, Randal had time to brood on the misery of his situation. Another wave of pain from the unanaesthetized wound made his teeth grit. Pain is just weakness leaving the body, he tried telling himself. More troubling than the wound was Ariane's fate. Had she escaped? Was she captured? Was she lying wounded somewhere, waiting for him to help?

Nightmare scenarios kept playing in his head. Time and again he clamped down on them, trying to find the austere comfort of Stoicism. Throughout the course of the war it had never failed him. He was as hard as he needed to be.

But it would not come. All his rationalizations and resolutions not to worry folded when faced with the prospect of losing her. If it was the end, they would never be reconciled. He wished he could go back—he would tell her she was right about everything. He'd tell her anything not to have this gulf between them.

She was right. Out of fear, or callousness, or something, he had held her at arm's length. She deserved better than the limbo he kept her in all the time. Guiltily, he admitted to himself that she was spot on about his faith as well.

Closing his eyes, he prayed. It was awkward at first; he felt guilty, like calling on a friend long neglected. But God was there in the stillness. Soon the feeling passed, replaced with a sense of homecoming.

Out poured all the fears and self-loathing he'd harbored for so long, all the anger. Being a commander was isolating. Always there was the need to seem in control. When it came to weakness or human frailty it came down to this: others may, the commander may not. For months

there had been a tightness in his chest so strong that at times he fought
to pull in a full breath. A centrifugal sense that if he loosened his grip for
even a moment, everything would fly apart.

But there, in the darkness, Randal remembered something he had
lost. God was there to listen, and more, His was the unseen hand behind
it all. Suddenly he saw the larger picture. A person must be faithful to his
calling, but he wasn't God. It was wrong and arrogant to imagine that
somehow he was the decisive factor.

He asked God for Ariane's protection. Then he asked for grace to
accept the answer, whatever form it took. Afterward, lying alone in the
tiny room, Randal's arm still throbbed. There was still a hard knot of
worry in his gut for Ariane.

Subtly, though, it was all different. For the first time in ages he
glimpsed another way. Rather than looking within for strength to per-
severe, he looked outside himself, beyond the space and time of the circumstances threatening to break him. The bleak equanimity of Stoicism
was replaced with a quiet peace.

Most of the candle was puddled in the base of the holder when the
scraping of moving furniture came through the wall. Randal took up his
sidearm from the nightstand, just in case.

The panel was pulled out and Goodwife Onodugo peered through
the opening. The dark skin of her face showed few signs of age, though
the tips of her hair were gone to gray. "A second of you has come looking
for shelter. I hope you don't mind sharing?"

"Of course not. Please send them in. Her in?" The last was a hopeful
question.

"Yes, a young lady. She looks to have been through a hard time. I'll be
back shortly." She disappeared before he could probe further.

A few minutes later the goodwife crawled into the tiny room, pushing a tray with tea and two shriveled baked potatoes. Considering the
famine, Randal knew what a sacrifice they represented. After setting the
tray on the nightstand, the woman checked his dressing and left.

Voices whispered outside and Ariane crawled into the cubicle. She
looked like her own ghost.

Thank God, thank you God, Randal thought over and over. A giddy
feeling of relief passed over him. Behind her the panel was replaced, the
hope chest slid back to cover it. "Ariane, I'm so sorry. You were totally
right the other night. I was a…"

She placed a soft hand over his lips. It trembled where it rested. "Don't
talk, please," she said in a whisper. "Just hold me."

Blowing out the candle, she eased onto the mattress beside him. Through the night he held her tightly with his good arm. For a long time he felt her shake with silent sobs until finally she drifted off.

Now that she was safely returned, he let sleep overtake him.

18

My advice to you is to get married;
if you find a good wife you'll be happy;
if not, you'll become a philosopher.
—Socrates

"*Izmenik*, what color are the ceiling tiles?"

Izmenik—traitor. That's all they would call him. The ridiculousness of the question irritated Nabil, but refusing to answer would only invite a beating. "They are white, doctor."

Hands settled on his shoulders and pressed downward. His knees hung over a metal bar, while his hands rested back on a second one, supporting his bodyweight. Around his neck looped a slender wire garrote, with no more than a centimeter's tolerance. The downward pressure forced the garrote tight. His throat spasmed to draw air.

"Wrong, *izmenik*. They are black."

The hands relented. When he could, Nabil gratefully sucked in lungfuls of air. He had no idea how long the session had continued. Five hours? Half a day? The best estimation he could muster was that he had been a prisoner for a week. The present interrogation was his eighth.

"Your friends in this terrorist band, how numerous are they?" The doctor rounded on him, pressing his face close and smiling. Now he would be kind. Doctor Gvozdyov had the most malleable face Nabil had ever seen—in an instant it could shift from apoplexy to kind concern.

Nabil refused to think of his compatriots, driving them as far from his mind as he could. He would forget them so he could not betray them. He would never become the *izmenik* the doctor named him to be. Never.

It became easier each day to forget them. His world was only the doctor now—the doctor, his cell, and the room they brought him to. Everything was still fuzzy. They woke him for most interrogation sessions with electroconvulsive therapy. That was something he expected. He had seen it used countless times on prisoners in Abkhazia. By awakening him with a mind-numbing electric charge, they hoped to render him groggy and suggestible. He vowed he would not break.

The doctor's cordiality faded. "How numerous are your friends, *izmenik*?"

Nabil managed a wan smile. "A vast host, from every tribe, tongue and nation. . ."

He steeled himself for the inevitable retaliation. Just so long as it wasn't more falaka. The soles of his feet still throbbed from the beating.

An elaborate show was made of deciding his fate. As the doctor opened his mouth to pronounce it, Nabil heard the door open. The garrote wouldn't allow him to see who it was. Regardless, the interruption was welcome.

"What news do you have for us, Doctor Gvozdyov?" The voice was quietly menacing, but there was a slight slurring to it. Nabil knew that voice. He felt his heart shrivel inside his chest.

"Nothing specific yet, Brigadier Tsepashin. But his will is weakening." The doctor smoothed the white lab smock nervously.

Brigadier Tsepashin. Nabil swallowed, barely pushing the lump in his throat past the biting wire. Then the man himself was squatting in front of him, his pale vampyr face nearly nose-to-nose with Nabil. "Here is someone I never expected to see again. . ." Tsepashin spoke almost wonderingly, the long, thin fingers of one hand scuttling down Nabil's face like a white spider.

"I still have the present you left me; I carry it with me wherever I go." The voice was almost kindly. Tsepashin untucked his fatigue blouse, showing Nabil the narrow scar between two of his ribs. "Every breath I take through this artificial lung reminds me of you, my dear friend. You were like a son to me. You were to be my successor. But you betrayed everything to go chasing after the God of the infidels."

The hand grasped Nabil by the chin, hauling his eyes upwards toward Tsepashin's. "Let us see your foreign God deliver you from my hand." Jerking Nabil's chin downward, he left him sputtering for breath, turning to the Scourge interrogator. "He's just sitting there. Burn him or something. Or let me have him alone for a few moments."

The doctor shook his head quickly. "The *izmenik* belongs to the Scourge. I will inform the Fist as soon as he is broken."

Nabil felt gratitude toward the doctor for rescuing him from Tsepashin. No, you idiot, he berated himself. That's what they want you to do, identify with your tormentor.

"These passive measures are unsatisfying and slow. Perhaps more . . . direct means of persuasion should be applied."

"This one is very strong, Brigadier. Beating him has only strengthened his desire to resist. Instead I have put him in a difficult position—he must hold himself up, or he chokes. It is not I who am inflicting pain; he does it to himself because he refuses to cooperate. Do you see?"

Tsepashin grunted. "Very well. I will monitor your progress."

"Of course, Brigadier. I...read the medical report on the nerve agent antidote in your system. I trust all is well?"

A pregnant pause followed. "I am almost fully recovered, doctor. However, if your viewing my private files is a reminder of how far the eyes of the Scourge can reach, I am aware of it. But they do not see everything. Especially where the Fist places the death mark. Remember that."

The doctor sketched a faint inclination of a bow. "All power to the Mogdukh."

"All power."

Relief flooded Nabil as the door closed.

"How many panes are in that window, *izmenik*?"

They were back to the nonsense questions. There were no right answers. For a while he would be peppered with them, but in time he knew the doctor would come back to the subject of his friends. "There is no window. There is only bare wall."

"Wrong! You only refuse to see it!" The choking lasted longer this time.

As he regained his breath, he fought down the black pall of hate welling inside. His hate was burned up in the flames of the refinery; he would not resurrect it. Hating the doctor would be the biggest victory his torturer could win, though the doctor would never understand that.

It was obvious to Nabil what they were doing. They wanted to destroy his will by destroying his mind. Why else take away his name? Why the random switching on and off of the lights, or the clocks which ran quickly forward and sometimes backward? Why the questions that denied what his eyes could plainly see?

His body shook. It was necessary to keep his elbows locked in place now—the muscles in his arms were nearly spent. The temptation was strong to just let go and let the garrote make an end of him. But the doctor would never allow it and it would only bring more pain.

"Doctor," he said, the voice unsteady in his ears. "I have something important to confess."

Gvozdyov clasped hands together, asking expectantly, "Yes? What is it, *izmenik*?"

"I confess that Christ is Lord, and that if you will fall to your knees and ask Him, He will forgive you for what you have done here today." Nabil braced himself for the punishment sure to come. He would remain faithful to the end.

꩜

Reluctantly, Randal tied off the last of the cords binding Nabil's bedroll. There were others who needed it. Already more than a week had passed since he disappeared; it was time to face facts. Nobody went up against a half-dozen Fists and lived. Pyatt's bedding was long since gathered up and redistributed.

Their absence was much more difficult to handle. Pyatt might have been a bit aloof, but he was a natural leader. Nabil was the only real black ops man on the roster. The loss of their powered armor was a disaster of similar scale.

"Onegin sends his congratulations. He was impressed with your work at the factory." Jeni stood in the entry.

"Did he send any food with his congratulations?" Randal patted the bedroll. "I can't believe they actually killed Nabil. If there was anyone I thought Death would take a shine to it was him."

"Funny you should say that…"

"Say again?"

"Onegin passed along something else for you. Nabil isn't dead—he's captured. They're holding him in the penitentiary with the other political prisoners."

"Oh blight. Poor devil." It would be better for Nabil if he were dead than to fall into the hands of the Scourge.

"They're interrogating him, and he's slotted for evolutionary experimentation when they're finished."

Randal looked up sharply. So the Khlisti were up to old tricks. They hadn't wasted any time, it seemed. Human experimentation was one of the key differences separating moderates from Purists. Both looked forward to the leap from flesh to pure spirit, but the Purists were Khlisti in a hurry—they hoped to jump-start the process through arcane and brutal human testing.

It made sense in their twisted worldview. Individual human lives meant nothing; they were only steps in the collective evolution of humanity. Killing an infidel was no crime, because it was merely the ending of a devolved throwback. It was no worse than a farmer culling a sick animal from his herd to protect the others from infection.

Paradoxically, the lethal experimentation was a "mercy." Infidels had no hope for an afterlife, instead simply ceasing to exist after death. There was always the chance, in the Khlisti mind, that the experiment would be a success and give the victim a chance to evolve to pure consciousness and escape the prison of the physical.

"Can Onegin help him? Lebedev could put together a suicide pill if your spy friend can get it to him."

The girl shook her head. "I asked. He'll kill Nabil if he can, but he's not hopeful. Security is drum-tight."

Practical concerns pushed aside worry for his comrade. "We'll need to order another evacuation."

Jeni sighed and nodded. "Just when I was finally getting my digs laid out comfortably. I'll get the HQ staff going with the packing."

"Thanks. Tell them to be ready to move out in two hours. Pieter has directions to the contingency HQ site."

Rather than leaving to carry out the orders, Jeni folded her arms and leaned against the wall, her expression darkening. Sadness was not common to her and it caught his attention. "Something on your mind?"

Jeni took out a rolled pack of bidis, sparking one up before answering. She dragged from it heavily. "I'm worried about Nabil."

"Well, of course. I am too, now that we know where he is."

"No, Randal. There's stuff you don't know anything about. Classified stuff. I guess that really doesn't matter now, does it? Security clearance and all that. . ." She took another drag, shaking her head slowly. "Didn't you ever wonder what a native-born Abkhazi was doing in our military? I mean, that's pretty rare."

"I just always assumed he got out on an exit visa. It happens sometimes. Well, it did before the Purists took over, anyway."

"I wish it was that simple," Jeni answered miserably. "Nabil and Brigadier Tsepashin go way back. I don't even want to imagine what the reunion must be like for him. Nabil was Tsepashin's aide-de-camp."

Randal stared at her in disbelief. She pressed on with the story. "Nabil was a Fist of the Mogdukh, a real fanatic. From what he said in his debriefing, he totally bought into the Khlisti propaganda about infidels being the source of Abkhazia's problems. You can't really blame him, he'd been sent away to a military madrassa when he was seven. He only saw his family in the summer and the rest of the time his head was filled with junk.

"What Nabil didn't know was that while he was busy helping Tsepashin kill off the infidels, his parents had converted to Christianity. They were discovered and shipped to the ghetto in Samarkand. When he found out, he took leave and flew down to try to talk them out of it, thinking they were being duped by foreign spies or something. Instead, he realized they were for real and that all the propaganda he'd been fed about infidels was probably nonsense."

"So he defected then?" Randal asked as Jeni paused to tamp out the bidi. She held up a hand for patience, chaining another smoke.

"No, it gets worse. Nabil goes back to 'work' and finds out Tsepashin has ordered the Samarkand ghetto to be liquidated. He confronts his boss in his chambers, somehow thinking he can help him see reason. Tsepashin tells him that the ghetto was already purged while Nabil was in transit and then denounces him as a heretic for defending his parents. He was just about to call for the guards when Nabil stuck him in the ribs with his guldor pichok.

"So Nabil escapes in the confusion and makes his way overland to the border. It takes almost a month with next to no food. This was back when the Huguenot Division was stationed on the Demilitarized Belt. He makes it through the Belt and surrenders to a forward observer. A friend of mine was on the team that interrogated him. We had to make sure he was for real. After that, all he wanted was a chance to get back at the Abbies. Even though he was Special Forces back in Abkhazia, we couldn't put him into anything requiring a security clearance, so he ended up in the scouts."

It took some time to digest. "To go through all that, and then end up back in Tsepashin's hands. It makes you wonder what God is thinking sometimes, doesn't it? There has to be some reason He let it happen." Even as he spoke the words, Randal realized he meant them.

"You got me, Randy. Listen, I'll go tell the HQ staff to start packing." She sounded resigned. It was the fourth time they'd been forced to evacuate because of captured Irregulars. Tsepashin was relentless in his pursuit, sending hunter-killer teams to follow up any lead on the Irregular's location. After the last incident, the Sergeant-Major had instituted the Guide Corps. Outside of the senior staff, only Guides knew the convoluted path to the HQ.

Nabil knew the path. Even now the Abbies could be moving on them. Nabil was tough, but no one escaped the Scourge unbroken. Images of beetle-like Fists of the Mogdukh scuttling through the tunnels played in Randal's mind.

"On second thought, have HQ ready to bug out in thirty minutes."

"Roger that."

Taking up a canteen, he took a sip of cold birch bark tea. The bitter concoction worked well as an appetite suppressant—an invaluable trait now that rations had dropped from one-quarter to one-fifth standard. Never one to carry extra weight, his frame could now most charitably be called sinewy.

Things could be worse, he thought. That was a quip he had heard several times lately: an Irregular optimist didn't say things would get better, he said things could always be worse.

One bright spot was his relationship with Ariane. The horrors of the ambush and its aftermath had fused them together. Gone was the awkwardness of before. They were a bit irresponsible, talking long into the night. For a long time he had been infatuated, but now that he wasn't pushing her away she revealed sides of herself he was sure others never saw.

A bigger surprise was Jean-Marie. Children were never his strong suit. They couldn't exactly talk books or history, they were too small for rugby, and they would rarely sit still for any length of time. He was usually at a loss with them.

Jean-Marie was different. It was fun teaching him to play soldier. He was definitely the most militant almost-two-year-old Randal had ever met, marching around the headquarters singing the first couple lines of "Lead on, O King Eternal" as best he could. In a way it made Randal sad to see a little boy who knew only war, but Jean-Marie seemed as well-adjusted as anyone could hope. In another year or so he'd begin teaching the boy his Catechism. If there was anything left in a year.

The other good news offsetting his desolate mood was the communiqué that had arrived that morning. Recruiting in the mountain villages was proceeding well. Apparently, word of the Irregulars had filtered out of Providence and many in the hills were anxious to get into the fight. When the thaw came in a few weeks the rural wing of the Irregulars would stand ready.

Laurent Mireault was cleaning his autorifle when Randal reached the room they shared. The aging weapon was broken apart, pieces surrounding the man on his pallet. After Mireault came over to the guerrillas, Randal had given him half his own room as a gesture of respect.

"Are you getting the feel of that weapon yet, sir?"

Mireault smiled sheepishly. "I always hated them. It still feels strange in my hands. Somehow, I think it can sense fear."

The change in the man still amazed Randal. Mireault reminded him of his own father in some ways—he was tough-minded and irascible, but once he made a decision he implemented it decisively. Now that he was an Irregular, the switch was made without a backward glance.

"Sergeant Diaz says you'll be ready to go topside soon." Randal started gathering up his personal gear. "But for now we need to bug out. Our poz has been compromised. Please get your stuff policed up and ready to move in fifteen minutes, sir." It was curious giving orders while remaining deferential.

Mireault nodded, taking the evacuation in stride. "I'll get started."

"Also, I wanted to thank you for your help at the refinery. It wasn't easy for you, I know."

The man waved it off. "I should be thanking you. A good kick in the seat of the pants was just the thing. I still don't believe this supernaturalism you and my daughter put faith in, but what you said that night was what I needed to hear."

Randal started to speak and then thought better of it. He should be focusing on the bug-out and not his personal life.

"You seem like there's something on your mind, Captain Knox."

"Um, yessir. Well, I'd like to ask you for courtship rights. I want to court your daughter, Monsieur Mireault." Until the words were out he hadn't been sure he could say them. He risked a glance at his prospective father-in-law. The man looked dumbfounded.

"You're serious? I assumed you two were just dallying. Why would the Prime Minister's son marry an immigrant's daughter avec un enfant bâtard?"

Obviously not all of Mireault's rough edges had been worn away, Randal thought ruefully.

"Because I love her. And Jean-Marie won't be illegitimate after I take him as my son." He folded hands behind him, pain shooting through his wounded arm. Lifting his chin, he said resolutely, "Monsieur Mireault, I request a suitor's right to court your daughter, Ariane."

Mireault regarded him pensively, fingers twisting at his goatee. "You are granted courtship rights, Randal Knox."

With a quick bow, Randal left to go find Jeni. A woman's point of view was definitely needed. Mireault's voice drew him up short. "If you break her heart I'll gut you like a carp, Captain or no."

꒐꒐

Bright light flooded the cell. Already awake for some time, Nabil covered his eyes against the painful flash. Blinking, he glanced at the clock. It spun lazily backward.

They would come for him soon, he thought. Often now his brain felt sluggish, a sensation like running in chest deep water. Sometimes he had to press hands to the side of his head; he could feel his brain splintering to pieces.

He screamed, pounding the floor. They were taking him away from himself; he could feel it. They wanted him to be them. They wanted to take his mind. He saw things now, things he knew couldn't be, but were there.

Every session now they would bring in other prisoners. Hold this bucket up; if you lower it we will kill this prisoner. But he could not. Every session another died. You killed him. You are no different from us, *izmenik*.

Always came the questions. Always about the past. But what was the past? There was no before, no after, only now. No day, no night, no long nor short, only sleeping and awake.

He nibbled at nails bit to bleeding. Thoughts came so quickly. He must keep control. Closing his eyes, he prayed. Praying held his brain together.

Paul preached to his jailers. Nabil tried to tell the doctor, but the doctor only laughed. The doctor said there was no God there, only the two of them. He said soon there would be no more *izmenik*—he would be the doctor, and the doctor would be him.

Clenching his fists, he shouted, the sound swallowed up by the padding coating the walls of the little room. The doctor lied. It was all lies. All the doctor's pills, all his needles and tricks couldn't kill God. Nabil would not hate, and he would be faithful.

꒐꒐

Randal glumly tossed the stack of hard copies into the burn bin. They were destroyed daily for security reasons. Not that there's anything valuable in that lot anyway, he thought, frowning.

In the two weeks since learning Nabil's whereabouts, Pieter's scouts had maintained cast-iron surveillance on the penitentiary. It was hoped they could find a chink in the structure's defenses. Each day it seemed less likely.

Jeni breezed in, tossing a stack of hand-written notes on his folding desk.

"Good news for me today? I could use some."

"I'll give you the bad news first." The slender Asian woman plopped down on a battered chair opposite him. "My network says the pyres for the dead don't even shut down at night any more. It isn't just the elderly and the sick these days, Randy. Granted, most of the deaths are from disease, but the famine is getting critical."

He wished Jeni wouldn't look at him like she expected a solution. Of all people, she knew his limitations. She was always the first person to point them out. "The Abkhazi are starving now, too. What little food they have they're guarding tightly. But I'll really see what I can do." She seemed unsatisfied with that, but he doubted she had a better idea. "So is there good news?"

Her face lit up. Leaning forward, she rifled through the notes, handing one across to him.

He read it by the light of his chemlamp. "The first supply convoy from Abkhazia muscled its way through the snow yesterday. Our recruits in the countryside annihilated it. The Abbies might as well have been on parade, for all the security they'd deployed." Randal grinned. "That's great! They won't be so easily surprised next time, but this has got to be a huge kick in the teeth for their morale."

"The other nice tidbit is this—I tallied the troop estimates I gleaned from each of my goodwives' spot reports. The Abkhazi really seem to be pulling troops southward. A few of the security sub-stations are closed down entirely."

That got his attention. "So maybe things really are going badly for them at the front. I didn't let myself believe it before."

"Exactly. I'd worried it might just be some Psy Ops ploy, but this is a very good sign." She examined her nails. "So... how goes the courtship?"

Despite his best effort, he felt blood warm his cheeks. "It isn't."

"It's been a week. You mean you still haven't asked her?"

"I'm going to. We build to that."

"Well, is this romance thing all it's cracked up to be?"

Randal grinned. "It's wonderful. I'd read everything written about love from the Greeks to Stendhal. It's nice to finally experience it."

"And you're ready for the instant daddy part, right?" She sounded skeptical. "I remember how agitated you were around Van Loon's kid."

He chewed his electronic stylus. "I think so. If I can be half the father Van Loon was, I'll be doing good."

"You'll do fine." A glance at her timepiece. "Oh! I have to dash. Onegin put out the sign for an emergency rendezvous this afternoon. The suspense is killing me."

Randal laughed wryly. "I think I'm not the only one with love on the brain."

She strolled to the door, flashing him a gesture considered rude in most inhabited systems.

≈≪≫≈

Jeni threaded the walking path, her boots scuffing through ankle-deep snow. She fiddled unconsciously with the insignia of her Abkhazi uniform as a trio of staff officer types walked by. Starched uniforms covered sleek, well-fed bodies, a marked contrast from the emaciated Abkhazi infantry she was used to seeing. Like in all self-proclaimed utopias, equality was a flexible concept among the Abkhazi.

Black limbs of the chestnut trees lining the path met overhead, coldly beautiful against the flat gray sky. Nearly every tree was stripped of bark by starving civilians.

The path split to circle the man-made lake slowly thawing in the center of the park. Gone were the ducks she remembered feeding. Onegin sat cross-legged at the water's edge, scanning a datapad.

She stopped a polite distance away, waiting to be recognized.

"Hello, Tatyana, my dear. Won't you sit down?" He patted the thermal blanket. "I brought a picnic if you're hungry."

Her eyes widened. Hungry? She was famished.

"That sounds nice," she said, trying not to appear desperate. Onegin broke open an insulated container, pulling out still-steaming shashlik, bread, a shallow bowl of beet soup and some fresh fruit. He poured them each a cup of tea—real tea from the smell, she noted wistfully.

With great effort she slid only one piece of meat or vegetable from the shashlik stick at a time. Besides making her look ridiculous, wolfing the food after such a long period of hunger might make her sick up. That would impress Onegin.

Silence always made Jeni jumpy. "So have you discovered anything about our friend?"

Holding up a finger for patience, Onegin reached into the container, and flicked a switch on the white noise generator concealed within. "Just because I haven't given them reason to suspect me doesn't mean I'm free of surveillance. With the war going badly, scapegoats are needed. They're purging officers left and right." Casting a wary glance around, he waggled a hand. "I haven't gotten to your friend yet. But there are a few angles I'm working."

"Thank you. And thanks for the chow." The suspense of why she was there was getting to her. "So, you wanted to meet?"

"I have something for you."

"For me?" That was a nice surprise.

"For your people. A memory chit." He palmed it to her while passing a pomegranate.

Jeni gave herself a mental kick. She was acting like a girl on her first date.

"On it you will find a recent holo of each of your targets, along with a brief bio. I assume you have a functioning holoprojector?"

"We do. Targets?"

"Targets. Each is known to reside at the Haelbroeck Chateau, approximately twenty kilometers north of Providence."

"I know the place. It's Abkhazi central command, after all." Jeni squeezed the memory chit, feeling the edges dig into her palm. "You want the targets flatlined inside the castle?"

Onegin shook his head, refilling her tea mug. "I don't want you anywhere near that deathtrap, dear Tatyana. But the powers-that-be want it. Very much. And they want it complete not before 2100 March the thirty-third, and not after 2300."

That was perplexing. "Why so specific, chumsley? Dead is dead, right?" Comprehension dawned slowly, and she flashed him a puckish grin. "New Geneva is planning a counter-offensive. It makes perfect sense—nighttime since we've got superior night vision. You want senior staff dead to paralyze the Abbie response time…" She was pretty impressed with herself.

Onegin's expression, however, was utterly level. "You didn't really expect a response to that, I hope." Then the corners of his mouth curled up in a way that told her all she needed to know.

Sitting back, she took some time to absorb the news. For so long they had fought with no end in sight, hoping only to bleed the Abkhazi to exhaustion. The prospect of a decisive counter-strike was dizzying.

"Can your people do it? My case officer will want my analysis."

Jeni shook her head to clear it. "Hmm? Of course they can."

He smiled approvingly. "That's very good news indeed."

It was a first-rate smile. Abkhazi men had never been her first choice, but there was something to him. He was either a good bad man, or a bad good one. Either way was fine with her - she always found a guy with a trace of wickedness more interesting.

"So," she said, leaning in a little closer. "If this goes well, everything should change. Any chance you might come in from the cold? Live a normal life somewhere sane?"

His face neared hers. "Regretfully not. If the soldiers win the war, it will be up to the spies to win the peace." Fleetingly he kissed her cheek, back near the ear.

Eyes still closed, it took her a second to realize he had risen to his feet. "Who knows, dear Tatyana, perhaps I'll look you up when all this is over. With an intelligence network to help me, I should have no difficulty finding you."

Flashing another of those smiles, he left without looking back.

Jeni watched him go, pouring herself another cup of tea. She'd see him again.

❧

Ariane lay on her pallet, legs extended up the wall and crossed, hands resting on her stomach. Soft brown hair fanned out on the pillow. In the dim yellow glow of the chemlamp Randal thought it looked like spilled honey. She was adorable in that position. Then again, there were few things she did those days that were not adorable. "What's the first thing you plan to do, After Everything?"

That gave him pause. When the Irregulars discussed "After Everything," it was usually in the vaguest terms and in the hushed tones one might use to talk about a baby arriving seven months after a wedding. Being Calvinists, no one really believed in luck, but talking about life after the war seemed like a jinx.

"After Everything?" Randal asked, considering the question. "Find a way to contact my folks, I suppose. It always seems too far off to think about. You?"

Her smile was winsome. "I'm going to find a house with a bathtub and a working stove. I'm going to sink into hot water with about a meter of bubbles floating on top. Then I'm going to read a novel with absolutely zero redeeming social value and eat sweets until I'm enormous. And I'm not getting out of the water for a month, no matter how bad I prune up. It won't have the glamour of bathing in underground puddles, but I'll make do."

"I'm changing my answer. That sounds pretty good."

"Doesn't it though?"

One of their long periodic silences settled in. Girls at cotillion had always felt the need to fill every second with chatter. Ariane understood that the context of a moment could sometimes say more than any words that might be spoken.

Stretching out on Jeni's pallet, he folded hands behind his head. It was hard to sound casual as he asked, "But what about after that? What do you hope to do?"

Fingers drummed on her belly. He knew it was as hollow as it sounded. "I'd always hoped to go to medical university and then on to relief work off-planet." A melancholy laugh. "After Jean-Marie was born it was more an escape fantasy than a plan. Being off-planet, no one would know or care who I was."

"I can understand that. The Defense Force was my escape hatch. The gray heads of the Founder's Party had the next thirty years of my life mapped out for me. Growing up, I tried for a long time to be what my father wanted, but I'm just not wired that way. Every time he gives a speech he's electrified. Me, I feel like I'm giving a part of myself away. There'd be nothing left of me when the crowds were done."

She tilted her head back to watch him upside-down. "So what do you want to do? Stay in the military? Become an officer?"

Randal shook his head decidedly at that. "No. I'm proud of what we've done here, but I've had my fill. My hitch was officially up over a month ago. I'm thinking of the Diplomatic Corps." He rolled to his side to face her. "Blessed are the peacemakers and all that."

"I can see you doing that. You kept Pyatt from killing Johnny for months. Preventing intersystem war will be… comment dites-on? Ah, small beans."

"It's funny you should ask about this." His throat was suddenly constricted and dry.

"Oh?"

"Well, yeah. I talked to your father. If you're interested, he's prepared to draw up terms of courtship for us." He bit down on his tongue. It was not the most compellingly worded proposal ever delivered.

Sitting up, he knelt on the pallet and asked again, pronouncing each word deliberately, eyes never leaving hers. "Ariane, if you're willing, I would be honored to court you. I want you for my wife and Jean-Marie for our son."

The girl knelt, facing him across the narrow divide separating the pallets. She searched his face, lower lip pulled in thoughtfully. Just when he began to fear he'd overstepped, she smiled gently. "Of course you may court me, Randal." She stretched a pillow over her lap, twisting bits of it absently. "And thank you for having the courage to do it right. To go to my father. It's important to me that it's done right."

"You know, my family's home church is the National Cathedral."

A hand rose to her hair, unconsciously straightening it. "That church is gigantic. It'll be gorgeous!"

"It'll be watched by half the country," he added wryly. "You'll have to get used to the screamsheets and trideodrones."

"All the more reason to go off-planet, n'est-ce pas?"

Leaning across the divide, he kissed her lightly. "It won't be official until I tell your father."

"Don't be long. I hope he allows for kissing."

"Me too. How about one more just in case?"

19

The tyrant dies and his rule is over;
The martyr dies and his rule begins.
—Søren Kierkegaard

Pain. Everything hurt now always. If only it would stop for a second. How would a second feel? Could a second stretch on like a day? A day is like a thousand years.

Nabil rubbed at the skin of his face. It felt thin, as if he were slowly losing his substance. It was harder to think now, to focus on any one thing.

A light appeared as the door opened and two guards entered. "*Izmenik*, on your feet," one of them said as they lifted him under his arms. They dragged him into the corridor, past the silent faces of guardsmen and workers. Where were they taking him? Lead me not into temptation, but deliver me from evil.

One guard rapped knuckles on a door painted in peeling green and then opened it. Hands twisted Nabil's arm behind him, shoving him into the room. Beyond the door was a desk. Behind the desk sat a man. "Wait outside. I will deal with the *izmenik*," the man told the guards. He smiled and sat on the edge of the desk. "Your Doctor Gvozdyov will not be coming back. He met with an accident."

The man crossed the room and locked the door. He motioned for Nabil to sit. Nabil fell into the chair. "You can call me Onegin when we're alone. Perhaps your friend Jeni mentioned me? I'm here to get you away from these cretins."

Nabil only stared at him slackly for a long while, memories of the outside world slowly resurfacing from the dark place where he had shoved them. "Jeni's contact. . ." he mumbled softly.

"Quite right," the man said, taking a seat on the edge of the desk. He held up a small sheaf of papers. "This is your full confession, where you admit to being a terrorist and tell us everything you know about the resistance. I've put in just enough half-truths to make it credible and enough false trails for the Abkhazi to stumble into ambushes trying to follow them. All I need is your signature and then I can help you."

"Help me?" Help was the farthest thing from his mind. Lot's wife had looked back; he would not. Nabil would gain the crown of life. It was probably all a trap anyway. He turned his eyes to the confession, but the words seemed to skitter senselessly across the pages like black insects. It did not matter. Whatever was on the pages had not come from him.

The man cleared his throat, shooting a glance at the door. "They have you slotted for genetic experimentation. I 'removed' your doctor from the case and replaced him, but there's only so much I can do. I can't get you out of here, but I can save you from a fate worse than death. . ." He spread his hands helplessly, the way Pilate might have.

The words hung in the air and Nabil nodded. He felt almost lucid after a few minutes away from the devised insanity of the interrogation chamber. "I understand." He took the stylus and scrawled his name on the document.

The man stood. "Rest here. I'll go make the arrangements."

Nabil sat quietly in the chair, his mind committing every detail of the drab office to memory. He was not afraid of what was to come; he only hoped it would be over quickly. Under his breath he prayed softly, giving thanks for the trials he had faced. Accepting Christianity had begun as another form of revenge against the Abkhazi, a change of loyalties but not of the heart. It had taken the war to teach him forgiveness of those he hated. Only after forgiving them did he start to comprehend the Forgiveness he had received.

Warm tears slid down his cheeks and he laughed a broken sort of laugh. It was funny. He had only just learned how to live his life and now it was over.

After perhaps an hour, the door opened again. Rather than Onegin, Brigadier Tsepashin entered, his black campaign coat trailing behind him like a cloak.

"The Scourge has decided to execute you rather than experiment," Tsepashin said in a voice cold with rage. "There is nothing I can do to change that. But I have the privilege of being your executioner."

He opened the door. "Come with me, *izmenik*." Nabil stood, meeting his eyes as he crossed to him. All his fear was gone. He felt pity for Tsepashin, striving so hard for something, something so far from the truth. He thought he had won, but soon Nabil would escape the fowler's net. Soon wicked hands would grasp in vain, for Nabil would be gone.

He was led out to a courtyard. In patches where the snow had melted, small tufts of grass were growing—once dead, but called back to life by the sun. Overhead, the sun itself was hidden behind thick clouds. He knew it would return.

An iron hand gripped his neck, pushing Nabil to his knees in the snow. Behind him, Tsepashin's guldor pichok slid from its sheath. He felt the sharp tip of the blade trail down his back. "When this blade enters your heart, you will cease to exist. I am taking away your last hope for immortality, heretic," Tsepashin said gloatingly.

"Whoever seeks to save his life will lose it. Whoever loses his life shall find it. . ." Nabil murmured, pressing folded hands to his lips.

"What did you say?" Tsepashin asked, nudging him with the blade. "I want to remember your final words."

Nabil smiled serenely. "I said I forgive you."

All was still and calm, Tsepashin's angry shouts a world away from him. The weapon shifted and Nabil knew it would come then. There was no fear—He was waiting for him.

A flash of pain, and then all was light.

20

A good plan, violently executed now, is
better than a perfect plan next week.
—General George S. Patton

The Quartermaster's monotone droned endlessly in Randal's ears. Though he could easily read the bad news printed on the hardcopy for himself, the man insisted on reading each item aloud.

"Oil, nil. Wheat flour, nil. Corn meal, nil. One hundred twenty-two kilos dry rice. Thirty cartons shelf-stable milk. Canned goods, nil."

Pieter lacked Randal's forbearance. "Skip the food part—you're making me hungrier."

Nonplussed, the Q-master continued his recitation, omitting the rest of the food items. "Lieutenant Lebedev seems to have solved the propellant shortage for now, sir. He's been working on formulating a crude propellant to reload expended shell casings. Two of the ingredients, sulfur and charcoal, were easy to secure. He's had difficulty locating the third, niter. Happily, this seems to be resolved. By boiling down urine, he's been able to crystallize usable quantities of niter." He flipped through a few sheets of the hardcopy. "There is an attached note requesting that you order everyone to save the contents of their bedpans for him, sir."

Pieter and Randal grinned at each other. Only Lebedev would have tried an experiment like that in the first place.

The sound of hard-heeled boots striking rock carried across the Tactical Ops Center. "Randy, I need you and Pieter. Q-master, get lost. Take everyone else with you."

Giving Jeni a dirty look, Randal dismissed the nervous Quartermaster. "Please excuse us. Good work, by the way. And tell Lebedev that we'll leave no bedpan unturned, so to speak."

Jeni watched impatiently as the Quartermaster gathered the rest of the staff and departed. She motioned Pieter and Randal in close. "Onegin just gave us a new mission. It's ugly." Her eyebrows arched dramatically. "We're going to take out the Abkhazi High Command. In the Haelbroeck Chateau, no less."

Randal felt like he'd just heard his own obituary read.

Pieter's expression was just as shocked. Shifting his stance, he tapped the side of his head. "That's my deaf ear. Say that again, because I know I just misheard you."

A memory chit appeared in the girl's hand. "A list of our targets is on here. Onegin asked if I thought we could do it. I told him of course we could."

Pieter boggled at her, spluttering, "Of course you think we can do it, the only thing you ever see of war is on a tridscreen!"

Afraid Pieter might just take a poke at her and aware that Jeni would probably incapacitate his much-needed lieutenant, Randal stepped in between them. "He has a point, Jeni. I grew up visiting the chateau. It has two hundred fifteen rooms and it's built like a fortress. Even if we got inside, how would we know how to find the targets?"

A blithe little shrug was her response. Chagrin wasn't an emotion Randal would ever associate with Jeni. "Maybe we should slot the mem chit."

They slipped the chit into the TOC's primary computer. This was powered by an omnifuel generator, along with the handful of other electronic devices in the command center. The computer functioned in many roles for them—tabulating recon reports, publishing propaganda leaflets, viewing the images collected by Jeni's Kitchen Klatch and a hundred others. It also supported the unit's sole functioning holoprojector.

The projector was flat and boxy, with a semi-opaque glass top. Jeni keyed up the chit, and the stern visage of an Abkhazi officer appeared.

"Field Marshal Mashkhadov, supreme commander of ground forces," came a narrator's voice. It was distorted, electronically masked. The voice gave a bio of the Field Marshal, along with known habits. Next was Vanguard General Assad, with the same sort of details.

"Cue it up a bit, Jeni. See if there's anything besides a to-do list."

Dizzyingly, the images blended and flickered as Jeni fast-forwarded the data.

"Stop, that's good." A figure sat in a high-backed chair, speaking directly into the camera. The data was edited, the figure digitally masked along with his voice. "At the time of your attack, all of your primaries should be found in the Great Hall."

"Wait." Pieter raised a protesting hand. The image froze. "How can this chap know where they'll be?"

Jeni's smile was impish. It irritated Randal. It was easy for her to be smug, she wasn't going to try and break into the place. "He's right, Jeni. Do they think I'm some kind of magician? This place is a fortress!"

"Randy, if you pull this off I promise it'll be the last rabbit you have to pull out of your hat."

"How do you figure?"

Casting a glance at the door, Jeni answered in a conspiratorial tone, "Because we're hitting these guys simultaneous with the New Genevan counter-offensive."

Pieter just stared, seeming gobsmacked. Randal's legs felt rubbery like after a run. "He told you that?"

"Uh-huh. That's how he knows where they'll be. With a counter-offensive launched against them, they'll all be sequestered in the command center."

The three of them fell silent. After so long a struggle, even the possibility of victory was almost too much to process.

The rest of the mem chit was devoted to overhead recon holos and a listing of the chateau's garrison, which was formidable. "I thought all the satellites were swatted down early on," Pieter said curiously. "These holos look fairly recent."

"Mesopheric Recon Drones," Jeni explained. "They're very new, very slick. Solar powered with a sensor cross-section the size of a cashew. It's got high-powered optics and a microwave burst transmitter to send back its findings. Virtually unlimited range. I want one."

Looking over the holo, Randal was relieved to see that, at least superficially, little had changed around the chateau. Built on the banks of the Zolotaya River, the chateau was an eclectic mix of Loire Valley styles ranging from Louis XIII to Henry IV. Just as mongrel were the decorative aspects of the structure, Renaissance frescoes commingling freely with French Classical cornices.

Though designed to look ancient, Randal knew it was barely forty years old, built by Grandfather Haelbroeck when the venerable patriarch made good at mining. To Randal the extravagance was all too arriviste.

The Knox family was content to live in a modest-sized mansion when not in the Prime Minister's residence.

For all Pieter's pretensions, the Haelbroecks weren't old money. Rather they'd earned it through work and entrepreneurship. Most of New Geneva saw that as something to be proud of, but Randal knew it always irked his friend.

The main body of the chateau was built around an open-air courtyard. From this central courtyard rose a freestanding tower, the "Lanternhouse." This was glass-domed, with the largest chandelier Randal had ever seen hanging at the top. One could see it for kilometers. Magnifying the image, Randal could see communications arrays covering the top of the tower. It was perfect for a commo center.

The front façade of the chateau faced southward. A drawbridge extended from its center to stretch across the demi-moat. Like the moat it crossed, the drawbridge was purely ceremonial—it was permanently affixed to the ground.

The guest wing of the building extended westward from the main body. It was built atop a mason arch bridge that spanned the river but led to nowhere.

On the east side, the demi-moat ended just out of view from the road. All remaining space was taken up by an enormous hedge maze. Around back the garden continued, mostly flowerbeds, sculptures and small trees, all in geometric patterns. Randal remembered vegetables being cultivated as well. Some group of monks back on Terra had done the same at an abbey, and Grandfather Haelbroeck had taken a liking to the idea.

What looked to be a security fence surrounded the chateau; that was a new addition. So were the hover tanks, scout cars and mobile artillery pieces visible in the holo. Parked in the garden out back was a small motor pool, likely skimmers for the staff officers.

"Jeni, magnify this section here," Pieter said, poking his finger into the holo and disrupting it.

The view zoomed to the ridgeline overlooking the chateau. That close, the image became a bit grainy, but they could still see details. Randal spotted what Pieter was getting at. "Good thinking. There's nothing more than that observation post up there."

"Exactly, Kipper. We can drop a double helping of hurt on them from that ridge."

Steepling fingers and tapping them together, Randal nodded. "You two keep all this under wraps. Pieter, start rounding up platoon leaders.

Jeni, please get me a secure channel with the rural wing. They have some hiking to do."

❧❧

The next few days were a flurry of activity at headquarters. Randal felt half-conscious most of the time from hunger and lack of sleep. There was just so much to be done: planning the raid, scouting the site, securing the equipment they would need. Just one aspect of their preparations, slipping rocket launchers and mortars out of the city to the rural wing, consumed hours of planning and organization by itself.

Worse, the longer they planned, the larger the operation grew. It was his own fault, really. He was the one who first conceived of Operation Jabberwocky. The name had seemed appropriate, since they planned to cut off the head of a monster. Ariane had been the only one to get the reference, declaring the codename to be "frabjous."

"It's ambitious, Captain Knox, I'll give you that," Sergeant-Major Wheeler had said, scratching at his bristly gray hair and poring over the map. "If it works it'll be beautiful, but you'll have the devil's time coordinating attacks on twenty sites at once."

Randal couldn't resist a smile. "I won't have a hard time, Sergeant-Major. . . You will. I'll be at the chateau when all this goes off." Randal tapped a spot on the map. "What's your advice: do we expand the raid, or just keep it simple and strike the chateau?"

The Sergeant-Major took a soggy lump of bark from under his lip, tossing it away. Many were chewing it against hunger as it had a way of fooling the belly. Drumming his fingers on the table, he grunted. "It's a gamble, but probably worth it. The more trouble we cause in the city, the slower they'll be to respond to the raid on the chateau. And hopefully the less relief troops they'll have available to send to the front lines."

"That's my thinking too. The Abkhazi are strong, but brittle. If the NGDF counter-offensive succeeds, I think they'll fall apart. Anything we can do to make that happen. . ."

Jeni wandered into the room as he was speaking, squinting to read a small scrap of paper in the dim light. The print looked tiny from what Randal could see. "Don't forget that their command structure is totally centralized," the girl contributed absently as she kept reading. "If you kill the leaders, it'll paralyze their entire army."

"A NATE report from one of your people?" Randal asked, sliding out a chair for her.

"Huh-uh. A dead-letter drop from Onegin," she said, still trying to decipher it. "Nabil's dead—Tsepashin did the execution himself. Whatever Nabil said to him, it really set off Tsepashin. Onegin says he spent the rest of the day bawling out anyone who looked at him." She read further, grinning at something. "He sent us a list of places to booby-trap. Apparently he cooked up a confession from Nabil full of phony Irregular bases. I love this guy!"

Randal spared a moment to mourn Nabil. He had never understood the turbulent scout, but he hoped the man had found peace in the end. He craned his head to take a look at the list of phony bases, but Jeni turned her back to him. "Aw, it says he's going to have to rabbit. Once the Abkhazi figure out the confession was bogus, his shelf-life is going to be short. He wishes us luck, and says he'll. . ." Her words trailed off and she folded the letter and stuffed it away. "The rest is for me."

The Sergeant-Major chuckled, sharing a look with Randal. "When you're done mooning, Lieutenant Cho, give me an update on the search for EGAs and wetsuits."

"We're tracking on that, Sergeant-Major. The Kitchen Klatch has found five dive suits so far, and a half-dozen External Gill Apparatuses."

Randal folded up the map. "It sounds like we've planned everything we can for tonight. Now all that's left to do is—"

"—the impossible!" Jeni finished for him brightly.

21

The starting point for the understanding of war
is the understanding of human nature.
—S.L.A. Marshal

Randal dug armored heels into the silty bottom of the riverbed. He and the other three in powered armor—Ariane, Lebedev, and Mayor Jowett—were each tethered to two or three divers in wetsuits wearing encrypted headsets. It had taken them two hours to get in position, entering the water far up-river and then making slow progress to the chateau.

While Mayor Jowett huddled with them under the river, the other members of the Burnley Gap militia augmented the Irregulars on the ridgeline overlooking the chateau.

They were just one of a score of rural militia cells taking part in Operation Jabberwocky. In addition to the raid on the chateau, almost two dozen strikes were simultaneously taking place on key Abkhazi transport, commo, and supply points.

They'd crossed H-hour about thirty minutes before entering the water. Prior to submerging, he had noticed smoke plumes in the direction of the city. Unless the unnatural glow was a product of wishful thinking, his people were already causing trouble for the enemy.

He was growing impatient with the wait. It was pitch black under the ice. Even on thermal all that registered was the even blue of frozen rock and water, broken only by the orange of the divers. The suit's sensors mapped the surroundings, overlaying green contour lines atop the monotonous blue.

They were sheltered under one of the enormous mason arches supporting the west wing of the chateau. There the river widened and shallowed; Randal could nearly touch the surface. Water conducted sound better than air and when the diversionary force on the ridgeline started shooting, his audio pickups had no problem catching it.

His comset squelched three times, banishing stray thoughts. The forward observer had decided the garrison was distracted and had signaled for Randal to move. Theoretically, it meant the way up topside was clear. "We're GO! Move out," he called to the others.

Extending climbing spikes, he slammed one into a bridge support and began to climb. Shortly, he broke the brittle surface of the ice. A quick visual scan revealed no one waiting to pounce on them. The other three armored bodies surfaced at his side.

Giving a tug on the rope around his waist, he ensured it was still secure. Then as quickly as possible he scaled the structure. Though the sound of the spikes driving into stone was damningly loud in his ears, he knew the din of incoming rocket and mortar fire more than compensated. He felt tension on the rope; the first of his three passengers was free of the water's grip.

He crabwalked his climb to avoid a wide picture window above him. Then he passed the first floor. Glancing below, he saw Shin and two other Headhunters swinging freely, attached by carabineers to the mountaineering rope.

Still no one was wise to them as he passed the second floor. The Abkhazi were likely more concerned with what was shooting at them from outside the walls than the slim probability of infiltrators.

Ariane and Lebedev were keeping up well, but the mayor lagged. The motions of his early-model armor were sluggish and awkward. Randal would never have brought him if the assault team hadn't severely needed beefing up. He imagined Pieter's complaints as the ancient suit jerkily hauled him up the wall, banging him into the rough stone.

The roof was only a few meters past the third floor. He grabbed a piece of cornice molding and started to pull himself on to the roof. His heart skipped as the plaster fleur-de-lis broke off in his hand. He hurriedly jabbed a spike into the wall and pulled himself up onto the roof—a copper-coated hump long oxidized green by the elements. Making some slack in the rope, he looped it around a gargoyle spout and hauled up his passengers.

A minute later everyone was assembled, perched on the narrow ledge abutting the curving roof. They were badly understrength. He had wanted more manpower, but they had only managed to scrounge seven dive suits in town. Mountain ranges made for lousy diving. They skinned out of the suits and pulled gear from their waterproof bags.

Spitting out his EGA, Pieter rubbed at his backside and looked over the edge. "It can't get any worse than that…"

Lieutenant Shin gritted pointed teeth. "Shut up and get out of the dive suit."

"Shin," Randal said, looking to distract him. "Go check the belvedere." He motioned for the others to stay low.

The wiry Korean drew out a double-edged blade, clasping it between his teeth. He slithered up the copper slope, disappearing from view.

Everyone pressed against the roof as a misfired rocket fizzled overhead, fishtailing and narrowly missing the group in its downward plunge. Rockets and shells were exploding regularly in the chateau grounds, lighting the night sky.

"All clear, Captain. I'm in the belvedere," came Shin over the comset.

They picked their way carefully up to him. In peacetime the turret-like belvedere gave lovely views of the nearby mountains. These days though, he and Pieter knew the Abkhazi would be using it as an observation point. As they climbed, the body of an enemy observer slid past them, plunging into the icy water, binoculars clattering after him.

"There was only one," Shin reported. He sounded disappointed. The twin panels of the belvedere's window were wide enough to admit the armored suits.

Randal's metal feet crushed the window bench as he entered. Down a short flight of stairs and he was in the guest wing's prayer chapel. A faded area on the wall marked where the family cross had hung. That angered him in a way he had thought himself inured to by now. As boys, both he and Pieter had been catechized in the chapel by Pieter's mother. It was like having his childhood invaded by the Abkhazi, along with his country.

"Okay, Team One. Form up on me," he said, taking position by the door to the hallway.

"Team Two is on me." Jeni pointed downward over her head. Originally, Randal conceived Shin leading the team tasked with destroying the Abkhazi commo array. Jeni had prevailed upon him to let her come along, telling him she had a plan. Once she was on the team, she had inexorably taken charge.

A glance showed the hallway to be deserted. All the combatants were likely defending the ramparts. At the end of the hall sat a majestic double-helix staircase, fashioned entirely in blue-veined marble. There were three such in the chateau, he remembered. The lines of the staircases were elegant and simple and Randal loved them. They were the only part of the chateau to escape Haelbroeck's parvenu hunger for the gaudy.

Reaching the base of the staircase, the two teams split up. "Okay, you know the layout. Down this next hall and 'round the corner. Then the dirty work begins," Randal said to his people. He pointed to the two Headhunters accompanying the mayor, Ariane and himself. "We don't have the luxury of being nice. We come across anybody, you put them down quick and quiet. Got it?"

The two solemn-faced Koreans nodded. One scratched at a neck covered to the jawline with skirling tattoos.

As Team One pushed into the long hall, Randal could hear Jeni's last minute instructions to her team: "Don't lollygag across the courtyard. I'll make catty remarks at your funeral and no one wants that."

Randal's team set a quick pace down the hall. It was short of running, since armored feet would echo even with their rubberized coating, but they wasted no time. The plush jade-green rug extending the length of the hall helped to muffle their movement. A silver griffin was woven in every four meters. It was the central figure of the Haelbroeck coat of arms, though Randal suspected it was as recent in origin as the Haelbroeck fortune.

He heard a surprised gasp from up ahead. The point man, Lee, fired a silenced burst into one of the bedchambers lining the hall. Passing the room, Randal saw an Abkhazi captain in dress uniform. He sprawled dead, the beige of his tunic blending with the Oriental rug his blood was staining.

The hall seemed endless. Sculptures, paintings and other objets d'art purchased more for objective than aesthetic value lined the walls. It was difficult for Randal to focus; all of it felt so surreal. How many times had he and Pieter played soldiers in that very hall as boys? And now he was there to kill for real.

Killing was the mission, plain and simple. Randal accepted it, but he would never like it.

At last they reached the corner. He raised a hand, calling for a halt. The mayor's old suit took a stutter step before complying. Randal prayed it would survive the mission. He prayed any of them would.

He and the mayor were too conspicuous. One of the Headhunters would need to peek and make sure the path was clear to the Great Hall, their ultimate destination. It was a mere thirty meters away and around the corner.

Just as he turned to motion for a look-see, movement flashed on his viewscreen. Reacting without thinking, he grabbed whomever it was, slinging him to the ground, nearly crushing him. The man fell with a clatter of shoes.

Randal recognized the bruised face staring dazedly up into his own. It was one of the servants. Bunches of shoes lay around him, their strings clutched in his fist. All looked freshly polished. The Headhunters dragged the injured man into the nearest room, leaving a swath of blood from his broken nose.

An arrhythmic clomping sounded from around the corner.

Lee leaned out a second and then pulled back, whispering urgently, "Two Fists. . . This way!" They were probably alerted by the commotion.

"Into the side room, now!" Randal called over the comset. He crouched in the doorway, training his targeting reticule in the direction of the sound. Across the hall the mayor did the same. If the Fists stopped to investigate the blood trail, they were his. If not, things would get interesting with a quickness.

❧ ❧

Jeni's team made a dash across the interior courtyard. Aside from the Lanternhouse tower, only a few benches and a handful of leafless trees broke the smooth plane of square-cut granite. Shin and Pieter led, the two Headhunters flanking. Bringing up the rear was Lebedev, running with his gawky, skipping gait as always. Jeni wondered fleetingly what someone like him was doing in the armored infantry at all.

They approached the Lanternhouse at an oblique angle, the tall wooden doors coming into view as they rounded the tower. Nearly windowless, the tower rose past the chateau walls, capped by a glass dome which showed off the huge chandelier to good effect. Round, gray communications dishes sprouted like mushrooms from the top.

A single Theocratic Guard trooper stood outside the entrance. His eyes were on the castle walls, as if expecting a mob of angry peasants to scale them any minute. Shin's flying kick took him in the head. Jeni had watched the Headhunters practicing taekwondo in the Catacombs. It never seemed practical to her—too much jumping around. The broken tilt of the enemy trooper's neck changed her opinion.

"So far so good! Everyone inside!" she called, giving Lebedev an impatient look. In a suit capable of making fifty kilometers an hour he still lagged behind.

"*Perestan*! Stop I say you!"

Jeni's eyes darted to the top of the wall. Blight! One of the defenders had them spotted. Others were turning to see what the shouting was about. She fired the submachine gun at him for nuisance value and followed the others into the Lanternhouse.

The foyer was empty. Pieter and Lebedev remained at the door. Jeni doubted they could hold it for long, but they would be good speed bumps.

Sprinting onto the main floor, what looked to have been a formal dining room, Jeni found cubicles filled with communications gear. She could just kiss Onegin. His intel was rock-solid as always.

The room was packed with commo techs, all babbling at each other. A senior officer was shouting orders over the noise. Everyone looked on the edge of panic –the counter-offensive in the south must be making progress. Jeni fired warning shots in the air and yelled in Russian, "No one move! Get down on the floor!"

The commo techs gave her pleading, confused looks.

"Reverse that. Down on the floor, then don't move."

Shin and the other two Headhunters assisted, snatching techs by their collars and hauling them to the tiles. She nodded to Shin. He pulled the officer to his feet, bending him over a desk and pressing a machine pistol to the man's temple.

"There we go," she said approvingly, motioning to one of the other techs. "You have something I need. Unless the Communication Officer's Instructions are in my hands in about ten seconds, you'll never get all the pieces of your boss out of that keyboard."

Blubbering, Shin's hostage gestured to an adjoining cubicle before anyone else could respond. That's showing faith in your comrades, thought Jeni. She flipped through the spiral-bound manual, memorizing that day's protocols almost as quickly as her eyes settled on them.

From the foyer came the sound of autofire and the lower chatter of Lebedev's arm-mounted LMG.

"Jeni!" Lebedev called over the com, the nasally voice almost womanish in his excitement. "Fists of the Mogdukh! We have two of them coming, plus many other soldiers. To hurry is obligatory!"

⋙⋘

The pair of Fists rounded the corner. Randal had gotten only a quick look at them in the warehouse. In a well-lit hallway they were even more horrific.

Growing up, he had once heard a theory that the "sons of God" in Genesis who coupled with the "daughters of earth" were demons. If so, their offspring must have resembled these hulking, black-coated monsters with grinning death's heads.

That was his thought during the tense second as they came to the blood trail. Neither Fist paused even a tic before their weapons came up, hungry for a target.

Randal cut loose, bringing his man down with a series of autocannon rounds to center-mass. The burst was cut short, and a flash on his HUD indicated an ammo misfeed.

Across the way, the mayor beat his man to the draw, surprising him with a long stream of LMG rounds, the archaic suit's only weapon. The ferocity of the attack put the Fist off-balance and his return fire went wild. It tore randomly through the walls around him. Unfortunately, the machine gun rounds didn't penetrate the thick breastplate of the Fist suit.

Randal added his own machine gun to the cause, further destabilizing the Fist. A near-miss shattered a vase next to him. Finally they whittled through the armor. The Abkhazi flailed, falling backward through a velvet-covered wall. Even the Haelbroecks resting outside in the family cemetery must have heard the ruckus. The team was pinched for sure.

"Team One, we've got to hurry. Any casualties?"

"A stray round got Harry Kim," Lee said stolidly as he stepped back into the hallway.

"I looked him over—he's gone," Ariane confirmed.

"I'm sorry. We've got to move before reinforcements arrive."

They turned the corner and made for the Great Hall, Randal taking point. A Theocratic Guard piled out from the hall, with several more on his heels. Spotting Randal, they scuttled back inside.

Team One hustled to the double doors, clustering to either side. Randal took a moment to mentally review the room he was about to assault.

The hall was long and open, with a cavernous vaulted ceiling. Overhead, the ceiling was paneled, each section holding a different rendering of a religious theme. Most of the paintings featured a Madonna and Child, but these were likely long-since defaced.

Twin rows of solid wood tables had previously lined the hall, though who knew what the Abkhazi had changed? On the far side of the room sat a raised dais, which could double as a stage. The senior commanders had likely taken the high ground for themselves. A plush velvet curtain covered the rear of the dais, and there was a small emergency exit behind the curtain. Thankfully, the Khlisti way of battle would not allow the enemy officers to flee through it. Nevertheless, the Abkhazi could use it to bring in reinforcements. A kitchen adjoined the room on one side, with an exit leading outside to the garden.

The room was practically windowless, except for some high, clerestory windows too small to admit an enemy counterstrike.

He and Mayor Jowett stood to either side of the double doors, with a Headhunter close on each of them. Holding up three fingers, he counted down to one, and then they kicked open the doors and ducked back behind cover. The two Headhunters popped out for the briefest of seconds, each tossing a smoke grenade into the hall.

Belated answering fire missed the Headhunters, instead shredding a luckless Dutch burgomeester whose painting hung facing the door.

After waiting a few seconds for smoke to suffuse the hall, Randal gave Mayor Jowett a thumbs up. Switching to thermal, the two men entered the room, Randal breaking left, the mayor right.

Rendered in thermal, the hall glowed psychedelically. The heavy dining tables were upended for cover, cool green in the HUD, while tangerine faces of enemy troops appeared and disappeared behind them. Ruby fireworks from enemy rifles were followed an instant later by the impact of light caliber rounds on Randal's suit.

"Follow my lead, Mayor."

Ducking, he sprinted for the front most table. Legs churning, he threw his shoulder into the thing, driving it backward along with the soldiers sheltering behind it. The first table took out the next, and that one the next. Out of the corner of his eye, he saw Mayor Jowett doing the same.

Engaging jump jets, he sailed over the jumbled tables, savaging the stunned Abkhazi with machine gun fire. While returning to ground, he saw that Ariane and the Headhunters had entered the fight.

A downed Abkhazi struggled up from behind one of the tables, poking a flechette rifle into Randal's face at point-blank range. Only his reflexes saved him as he stiff-armed the man, sending him flying onto the dais.

Turning his attention to the dais, Randal took down the handful of defenders still standing. Belatedly, he noticed a man in the back shouting into a comset. Mayor Jowett took him out a moment later.

With no one moving except the wounded, Randal shifted to the unpleasant business of identifying the fallen. "Let's get some air in here!" While the team shot out the windows, Randal activated the facial recognition application on his target acquisition system. Before the operation, Jeni had uploaded the mug shots of the Abkhazi High Command provided by Onegin.

"Don't wait for all the smoke to clear—start grabbing bodies and identifying. Priority is on lieutenant-general and above."

Switching to standard optics, he felt his way carefully through the room, holding the victims up close to his visor, watching as the FR application cycled through the faces chosen by some administrative reaper back in New Geneva. The first one came back as a master sergeant. Randal set him carefully aside. Next came a major, eyes staring sightlessly into his own. He knew these faces would never leave him.

"Vanguard General Assad," Lee reported, moving on to the next body.

Soon after, the other Headhunter called out cheerily, "Lieutenant General Yerikuly, assuming room temperature."

Randal saw Mayor Jowett heading for the dais and moved to follow. Just then, something stirred on the raised platform. The smoke cleared enough for him to see a wounded officer scuttling for the emergency exit. Even with a partial view, the FR application went to work. "It's Field Marshal Mashkhadov! Stop him!" He triggered the light machine gun, but got nothing in return. Only then did he notice the empty ammo gauge on the HUD.

Jowett fired, but the shots went wide. He lumbered after the fleeing Abkhazi commander, hard on his heels as the man tore aside the velvet curtain and threw wide the emergency door. Jowett grabbed the Field Marshal, pulling him into a lethal bear hug.

The first thing Randal saw through the open door was burning shrubbery. The second thing was Brigadier Gregor Tsepashin.

❧

Shin held the communication officer face-down on the keyboard, a machine pistol caressing his scalp. Jeni Cho produced a memory chit from her pocket and pressed it into the officer's hand. "Okay, Shin, let him up—he's going to behave." Switching back to Russian, she pointed to the chit. "There's only one file on there, an audio file. It needs to go out over your Command Net now. You make sure all the protocols are satisfied. Turn up the volume so I can hear."

Shin moved back to help cover the door.

With shaky hands the officer complied, hailing over the ComNet, giving and receiving authentication codes. Jeni made a show of reviewing the Communication Officer's Instructions to keep him honest, but she already had the codes for the day memorized. She would know if he betrayed them.

Watching her with fearful eyes, the man wet his lips nervously and then entered the command to transmit the audio file over the command channel.

"Attention all units! This is Field Marshal Mashkhadov. I have just received orders from the Guardian Council to surrender at once. I repeat: surrender at once. It is with the deepest regret that I order you to lay down your arms, and to surrender to the nearest organized New Genevan unit. May the Mogdukh have mercy upon our spirits."

The officer wept openly, staring at her in horrified wonder. "The Field Marshal would never..."

Jeni cut him off merrily. "Of course he didn't. It's called voice manipulation and intrusion."

The ComNet was flooded with requests for confirmation. No one wanted to believe the news.

"Well, answer them. Tell them to surrender and play nice." She frowned thoughtfully. "Play nice" wasn't exactly in the Abkhazi idiom, and she wondered how his mind would translate the phrase she had imported. It didn't really matter, so long as he didn't sell them out.

One of the Headhunters must have had the same thought, tickling the nape of the man's neck with the cold muzzle of his SMG. The tech shuddered and said over the comset, "No, no. That's correct, you are ordered to surrender. Authentication code *Arlekino—Gromov—Lyotchik*."

An explosion just outside the entrance sent a rush of noise and air through the chamber. Jeni heard Shin yell—it sounded more out of anger than pain.

Lebedev called back to her. "Jeni! One of the Fists is still out there and there are no more autocannon shells. He will try again soon, I think. Also, Shin is hurt badly."

"I scan, Lebedev. Don't worry, we're almost done here." After allowing the communications tech time to authenticate twice more, Jeni blasted the machine. The commanders who were going to buy the deception would be convinced by now; those intent upon fighting to the bitter end wouldn't care a fig about authentication codes anyway.

She and the two Headhunters shot holes in the rest of the commo equipment. "Okay, people, time to evac the area. Don't bunch up crossing the courtyard." She felt silly giving them tactical advice. Of the team, she was the only one with no real combat experience.

"Um, Jeni, Plan A is a no-go." That was Pieter. He sounded scared. From the stairs she saw why. He and Lebedev were firing blind, the volume of incoming rounds too thick for them to reveal themselves long enough to take aim. The only things saving them were the thick walls of the tower and Abkhazi reluctance to destroy their communications center by firing rocket grenades.

Plan A was to sneak in, sneak out, and use the wetsuits and EGAs to swim downstream to safety.

There wasn't really a Plan B.

"Now what?"

"How should I know? You're in charge!" Pieter fired another burst to keep the Abbies at bay. "Wait! Run back to the room beyond the swinging doors. It's a kitchen area. See if there's still a dumbwaiter."

Jeni did what she was told. The kitchen was all prep tables, trays and the like. At the back, set into the wall, was a lift no more than a meter in height. The controls were set into the wall nearby.

"Yes!" Jeni called to Pieter over the headset. "And it looks in working order. Where's it go?"

"To the wine cellar. I've got Shin—we're pulling back to you."

Seconds later the doors swung open, Pieter lugging a bleeding Shin inside. The others followed, firing on the move. Jeni could hear the screams of the techs caught in crossfire.

Standing by the controls, Jeni motioned a Headhunter to the lift. "Get in, no arguments." She engaged the dumbwaiter once he was inside, sending him down.

"You're next, Sergei."

"I'll have to abandon my suit," Lebedev said unhappily. Then, a moment later, "Autodestruct is set. We will not want to be in here in about, oh… three minutes and twenty-five seconds." His helmet flipped back, the knees bent, and the breastplate opened. The little man climbed out. Jeni always thought the process resembled an alien form of reproduction—like mitosis only weirder.

Shin lay by the doors, bleeding from multiple shrapnel wounds but still on the job. "They're charging! Get everyone down quickly!"

She pressed the button, lowering Lebedev. As the lift returned to the top, Jeni heard the pounding of booted feet. The fools were rushing them, vibro-bayonets fixed. A clot of men was trying to squeeze through the door, dying in droves in the narrow space. Three made it into the kitchen. Jeni fired on them, feeling strange as she did. It was one of the first times since Basic Indoc that she had fired a weapon.

Two of her assailants fell. The last thrust his bayonet at her, the weapon level with her stomach. She froze, entranced by the humming blade about to impale her.

Then the man was falling, the tip of his bayonet striking tile, the rifle flipping from his hands and clattering away. He fell at her feet, unmoving. Shin stood over him, breathing shallowly and flashing a bloody smile.

If her SMG was not fastened to a sling she would have dropped it. "Oh God, oh God… I'll go to church more. I'll even give up swearing. Honest." In that moment she actually meant it.

With the bayonet charge repulsed, the Abkhazi took time to rethink things. She imagined the Fist would lead next time. That would roast the team's chestnuts for sure.

"Pieter, into the dumbwaiter, go!" Pieter was many things, but recklessly brave was not among them. He was crammed into the dumbwaiter quicker than she would have imagined possible. She sent him down.

The other Headhunter grunted as a ricochet caught him. Shin checked on the downed man and shook his head. "Just you and me now, Cho," he told her in Korean.

Jeni swallowed. Someone had to stay behind to operate the controls.

Shin hawked, spitting blood. "Get in the lift." He shuffled over to the controls. His shirt clung to his bantam frame, shiny with blood. The mad smile he gave her was garish, all sharp teeth and bloody gums.

For a moment she hesitated. She should say no, should offer to stay instead—the team was her command. But she didn't. "Thank you, Shin."

A torrent of thoughts and emotions flew through her mind during the descent. Was she wrong to go? She felt shame for leaving him to die alone.

Perhaps it was for the best. She imagined him after the war—no family, his mind bent toward death and killing. What sort of life would he have? He would be like a primitive plucked from the wilds and forced to wear pants. Whatever Shin was before the war, he was a killer now. There was no reason to feel guilty.

She grinned the sardonic grin she used on the rest of the world. Only this time it was for herself.

ॐ९०

The black armor seemed to suck all available light into itself, its bulk making the contents of the room seem sized for children. Even as Randal triggered his autocannon, he remembered it was jammed.

Tsepashin killed with clinical efficiency, a single rocket flaring from the shoulder rack toward the mayor while a precise three-round burst from his chain gun eliminated Lee. The mayor's first-generation armor never stood a chance, the blast knocking him back several meters. He didn't get back up.

Randal was scouting for cover when the wall next to him imploded. The world went dark as he sprawled out beneath a fall of shattered brick and mortar. Stunned, he had enough presence of mind to scrabble for the kitchen, croaking out, "Run! It's Tsepashin. . ." Through the newly-formed hole in the wall he saw a hovertank and a squad of Theocratic Guards heading for the breach.

Somehow still standing, the last Headhunter lobbed a smoke grenade at Tsepashin, shouting something in Korean. The Abkhazi contemptu-ously kicked the grenade aside, gunning down the Headhunter almost as an afterthought.

Randal silently thanked the Headhunter, using the distraction to break for the door. Ariane stood stock-still, frozen in place. "Move!" he said, snatching her arm in passing and dragging her toward safety.

Smoke from a cooking fire obscured the kitchen as they entered. The floor tile ran with water from an overflowing sink, the mess crew long since fled. Ariane ran blindly through the room, knocking aside a work island, upsetting a rack of drying pots. He could tell she was terrified. She had never told him what happened the night of the ambush, only that Tsepashin had found her.

Now he was back, and after her once more.

They ran out of the kitchen and into the garden. Rocket and mortar strikes from the Irregulars had set the foliage alight. The ground was sodden, one of the reflecting pools breached and spilling water every-where. Dirt and rock erupted ahead of them as another mortar shell struck home.

In the orange glow of the flames he could see the silhouettes of staff cars up ahead—mid-sized, sleek-looking skimmers.

Ariane pulled up short. "Which way?"

Momentarily unsure, Randal debated internally. Could they reach a skimmer before Tsepashin caught them? Was it better to evade on foot and try to reach the friendlies on the ridgeline?

A clatter from the kitchen decided for him. "This way," he said, giving her a nudge toward the maze. The two sprinted for the hedge wall, the rear of the chateau looming over them.

Ahead lay a pair of broken Abkhazi corpses, the snow around them stained crimson. From their postures he could see they had been blasted from the wall. Randal feared Ariane was hit as she dropped behind. Half-turning, he saw her bend down, scooping up a collapsible rocket launcher from one of the corpses. "I'm coming!"

"Hurry!" Behind her Tsepashin emerged from the kitchen, death's head swiveling, claws flexing and eager to rend.

Randal set his targeting reticule on the thing. Achieving a firm lock, he let loose with his LMG. "Jump, Ariane! Into the maze!"

The slugs rebounded harmlessly from the near-impervious hide of the beast. They did unbalance it, long enough for Randal to follow Ariane into the labyrinthine hedges. These were snow coated, rising three meters into the sky and nearly as thick. The two ran blindly through them, hoping to lose Tsepashin in the maze.

Randal felt as if he were running down a chute to slaughter, like one of the massive, gen-engineered cattle he'd seen out on the Dry Flats.

It was no problem for Randal to outrun Tsepashin. Fist suits sacrificed speed for armor. Medics, though, were never intended for combat and Ariane's suit was woefully slow. It was only a matter of time until he caught them. Randal would buy as much time for her as he could, but short of a miracle...

A dry, rattling laugh rolled over the maze, amplified by speakers.

Ariane stopped, pressing back into the hedge. Randal nearly fell, skidding to a halt on icy granite. "We can't stop, we have to keep moving."

"Promise me you won't let him take me alive." Panic fluttered in her voice.

"I promise. Please come on."

"I mean it, Randal. We both know he's going to catch us. Promise me!"

"When the time comes, I won't hesitate." And he would not. Tsepashin would never touch her.

She seemed satisfied with his answer, setting off at a run. They rounded a corner, skidding to a halt as a black blur flew overhead several meters down the path. The two instinctively ducked as Tsepashin passed out of sight, jump jets flaring. "Do you think he saw us?" Ariane asked in a small voice.

Randal didn't answer, pulling her in the opposite direction. His heart thudded in his chest. It was the worst feeling in the world to have the woman he loved threatened and to know there was almost nothing he could do about it.

They ran down a short straightaway and into a dead end. The crunch of snow underfoot behind them was so faint Randal barely recognized it for what it was.

"Step away from the medic. It would be a pity if she were accidentally damaged." The voice was like cold fog on bare skin.

Randal turned to face Tsepashin. He shifted as if complying with the order, the arm with the machine gun rising subtly. It would be a headshot. She wouldn't have time to hurt with a headshot

Randal nearly swallowed his tongue in shock as flame blossomed around Ariane.

When his visor's flare dampeners reduced the opacity an instant later, he saw the compact rocket tube smoking in her hand. Ariane had fired it from the hip. Tsepashin was sprawled supine in the snow, tendrils of smoke curling from the crater in his breastplate, right over the heart.

Both stared at the downed monster, neither quite comprehending.

"Bloody hell. That was amazing. . ." Randal said when he found his voice again. He rested an armored hand on her shoulder. "We'd better keep moving. There might be others."

"Of course."

With an unearthly snarl, Tsepashin bolted upright. They could see where the warhead had spiderwebbed the armor but failed to penetrate. Ariane had only stunned the beast.

Pushing off from the ground, he clambered to his feet. "Now you will hurt before I kill you, Captain Knox." The voice was pure contempt. "For the girl, I have other plans." A clawed hand rose, the chaingun barrels impossibly wide as Randal stared into them.

Randal crouched and then leaped, engaging his jump jets. He sensed the air being ripped apart above him as Tsepashin fired high, surprised.

With a wrenching sound the two armored figures collided, falling to the ground. A hand caught Randal's helmet in a viselike grip, claws fracturing the edges of his viewscreen. Randal hammered a fist into Tsepashin's helmet. The Abkhazi rolled to the side, tossing Randal into a nearby bench. The two scrambled to their feet, Randal a moment faster. He charged before Tsepashin could raise the chain gun in his direction.

A massive claw sliced at him. He ducked under it, coming up inside his enemy's guard. Randal screamed defiantly, snapping a climbing spike into place and stabbing at the thing's chest. The spike punched cleanly though the pock made by Ariane's rocket. It slid deep into Tsepashin's chest and came out wet, the blood dripping like ichor in the dim light.

Tsepashin shuddered with reflexive movement, a claw scratching feebly across Randal's faceplate. He toppled to the ground.

Randal turned from the body and ran to Ariane's side. They backed away, unable to believe Tsepashin was really dead. Randal was so intent upon the downed foe that he barely noticed when the comset squelched.

"Randal, what's your status?"

"Jeni?" His voice cracked with tension. Clearing his throat, he tried again. "Jeni? We're in the hedge maze. Where are you?"

"Why in the world are you there? We're holed up in the wine cellar. Pieter's puzzling a way out."

Why in the world would they be there? "Tell Pieter to lead your team out the cellar door near the gardens. We'll rendezvous at the staff skimmers."

"Roger that. Should we expect unfriendlies?"

"Resistance should be minimal. But there's a hovertank on the prowl, so move smartly."

Ariane stood rooted in place, her eyes never leaving Tsepashin. They needed to run. It was only a matter of time until someone on the roof spotted them.

"C'mon, love. It's over."

"Over?" Her voice was plaintive incomprehension.

"All over."

Hesitantly, she followed him as they jumped out of the maze. It was a quick sprint to the skimmers and no one intercepted them. The largest of the vehicles was marked with the crescent and star of a field marshal. It looked big enough to hold all the survivors. Randal took satisfaction in using Mashkhadov's personal skimmer.

The doors were too narrow to admit their suits. They hunched down behind the vehicle while Randal walked her through the autodestruct sequence.

After buckling the shell-shocked girl in the rear of the craft, Randal clambered into the pilot's chair. Lacking Johnny's larcenous abilities, he was thankful the staff car needed no keycard—military vehicles seldom did. He powered up the skimmer, giving it a quick preflight.

His hand dropped to his sidearm as a face appeared, peering in the side hatchway. "Whoa, Kipper. Easy there. Have room for four more?"

"Pile in quick. Hey, you fly this thing. You're better at it." Randal climbed through the interior hatch and settled in next to Ariane.

Bullets spanged from the skimmer's shell. The Headhunter returned fire while the others bundled into the passenger compartment. A round followed them inside, burying itself in the hardwood paneling.

Firing a last burst, the Headhunter hopped into the skimmer, flashing a "Go" signal to Pieter.

The door slid shut as the craft lifted off raggedly, rear first followed by the nose. Pieter cackled as he flew. "Hopefully the air defense guys won't fire at this thing. After all, who'd shoot at a Field Marshal?"

Ariane glanced up at Randal. There was an ethereal look to her, cheeks blanched pale, dark eyes unblinking. She took his hand, holding it tightly and managing a weak smile. "Let's not wait for the cathedral. Let's get married tomorrow."

"The minute I can find a chaplain."

The skimmer gained altitude, listing to the side and giving the occupants a view of the chateau.

Randal's lips twisted into a bitter smile, his eyes blurring with unshed tears. The Abkhazi, like so many ideologues before them, tortured and killed in the name of perfecting humanity. How many innocents had died in Soviet gulags, Islamic holy wars, or Abkhazi experiments?

Man was unchanged since his Fall—twisted from what he was and always one malignant idea from barbarism. A millennium ago, men were killing each other in castles like the one below. They were still doing it. Man's technology changed, but his nature was a constant. The worst atrocities in history came when he forgot that fact and tried to create a terrestrial heaven.

With such flawed stock, what hope was there?

Ariane rested her head on his shoulder, her soft brown hair crushed against his cheek. Faith, hope and love; these three remain. God wouldn't allow his creation to suffer forever.

The chateau grounds passed from view as they traveled to the nearby mountains, to safety. Kissing Ariane's temple, he slipped an arm around her shoulders and held her close.

EPILOGUE

Blessed are the peacemakers: for they
shall be called the children of God.
—Matthew 5:9

The office of the Abkhazi Interior Minister mingled the ugly joylessness of Khlisti aesthetics with the conspicuous consumption of a bribe-taking official. Heavy, brocaded curtains of mud brown flanked the windows, and the furniture was massively constructed from some dark wood. On one side of the room hung a gold-framed painting of the minister himself, while a portrait of the Abkhazi president smiled paternally from the opposite wall. On the minister's desk sat a gold pen set, a guldor pichok letter opener, and a globe done in ruby, topaz and other gemstones.

Interior Minister Ghorbani had occupied his chair for only thirteen months, ever since the end of the civil war. When the New Genevan counteroffensive smashed the Abkhazi army, it also broke the Purist hold on power. The army returned angry and radicalized by their experience. Generals, politicians and prophets each claimed a slice of the military, and the country fell in upon itself.

In time, Moderates triumphed and restored relations with New Geneva. Randal and Ariane Knox were among the first to repopulate the New Genevan embassy. Peace was, if anything, more challenging than war: Moderates might renounce violence, but many still despised "infidels;" the economy was backward and awash in red tape; and Khlisti bitter-enders plagued Abkhazia with terrorist attacks.

"Your Excellency, I must remind your government that these agricultural technology transfers were contingent upon several factors," Randal told the Minister. "Most important was the restoration of full civil rights to ethnic and religious minorities here in Abkhazia. We are sensitive to the complexities of the situation, but there has been insufficient progress, in our view."

Minister Ghorbani rotated the globe lazily. "If you are sensitive, then you know how unpopular such a change would be. We Moderates now control the government, it is true. But fanaticism still rules the hearts of many in Abkhazi. Would you inflame them further?"

Randal rubbed the corners of his eyes with thumb and forefinger. What should have been a simple demarche had turned into a two-hour debate. *Things were so much easier when we could just shoot them*, he thought ruefully. *Abkhazis made for good enemies and difficult friends.* "We would have you honor your treaty agreements. Your country slaughtered a quarter of a million innocent people. You can't bring back the dead, but you will pay back the living."

"Look behind me," the Minister said. "Do you see the holes in the plaster? I leave them as a reminder—if not careful, I will be as dead as my predecessor."

"Without our aid, your government will topple in a month. You may not like us, Your Excellency, but you need us."

Randal collected his comset on the way out of the Ministry of the Interior, and found six messages awaiting him. One was from Ariane, reminding him about lunch. Colleagues in the Political Section had sent three requests for information, and another was the Consul General asking about a visa issue.

A DiploSec officer opened the door to his hovering staff car, while another scanned the surrounding rooftops for snipers. Randal took a seat in the armored vehicle, and they set off for the Embassy. A reflexive glance verified the security follow car was, indeed, following. The streets of Chimkent slid by in all their depressing grandeur. Always fearful of uprisings, the Abkhazi had built their streets wide, the better to bring in tanks and crush rebellion.

Randal read the last message on his comset. It came from Youth for Justice, the group which gave him the most hope for Abkhazia's future. From what he had seen, the older generation would forever mistrust New Geneva, but young people could still be reached. His diplomatic portfolio included youth issues, and the group was his first real success. "New chapters have formed in Astrakhan University, Chimkent Polytechnic, and the Military College of Abkhazia," the message read in part. "We're also pleased to report thousands of applicants for the Study in New Geneva scholarship program."

Small steps, to be sure, but Randal was thankful for them. The staff car arrived at the Embassy gates and was admitted after several minutes of security scans. Three checkpoints later, Randal entered the chancery and hurried to lunch. Jean-Marie's happy shout greeted him at the canteen door.

"Hello, little man," Randal said, scooping up the boy and planting him on a hip. "Where's your mum?" Jean-Marie pointed a plump finger, and Randal spotted his wife by the window.

Ariane stood as he approached, and he marveled as always at the gentle roundness of her belly. In a few short months, Jean-Marie would have a sister.

The canteen was practically deserted that late in the afternoon, so he slipped an arm around her waist and pulled her in for a kiss. Jean-Marie made a disgusted sound. "Did the demarche go well?" she asked as they sat.

Randal laughed. "The Minister will do what we ask. If we don't send aid payments, how can he embezzle them?" He paused as the waiter brought a menu. "How are things at the veteran clinic?" Ariane worked part-time at an outreach for disabled Abkhazi soldiers.

"Formidable! The Ambassador visited today, so we had a lot of visitors to work around, but it's good. We finally received that shipment of prosthetics from Pieter's factory." She took a sip of coffee, and added brightly, "Guess who I saw today?"

"Who? Did Pieter accompany the shipment?"

"Non, but just as good." She pitched her voice low. "Jeni and Onegin. Though they're traveling as Monsieur and Madame Izmailev—tourists from off-planet."

"Did they seem happy?"

"They look like they're in love. It could just be part of their cover, but I don't think so." She grinned and gave his hand a squeeze.

"We should have them over one of these days, when they aren't here on business," he said, setting the menu aside. "The new diplomatic bid list came through this morning. I thought we could mix up some cocktails tonight and dream about our next posting."

Ariane glanced through the reinforced blast windows of the Embassy and then rolled her eyes playfully. "And give up all of this? Were there any good posts on the list?"

"A few. Any chance you might like to see Earth again? Our mission to the Terran Hegemony has a public diplomacy job I can definitely score."

"Vraiment? I could show you Geneva! My family, my home."

Randal brushed bangs from her eyes and traced the curve of her cheek. "It's settled then. One more year of repairing Abkhazia, and then off to another adventure."

About the Author

J. Wesley Bush currently lives and works in Kiev, Ukraine, where he reports on economics. He has previously served as an airborne infantryman, military intelligence cryptolinguist, NGO worker, and historian. He also spent two years as a unicyclist in a circus. He is the husband of a lovely wife and the proud father of five boys.

Connect on:

 Facebook: jwesleybush

 Twitter: @jwesleybush